TENNIS SHOES
ADVENTURE SERIES
THE GOLDEN
CROWN

TENNIS SHOES ADVENTURE SERIES

Tennis Shoes Among the Nephites

Gadiantons and the Silver Sword

The Feathered Serpent, Part One

The Feathered Serpent, Part Two

The Sacred Quest
(formerly *Tennis Shoes and the Seven Churches*)

The Lost Scrolls

The Golden Crown

OTHER COVENANT BOOKS BY
CHRIS HEIMERDINGER

Daniel and Nephi

Eddie Fantastic

COVENANT TALK TAPES BY CHRIS HEIMERDINGER

Chris Heimerdinger's Adventures with the Book of Mormon

The Name That Matters Most

TENNIS SHOES
ADVENTURE SERIES
THE GOLDEN CROWN

a novel

CHRIS HEIMERDINGER

Covenant Communications, Inc.

Covenant
Communications, Inc.

Cover illustration by Joe Flores

Published by Covenant Communications, Inc.
American Fork, Utah

Copyright © 1999 by Chris Heimerdinger
All rights reserved

Printed in the United States of America
First Printing: October 1999

06 05 04 03 02 01 00 99   10 9 8 7 6 5 4 3 2 1

ISBN 1-57734-498-7

For my daughter, Alyssa,
the prettiest jewel in my crown

PROLOGUE

The two worlds weren't so very different, you know. That is, the world of our Savior in the first century, and the world of Joseph Smith in the nineteenth.

Perhaps I should identify myself. My name is Jim Hawkins. I'm the father of three beautiful, brilliant, wonderful children—two of whom are safe and one who I hope soon will be.

It's actually astonishing how similar the two time periods were. Though separated by eighteen hundred years, the technology was almost identical. The daily lives and routines of the people were, for all practical purposes, mirror images of each other. Both depended on horse, carriage, and foot for transportation. Houses were heated by wood, coal, and dung. Water was fetched from wells, unless, like for certain wealthy Romans, it was piped into your home from the local aqueduct. Both had stock markets, an international postal service, and their populations whiled away the hours reading the world's great books—many of which had exactly the same titles.

By the 1800s, the treatment of disease was still much the same as it had been in the days of Galen, the old Roman physician. Many doctors still used his textbooks. Even where technological advances were obvious, like the printing press or gunpowder, Roman superiority in civil engineering more than balanced it out. The truth is, when Joseph Smith was born, the world had been struggling to reacquaint itself with Roman technology for three hundred years. By 1830, they were just about there.

And then suddenly, overnight, technology exploded: Railroads and steam engines. Telegraphs and telephones. Automobiles and airplanes. Computers and cosmonauts. All in a little over a hundred and fifty years.

The coincidence seems undeniable. As the Lord poured out spiritual knowledge upon the Latter-day Saints, He poured out every other kind of knowledge upon all the nations of the earth. The two worked hand in hand, inseparable. One led to the other. After all, this is the dispensation of the fulness of times. Knowledge is knowledge. Truth is truth.

Maybe this also explains the other coincidence—how when the Church of Jesus Christ fell into apostasy, the world descended into a period of ignorance and chaos known as the Dark Ages, a state from which it took fifteen hundred years to recover.

Maybe it's an oversimplification. Certainly there are points of light in every century. But the overall the picture seems clear. The dispensation of the fulness of times means more than just a restoration of heavenly truth. It's a universal enlightenment destined to bless all the nations of the earth. Gospel knowledge and technological advancement are flames that burn as one. But who will acknowledge that the initial spark for both revolutions was ignited in 1820 in a quiet grove near Palmyra, New York? Perhaps no one. At least not yet.

So I'm led to wonder: If the Saints who lived in Christ's day had *not* apostatized, would this technological revolution have taken place two millenniums earlier? If the Church had continued, if the Empire had let it grow unmolested, if the members had held to the iron rod, might combustion engines, electric lightbulbs, microwave ovens, and VCRs have been invented sooner?

It seems logical. God might have doled out such inspirations long ago. The Romans might have transformed their excellent highways into the first eight-lane interstates for motor cars. The Emperor Constantine might have rolled his army across the Mulvian Bridge in tanks instead of on horseback. The philosopher Origin might have written his spiritual essays on a word processor instead of papyrus. Rome's last emperor, Romulus, might have eliminated the conquering hordes with F-15s, cruise missiles, and atomic bombs. And by the time of Columbus, technology might have been so advanced that instead of discovering America, he'd have charted a course to a distant galaxy.

But of course such speculations are pointless. If the Church *had* survived, the Second Coming likely would have already occurred. The goal to prepare a Zion people to receive the Savior would have already been accomplished. It just didn't happen that way. The Lord knew it wouldn't. He told us so by the mouths of His apostles—Peter, John, and Paul. But it *could have* happened. That's the key. It's also the key to letting us know the responsibility still before us. We are the framers of the future. If we desire all the gifts of God, if we seek to win the Golden Crown, we can't just sit back and watch. We have to make it happen.

Perhaps that's my problem. I've been sitting back and watching for far too long. Waiting and watching for six unendurable months. It was a mistake. That, I now believe, was the message—the *warning*—of the dream.

I had the dream a short time ago. It happened one morning in a Shoney's restaurant in West Valley City. I was exhausted; I'd dozed off while reading the menu. In that dream—that horrible dream—I saw my son, Harry. He was no longer a boy of fifteen years, but a man in his early thirties. It crushed my soul. After all, Harry had only been gone for six months.

The dream seemed so clear, so detailed. And yet I refuse to believe it was real. When I see Harry again, he *will* still be my teenage boy. As I've said before, reality is what we make it. If this dream was indeed some sort of reality, I will exert all the energy within me to turn it back into a dream.

My only fear is that I've already waited too long. It was my daughter's condition that forced me to procrastinate. Six months ago, Melody was diagnosed with ovarian cancer. Her treatments have concluded now, and she is growing stronger every day. More importantly, she has Marcos, her true-blue Nephite hero, at her side.

I can't wait any longer. Thanks to Marcos, I know where Harry is. I even know *when* he is. At this moment he's in that very world now teetering on the brink of apostasy. Something has detained him. I'm resolved to find out what it is. My supplies are already purchased. My departure date has been set. In two days, I will enter a cavern in northern Wyoming and descend to another place and time.

And yet something inside me hesitates. What could it be? It's as if I sense that some event is about to occur. Something important. Still,

I can't let such premonitions slow me down. There's too much to do. I have too far to go. If a crucial piece of information is about to reveal itself, it has about forty-eight hours to do so. After that, I, too, may become lost in time.

I sense that I won't have to wait that long. Something tells me it's coming even now. Something in the wind . . .

PART ONE

CHAPTER 1

Okay, Meagan, you like to talk. Why don't you fill us in on what's happened.

Why, thank you, Harry. Does this mean I get to tell most of the story?

Nah, we'll need a breath of sanity from time to time. I'll step in whenever we can't take any more.

Very funny. Have I ever told you how funny you are?

I think you were referring to my looks.

I'm sure I was. Still, somebody has to love you, bro.

Yes, I know. How could you help yourself?

I couldn't. I love you like a kitten loves a ball of lint.

We sound like brother and sister already.

We do, don't we? But not yet. We still have the most incredible journey ahead. And yet I cringe to think about it. It never needed to happen. We were so close, Harry. So close to going home—you and I and your Uncle Garth. It might have been so easy.

It just wasn't meant to be. Fate had other plans. I understand now. I only wish I had understood then.

You'd better start at the very beginning. Remember when that was?

Only too well. It was the day my sister, Melody, became sick. A few days later she was diagnosed with ovarian cancer.

A diagnosis which led you to embark on a grand adventure to find her one true love, a Nephite named Marcos. I got involved purely out of curiosity—a rather quirky strain in my personality. I followed Harry into a dark, dank cavern near Cody, Wyoming, which hours later spat us out in the middle of the land of Jerusalem in 70 A.D. From there, it gets rather complicated.

Give the Reader's Digest version.

Harry and I found an ancient scroll near the ruins of Qumran that appeared to be the only existing copy of the Book of Matthew. It was brought to Qumran by a man named Barsabas, who had rescued it from a secret vault in Jerusalem. Barsabas later died from an arrow wound, leaving the scroll, as well as his nine-year-old grandson, Jesse, in our care.

Not that Jesse needed much care.

No. Much of the time, he took care of us. Jesse helped us to keep the scroll from falling into the hands of Simon Magus and his band of quasi-religious freakazoids. We fled to a city called Pella, where we met a cousin of Jesus Christ named Symeon Cleophas. Symeon also had a sixteen-year-old daughter named Mary. Harry could probably tell you more about Mary.

You're digressing.

Sorry. Suffice it to say, Harry went ga-ga over her at first sight. Unfortunately, the elders of Pella tried to burn the scroll of Matthew and forced us to leave. On our way out of town we met an old prophet named Agabus, who told us to take the scroll to the Seven Churches in Asia Minor and give it to John the Beloved. It was a long way. We weren't sure if we could make such a journey. But before we could even decide, everything was turned upside down. The next morning, Jesse and I were kidnaped by Simon Magus. Harry was told if he wanted to save our lives he would have to obtain for him another scroll called the Scroll of Knowledge. Like the scroll of Matthew, this mysterious book was also hidden in a secret niche in Jerusalem. Simon was convinced it contained the secrets of the universe and dreamed it would give him ultimate power.

Without delay our hero, Harry Hawkins, began his journey toward Jerusalem. He was briefly sidetracked, however, to rescue Marcos and another Nephite warrior named Gidgiddonihah before they were torn apart by a five-hundred-pound lion in a gladiator pit.

I succeeded, of course.

Oh, of course. Was there ever any doubt?

Well, maybe a tiny speck.

After we escaped, I told Marcos about Melody. Grief-stricken, he set out for the modern century to be with her while Gid and I continued on to Jerusalem to find the Scroll of Knowledge.

Meanwhile, Jesse and Meagan were imprisoned in a dungeon somewhere in Samaria.

It was a catacomb, actually. Do you mind if I tell my part of the story?

In a sec.

On the way to Jerusalem, Gid and I hooked up with Bishop Symeon and his daughter, Mary. Symeon was also headed to Jerusalem to find any sacred manuscripts still left in the secret vault. When we arrived at the city, we found it surrounded by tens of thousands of Roman soldiers, who'd managed to turn the landscape into a wasteland. To get inside Jerusalem we were forced to seek assistance from an old friend of Symeon's named Joseph ben Matthias, or Josephus.

Josephus, with considerable reluctance, directed us to a subterranean passage that wound its way beneath the city, finally emerging inside its walls. But the Jews were no less hostile than the Romans. They called us spies and imprisoned us inside a tall tower called Phasael—all except the slippery Gidgiddonihah.

We learned that the Jews had captured another Christian the week before. To my ultimate surprise, our cellmate was none other than my Uncle Garth, who had journeyed from the modern century to find us. Shortly after our splendid reunion, the Romans set fire to the great temple of Jerusalem.

During the confusion, Gidgiddonihah freed us from our prison. We located the secret niche and found no less than ten sacred scrolls, all written by apostles and prophets, including the most sacred of all— the Scroll of Knowledge.

With this scroll in hand, the five of us set out for Samaria and the summit of Mount Gerizim. It was here that I was to give the Scroll of Knowledge to Simon Magus in exchange for Meagan and Jesse.

Okay. You've rambled long enough. My turn.

Jesse and I managed to escape the catacomb by swimming through a dark, underwater tunnel. But as we tried to flee, Jesse was shot through the hand by an arrow. We spent the night in the hills, poor Jesse losing more blood and strength by the minute. Then came our unlikely rescuer— a virtual knight in shining armor—

Oh, brother.

His name was Apollus Brutus Severillus—a nineteen-year-old Roman centurion riding a shimmering white stallion.

You're kidding. The horse was white?

There may have been a few brown patches.

Anyway, Apollus took us to his army camp below Mount Gerizim, where Jesse received medical treatment for his wound and I was treated like a true princess.

Princess? I thought you said you'd made up a story about how you were the daughter of a Roman shipping merchant from Sicily.

Same dif. The point is that Apollus' father, the commander of the fort, was deeply moved by my plight and agreed to help me find Harry.

With Apollus and twenty Roman soldiers at my side, we rode up Mount Gerizim. Enroute we were attacked by Simon and his men. Apollus was struck by an iron ball attached to a chain. He was bleeding and barely conscious. I managed to half-carry him to a shallow cave, where he quickly fainted.

We hid there for three days, unsure if Apollus would live or die. At last, with my constant care, he recovered enough to try and reach the Roman fort. During his absence I made the foolish choice of climbing to the summit to try one more time to find Harry. Instead, I came face to face with Simon and the Sons of the Elect. Once again, I was his prisoner.

When we arrived at Mount Gerizim, we found over a thousand Roman soldiers at its base, prepared to set fire to the mountain to flush out Simon's raiders. We were taken to the Roman camp where we met Apollus and his father, Commander Severillus. Because of Meagan, the Romans knew exactly who I was. We were given until sunset to stage our rescue. With Apollus and two hundred Roman cavalrymen close behind, Garth, Gid, and I set out for the summit.

The exchange turned out to be a fiasco. Simon and his men forced Harry to turn over the scroll without releasing anyone. In fact, it was Simon's intention that all of his followers would commit suicide rather than submit to the Romans. They fully believed the Scroll of Knowledge would guarantee their salvation. The first ones lined up to drink the poison were the five of us.

Just then my Roman knight, Apollus, came thundering up the slope with his horsemen.

But in the confusion of the battle, Meagan disappeared.

Simon dragged me down the slope. As promised, the Romans set fire to the mountain. With the forest around us in flames, Simon tried to get me to take him to the cave where Apollus and I had hidden for three days. Before we arrived, Apollus, Harry, and the rest of my heroes surrounded us. Jesse threw a large rock into Simon's back, causing him to fall forward into the blazing undergrowth. The days of Simon the Sorcerer were over.

Garth saved the Scroll of Knowledge. We fled safely down a rocky corridor and joined the soldiers at the bottom of the mountain. As we watched the fire engulf the summit, Garth revealed to me the answer to the great puzzle. The Scroll of Knowledge did not contain the secret powers of the universe. Actually, it turned out to be the simple, sacred covenants of eternal life from the holy temple.

Two days later we reached the seaport at Caesarea and said our final good-byes to Symeon, Mary, and little Jesse. Symeon would journey by ship to the region of the Seven Churches and give the lost scrolls to John the Beloved. Jesse was to become his adopted son.

It wasn't easy saying good-bye to Mary. And yet something gnawed at me, telling me that I had not seen the last of her. Somehow, somewhere, I would meet up with her again.

I was sure I was about to see Apollus for the last time as well. I'd expected to say good-bye forever in Caesarea. Who could have known what was about to befall us, or how our lives would spin more out of control than ever before?

So here we are. Precisely where we left off.

Should I tell what happened next?

No, I'll tell it. It's my responsibility. And my fault. After all, I was the one who made the fatal choice to stay in Caesarea one more night.

Five days. That's how long I'd figured it would take. Uncle Garth had figured seven. But as it sank in that we were finally going home, I was sure we'd suddenly find more energy than ever. Yes, I was certain we'd reach that cavern near the fortress of Masada in five days or less.

Besides, the faster we traveled, the safer we'd be. This was still a hostile world, filled with bandits and soldiers and starving countrymen. Anything could still happen. I told myself this, but I didn't really believe it. It wouldn't have made sense. We'd just capped off the perfect ending. Everything had been wrapped up as neatly as a Christmas package. We'd defeated the bad guys, saved the girl, and ensured the future of the Holy Bible as we know it. How much more can a guy be expected to do in two and a half weeks? No, we'd fulfilled our quest. Now God was going to whisk us through any further danger and deposit us safely back in the twenty-first century. I was sure of it. Nothing could have convinced me otherwise.

This confidence was surging inside me that next morning as I awakened in our hotel room on the oceanfront. I threw off my bedding, climbed into my linen shirt and freshly washed blue jeans (the only stitch of modern clothing I still had left), and practically skipped down to the first floor and out into the yard to greet the rising sun. It was still a little early. The sun had yet to poke its rays out from behind the hills. The light was fairly dusky, with most of the buildings and objects slightly obscured. I was far from being the first person up. There was some sort of temple across the street, and I could see about a dozen silhouetted figures inside the open, pillared compound. I could see a tiny flicker inside a stone basin at the foot of a silhouetted statue with outstretched arms. The people were lined up to make an offering of some sort while a priest in heavy robes chanted a prayer. It was the temple of a Roman god, I presumed.

My attention was drawn toward the hotel stables, where I heard the whinny of a horse and saw six men securing bridles and provisions to their mounts. I recognized the men at once. It was Apollus and the other five Roman soldiers who had accompanied us from the fort at Neopolis. I interpreted their actions immediately. They were leaving.

The sight was a little disconcerting, though perhaps it shouldn't have been. We'd pretty much said good-bye the night before. It had already been decided that today we would part company. I guess I'd sort of envisioned riding together to the outskirts of town and giving each other a final salute; Apollus and his men would go one direction while we went another. This vision might have been more for Meagan's sake than anything else. I felt she should have the opportunity to give her Roman warrior a final farewell and watch him ride into the distance. It just seemed more fitting. I knew Meagan was counting on this, despite the fact that the two of them had talked and held hands until late into the night. Maybe it was also disconcerting because I knew that as soon as Apollus left, we would truly be on our own.

As I approached, one of the other soldiers nudged Apollus. He turned to face me. He looked relieved—glad, I think, that I wasn't Meagan.

"Harrius," he said warmly. He always called me Harrius, convinced that to call me just "Harry" was somehow disrespectful, like calling Julius Caesar "Julie."

"Are you leaving already?" I asked.

"Yes," he said soberly. "I think it would be better this way."

"Meagan will be disappointed." It was an understatement. Meagan would be devastated. But as I thought about it, I realized Apollus was probably right.

"Your sister is a beautiful girl," said Apollus. "None like her in all the world. I'm sure she'll soon grow out of her infatuations with the likes of me and find herself much more suited to someone of her own class."

"Her own class?" I asked.

"Yes. The son of some wealthy merchant, like her father. Not the son of a sixth-generation headcount Italian soldier."

"Meagan doesn't think like that," I replied. "She doesn't judge people for their class. She judges them by their heart."

Apollus chuckled. "That's the way all young girls see the world. Their fathers usually set them straight. I'm sure your father is anxious to know you are safe. I hope you find him well in Alexandria when you arrive."

I was confused for a second, until I remembered Meagan's tale that our father's merchant ship was stationed in Egypt at this time of year. She told Apollus this story to discourage him from following us to the Dead Sea and discovering that she'd been lying about her true identity all along.

"I've given your uncle all the references you'll need to attach yourselves to one of the imperial caravans headed south on the *Via Maris*," Apollus continued. He reached out and took my forearm in his grip. "Farewell, Harrius. May Mercury make your journey swift, and may Fortuna give to you and your family all the bounties of life."

I gripped his forearm in the same manner. "Farewell, Apollus. May our Father in Heaven give you all the same blessings."

He smiled, then turned and mounted his horse. A kick to its ribs, and Apollus and his companions rode off into the misty light. Within seconds they were out of sight. I sighed deeply. Now it would be my unenviable job to tell Meagan.

The moment came an hour later when we met in the eating house next to the hotel. As she stepped inside, her eyes barely skimmed over Gid, Uncle Garth, and me seated at a corner table. Apollus had promised to meet us here for breakfast. As she noted the concerned expression on my face, her shoulders slumped. She knew instinctively what I was about to tell her.

She took the news better than I might have expected—at least on the outside. The only hint of her inner turmoil was the sharpness in her voice as she demanded to know when we were leaving.

"Gid and I are going to buy some supplies in the market," I told her. "It shouldn't take more than an hour."

"Good," she said, stiff-lipped. "I'll be ready."

"Meagan," I said, "I'm sorry."

"About what?" she said defensively. "We knew he was leaving. Last night, this morning, tomorrow morning—what difference does it make?"

She turned to leave, nearly forgetting the French toast-like pastries that had been laid out before us. At the last instant she turned back and asked, "Are one of those mine?"

"Yes," said Uncle Garth.

She snatched it up and left, but she didn't eat it. I think she just took it to make us believe she was all right. When we went outside, I saw one of the hotel stewards, likely a slave, munching on it as he leaned against a statue of the Emperor Augustus in the courtyard. Obviously poor Meagan didn't have much of an appetite.

In addition to buying passage for Symeon and Mary on yesterday's ship bound for Athens, the red ruby in the hilt of Gidgiddonihah's sword had also afforded us the use of the four horses we'd brought from Neopolis. We hadn't bought them, exactly. More like rented. Apollus had asked us to turn them over to the nearest Roman garrison when we reached our destination. As Uncle Garth went to make sure they were well fed and cared for before our departure, Gid and I made our way toward Caesarea's main market about three blocks inland from the hotel. The cobbled streets were dry and dusty from the long, hot summer. They heated up quickly as the sun rose into the morning sky. I still marveled at how clean and new the city looked. This was the crown achievement of Herod the Great—the same Herod who had tried to kill the infant Jesus. The blocks were all laid out in a nice, neat grid pattern, almost as symmetrical as Salt Lake City.

The market was already a flurry of activity. But the sights were anything but cheerful. The large square in front of the city's amphitheater was a sea of Jewish war captives, all divided into individual chain gangs that a company of Roman soldiers had tried to organize into straight rows. My stomach knotted up as I looked at them. The slaves were skinny and ragged, their spirits and their hearts shattered. Many of them wore little more than a filthy cloth about their loins. Some had Roman numerals drawn on their backs, the red paint still dripping as if they'd been lashed by a whip. The numbers were meant to distinguish particular groups for the slave buyers who paraded up and down the aisles in their richly colored costumes.

The regular customers of the marketplace generally ignored the scene, laughing, speaking of the weather and whatever other gossip was prevailing in their lives. The suffering masses didn't even faze them. Just another day at the market. I found myself loathing every one of them.

My gaze fell on one of the younger slaves as we passed by. He was just about my age. His hair was fair and sandy. Every other feature, however, was very Jewish. As I continued to stare, he straightened up a little taller and looked almost defiant. I think he wanted me to know that I was no better than he was. I turned away, feeling a sharp stab of shame. I guess it was just the guilt of knowing that I was going home today while he was likely setting sail to some foreign land, never to set eyes on his home again.

Gidgiddonihah put his hand on my shoulder. He'd read my thoughts perfectly.

"We save who we can," he said. "I wish we could save them all. Fortunately, their souls are in the hands of a Being far wiser than any of us."

I nodded at Gid. Still, I wished we could do something . . . the thought was overwhelming. I stole a last glance at the young Jew, sighed, and continued to follow Gidgiddonihah.

We entered a street with leather shops and food stalls. It appeared that this was where we would find everything we would need for our journey. We'd been living pretty high on the hog these last couple of days—pastries, fish, and fresh vegetables. Those days were over. Tomorrow it was back to dates, dried fruit, and heavy breads. Not that I cared. Soon enough I'd be able to have my fill of McDonald's and Pizza Hut and Subway sandwiches whenever I wanted.

Gid was also interested in getting a couple of sturdy leather canteens and head cloths to shade us from the September sun, as well as a good road map of Judea. We pretty well knew the course we were going to pursue—down to the seaport of Joppa and then overland, bypassing Jerusalem on the south—but we still wanted to be sure we didn't wander in circles. No sense getting lost in a land where strangers might easily be suspected of being Jewish rebels.

We hadn't lost our papers from Commander Severillus vouching for our good character. Still, I had a suspicion that Uncle Garth was terribly uneasy. If it had been his choice, I think we'd have left the day before, right after Symeon and Mary's ship had left the harbor. *I* was the one who'd pushed for a good night's rest in a clean hotel. Besides, I knew Meagan had wanted those last few hours with Apollus. But now that all our business was concluded, wild horses couldn't have kept me here another night.

All around us dozens of merchants and customers yelled at each other in sing-song tones, haggling over the price of everything from incense to olives. Not everything was bartered; some prices were fixed, like grain. I found myself gravitating over to those stalls just to hear myself think. As I stood there, mentally recalculating the quantities of food we would need, I became vaguely aware of a group of men gathering in the vicinity of Gidgiddonihah. The Nephite stood about a dozen feet away from me, leaning over a table piled high with leather goods.

I registered that the men were armed, but for some reason I didn't think much of it. There were armed men everywhere, mostly soldiers. Then, out of the corner of my eye, I saw one of them separate himself from the others and approach Gidgiddonihah from behind. He reached out and casually tapped him on the shoulder.

"Excuse me," he said matter-of-factly. "I believe you have something that belongs to me."

Gid turned. As soon as their eyes met, the man ended his act. A menacing look darkened his features. He was a crusty-looking man with gray hair and taut muscles. His arms and calves were squeezed into leather bands, while his chest was draped in a cuirass of silver mail. At last it registered. The armed men were gladiators.

My heart froze. I could hear the blood curdling in my ears. Suddenly the face of the man who stood before Gidgiddonihah zoomed in with blazing clarity. A million faces from this ancient world must have etched a place in my memory these last few weeks. This was one I'd prayed that I would never see again. His fingers gripped the hilt of his undrawn sword so tightly as to make them white and bloodless.

His name was Problius of Berytus.

At one time he had owned the sword that hung on Gidgiddonihah's back. Gid had actually impersonated him in order to gain access to the secret passages leading inside Jerusalem. I knew that Gid had recognized him, yet his face showed hardly any reaction. The Nephite's eyes flashed me a warning glance. The other gladiators hadn't yet placed me as one of the instigators of all the trouble at Salim. Then Gid stared hard into Problius' eyes. He smiled slightly, as if to say, "Yes, I remember you. I bonked you on the head and laid you out flat as a tortilla once before. You know full well I could do it again." But there was something else in Gid's expression—something that made me shudder. It was a look of resignation. A look that suggested the fight was over before it began. There were too many of them closing in now.

However, if those were Gid's thoughts, they certainly didn't parallel his actions. The sword behind Gid's shoulder came out of its scabbard like a flash of lightning. Problius drew his own with virtually equal speed, though his was a Roman battle sword, only half as long. If that sword had been just an inch or two longer, Gid's belly might have been split wide open right before my eyes. As it was, he managed to parry the smaller blade and even cause Problius to stagger back, off balance. But the two weapons never clashed again. Problius' men raised a forest of clubs and fell on him like wolves.

One, two, three men were cut down by Gid's thrusts and parries. The men just kept coming. I was astounded. In any other situation, a fallen comrade would have caused the others to hesitate, reassess their footing. Not these gladiators. They seemed to have no thought for pain or death. They poured all over him. Finally Gid had no room to raise his weapon. The clubs began to come down, and I heard the dull thud of wood striking flesh. "Gid!" I cried.

My rage exploded. I dove into the fray, wrapping my arm around a gladiator's neck. I shoved my palm into his face and threw him toward the table piled high with leather. The table tipped, collapsing the shade awning overhead. The shopkeeper and several other bystanders scattered. I wheeled around to pull the next man away from Gidgiddonihah's collapsed body. But now the whole group turned on *me*. A man at my left raised his club. I caught his arm and plunged my fist into his mouth. Someone seized me from behind. A rough hand grabbed my hair and pulled back my head. I caught a brief glimpse of the blur of wood flying at my face, but I never saw who swung it. Only the blur. The image still hangs in my memory like a shimmering phantom.

I was spared the memory of its shattering impact in my right eye. Just as I was spared the memory of anything else for the next several hours.

CHAPTER 2

Garth found me sitting on a wooden bench on the second floor with my knees curled up into my chest overlooking the street, the temples of Juno and Augustus, the Hippodrome and Palace and Amphitheater of Caesarea, and the dusty hills to the east cut in half by a long aqueduct that brought fresh water to the city's inhabitants. The view was obscured by a mesh screen that the owners of the hotel had put up to keep the guests from tossing their waste over the balcony. I knew this because when we paid our fee, the innkeeper expressly told us to give our chamberpots to his steward who would take them, I assumed, to a place where they could be emptied into the city sewer. Now that's service, I said to myself. Chamberpot Delivery Incorporated. For the moment, however, my mood was anything but humorous. The obscured view was just as well. I couldn't think of anything more infantile than trying to spot six Roman horsemen riding off into the distance along the highway leading to Sebaste and Neopolis.

Yet who was I kidding? When I'd first sat down, that was exactly what I'd been trying to do. Now I was just wallowing in self-pity. Maybe it was just numbness. I didn't know what to feel, or what to think. Apollus had left. He'd left without saying a single word. My last words to him were, "Good night. I'll see you in the morning."

"Yes," he'd replied. "Good night."

Good night.

Not good-bye. If I'd known—if only I'd known—I'd never have gone to bed. I'd have cherished every last moment. I was sure now that he'd been planning this exit all along. I'd intended to give him my garnet ring, the one I'd bought for myself at the Utah State Fair. Not exactly a valuable gift, but it was something. Something to remember me by. Maybe in response he'd have given me something in return. One of the hobnails on his sandal—I don't know. Something! *Now it was too late. He'd ruined the moment. Better that I was rid of him. Yes, that's what I told myself.*

Oh, but what was the use? My heart felt like it had been bowled under by a steamroller.

As Garth sat down beside me, I hardly reacted. I might not have even noticed him, but it was hard to ignore his bright green eyes, full of caring. He put a fatherly arm around my shoulder.

"How are you feeling?" he asked.

I tried to perk up. "Great. Why wouldn't I? We're going home."

"That's right," he replied.

I felt him tense a little. Garth was uneasy. He looked out through the mesh toward the forum and the market. Nevertheless, his words remained positive. "The horses are all ready. We'll start as soon as they return. The stable boy thinks we can reach Joppa by tomorrow afternoon."

I didn't reply.

"I know it hurts, Meagan," he said. "I wish there was something I could say."

I considered giving him another defensive reply, like I'd done in the restaurant. But I'd given up. My true feelings were bound to come to the surface sooner or later. When they finally came out, it was all at once. I felt the blood rush to my face, and within seconds I was a blubbering idiot. Big, embarrassing, gulping sobs. What was the matter with me? Heavenly Father had given me so much. Even Apollus had been a gift. He'd saved all of us that night at Mount Gerizim. I hated myself for crying. Yet Garth, who held me against his shoulder, didn't appear to judge me in the least.

"There now," he said. "You'll be all right."

"I feel like such a putz," I sobbed. "I'm sorry, Brother Plimpton."

"Call me Garth. Uncle Garth, if you prefer. After all, we're almost related."

"Do guys ever feel like this?" I asked. "I don't think they do. I don't think they know how to feel anything."

"Don't worry. They know. They just don't always know how to show it. Or they don't want to show it."

"He just left. No good-bye. Nothing."

"That's how they do things sometimes. It doesn't mean they don't feel."

"I'll never let myself care about someone like that again. Never."

"Sure you will."

"No. I'm serious. I've learned my lesson. It's not worth it."

"Oh, it's worth it. At the right time, with the right person, it's worth everything in the world."

"No way. There's no way."

He grinned and hugged me tighter. "You'll see."

I wiped my eyes and tried to collect my wits. "You won't tell Harry and Gid, will you?"

"Tell them what?"

"That I made such a scene."

"No. It's our secret."

I hugged him. Garth was craning his neck, his eyes searching the street below.

"What's the matter?" I asked.

"Nothing," he replied. "Why don't we wait down by the horses. I'm sure they'll be along any minute."

We descended the stairway and waited by the stable, but Harry and Gid didn't return in a few minutes. We waited an entire hour. Garth had now become so nervous he couldn't stand still.

"Maybe we should take a walk toward the market," he suggested.

"Do you think something's wrong?"

"I don't know," he said. "I really had expected them back by now."

My own pulse rate started to increase. All at once my heartache evaporated, and a feeling much more ominous took its place. I drew a deep breath to try and relax. It was silly to be nervous. We had no enemies here. Besides, I knew that Harry was carrying the letters of recommendation from Apollus and his father, Commander Severillus. We'd been assured that if we ever got into trouble, all we had to do was show our papers. There had to be a reasonable explanation. Maybe to find the map that Garth had requested, Harry and Gid had had to walk to a shop in another part of town.

As we neared the central market, Garth was walking swiftly. I practically had to run to keep up with him. In front of the forum and east of the amphitheater, there was a large open square where some big to-do was just breaking up. Hundreds of Jewish slaves wearing shackles and chains were being herded toward the Caesarea docks by taskmasters with whips. It was a sickening sight. I managed to ignore it and focus my energies on trying to spot Harry and Gid. We stopped at the intersection of two market streets.

"Where might they have gone?" I asked Garth.

He closely assessed the street going off to the right. It had food stalls and stacks of leather goods. "Let's try down here."

We pushed our way through the other shoppers loaded down with satchels and bundles, our eyes searching every direction. I bumped into an old man in a leather tunic, nearly causing him to drop his basket of lemons.

"Excuse me," I said.

He grunted and moved away. Garth approached the shopkeeper at a large food stall.

"Hello," he began. "Have you seen two people—a large man with long, dark hair and a younger man? He would have been the same age as this girl, light hair, strong build, with the same color skin."

The man looked us over from head to foot. For a moment I felt certain he knew something. His eyes darted about. But then he lowered his gaze and shook his head, fading back into the shadow of the market stall.

Garth pressed on. "Please. If you know anything—if you've seen them . . ."

But the man ignored him. I turned to see what might have spooked him. There were two Roman soldiers across the street, fingering through a collection of clay figurines. I started to feel queasy. Something bad had happened. I knew it by intuition.

I was just about to march right up to the soldiers and ask the same question Garth had asked, but then I realized Garth had moved up the street. He was approaching a stall where some sort of disturbance had taken place. A table had been overturned. The shopkeeper, a short man in a crimson robe, was just tying off the corner of his collapsed awning. As I drew closer, I stopped dead in my tracks. There was blood on the cobblestones, black and coagulated, having mixed with the dust. I latched onto Garth's arm.

Garth interrupted the shopkeeper. "What happened here?"

"Just a scuffle," the man in the crimson robe replied. "I'll be open for business in just a few minutes."

"A scuffle between who?" I asked.

"Gladiators. The soldiers broke it up. It's all over now."

"Gladiators?" asked Garth, perplexed. "Why were they fighting?"

"Wouldn't know. That rabble are always fighting. Usually over some

gambling debt or a woman. These gladiators looked like they were settling an old score."

"*Did you see a big man with black hair?*" I asked. "*Or a boy whose hair was light-colored?*"

We had his full attention now. "*Light? Yes, I believe so. I didn't see too much. As soon as swords flashed, I cleared out.*"

My heart was pounding. "*What happened to the boy? Where is he?*"

"*Dead, I would guess. There were three or four of them dead. The Romans hauled them away.*"

"*Was the boy one of them? Did you see him for certain?*" asked Garth, his face as white as a sheet.

"*I believe so. My eyes are dim. They don't see too clearly past my hand.*"

"*Please,*" said Garth. "*You have to tell us exactly what happened.*"

The man suddenly became tentative, just like the shopkeeper down the street. "*You'd better ask someone else. I don't want any trouble.*"

"*We won't give you any trouble,*" I pleaded. "*We just need to know what happened to our friends.*"

At that instant a squad of Roman legionaries—twelve in all—marched past the stall on their way toward the forum square. I watched them for several seconds. When I turned back, the shopkeeper was facing away from us. He finished tying off his awning. This was crazy! Someone had to help us. We had to find out what happened! If the citizens wouldn't talk, that left only one option. I had to ask the soldiers.

As Garth tried to coax more information out of the shopkeeper, I followed after the dozen legionaries. I was determined to stand right in front of them if I had to. I'd demand to know every detail of what happened. Maybe the scuffle had nothing to do with Harry and Gid. The man had said his eyes were dim. Nothing he told us would have been reliable anyway.

I dodged through shoppers to catch the soldiers. I was just about to grab the arm of the one marching at the rear when I heard a strange, familiar voice.

"*Meagan.*"

I stopped cold. Something about the voice froze my blood. As I looked toward the source, I squinted to try and see into a dark building with a wide, open front. Because of the bright sunlight, I could only see a vague silhouette. All my senses were on alert. My first temptation was to run.

And yet I could see the person well enough to know that he wasn't threatening me. As far as I could tell, he was seated at a small table just inside the shadow, sipping from a clay cup as daintily as any British gentleman might sip a cup of tea.

I took a step toward the edge of the shadow, still squinting. The voice spoke again.

"I wouldn't bother the soldiers if I were you. There were several arrests made in connection with that incident up the street. You wouldn't want to get mixed up in all that, I assure you."

I felt a shiver from head to foot. The voice stirred dark memories. I knew it now. It was the voice of a ghost. A voice from the dead. I took another step and the shadow fell over my face. The smells of smoke and sweet spices whirled around me. It was some sort of café. There were about six tables. All of them were empty except for the one where the man was sitting. A broad, leering smile lit up his face. He seemed pleased that I'd recognized him. Indeed I had. His smooth features had been burned into my brain. The stiff, greasy-blond hair. The handsome, plastic face.

"Cerinthus," I whispered incredulously.

"Hello again," he replied.

"But . . . I thought—"

"You thought I was dead? Is that what you were about to say?"

"Y-yes," I stammered.

"Sorry to disappoint you."

"I thought you perished with Simon and Menander and everyone else on the summit of Gerizim."

"What makes you so certain any of them are dead either?"

My heart stopped. Minutely, I shook my head. I knew what I had seen.

He smirked. "Don't look so distraught. Yes, Meagan, they're all dead. All but me. I'm the only survivor of that fiery night. That is, besides yourselves. Though unlike you, it appears that I was the only one who took with him such a painful reminder."

Carefully, he lifted back a portion of the collar on his tunic. There was a large red area on his neck, about the size of my fist, blistered and sore. The wound caused him to flinch. After all, it had been less than a week. The way he moved, I suspected that a portion of his left forearm had been burned as well.

"Don't worry," he said. "It's not as bad as it looks. Actually, it's heal-

ing quite nicely. Balm of Gilead doesn't work nearly as well as my own salves. Though I do expect a bit of a scar."

"But how?" I asked, my heart still hammering. "How did you survive?"

"I took cover inside the same cubbyhole of the ruined temple wall where Simon first found you. The soldiers didn't notice. I waited out the fire and smoke, and in the morning I made my way to safety. I believe I was spared by God."

I scrunched my forehead. The words struck me as grossly out of character. The last time I'd spoken to this man, he'd called himself Cerinthus the Divine. He'd proclaimed himself a god. I also found it curious that he'd failed to include the adjective "unknown" when he mentioned God, though I suspected this was just an oversight.

His eyes crawled over me again. "It's good to see that you're doing so well. It's more than I can say for your companions."

My body stiffened. "What happened to them? What did you do?"

He shook his head. "I didn't do a thing. It all happened without my help."

"Where are they?" I demanded, my voice cracking with desperation.

"I wish I could tell you."

"You don't wish any such thing!" I seethed, clenching my fists. "You're responsible for this. What have you done with them?!"

"Keep your voice down. You give me too much credit, Meagan. Do you really think I'd try to conspire with the Romans after what happened at Gerizim? I'd be arrested in a heartbeat."

Garth appeared outside the café. I realized he'd been searching frantically for me. I called to him, and he came into the shadows.

"Meagan, what are you doing!? We have to keep together—" His focus settled on Cerinthus. As he recognized Simon's young apprentice, his eyebrows rose in astonishment. He stepped close, as if to protect me. "What's going on?"

"Garth," I said, "he saw everything. He knows what happened."

Garth narrowed his eyes. "Where are they?" he demanded.

"I was just telling Meagan, I don't know. They were set upon by gladiators, and then by soldiers. Both were carried away. I assure you, I was only an innocent witness."

"Were they alive?" Garth demanded.

"I'm not quite sure. Both were badly beaten."

My body started shaking. "And I suppose you just stood there and watched the whole thing, gloating."

"On the contrary," said Cerinthus, *"I'd been following them for several minutes, trying to decide how best to approach them. I'd wanted to express my regrets for what happened at Gerizim."*

"Your regrets!?" I said accusingly. *"You tried to kill us! You tried to make us drink poison!"*

"I did no such thing," he replied firmly. *"I only delivered the poison into Simon's hands. My actions were those of a misguided subject. When I heard of Simon's death, it was as if some great chain that had been binding my soul shattered into a thousand pieces. You people are Christians, are you not? I had always understood that it was one of your principal tenets to forgive. So that is what I sought from them. It's also what I seek from you. Forgiveness."*

My mind was reeling. Harry and Gid were gone. I couldn't think about forgiving this man. I was shaking with fury. "You're a liar! A sleazy, slimy insect! You told me you were divine—a god! Simon was your father! You believed everything he taught!"

"Simon was *not* my father," he said defensively.

He sounded almost vulnerable, as if my accusations had stung. I wasn't buying it. If Garth hadn't been holding my arms, I might have tried to gouge out his eyes, just as I'd tried that night when Jesse and I escaped from Simon's villa. Garth couldn't know what this man had done to me and Jesse. How he'd tried to humiliate me and prove that his gifts of prophecy were greater than mine. Or how he'd tried to seize us in the villa courtyard as Jesse and I were trying to escape.

"Simon had proclaimed himself the father of my spirit," Cerinthus continued. "But he was not the father of my flesh. My mother, Helena, was a harlot. She met Simon after I was born. I've been under the heel of the Standing One all my life. For the first time, since as far back as I can remember, I am free."

I couldn't listen to any more. There was no way such a corrupted heart could have changed so suddenly. Something was black and twisted about all this. But the plain truth was, I really didn't care. We had to find Harry and Gid. My heart was sick with panic.

"Did you see which way the soldiers carried them?" asked Garth.

"Toward the docks," said Cerinthus. "I certainly hope they're still alive."

His eyes were unflinching, as if his words were insincere. And yet I wasn't sure. Was my judgment clouded by my hatred? It was so murky.

Still, what did it matter? For all I cared, Cerinthus could rot.

"We'd better go now," said Garth, preparing to lead me from the café.

"I wouldn't go after them, if I were you," said Cerinthus. "Get out of Caesarea. Save yourselves."

I felt another surge of anger. "Of course you wouldn't go after them. You don't care about anyone or anything—"

"Come on, Meagan," Garth said gently. "Let's go."

"Do I have it, then?" asked Cerinthus.

Garth glanced back. "Do you have what?"

"Your forgiveness," said Cerinthus.

Garth studied him a moment. "Our forgiveness is easy. It's God's forgiveness that matters most. Seek to make your heart right with God."

"Oh, I will," said Cerinthus, his tone dripping with far too much confidence. "In fact, that's where I'm headed right now—to make my heart right with God. I'll be boarding the first ship that can take me there."

"You don't have to go on a journey to do it," said Garth.

"In this case, I do," said Cerinthus. "I'm going to Ephesus."

We stared at him. He enjoyed seeing our surprise. The implications of such a destination were clear. He was headed to Asia Minor. He was following directly on the heels of Symeon and Mary and little Jesse. A chill ran up my spine. His destination was the region of the Seven Churches. What havoc could a man like Cerinthus wreak in the midst of God's faithful Saints? I cringed to think of it. I feared the Saints of the Seven Churches had a storm coming the likes of which they had never seen.

* * * * * *

We wandered along the waterfront of Caesarea's busy harbor, passing dozens of warehouses and slave pens where war prisoners were being processed before they were put on board ships bound for hundreds of destinations throughout the Roman empire. Our search became more and more frantic. There were just so many of them—so many slaves and slave dealers and Roman soldiers.

I was brazen enough to ask several legionaries standing outside a tavern, "Have you seen my brother? Please, help me. He was beaten in the marketplace by a gang of gladiators and carried away by soldiers. His name is Harry. He was with another man named Gid. Both of them would have looked very different from anyone else around here."

"You look very different yourself," said one of the soldiers. "Unusual hair color. Are you from these coasts?" One of them tried to touch my hair. Over the weeks, my black hair coloring had started to fade. The reddish-brown roots were showing through.

Garth whisked me away before the soldiers could become more aggressive. I had a feeling that around here, women who dyed their hair were either very rich or belonged to the same occupation as Cerinthus' mother.

"Someone has to know what happened," I said to Garth. "It's impossible that nobody would have seen."

We posed the same question to a man in a silk cape who I suspected was a slave dealer.

"Couldn't help you," he replied. "But I did see a cluster of gladiators down at the north end. There's a slave yard over there. Biggest one in Caesarea. That's where I'd look."

It was our first decent lead. We made our way at a run toward the north end of the harbor. The gladiators the man had described were nowhere in sight, but we did see a large encampment surrounded by spiked poles. The poles were so tightly knit that we could hardly see inside. I wandered along the perimeter until I found a wide enough space, but the view through the gap was no better. Inside the first fence there was another fence with the same kind of spiked timbers. All I could see were a few Roman sentries pacing along the inner corridor. Beyond the second fence I could hear people muttering. I could smell the strong odor of human waste, but I couldn't see a single prisoner. I was tempted to cry out Harry and Gid's names. If I could just get a response, at least we would know they were here. I thought better of it and followed Garth around to the compound gate. There we found several alert Roman guards armed with long javelins.

"Please," Garth pleaded with them. "We think there's been a terrible mistake. Members of our family may have been arrested."

The guard seemed irritated. "This is a compound for war prisoners," he said gruffly. "Debtors and malfeasants are kept at the facility near the forum."

"We were told that soldiers might have brought them here," Garth persisted, "accompanied by several gladiators."

The guards raised their eyes and glanced at each other. They knew something! I was sure of it!

"Are they here?" I asked desperately.

"Two men?" asked a second guard.

"Yes," replied Garth excitedly. "One is fifteen. The other in his early forties."

"Foreigners?"

"Yes, they're both foreigners," said Garth. "Like ourselves."

"They're here," the guard confirmed sourly. "If they're still alive."

I swallowed, my heart breaking. "Can we see them?"

He shook his head. "These men are charged with crimes against Rome."

"What kind of crimes?" Garth demanded.

"Sedition. Disturbing the peace. Murder."

"Murder!" I repeated with surprise. "This is ridiculous! They're inno-cent. They've done nothing against Rome. I know they haven't."

"Of course they haven't," the first guard smirked. "I have a whole camp filled with innocent people. We have no enemies here. Why, all the people in this land love Rome like they love their own mother."

The other guard laughed derisively.

"You'll have to take up the matter with the prefect," said the first guard succinctly.

"Who's the prefect?" I demanded.

"Tiberius Aristus."

"Where can we find him?" asked Garth.

"At the office of the magistrate," the guard replied.

"Where is that?"

"Back that way," he pointed. "White building. East of Agrippa's palace."

We wasted no more time with these imps. Fifteen minutes later, Garth and I found the office of the city magistrate. It was a clean-swept, marble-pillared building just adjacent to the magnificent palace now occupied by the puppet-king, Herod Agrippa, grandson of Herod the Great. The offices were hot, stuffy, and buzzing with flies. It took us almost two hours to get an audience with one of the prefect's secretaries, who summarily told us that the prefect only heard civil petitions on Wednesdays—two days away.

"But by then it might be too late," I cried.

"What is your petition?" the secretary asked.

"The release of two innocent men," said Garth. He explained what had happened in the marketplace, passionately insisting that it was all a mistake.

"You say they're in one of the slave camps?" asked the secretary.

"Yes," I confirmed.

"Then it's not a matter for the prefect anyway. It's a military matter. You'll have to take it up with the garrison commander."

Seething with frustration, we got directions to the garrison headquarters. It was located west of town, a good half-hour away, even on horseback. We arrived sweaty, tired, and hungry—only to be told, after waiting another three hours, that we would have to file a written complaint with the sergeant-at-arms, who would then take up the matter with the officer in charge of the slave camp and schedule a hearing with the garrison commander, though he doubted if the plight of two foreign criminals would warrant the attention of any of these men.

"Where is the sergeant-at-arms?" asked Garth, his face a mask of exhaustion.

"At the office of the magistrate," said the commander's orderly.

I groaned inwardly. "But we were just there. Why didn't they tell us this when we were there?"

The orderly shrugged. "If you'll excuse me, I have other business."

That was it. We were brushed off like stray cats.

Back outside, I sank down onto the ground beside my horse, hugging my knees. I started to cry. I'd never felt such frustration. Give me a dark catacomb or a burning mountain over Roman bureaucracy any day. I couldn't believe I'd ever wasted one moment of the day mourning over my loss of Apollus. This had become a matter of life and death. I shuddered to think of Harry and Gid inside the walls of that terrible camp, battered and bruised, maybe even dying or dead. Garth put his arms around me.

"What are we going to do?" I wept. " What can we do?"

"We can pray," said Garth solemnly. "When every other option is expended, we always have that."

"But I've been doing that all along," I said. "What does God want us to do?"

"That's what we have to find out," said Garth. "If we have to ride back to the magistrate's office and file every petition they have, even if we have to use the rest of our resources to hire a lawyer, we'll do it."

"A lawyer? They have lawyers here?"

"Of course. Any civilization governed by human laws has lawyers."

"But it could take forever. Days. Weeks. We can't let them rot in there another day."

Garth glanced at the sun. It was already setting over the ocean. It appeared that Harry and Gid's overnight stay in the slave camp was inevitable.

"I don't think we can do much more before morning," said Garth.

"Then I know what we have to do," I blurted out.

Garth raised his eyebrows, waiting for an answer. I hesitated to be sure that I was following my head and not my heart. It didn't take long to decide. I was following my head. Not that it mattered. Either way, I was sure it was the right decision.

My hesitation told Garth all he needed to know. He nodded and sighed.

"Yes, I know what you're thinking. It's crossed my mind as well. But even if we rode as hard as we possibly could, we'd still be looking at a delay of several days."

"But what other choice do we have? No one here will listen to us. We might as well be invisible. But they'll listen to Apollus. They'll listen to his father."

"Maybe," said Garth, not entirely certain. "That is, if the commander and his son are willing to help."

"They have *to help us," I insisted. Then, more subdued, I added, "It's our only hope."*

Garth sighed. My mind was set. It was the only logical choice left. Garth seemed to know by instinct that if he disagreed, I might easily ride off without him.

I held back my tears, determination boiling inside me. A minute later we were back on our mounts, riding hard into the night toward the tiny Roman fort at Neopolis.

CHAPTER 3

When I started to come to, I wished somehow I had remained unconscious. The pain was almost unbearable. The gladiator's club had struck me in the same eye as the Jewish soldier's fist when I had been captured inside the city of Jerusalem a little over a week ago. Even before the club came down, there had still been evidence of black and blue. Now I couldn't open my right eye at all.

I hardly dared to open the left eye. Each time I tried, it pulled at the muscles around my swollen right eye, heightening the pain. Better to keep it closed. Not that this mattered. What little vision remained in my left eye was all blurry and watery.

I desperately feared there was no vision in my right eye at all. There was so much swelling and blood. The blood was mostly from my nose; I was sure the bridge had been broken. I had to breathe through my mouth. The club had come down full force on my face. My ribs on both sides of my chest were also numb. The gladiators had been ruthless, unleashing their vengeance like dragons.

Gidgiddonihah! Where was Gidgiddonihah? Was he still alive? I didn't know. I pried open my left eye again. The pain was dizzying, but I perceived enough to conclude that I was no longer in the market street. I was inside some kind of compound, lying on my back in the shade of a surrounding fence. More people were lying beside me, some groaning in agony. I couldn't keep my eye open long enough to see if one of the wounded men was Gidgiddonihah. There were other people milling about, but they were all a blur. I also heard the unmistakable voice of a Roman guard somewhere across the yard.

"Get away from there! You! Get away from there!"

The voice was directed at other men, but it filled my veins with ice. It confirmed what I had feared: I was inside a prison. For the third time since arriving in this wretched land, I was someone's prisoner.

All at once, my mind flashed back to that immense gathering of Jewish war slaves I'd seen in the forum square. Had I become one of them? I opened my eye one more time to confirm it. Yes. The raggedly dressed men all around me were Jewish POWs.

I shut my eye again. The throbbing in my head was worse than ever. I braced my skull between my palms. A part of me wished it would all end. Immediately, I felt ashamed. Where was the incredible faith that had sustained me for so long? Where was the conviction that everything was in the Lord's hands? It hadn't gone anywhere. It was still with me. I just had to dredge a little deeper.

I worked up the nerve to touch my injury—very lightly. The right side of my face felt like twice its normal size. I felt powerless. Too weak to stand. Suddenly I was very thirsty. I tried to wet my lips, but all I tasted was blood.

And then, as if someone had read my thoughts, I felt a cool drizzle on the side of my face. I tasted water in the back of my mouth. I swallowed. The water caressed and soothed my injury. I forced my eye open again. A face was leaning over me. A young face, still too blurry to recognize. But then the blurriness cleared for just an instant. I'd seen this face before. It was the sandy-haired boy with defiant eyes who I'd noticed as I was crossing the forum square that morning.

The look of angry defiance was still there, only slightly softened. He continued to drizzle cool water on my face and in my mouth from a rusty-looking cup. He looked almost smug, as if he was gratified to see me in a worse predicament than he was.

He stopped pouring and put the cup to his lips, guzzling down the remainder.

"More," I whispered hoarsely.

"Sorry," he said, wiping his mouth and then licking the residue from his dirt-blackened hand. "The trough is empty. They won't fill it again until tomorrow."

I shut my eye again, cringing as more needles of pain shot into my brain. "I can't . . . I can't wait that long."

"You'll make it," the young POW proclaimed. "But you'll have to get your own tin cup. I won't share mine with you again."

His voice had an edge of spite. I tried not to draw any conclusions. After all, he'd just shared a precious portion of his daily water ration.

"Thank you," I said.

There was no reply. I peeked again. The boy was no longer there. He'd disappeared into the sea of other prisoners. I wasn't sure he'd even heard my thanks. Depression crept over me. I wanted desperately for him to come back. I needed the company. I felt so alone.

I noticed that the man lying beside me was shivering. It must have been a hundred degrees. The man was dying. Several of the men farther down appeared to be already dead. With alarm, I realized they'd lined me up in a row of men who were not expected to live. Terror gripped me. Was my injury really that serious? Had my face been completely destroyed?

Adrenaline rushed into my joints. I pushed myself upright, ignoring the waves of nausea and dizziness. I was not going to lie back down. I was not going to be numbered with those who were without hope. *Please, God*, I prayed. *Give me the strength to stand. Give me the will to stagger to some other part of the compound, away from these dying men.*

I brought up one knee. Immediately, the dizziness became overwhelming. I fainted and fell to the ground. Several seconds later, I came to my senses. The dizziness faded. I became fully coherent, though the pain was nearly unbearable. I tried again to push myself to my feet. This time, I succeeded.

I stumbled forward along the row of dying men who lay in the shade of the fence. The smells of death and sweat and human feces were everywhere. The sound of flies and other buzzing insects almost drowned out the groans and mutterings of the men. My vision remained obscured; nevertheless, I searched the row of men for Gidgiddonihah. He did not seem to be among them. At first I was relieved to see it. Then a horrible, drowning sensation came over me. Was Gid already dead? Had his body been disposed of? Who could I ask? Who would know?

I felt sure if Gid was here—if he had any strength whatsoever—he would have already found me. It would have been *his* face I'd have seen when I opened my eyes. That left only two options. Either Gid wasn't here, or . . .

I couldn't think about the second option. It was too awful. It wasn't true. Gid was invincible. But where was he? Maybe he'd escaped. Gid was an expert at that. That was it. He must have escaped.

I stumbled to my left, into the sea of faces. Most of them were sitting on the ground, stretched from one end of the yard to the other. I saw children among the faces. All boys, no girls or women. The compound seemed to have been divided. The mothers and daughters were kept in another yard to the north, on the other side of the fence. Men were over there leaning close to the timbers, as if speaking to someone on the opposite side.

As I passed through the crowd, I noticed many of the men turn to stare at me. Some had expressions of wonder, seemingly surprised that I was able to walk at all. Several cleared the way, as if touching me was the same as touching a corpse. No one came over to help. I guessed it was obvious that I wasn't a Jew. Most of them were probably wondering what I was doing in here in the first place.

I couldn't see very well. At the edge of the yard stood a kind of tower on stilts. Upon it was a man in a uniform who I presumed was a Roman guard. I approached the tower. I felt a little better. My blood was flowing again. The pain in my head had lessened. I felt strong enough to call up to the guard.

"Hey!"

I couldn't tell if he'd reacted or not. It was so hard for my eye to stay focused.

"Hey!" I cried again, leaning on the tower. "My name is Harry Hawkins. I need—"

Instantly, I felt the whack of a long wooden rod against my elbow. It hit me right in the funny bone, causing the limb to instantly ring with numbness.

"Get your hands off the tower!" the guard called down.

I backed away, holding my arm. "Please," I begged. "I need help. Where am I? Where is the man who was with me?"

"Get back with the others!" he spat. "Or you'll get another!"

"I need to speak with someone in charge," I insisted. "There's been a mistake. I shouldn't be here."

I heard some of the other slaves snicker. They were laughing at me. I felt their resentment.

"You're the property of Rome now," blustered the guard. "I warned you!"

I cringed, knowing the strike was coming. It hit me hard on the shoulder, but it wasn't nearly as painful as the first. Frustrated, my spirit crushed, I did as I was told and faded back into the midst of the other prisoners. I found another spot that received a bit of shade. It was occupied by several men, but as soon as it became apparent that I had chosen to collapse here, the spot was vacated. Being judged as a man near death had its advantages. I dropped down and lay on my back.

The property of Rome, I repeated in my mind. What did that mean? Had I been earmarked to become a slave? Was I to be sold to some slave dealer and shipped across the sea? I couldn't imagine it. I'd endured so much already. God would never allow it. Garth and Meagan would get me out of here. Or Gid. It was only a matter of time. I just needed to believe. Keep the fires of faith burning. I trusted God. I knew that He was with me.

What I didn't know was what God had in store.

CHAPTER 4

We pushed the poor horses too hard. We rode them half the night, giving them only a few hours to rest. At daybreak we were at it again. Just a few miles short of our destination, Garth's horse gave out. It just stopped running, its lungs heaving and its mouth foaming. Mine took the other's cue and stopped as well. I felt terrible, fearing that we'd ruined them for any other riders.

In the distance I could see the scorched hump of Mount Gerizim. We walked the rest of the way to our destination, practically dragging the horses by the reins. Just before the day was over, the walls of the fort appeared above the tiny village of Neopolis. As we approached the front gate, several of the sentries recognized us immediately. We were brought inside and escorted to the central compound where the offices of the garrison commander were located.

I was exhausted to the point of fainting. I knew I must have looked like something the cat had dragged in. Garth and I were both caked in dust and sweat. We must have smelled no better than the horses. My mind was still consumed with anxiety over Harry and Gid. If they were still in that terrible slave camp, they'd been there for two eternal days. Heaven only knew what condition they were in, or if both of them were even alive. Yet I knew a part of the reason my heart was racing had to do with my anticipation of seeing Apollus again. I wasn't even sure he'd gotten here ahead of us. All during our ride I'd wondered if we might overtake him. But one of the guards confirmed that he'd arrived just an hour earlier. His father, Commander Severillus, was just now taking his report.

I'd anticipated the look on Apollus' face when he saw me. There would be shock, of course, and deep concern. But then I was sure he would take me in his arms as I unleashed a waterfall of tears.

The men of the Neopolis garrison were up to their usual activities for this time of the evening—gambling and consuming ale by the barrel full. All activity stopped as Garth and I crossed the central square. Something was up and they knew it. A few of them followed us to the doorway of the commander's office, hoping to overhear some tidbit of gossip that they could pass along to the others.

Commander Severillus and his son had not been warned of our coming. They didn't know we were here at all until the sentry was sent inside to fetch them. Finally, they emerged. Their faces were set in surprise, just as I'd expected.

"Meagan!" Apollus exclaimed. "Garth!" He stepped off the boardwalk and came to me. "What's happened? What's wrong?"

I couldn't even wait for him to take me into his arms before my tears began. I reached out to bury my face in his chest. Instead, he took me by the shoulders and stood me up as straight as a post.

"Where are Harrius and Gidgiddonihah?" he demanded.

He quickly realized that I was too overwhelmed with emotion to answer right away. Impatiently, he turned me aside and faced Garth. Garth unloaded the whole story, from the moment Apollus and his companions had departed to our frustrating meetings with officials at the office of the magistrate and the local garrison. I simply looked on, practically ignored, while I brought my emotions under control.

"I don't understand," said the gray-haired, kind-eyed Severillus. "Who were these gladiators that accosted them? Why didn't Harrius show the Roman soldiers the recommendations I wrote?"

"We don't know," said Garth. "I'm not sure he ever got the chance. They were beaten and taken to a slave camp along the harbor. Beyond that, no one would give us any information."

"What I don't understand," said Apollus, "is why they were taken to a slave camp at all. If they were involved in some sort of disturbance, there are civil facilities for such matters. It's almost as if these gladiators had accused them of high crimes against the Empire."

Garth and I became very uncomfortable. I didn't know a lot of the details of what Harry had done during the time he and I had been separated, but I knew there might have been dozens of incidents to justify such accusations. Hadn't Harry mentioned some sort of fight in a small village involving gladiators? Yes, I remembered now. It was in this village that

Harry had rescued Gidgiddonihah and Marcos. Was it possible that the men who'd attacked them were these same gladiators?

"Those camps turn over their inventory of slaves every few days," said Severillus. "With all the thousands of captives coming in daily from Jerusalem, they ship them off as quickly as possible. They have to. In a few weeks, shipping on the Middle Sea will come to a standstill in anticipation of winter."

I shuddered. Apollus must have seen me shiver. Finally showing me a small sampling of compassion, he took off his red cape and put it around my shoulders. What I really needed was to be held, but I guess I understood his hesitation. Half the men in the garrison were looking on. It couldn't have been good etiquette to make such a display. Actually, it was his father who recognized my need even before his son. He descended from the boardwalk and wrapped his arm around me.

"There, there, child," he said. "If anything can be done, I assure you I will do it. I know the commander at Caesarea, Sextus Aquinius Rufus. I'll have my secretary write a strong letter to him on this matter, and it will be delivered by my son." He directed a stern finger at Apollus. "I want this situation resolved. This time you will stay with this girl until you know that she and her companions are safe."

Apollus reddened. I wasn't sure if he was embarrassed because his father had reprimanded him in front of his men, or if it was because he felt guilty for having left us before his mission had been completely fulfilled. I almost wondered if he was embarrassed for his father, that the old soldier would show such overt sentimentality over the case of a young girl he'd only met a week and a half ago. Apollus had said that his father's favor toward me might have been due to the fact that he'd once lost his own daughter in a carriage accident. She would have been my same age. The reason didn't matter; I was overwhelmed with gratitude that Severillus had become such a fervent ally. But what was up with Apollus? Why had he suddenly grown so cold and official?

"But sir," he protested, "you were just saying how you needed my help to round up any other Samaritan villagers who may have conspired with Simon Magus to—"

"You said this girl saved your life!" the commander interrupted. "There is no greater priority than her safe delivery into the hands of her father."

"But that might mean I'd have to travel to Egypt, or—"

"I don't care if you have to travel to India! Ready your men. You'll depart in the morning."

"Yes sir," said Apollus feebly.

Severillus barked more orders for Garth and me to be fed and given a bath and fresh clothes. I glanced at Apollus before we were led away toward the mess tent. His eyes were fixed on mine, but he couldn't hold them there for long. He looked down at the ground and then turned and walked away. My heart shriveled. The hurt was so bad my teeth were clenching. Why was he acting this way? What had changed?

As I looked back into the yard, I realized that some of the men in the garrison were chuckling among themselves. Apollus stepped up to one of the men and said brusquely, "You have a problem, soldier?"

"No sir," said the man. "Sorry sir."

It was then that I realized why they were snickering. They were laughing about Apollus' assignment. I guess I just didn't understand how the male mind worked sometimes. I knew that Apollus felt deep resentment at not being allowed to take part in the siege at Jerusalem. His father had already lost two sons in battle and didn't want to lose a third. To me this made perfect sense. But to Apollus it seemed to be a source of grinding humiliation.

Apollus had been wonderful when he'd escorted us to Caesarea the first time—so kind and grateful after all we'd been through together. I realized now that he'd also been all too glad to be rid of us. He was anxious to get back to business, fighting the war in Samaria, what little war there was. Some of the men must have seen how close the two of us were becoming. Surely Apollus had taken some flack. I guessed a nineteen-year-old warrior with a little lost Sicilian girl hadn't helped his image. The more I thought about it, the more I steamed. Oh, I hated guys. I hated them all.

I forced my mind back to the situation in Caesarea. Who cared what Apollus said or did or felt? He'd been ordered to help us free Harry and Gid. That's all that mattered right now. That's all that mattered ever. I resolved that beyond this, my heart was going to turn cold.

I didn't see Apollus again all the rest of that day. Part of it might have been my fault. I ate and refreshed myself as speedily as I could, anxious to curl up in the blankets of the soft bed in the guest quarters and forget about all our trials and trauma for a few hours in the oblivion of slumber. Before I fell asleep, I heard the voices of Apollus and two of his men through the wall of the quarters next door. They were grilling Garth for more information and devising strategies for how they would proceed. I felt insulted that I hadn't even been invited to the meeting. Maybe they're just being considerate, I told myself, by allowing me to get some rest.

No, that wasn't it. It was one of those male superiority things. No self-respecting Roman soldier would have considered that a woman *might offer any valuable insight into matters of strategy. Heaven forbid! I had a mind to march over there in my nightgown, storm through the door, and insist that I be included.*

Oh, what was the use? I lay back on my pillow. I could hear everything they were saying well enough. Apollus was telling Garth about how politics worked in Caesarea, and how best to earn the favor of the procurators and magistrates. There really wasn't much I could have offered. I might have expressed my theory as to why the gladiators had accosted them, but that would only have opened a new can of worms. Up until now, Apollus had been convinced that we were Roman citizens from Sicily. Telling the story of how Harry had rescued Gid and Marcos in that small village in the Jordan Valley would have inspired many probing questions. Undoubtedly it would have blown our cover. Still, how long could we keep this up? I was sure that sooner or later Apollus was going to catch me in a lie. Something was going to give us away. It seemed only a matter of time.

We rode hard the following day. There were five of us. Apollus had only brought two other soldiers, as opposed to the five he'd brought before. I knew their names from our first trip to Caesarea—Graccus and Lucullus, both of them fierce-looking men, and from what I gathered, close friends of Apollus despite the fact that they were at least ten years his senior.

Apollus had carried all the necessary letters from his father to garner the most influence with the local leaders. He also had a writ of authority granting us the right to exchange our horses at several outposts along the way. My rear end was about as sore as a rear end can ever get. I now had first-hand knowledge as to why cowboys walked bowlegged.

When I dismounted at our last exchange outpost of the day in a village called Narbata, my leg muscles simply gave out and I stumbled, landing on one knee. Apollus jumped to my aid. He reached under my arms and helped me stand.

"Are you all right?" he asked.

"Fine," I said bluntly, not looking at his face.

Apollus' indifference toward me all of yesterday and today was incomprehensible. It was as if the two of us were suddenly strangers. Not as if we'd spent three days in the hollow of a cave, where I'd nursed him back to health after being whacked on the head by an iron ball. Not as if three nights ago we'd spent the evening together, preparing our hearts for the inevitable moment of good-bye. I was hurt and confused. As soon as I'd steadied my legs, I broke away from his grip and made my way over to a well on the far side of the stables. I'm sure my walk was the most unfeminine-looking walk on the face of the planet. More like a funky chicken. I half expected to hear Apollus and his men laughing uproariously as I massaged my thigh, trying to rub feeling into it. They courteously restrained themselves, though as I cut back a glance, Graccus and Lucullus wiped away a smile.

I didn't care. Let them think of me as a spoiled little rich girl. It didn't matter what kind of harrowing experiences we might have endured together. These Romans would never think of me as one of the gang.

Apollus followed me to the well—which was shocking enough—but I noticed he acted self-conscious about it. His men continued looking on, no doubt to tease him later. He called back to them to help ready the new horses. They snapped to it. Garth joined them.

An old toothless woman at the well graciously lowered the bucket and raised it up full and dripping with cool water. Apollus gave her a few coins as I drank from a ladle. Helping travelers and soldiers obtain a drink was probably this woman's only livelihood. When I was done, I smiled at her gratefully. She bowed and moved away to sit in some nearby shade, anxiously watching for anyone else who might come near for a drink.

Apollus and I stood alone. I still refused to look at him.

"We'll only ride a few more hours, until just after dark," he said. "Then we'll make camp and you can rest your . . . your legs . . . until morning. We should reach Caesarea by the fifth hour. I expect to have an audience with the garrison commander and have your brother and Gidgiddonihah released before the end of the day."

I nodded. "That's good. Then we can be on our way. And you can be on yours."

He leaned back against the well, his broad shoulders hunched forward beneath the leather and bronze of his uniform. "Unfortunately, I can't do that. My father's orders were quite explicit. My men and I are to accompany you all the way to Egypt, until I can deliver you safely into the hands of your father."

"That won't be necessary," I said. "Just get us hooked up with one of those military caravans you told Uncle Garth about. After that, I'll release you from all obligations."

Apollus read the coldness in my tone and fidgeted a bit. "I think I must . . . owe you an apology," he stumbled out.

"You mean you're not sure?"

"It seems that over the last week I must have . . . given you the wrong impression."

"Oh?"

He stewed over his words another moment, then let it blurt out, with no tact or sensitivity whatsoever. "It's not that I'm ungrateful for all you've done. Quite the contrary. But I am, after all, a centurion in the army of Rome. A soldier does not entangle himself with the affairs of women. Well, that is, beyond a man's natural physical needs. But as for the kind of woman that a man might marry, we don't seek those sorts of entanglements until we have concluded our service to the Emperor. After that we are given a comfortable tract of land in a province of our liking, where we can settle down and raise a family. By then a veteran may be forty or fifty years old, depending on the fortunes of his career. If a soldier finds himself permanently based at some foreign outpost, he may settle down with a foreign bride if she suits him, but from what I've seen, such relationships are generally abandoned when a veteran is released—"

"Hold on, bucko," I interrupted. "You thought I was looking for a husband?"

"Well, for someone so young, it's only natural that you should become so infatuated—"

"Infatuated?" I shrieked. "With marrying you! Give me some credit! I'm fifteen years old!"

"Yes, I know. But in Sicilia I've heard—"

"Well, you heard wrong. I'm not marrying anybody! Not for at least ten or twenty years."

He smiled shrewdly, as if he didn't believe a word of it—as if this lout was convinced that every woman he ever met would have been willing to lay down her life for the chance to marry him. "It was not my intention to offend you," he continued. "I'm actually quite fond of you, Meagan. But let's be realistic. You are a Roman of the second class, whereas I will always be of the fourth or fifth class, no matter my rank. I am a man. Whereas you are . . ." He paused to find the right word.

"A child?" I snapped.

"I was going to say a girl.*"*

I threw up my hands as if shooing off some great flapping bird. "I've heard enough of this. A man? *What delusion convinced you of* that? *If you're a man, then someone like little Jesse must be a wise old sage."*

I started back toward the stable. Apollus remained there at the well, red-faced. After a moment, I heard him curse. I wasn't sure if he was cursing me or himself. Either way, the two of us didn't speak again until we arrived at Caesarea.

* * * * * *

Our first stop was the garrison fort at the edge of town. Apollus sought an audience with the commander, Sextus Rufus. He was received almost immediately and presented his father's letter. It stated, in short, that a great injustice had been committed against one Harrius Hawkins, citizen of Rome, and his friend and manservant, one Gidgiddonihah. The letter commended these two individuals for their courageous exploits in the service of the Empire with regard to the recent uprising on Mount Gerizim and recommended that they be remanded at once to the custody of his son, Apollus Brutus Severillus.

Apollus emerged from the commander's offices looking enthused and optimistic. "The commander is drafting an order for us to carry to the slave camp and hand to the officer in charge," he told us. "He's first advised us to carry it to the magistrate's office to be stamped by the city prefect in case the matter for which they were arrested comes under civil jurisdiction. His first officer, Gaius Mitellus, will join us. Just as I predicted, we should have them out of there before nightfall."

Apollus beamed a smile at me, half-expecting that I might jump up and down and give him a big hug. I saved that reaction for Uncle Garth. It was marvelous news, but I withheld any real celebration until I could wrap my arms around Harry and Gid. Again I cringed to imagine what shape they might be in. Maybe I wouldn't be able to hug them. Maybe we'd have to carry them out on a stretcher. Nervousness erupted inside me all over again. The wait in the anteroom of the municipal offices while Apollus and the first officer, Mitellus, met with the prefect was only about half an hour, yet it seemed an eternity.

At last Apollus emerged, but this time his expression was different. He looked deeply concerned. Even disheartened.

"What is it?" I demanded. "What's going on?"

Apollus paused before answering. His eyes peered into mine in a way they never had before. I swallowed. Was it suspicion I saw in his face?

He shook off this emotion and tried to sound positive. "It's all right. Things are just a little more complicated than we first anticipated. I've seen the arrest report now. It seems your companions were accused of far more than some sort of civil disturbance. As I first surmised, they were arrested for crimes against Rome."

"What?" cried Garth in astonishment. "What are they accused of doing?"

Apollus turned to me. "Do you know the whereabouts of your brother while you were being held by Simon Magus in Samaria?"

I fought down a tremor of hysteria. "Yes. It's like I told you. He was in Jerusalem, obtaining the sacred scroll that we gave to Symeon and Mary."

"Do you know the origin of his companion, Gidgiddonihah?"

Garth stepped in. "We've known Gidgiddonihah for years. He's not from this land, but I can assure you, he would never intentionally commit any sort of crime against Rome or anyone else."

Apollus let this sink in. He studied Garth's face, I think trying to determine if he, too, was hiding a lie. "The gladiators who attacked Harrius and Gidgiddonihah were none other than the fighting troop of Berytus, under Problius the Syrian himself. Problius claimed that Gidgiddonihah was a common Jewish slave, and that Harrius helped him to escape. It happened in a small village in the Jordan Valley. Apparently it was quite a fiasco. Several spectators, as well as a slave dealer, were killed. Two Roman soldiers were seriously injured. The story was corroborated by an agent of the Syrian governor, Quintus Lutardius. Were you aware that your brother was in the Jordan Valley?" he asked me.

"Well, yes," I said. "That's where I was kidnaped by Simon Magus.

That slave dealer made Gidgiddonihah a slave without any cause. If Harry helped him to escape, I'm sure it was only to save his life."

Apollus frowned. "You told me you were kidnaped here in Caesarea."

For an instant I froze. I'd been caught. How could I have been such an idiot—forgetting the details of my own lie? Did Apollus perceive that instant of panic?

Immediately, I began to reply with perfect confidence. "That was where we were originally *kidnaped. Harry and I escaped once from Simon's palace in Samaria and made it all the way to the Jordan Valley. It was there that Simon recaptured us and threatened Harry that if he didn't journey to Jerusalem and find the Scroll of Knowledge, Jesse and I would be killed. What's the matter with you? You think I'm lying because I forgot a few irrelevant details? Yes, I knew that Harry had rescued Gidgiddonihah. If he hadn't, Gid would be dead right now. And if Gid had died, you'd be dead too. He saved your life on Mount Gerizim, didn't he?"*

Apollus eyed me warily. "How did Gidgiddonihah come to be in possession of Problius' sword?"

"Sword?" I repeated.

"Yes," Apollus persisted. "I remember seeing it and thinking it was quite unusual. I guess in all the commotion I started to take it for granted. Were you aware that he had stolen this sword and sold off several of the jewels in the hilt?"

I stood there dumbly. What was I supposed to say to this? *Everything was unraveling. Father in Heaven, what was I supposed to say? My response was something totally unexpected. I told the truth.*

"I don't know anything about that," I admitted.

Apollus' face was unreadable. Was he buying a single word of this anymore? Who could blame him? My heart was quaking. I was ready to explode into tears.

Then a flash of sympathy entered Apollus' hard eyes. Did he really believe me? Or was it that he made a conscious choice to ignore his doubts? Something told me it was the latter. He chose *to believe me, at least for now. But shortly I knew I'd have to face all my own lies again.*

"All right," said Apollus. "I'll vouch for their character. Surely their heroics at Gerizim will stand for something. But neither I, nor my father, nor Commander Rufus has the authority to order their release. There will

be a hearing, and then the matter will have to be taken up with the governor of Syria. Right now he's in Antioch."

I felt the blood rush from my face. "The Governor of Syria? Why can't it be handled here? Can't we take it up with the King? He's right next door!"

Apollus looked surprised that I seemed so ignorant of protocol. "Your brother is a Roman," he said, as if that should have explained it. Apparently the King had no authority over non-citizens of his own lands.

I clenched my fists, trying to steady my nerves. "How long will that take?"

"Several weeks, I'm afraid."

"Several weeks!" Garth cried in exasperation. Indeed, I'd never seen Harry's uncle so beside himself. "What are we supposed to do in the meantime? We were told they'd been badly beaten. The guard at the camp wasn't even sure they were still alive. We need to see them!"

"That's our next order of business," Apollus assured. "I've been granted leave to have them removed from the slave camp and brought here to the municipal dungeons. They'll be much better treated, and if necessary, the prefect will see that they receive care for their injuries. I've convinced Aristus to allow us access to the prisoners as long as they're here."

"Then let's go to them," I said anxiously.

Apollus, Garth, and I went on ahead as the first officer of the garrison assembled the armed embassage that would escort Harry and Gid—in chains—to the cells of the municipal dungeon. We were on horseback this time, which made our presence before the guards outside the gates a little more intimidating. Apollus handed over the order to allow us entry into the camp. The guard read it perfunctorily, then handed it to another guard who must have been his senior. After this man had perused it, he glanced at Apollus, then at me and Garth, and said, "You'll have to show this to the camp warden, Centurion Orientus."

"Undoubtedly," said Apollus gruffly.

The gate was opened and we were led inside. I expected the camp warden to be a bloated, grim-faced man with an underbite like a halibut. He was, in fact, quite short and mousy-looking, not much older than Apollus. He sat there behind his desk, scratching his stubbled chin and reading the order several times over. At last he looked up at Apollus.

"You say a police guard is on its way?"

"Yes," said Apollus. "My men are with them. They should be here within the hour. We'd like the prisoners readied for transport immediately."

Garth leaned in toward the warden. "Do you know which ones they are?"

The warden scoffed in amusement. "We bring in five hundred slaves a day. Honestly, they're all starting to look the same. But I'd certainly remember if anyone had invoked his rights as a citizen of Rome."

"Where are they?" I demanded. "How can we find them?"

The warden shrugged. "They're out in the yard, I presume. I'll have my guard take you to the south tower and—hey, wait!"

I stomped back outside. The inner gate leading into the central compound was wide open. Two chain gangs of slaves—at least a hundred people long—were being lined up at the crack of a whip and herded inside. There were Roman guards on either side, but the path directly between them was open. I realized I could pass through and enter the yard before anyone could stop me. I found the tail end of the two chain gangs and dashed down the middle.

"Girl!" cried a guard. "You can't go in there!"

The warden blustered behind me, "Stop her! It's too dangerous!"

"Meagan!" shouted Apollus.

I didn't stop. I'd had enough of orders and waiting and Roman bureaucracy. I had to know if they were all right—if they were alive. For some reason I had no fear of the thousands of Jewish prisoners as I pushed my way through them toward the center of the compound. For the most part, they seemed far more terrified of me than I was of them, nearly climbing over each other to get out of my way. My eyes scanned the weary, broken-hearted faces. That calloused warden had thought all these people were starting to look the same. What an imbecile! In those faces I saw a million separate tales of suffering and humiliation. And yet none of the faces belonged to Harry or Gidgiddonihah.

I continued across the sun-hardened yard. It was reeking with human excrement, and I swallowed a lump of nausea. Several bodies were lying out in the open, swarming with flies. Despite the horror, it was these silent faces that I peered at most closely, my heart pounding like a drum. Please, God. Don't let any of them be Harry or Gid.

At last I reached the far side of the yard. A long row of sick and injured men had been laid out. My stomach knotted. If Harry and Gid had been beaten, this was where they would have been laid. I realized some of the men were dead. Even the living had flies crawling on their faces. The horror was too much. Somehow I numbed my senses enough to endure the ter-

rible sights and keep my head clear enough to finish what I'd come for.

I reached the end of the row. They weren't here! My eyes searched the whole of the yard one more time. "Harry!" I cried. "Gidgiddonihah!"

Apollus arrived with three other Roman guards. He'd have reached me sooner, but his eyes were also searching among the faces. He put his arm around my shoulder.

"Come on, Meagan—"

"Get away!" I shrieked, shaking him off. "I don't see them. Did you see them?"

"No," said Apollus. "We'll look again on our way back."

The guards cleared the pathway back through the prisoners. I shouted Harry and Gid's names three or four more times. The prisoners, and even the Romans, were looking at me like I'd lost my mind. Frankly, I was just on the verge of doing exactly that. Harry and Gid were not inside the compound.

"They told us they were in here," I wept to Apollus. "The guards at the gate—they said they remembered them!"

Apollus tried to calm me down all the way back to the warden's office. When I saw Garth, I broke away from Apollus and clung to him. "They're not here, Uncle Garth. Where could they be?"

Apollus slammed his fist on the warden's desk. "Where are they?"

"As I was trying to explain before everyone ran off," said the warden, "we receive over five hundred slaves a day. Most of them we dispose of almost as quickly. Look here—" He shuffled through some papers on his desk. "I have an order here for three hundred mine workers in Egypt. Here's another for four hundred and fifty stone quarriers in Macedonia. Another for seventy-five nursemaids in Capua—"

Garth was nearly hysterical. "Are you saying they've already been shipped out?!"

"Most likely," he calmly replied.

"But they'd been beaten!" I raged. "They might have been in no condition to travel anywhere!"

The warden made a small smile. "We always pad our orders by twenty percent to allow for . . . anticipated losses."

A sound retched out of my throat like a wounded crow. I reached across the desk and began pounding him with my fists. I'd gotten in several blows to his face and chest before he seized my wrists and Apollus pulled me back. I buried my face in Apollus' leather tunic, howling almost to delirium.

"Where were they shipped?" Garth demanded. "You must have records!"

"No names," said the warden, testing his fattened lip for signs of blood. "Only numbers. Jupiter, man! You really expect us to document every shackled Jew who comes through those gates? Get out of my office—all of you! Take to the tower if you want. Search till your eyes burn out of their sockets. But leave me and my guards out of this! We have work to do!"

Our minds swimming in desolation, we made our way out of the slave camp. We headed toward the docks—our last flicker of hope. The man-made harbor, enclosed by a circle of large, arc-shaped stones, was filled with ships—massive hulks of wood and paint anchored to thick ropes that snaked into the blue water. Some were sailing though the inlet on the north and into the sun, propelled by a hundred sleek, white-washed oars shooting from three separate banks along the ship's bulbous sides. Smaller boats along the shoreline unloaded goods by means of bronze-skinned slaves and bulky apparatuses with pulleys and cranes. After they were unloaded, the same boats, refilled with chained men, women, and children, sailed out to the larger ships to stow their cargo somewhere under the deck. I noticed that the chains in these smaller boats were secured to strong metal hooks fore and aft. If the slaves tried to escape or overturn the boat, everyone would drown together.

We wandered back and forth along the seawall at ocean's edge until well after the sun had been extinguished beyond the waves, hoping just one face might shine out at us, maybe even wave his arms or cry out our names in tearful relief. It didn't happen. They weren't here. Harry and Gid had been taken away. Somewhere out there, one of those hulking ships was rowing them toward a destination that we had no possible way of knowing.

I wept into my hands after I'd collapsed at the end of the pier farthest north along the Caesarea shoreline. "What do we do, Uncle Garth? They're gone! They're really gone!"

"We find them," said Garth. "We find them however we can. We'll go back to the camp and find out the destinations of every slave ship in the last three days."

"You might have a list with over twenty possibilities," said Apollus. "You could find yourself searching in every corner of the world."

"Then we'll search every corner of the world!" said Garth.

Apollus sighed. "I'm sorry. I'll do whatever I can for you, but . . ." He didn't finish the statement. He didn't have to. We knew what he wanted to say. He couldn't help us forever. There were limits. Finally he added, "I think our first obligation is to get Meagan home to her father."

"Father?" I said dazedly.

"Yes," said Apollus. "You said your father is very rich. You're going to need that wealth, Meagan. If you intend to carry on a search as wide as this, you may need every spare sesterces in your father's coffers."

The dark tunnel of my emotions grew darker still. Rich father, shipping merchant—it was all a lie! We had no wealth! We had no resources at all to fund such a search. We had nothing. Any money we'd had was in the possession of Harry and Gid. We didn't even have enough to feed ourselves for one more day.

Apollus pleaded his cause with Garth. "Do you agree?" he asked him. "In my opinion, we should now travel to Alexandria. Our journey should begin immediately—tomorrow morning."

Garth didn't reply for quite some time. I studied his eyes. Up to now, Garth had regretfully said nothing about all the lies I had spun. I knew it was against all of his better judgments, and he wasn't going to tolerate it any longer. I braced myself. Heaven help us, I thought. He was going to spill every last detail.

"We do have a journey to make," Garth began. "But not to Alexandria."

Apollus drew his eyebrows together. "But isn't that where Meagan's father is stationed?"

"To find the resources we'll need," Garth said, "we will have to travel to another destination."

"But my orders are to return Meagan safely to her father's hands."

"Oh, she'll be safe enough when we get to where we're going. That I assure you."

"Where is it that you wish to go?"

Garth faced Apollus. He laid his hands on the Roman's shoulders. "Apollus, I know you've had suspicions about everything we've told you about ourselves these last few weeks. I'd like to tell you everything. I know Meagan would like to tell you everything, too."

Apollus eyed me guardedly. I'm sure I was as white as a ghost.

Garth continued, "I'm asking you to trust us, Apollus. I know you have no reason to do so. There are no debts between us; we saved each other's lives on Mount Gerizim. I'm asking you to search your heart for another reason. A more powerful reason. Friendship, loyalty, duty—I don't care what you might call it. We need your help, young man. But we have to know if we can trust each other. You have to trust that we have good reasons for going to where we're going and doing what we'll do. Our goal is to save Harry and Gid. Perhaps even save ourselves. But you can't expect to understand it all right away. In time I promise that you'll understand everything, but until then, we need to have your trust. If you can't give it, that's all right. There will be no ill will. But I'll have to insist that we part ways. Now. Tonight. In spite of any orders from your father. So I'm asking you, Apollus. Do you really want to help us? Can you trust us?"

Apollus' eyes were wide with a look of absolute uncertainty, even a thread of contempt. He looked from me to Garth and back again. Finally, he started to rise to his feet. My heart sank. He was leaving! He was going to turn around and walk out of our lives, leaving all this mind-boggling business behind forever.

Indeed, he did turn away. But an instant later he turned back.

"If I'm to help you, I must at least know where we're going."

Garth hesitated, then replied, "Masada."

His eyebrows shot up even higher. "Masada? Herod's fortress?"

"Yes. Well, not the fortress itself, but very close by."

The young Roman was growing more confused by the minute. "Near Masada there is only wilderness and wasteland. What could you possibly be looking for near Masada?"

Garth closed his eyes. "A cave," he replied.

Apollus was silent, studying, stewing, considering. "And this is your final destination?"

"Beyond this, I can't say," said Garth. "This is where I'm asking you to trust us. But I can promise you this, Apollus: if you come with us, you'll embark upon an adventure beyond your wildest dreams."

The wheels of his mind continued to spin. The Roman was still trying to decide what it all meant. But there were flecks of light in those bright blue eyes now. Garth had selected the perfect words—"an adventure beyond your wildest dreams." Though Apollus remained dubious, if there was any chance that somehow he might find with us the adventure that his overprotective father had so long denied him, he was powerless against the temptation.

"All right," he said resolutely. "I will trust you. And you can trust me.

But when the time comes, I'll expect you to share with me all that can be shared. Do you agree?"

"Yes," said Garth. "We agree."

I was still trying to digest it all. "What about Graccus and Lucullus?" I asked.

"My men are my men," said Apollus. "You let me worry about them."

And so the terms were set. The deal was sealed. We were really going home.

I stared out again at the vast Mediterranean, its surface glittering with the last purple shards of the setting sun. Again my heart sank into the blackest oblivion. There was nothing to celebrate. Nothing about this journey that could bring any peace. Somewhere out there on that infinite ocean were two of the people I cared about most in this world. Perhaps they weren't even on the same ship. Perhaps, I thought darkly, we'd missed them entirely and they weren't out there at all.

Garth and Apollus were right. To find Harry and Gid, we needed far more than anything we currently had. But what was there in the modern world that could possibly make this quest any easier? Garth must know, I told myself. He must have had some tangible idea, some clear plan. I saw no solution whatsoever. If I thought about it, my thoughts just closed in on themselves and my eyes overflowed. What if Garth really didn't have any answers either? In that case, maybe his decision to go home made the most sense of all. There was only one last bitter obligation remaining.

The obligation of telling Harry's father.

CHAPTER 5

My ankles chafed under the heavy iron bands they'd chained to the baseboard of my narrow wooden bunk. The crown of my head was set directly against the inner wall of the ship. I think I was a little taller than most of the slaves who had been locked into this claustrophobically small space. As a result, the hair on my head was always wet and covered with a sticky film. Sea water apparently seeped through the boards—or else it was just the condensation from the sweat and breathing of a hundred and fifty other prisoners trapped inside the ship's hold with me.

The bunks were stacked three high along both sides of the ship, with an aisle down the middle. I was on the second row from the bottom. Only my ankles were manacled. The chain ran through several bolts, locking the manacles on my legs with those of the slaves above and below me, meaning that I couldn't be set free without also freeing two others. Once a day the three of us were released for three or four minutes to stretch our legs while our chamberpots were emptied and our bunks wiped down with some kind of lye that smelled more obnoxious than the odors of human waste. The men who cleaned our bunks were slaves themselves. Somehow they'd earned the privilege of moving about rather than being stuck in a prone position for twenty-three hours and fifty-seven minutes a day.

Actually, about half of the men were unlocked at regular intervals, every four to eight hours. These men were then taken to the level just above us to fulfill their shift at rowing one of the ship's oars. The constant creaking of the oars and the steady beat of a drum were the main sounds that occupied my thoughts. The drum, I assumed—if I'd learned anything from the movie *Ben Hur*—was to keep the rowing at a constant pace. Others sounds were coughs and moans from other men in the hold.

For the last three days, I'd been passed over when it came my turn to row. I guess my swollen face and signs of other bruises had led them to conclude that I wouldn't be of much use. In reality I felt that much of my strength had returned, though I still couldn't see clearly out of my right eye. I was starting to accept that I might never see clearly out of it again. Days ago I'd thought several of my ribs had been broken, and two spots along my sides still felt tender. They might have been cracked; I wasn't sure. Nevertheless, I was convinced they were healing just fine.

My heart and soul ached worse than any part of my body. My memory of being herded down to the city docks to be boarded onto a large black ship flying a Roman flag was all a blur. I still couldn't believe it had happened—and I couldn't believe that Gidgiddonihah, Meagan, or Garth hadn't come to my rescue. What had become of them? My faith was waning that Gidgiddonihah still lived. The thought ripped at my soul, but it was harder and harder to deny. As for Meagan and Garth, I could only hope they had somehow escaped. Perhaps they were even now on their way back to the modern century. I realized now that I was beyond anyone's rescue. Anyone except God.

But I wasn't bitter or angry. Just confused and scared. I fully believed my fate was still in Heaven's hands. I just wished I understood what that fate was. Why was it necessary that I endure so much more pain? I wanted to think this was all some kind of bad dream; that it wasn't real. It was easier that way. I understood the temptation some people had to reject reality altogether and let their minds sink into a kind of no-man's land. It took great self-control to hang on. Every hour I reminded myself that I could still feel, still think and breathe, and that I was still loved. Somewhere out there, people still cared for me. They were praying for me. I wasn't alone.

I didn't have the vaguest clue where our ship was headed. I felt its rocking motions and tried to imagine that it might be headed to Athens, where I might find Symeon and Mary and little Jesse. Or Ephesus, where I might find the Apostle John. Somewhere that I could find friends. There were so many destinations in the Roman world, and I knew it was unlikely that I'd wind up in any location that had a name I would recognize. Maybe I was going to Rome itself. At any other time, seeing the great capital of the Empire would have filled me with wonder. But at the moment, no ancient destination in the world would have gratified my imagination. I just wanted plain, boring Salt Lake City, Utah. I just wanted to be home.

There was about a six-inch space beside my head that allowed me to see into the neighboring bunk. To my left was a man with a terrible, wheezing cough. His name was Joshua. He was about my father's age, early forties. At least this is what he told me. I'd have guessed he was closer to sixty. He'd been a slave for several months already; the lack of proper nutrition had taken its toll. His body was as thin as a rake, and his eyes looked as if they might roll out of their sockets like a pair of cat's-eye marbles. For the most part he was too weak to talk, but I learned that he was an Idumean from Hebron, south of Jerusalem. He'd been arrested for aiding and abetting soldiers held in a fortress called the Herodium. Idumeans, as far as I could determine, were just another branch of the tribe of Israel, though they liked to consider themselves distinct from the Jews.

For the first three days, the bunk on my right had been occupied by a Zealot soldier captured near Jerusalem. I never learned his name. He wasn't very friendly and had little to say. He didn't like to look at me; the injury on my face seemed to offend him. Every eight hours he was gone anyway, taken up top to do his shift at rowing the ship.

The loneliness I felt had become physically painful. I could feel it throbbing in my chest. Very few of the Jews spoke to me much at all. They were such a sour, doleful lot. I guess I could understand that, considering our circumstances. But my gosh! We were all in this together. Couldn't we lean on each other? Draw strength from each other? It was as if they believed they were already dead.

"Hey," I once asked the Zealot on my right, "why was Cleopatra so negative? Because she was the Queen of Denial. Get it?"

I said it more to be mocking than to make a joke. Something was lost in the translation. The soldier pressed tighter into the other side of his bed. I sighed and tried to fall asleep.

When I awakened, the bunk on my right was empty, but I heard the clink of chains as someone else was being forced to climb inside. As the head slid awkwardly into view, my heart flipped. It was the boy!—the boy who had given me water back at the slave camp. Someone had mixed up the sleeping arrangements. His face was the most welcome sight I had seen in three days. I wasn't sure why I felt this way; our last encounter hadn't been all that encouraging. Nothing had told me he had any desire to become my friend. I didn't care. He was going to become my friend whether he liked it or not.

He looked weary, having just finished his turn at the oars. He smelled of fish oil, like the rest of the men. It must have been some sort of lubricant used to grease the eyelets that held the oars in place. He closed his eyes without even acknowledging his new neighbor, as if he intended to fall asleep immediately.

"Hello," I interrupted.

The eyes opened reluctantly. As soon as he recognized me, they rolled upward and closed again. "Oh, it's you," he said with obvious contempt. "Ever get yourself enough water to drink?"

The contempt was *too* obvious. I was sure he was pleased to see me.

"No," I replied. "You?"

He laughed scornfully. "No. And I don't expect to. Especially now. At sea they'll give us only enough to live. Not a drop more."

He stopped speaking and became still. I wasn't about to let him fall asleep so easily. Not after being in this horrid isolation for so long.

"My name is Harrison," I said, feeling the need to give my name its more distinguished ending.

He didn't reply.

"What's yours?" I persisted.

"Why do you want to know?" he asked. "Were you hoping we might end up in the same household? The twin slaves of some rich Roman landlady? Don't count on it. We might as well forget our names. They'll never mean anything to anyone again. You and I are slated to die."

What a cheerful fellow, I thought. But I wasn't to be defeated. "I'd still like to know. It might mean something to me."

He was silent another moment, then gave up. "Micah."

"Micah," I repeated. "Cool. Micah was a prophet, right? Of the Old Testament?"

"The old what?"

"Never mind. It hasn't been compiled yet. But it's still a good name."

"How would you know or care?" he asked. "You're not a Jew. You're not even an Israelite."

I was tired of this distinction—tired of the lower tier it seemed to put me on. "How can you be so sure?" I asked, just to be ornery.

He huffed. "You're a Sarmatian or a Scythian or a Celt, or some other barbarian if I ever saw one."

"Then how do you explain my being here with all you captive Jews?" I asked.

"Your father is a drunk, and he sold you for a flask of wine," he answered smugly.

Boy, this friendship wasn't going to be easy.

"Okay," I admitted, "I'm not a Jew. But you *know* I wasn't sold by my father. You saw me that morning before I was arrested. You saw me with my friend, Gidgiddonihah."

"Ah, yes," he said. "The big man with the sword. Yes, I remember."

I felt a jolt of anxiousness. "Did you see Gid after we were attacked? Did you see what happened to him?"

He scrutinized me, eyes taunting. He *did* see something!

"Please!" I begged, "If you know anything—"

"He's dead," Micah said bluntly. "He must be, after what they did to him."

"*What?*" I asked, horrified.

"Doesn't matter," he said wearily. "He's better off. You should envy him."

If I could have reached into his bunk, I'd have throttled him. I had to calm myself. Getting angry wouldn't get me anywhere. Be calm. Be nice.

"Please . . ."

He relented. "They beat him. Same as you. Beat him to a pulp. You wouldn't have recognized him. For a while he was right beside you in the yard, lined up with the others waiting to die."

"But he *wasn't* dead," I said, as if trying to persuade him. "You never saw him die."

"No," he admitted. "He was still alive when they took him, though I doubt he knew his own name."

"*Who* took him?"

"The arena men," said Micah.

"You mean gladiators? The gladiators took him?"

"Yes, yes," said Micah, growing impatient.

"Why? What were they going to do with him?"

"Dump his body in the sewer! How should I know?"

He shut his eyes again, determined to sleep. He'd told me every-thing he knew. Despite what he'd said about Gid's condition, I felt a renewed sense of hope. Micah hadn't seen him die. But what did Problius want with him? Was he taking him back to Berytus to train him as a gladiator? Gid would never cooperate. Maybe Problius want-ed to torture him—make him a training dummy for his men. Maybe he just wanted the pleasure of executing him personally. I shuddered. That seemed the most likely conclusion. After all, he'd stolen and defaced Problius' precious sword.

God would protect him, I thought. Then I felt guilty. Gidgiddonihah wouldn't be the first righteous man to die at the hands of villains. If it was Gid's time, there was nothing anyone could do. But it *wasn't*. I knew it. I would see him again.

I was offended by Micah's flippancy, yet I tried to understand. Obviously he'd also been cut off from everyone he'd ever cared about. Every slave in this ship had lost loved ones. The concern I'd expressed over the loss of a friend would have seemed trivial.

"I'm sorry," I said, resenting a little that I had to apologize. "I just wanted to know."

He didn't respond, just drew a long sigh and turned his head away. I let him sleep. He was out for about three hours. The instant I heard him stir, I spoke again, as if there had been no break in our conversation.

"What about you? How did you become a slave?"

He looked at me. Sleep seemed to have settled his mood. "I vol-unteered," he said.

I thought he was joking. As a joke, it would have been rather clever. But something in his tone sounded perfectly serious. "Volunteered? You *volunteered* for this?"

Micah answered soberly. "They demanded twenty young men. There were only twenty-three in our community. I knew my destiny. It was written long before I was born. If I hadn't gone, those scum, the

Syrian auxiliaries in their Roman rags, would have burned our community to the ground."

"What community is this?" I asked.

"No name," he replied. "It's in the hills above Betharamptha in Perea. We just called it the Place of the Fathers."

I started to feel uneasy. I hoped he wasn't part of another one of those creepy cults, like Simon Magus.

"I've never heard of it," I said.

"It's just above the Jordan plain, near the Salt Sea."

"Really?" I said, intrigued. "Is it like Qumran?"

He scrunched his forehead. "I don't know this place."

I fumbled to clarify myself. "The City of Salt—I don't know what else to call it. It was in the hills above the Dead Sea along the northwest shore. We were there just a few weeks ago. It's in ruins now."

"Yes," said Micah. "It's like the City of Salt. Only our order was much more strict and holy. The priests at the City of Salt had perverted the right way. That's why they were destroyed."

Oh dear, I thought. Another fanatic. Why couldn't I just meet a nice, normal kid?

"To the Pharisees and Sadducees we are called Essenes," he continued. "To ourselves we are the Sons of Light."

"I see." Man, I didn't want to talk about any more goofy religions. At the same time, I was desperate to nurture a friendship. "So what about your mother and father? Are they Essenes, too?"

"I don't remember my mother," he said, almost with pride. "My father is one of the Teachers of Righteousness. Women are not a part of our community. I was carried to the Place of the Fathers when I was a small boy. I accepted the Covenant of Moses two years ago. I was to be inducted into the Holy Congregation next summer."

"No girls?" I said with surprise. "You mean no one gets married?"

"Marriage is for the weaker children of the Covenant."

"Then how does anyone . . . how do you repopulate the community?"

"We don't need to repopulate it. Seekers of truth come to *us*. If they prove themselves worthy, they may join us. It's the sacred duty of the Sons of Light to pave the way for the coming of the Messiahs."

"*Messiahs?* You think there's more than one?"

"Of course. The prophet, the priest, and the king. The scriptures are very clear."

Boy, I thought, folks could sure screw up some perfectly good doctrines. There had to be something else we could talk about.

"Do you miss your father?" I asked.

It struck me that this might be an insensitive question—the kind where the only reply I might get would be, "Duh!"

Micah, however, took it in stride. "Of course not. Neither would he miss me. Such emotions are frivolous. We are trained to focus our minds on more important things."

Okay, I thought. *I was trying to befriend a non-human.*

"Your father doesn't happen to be Mr. Spock, does he?" I asked.

The point was lost on him.

I thought another moment, then said, "I don't believe it. I think you miss your dad very much. That's what I think. I think you miss a *lot* of the folks back in your community."

He didn't reply, either because I'd struck a chord, or because the Vulcan thought my statements were illogical. Once again, I decided to change the subject.

"What did you mean when you said you and I are slated to die?" I asked.

"It's our destiny," he said. "We cannot change it. God's will is written in stone. You and I are to become canal diggers at the straits of Corinth. They work slaves at the straits until they're dead. It saves them the trouble of having to resell our broken bodies after they've outlived their usefulness."

"How do you know that's where we're going?"

"I heard them talking up top. Don't worry. If God wills, we'll never reach Achaia. The storms of October will be upon us before we arrive. No slaves ever survive a shipwreck."

That seemed obvious enough, considering our chains. I thought about his words. A canal digger, eh? So that was God's destiny for me. I had a hard time believing it.

"Don't you think we have the power to change our destiny?" I asked.

"Of course not," he replied.

"That's stupid," I said, growing tired of such nonsense. "I might have believed my fate was set in stone a dozen times. I always changed the outcome."

"You only *thought* you did," he said arrogantly. "You were still fulfilling the plan set by God before the foundation of the world."

Now I was getting irritated. "That's hogwash. We can change anything we want to, if it's right, and if we have enough faith. If you want it bad enough, you can be anything you want to be."

"But it would still not change your destiny," he said.

I stewed for several minutes. I couldn't have changed this guy's opinions with a sledgehammer. I was starting to doubt if I wanted him for a friend or not. But then, to my surprise, Micah asked his first question.

"So are you a Pagan? A worshipper of the sun, moon, and stars like these vile Romans?"

"No," I answered. "I'm a Christian. That is, a Nazarene."

"Ah, I see," he said with genuine interest.

"So you've heard of us?"

"Yes, of course. The founder of your sect was an Essene."

"Oh, is that so?"

"Yes, it's so."

"Our founder was Jesus Christ."

"There you're wrong," he insisted. "Jesus of Nazareth did not found your sect. It was John ben Zacharias, who for a time dwelt with the Holy Ones at Jericho and elsewhere, until he was beheaded at Machaerus."

"That's not true. John the Baptist didn't think he was worthy to loose the Savior's boot latchet. He was great prophet, but he didn't start Christianity."

"But even your priests teach that John paved the way as the voice of one crying in the wilderness, as it is written in Isaiah, do they not?"

"Well . . . yes."

"Then your beginnings sprang out of the communities of the Essenes."

"That's ridiculous. John the Baptist wasn't an Essene. Or if he was, he didn't *stay* one. He may have lived like one for a while, but—"

"If he lived as one, then he was one."

"I didn't say *as*. I said *like*. John believed in just one Messiah—the Savior Jesus Christ. He baptized Jesus in the River Jordan."

"The ceremony of rebirth by water. He learned this ceremony from us."

I started to wonder if I was arguing with the wall. I'd learned somewhere that it was better to attract flies with honey rather than vinegar. Maybe now was a good time to try it out. We needed to celebrate what we had in common. Not our differences.

"You may be right," I said. "But let's face it. The ceremony began a long time before that. It was started with Adam. Wouldn't you agree?"

He seemed reluctant to agree with anything. Then finally he said, "Yes. It began with Adam."

"We believe it symbolizes death and rebirth into the Kingdom of God," I added. "A washing away of our sins."

He didn't comment. I had a feeling he believed the exact same thing. But his next statement revealed to me how little he actually knew about Christianity. "So does your sect still keep the Sabbath?"

"Yes," I said. "Very much so."

"To the letter?"

I became cautious. "What do you mean?"

"Do you fast? Do you keep your mind and body pure? Do you refrain from speaking, except to utter prayers? Or from moving about, except to raise your arms or prostrate yourself before God? Do you have the self-discipline to refrain from all bodily desires, including sleep and even relieving your bowels?"

My eyes widened. "You've gotta be kiddin' me! You think that's what it means to keep the Sabbath?"

"Of course. One day in seven we give wholly to God."

"We *do* fast once a month," I concurred. "We like to make an extra effort to keep our minds and bodies pure, too. But the rest of it . . . we believe the Sabbath was made for man."

"As I thought," he said smugly. "You Nazarenes could never display the same discipline as an Essene."

"I said we didn't believe all that was *necessary*. I didn't say I couldn't do it."

"We shall see," said Micah. "The Sabbath begins shortly. Let's see if you Nazarenes can be as holy as the Sons of Light."

I opened my mouth to protest, but nothing came out. This was ridiculous. I wasn't going to let this kid coerce me into some kind of

Sabbath-day competition. It was sacrilegious! And yet . . . what harm would it do to spend a day in fasting and prayer? Considering how little I was eating anyway, was it wise? Staying in one place wouldn't be a challenge. Staying awake didn't seem difficult either. But refusing to relieve myself? *For twenty-four hours?* When I'd called this guy a fanatic, it was the understatement of the century!

"All right," I said. "I'll fast with you. But it's not a contest. Just a day of prayer and meditation. A day devoted to God."

He smiled impishly and closed his eyes.

I glanced toward the far end of the hold, where slivers of sunlight penetrated the boards in the ceiling. From this I'd be able to determine when the sun went down. I knew the Jewish Sabbath began at sundown, not at daybreak, then ended at sunset the following day. The light was already dimming.

A few minutes later they brought us our food—a bowl of gruel. Barley, I think. And a wooden cup filled with water. It wasn't technically the Sabbath yet. Still, I was afraid to eat or drink. I knew it wasn't right to fast the way Micah was fasting, but oh, pride can be a terrible thing sometimes.

Micah ate without hesitation. That cinched it. I scooped up the gruel with my fingers and washed it down with the water in my cup.

As the light of the sun disappeared, Micah began to sing. The melody was quite dreary. Micah's singing prompted other voices to start singing or chanting or mumbling. I was sure they weren't all Essenes—just Jews. But it still amazed me to hear my fellow prisoners so determined to keep up the rituals of their religion. Not everyone sang or prayed. Joshua, on my left, was as quiet as a dormouse. I feared he wouldn't survive this journey, but at least for now I could hear him breathing.

Micah was singing the Book of Genesis:

"In the beginning God created the heaven and the earth. And the earth was without form and void . . ."

He kept going verse after verse after verse. Had he memorized the entire book of Genesis? It seemed to me he was making up the melody as he went along. But maybe not. Maybe the Essenes had created a song for every scripture. Maybe he wouldn't stop at Genesis. Maybe he'd sing the entire Bible!

Obviously the Essenes had way too much time on their hands. Then again, there probably wasn't much else to do out there in the desert. After an hour, Micah was singing about the Tower of Babel. Other voices in the hold went quiet. They were listening to Micah.

Was this what Micah meant by prayers to God? This wasn't talking to God. Any parrot could do this—well, any particularly *intelligent* parrot. I'd always been taught that prayers should be from the heart. So that's what I tried to do, though with all the singing and chattering, it was hard to concentrate.

I talked to God about every subject under the sun—my pains, my hopes, my fears. Even my future dreams and expectations. The feelings were glorious, despite the discomforts, despite the continual rocking motions of the ship. But sometime in the middle of the night, my eyes opened wide. I began to feel that familiar pressure. My chamberpot was still beside my hip.

I pinched my eyes shut. *I could do this,* I told myself. *Just hang in there.*

It might be best at this point if I made a long story short. Let me just confess that I failed in my efforts to match Micah's self-discipline. Micah, whose song was now well into Exodus, I'm sure was over there gloating.

Still, I continued my fast in my own way—the way I felt was right. But the next morning something happened that I knew would spoil Micah's Sabbath as much as mine. The key-keepers returned and began unlocking the three men of Micah's bunk. His turn at the oars had come around again. This ship apparently didn't have any work policy respecting religious rights. As the chain began sliding through the metal loops, I could see the stress in Micah's face. He continued to lie there while the other two men climbed out of their bunks. Would Micah refuse? It seemed unthinkable. I noticed that all of the other Jews—even men who'd been chanting prayers—were willingly submitting. Somehow I knew instinctively that Micah was different. This could well have been a matter of life and death. Or at least of bitter humiliation and defeat. He'd be compromising one of the most important tenets of his faith.

"Let's go!" barked the key-keeper.

Micah faltered in his song. His singing voice, already more subdued than when the night had begun, cracked with tension.

"Wait!" I said to the key-keeper. "This man is sick. I'll take his place. Let him rest today. I'm sure he'll be fine tomorrow."

The man and his fellow jailers looked me over, no doubt assessing my bruises. One of them laughed. Suddenly the matter became very humorous to all of them.

"Fine," said the key-keeper. "You take his place. But if you can't pull your weight, don't expect to be loosed from your oar. Not unless it's to toss you to the sharks. Understand?"

I nodded uneasily. "I understand."

The chain that attached me to the bunk was removed. I climbed out and stood in the narrow aisle, my legs a bit wobbly. My ribs still felt tender. I glanced inside my bunk, where my bowl of breakfast and cup of water sat untouched. The men were already pushing me on. For the next eight hours, I'd continue my fast whether I liked it or not.

As I turned to follow the key-keepers, I looked in briefly at Micah. He was still singing, still reciting his Sabbath day hymn. But he was watching me. In his eyes there was a look I hadn't seen before. Maybe it was too much to call it gratitude. It might have just been astonishment. Whatever it was, I felt confident that I had indeed earned a friend.

CHAPTER 6

The massive fortress of Masada shimmered on its rocky precipice in the afternoon heat. The five of us sat on our horses in a gully about three miles to the southwest. We could clearly distinguish all of the buildings and structures on the flat mesa summit. The three-tiered palace of King Herod and its balconies on the northernmost edge were breathtaking, a marvel of ancient engineering. Especially considering that the surrounding landscape was as barren and dead as any desert on earth. It seemed to me that the summit even showed a bit of green. The Jewish rebels who had taken control of the place from the Romans were actually growing crops.

"Where do they get enough water?" I asked Garth.

"Rain," Garth replied. "They have a whole network of ditches and pipes that catch every drop and store it in large cisterns at various places inside the mountain."

Fascinating, I thought. From where we stood, I could see the tiny shapes of sentries overlooking the battlements. All was very quiet on the surrounding plains up to the shores of the Dead Sea to the east. According to Garth, the Jews had taken the fortress from the Romans in a single day near the beginning of the war. They promptly executed all legionaries who had been stationed there. I knew in a few months the barren plains would be teeming with Roman soldiers determined to take the mountain back. At the moment, the Zealots were enjoying a fine respite. But even I'd been taught the fate that would eventually befall them. After several grueling years, the Romans would succeed in their campaign to breach the battlements. Nearly a thousand men, women, and children would commit suicide rather than allow themselves to be executed or enslaved.

"How do you know so much about Herod's fortress?" Apollus asked Garth suspiciously.

"That's another of those questions," Garth replied, "that will soon be answered in one blinding moment."

Honestly, Apollus actually hadn't asked many such questions. Neither had his men, Lucullus and Graccus, though in the evenings I could sometimes hear them whispering questions to Apollus. I found it naggingly curious why Apollus had been as consenting as he had. I was sure it wasn't because he had any great love for me. Though he had been very cordial to me throughout the six long days we had traveled across war-torn Judea to reach the wilderness of the Dead Sea, he hadn't made any effort to reestablish the closeness we had enjoyed that first night in Caesarea, or those three days we had been alone together on Mount Gerizim. Maybe his cooperation went back to fulfilling the promise he had made to his father to watch over me until I reached safe hands, but I was beginning to doubt that as well. Perhaps it was just his yearning for adventure, but I wasn't sure there was enough motivation there either. Something else was driving Apollus to be so patient with this bizarre escapade into these thirsty hills, though I sensed he wasn't all that comfortable with his reasons. Call it female intuition, but I had a gut feeling that Apollus felt guilty.

It was a strange conclusion to draw. I almost hoped I was wrong. If I had been certain, I might have feared that Apollus was planning to betray us at the last moment. Or turn on us in some other way. But the vibes I got weren't quite that threatening. It was as if the big Boy Scout was afraid he was about to do something that wasn't entirely honest.

"Where is the cave?" Apollus asked a little too eagerly.

Lucullus and Graccus perked up as well. We all knew that we were very close to our destination.

"Over this rise, then down a steep escarpment, and through a canyon," Garth replied. "We should leave our horses in this gully. From here, we should reach it on foot in about an hour."

Apollus nodded. His face betrayed that guilty look again. When our eyes connected, he looked away. Lucullus was grinning. I actually saw Graccus lick his lips. What was going on? They all looked like gluttons staring down a Thanksgiving turkey.

Suddenly it hit me. A rather bizarre statement that Apollus had made before we left Caesarea flashed through my mind—"When the time comes, I'll expect you to share with me all that can be shared."

At first I'd thought this meant information—a revealing of secrets.

Oh, my gosh. It was all becoming clear to me. Mysterious secrets, caves near the Dead Sea—now I understood Graccus' need to tell his little anecdote that night in Joppa about a Roman soldier in the days of Pompeii discovering a cache of treasure in a cave near Bersabe. The money had turned out to be part of the royal treasury of old King Solomon. Roman folk tales were rife with stories of ancient treasures located in caves. Garth had mentioned that our destination was a cave near the fortress of Masada right after Apollus had suggested that my father's wealth might be the only way to find Harry. Oh, my gosh! *He thought we were on our way to recover* a *secret treasure! Now that I thought about it, what other conclusion could he have drawn? Why, that low-down, greedy pile of Roman drool. He expected to* be paid *for helping us get here. So did his men.*

As we climbed down from our horses, my face was bright red with anger.

"Maybe we should leave them here," I said sharply to Garth.

I sounded accusing, which made Garth raise an eyebrow. Graccus and Lucullus looked stricken. Apollus waited to hear Garth's reply.

"We really can't force them," said Garth. He faced Apollus. "You shouldn't feel any obligation. If you join us from here, I can't guarantee that you'll ever return to the world you know. Only that your life will never be the same."

Apollus' men smiled. They took it as a metaphor for a life of riches. Apollus looked slightly more sensible. He turned to Lucullus. "You and Graccus stay with the horses," he commanded.

"But," said Graccus, heartbroken, "won't you need our help?"

"Yes," said Lucullus, "things could get . . . heavy."

That confirmed it. My suspicions were correct. "I think they should all stay," I said. "If they came, they'd only be disappointed."

That drew some stares. Now Apollus' men really were curious. Even a bit defensive.

Apollus said, "If you wish us to stay, we'll stay."

I studied his face. Maybe I'd judged him too harshly. He seemed to mean what he said. It was up to us. Apollus may have harbored secret desires of becoming rich, but for now he appeared willing to leave it to our discretion.

Garth hadn't picked up on the hints of what was really going on. "After all we've been through," he said to me, "I feel we should leave it up to Apollus. The choice should be his."

Apollus looked gratified, but the look on my face made him uncertain.

"I will let Meagan decide," he said. "I have no intention of intruding where she may not feel that I belong."

His sincerity softened me a bit. I really wanted to believe he'd come for reasons other than money. But how would he respond when he entered a cave with no signs of glittering loot? When that moment came, I was sure I'd see his true character. I desperately had to know. It was totally selfish. Of course there was still a part of me that winced at the thought of leaving him behind, despite all I'd done to try and suffocate such feelings. I tried not to think about that. Maybe I just wanted to see the look on his face as we stood within the glorious, swirling wonders of the Galaxy Room.

"It's all right," I said. "He can come."

Lucullus and Graccus reluctantly consented to remain behind. I almost amended Apollus' orders. I wanted to tell them if we were gone for more than three days, they should pack up and go home. It seemed too cruel to expect them to stay any longer. Then again, they were grown men. They'd certainly draw those conclusions on their own. I didn't believe they would follow us. Garth's directions sounded complicated. But even if they found the cave, I was convinced that the sight of something like the Galaxy Room would send their ancient minds squealing home. The only reason I didn't think Apollus would react the same way was his association with us. Our presence would give him all the confidence he needed. Maybe I was completely underestimating the limits of the ancient imagination.

Garth unstrapped his backpack from his horse and looped the straps over his shoulders. It was the same backpack we'd recovered from the Mount of Olives as we were escaping from Jerusalem. I knew it contained flashlights and many other supplies that would prove invaluable inside the cave. Up until now, Garth had successfully kept all of its contents hidden from view. In about an hour, such discretions would come to an end.

We took other supplies—plenty of food and water. Apollus also carried several torches soaked in a black tar called bitumen. Lucullus and Graccus kept their eyes directed at our backs until the last possible moment as we dropped out of sight behind the first escarpment.

"Meagan," said Apollus as we scrambled down the rocky ravine, kicking up dust, "I've come to a decision. I wish you to know it before we reach this cave."

"Really? What's that?"

He hesitated, almost as if he was about to change his mind. "It's quite difficult," he said.

"The decision?"

"Yes. My family is not rich. We have some holdings in Italy. Some scant shares in a bank at Pergamum. But my father's debts when he retires from the army will well exceed his pension. I must confess, when your uncle first made his proposal to me in Caesarea, the temptation was overwhelming."

I listened without interrupting. Garth was a few yards ahead of us. The grinding of stones kept him out of the conversation.

"I just wanted you to know," he continued, "—though I have no idea what we are about to behold—that I would never cheat you out of your rightful find."

"Cheat me?" I asked, as if flabbergasted. "Whatever do you mean?"

"Well, no doubt you are aware that whatever treasures are unearthed in Roman lands are the property of the Emperor. It would be within my duties to confiscate the whole amount and accept a commission from the royal treasury. This, of course, would hinder you in your efforts to find your brother, so I just wanted you to know that I will not accept any more than might be necessary to satisfy the demands of my men."

"What are you talking about?" I asked in utter perplexity.

Apollus looked confused, then he smirked. "I think we both know."

"Let me see if I've got this straight. You were actually tempted to confiscate everything that might be in this cave and leave us high and dry?"

"No!" said Apollus, offended. "I mean—it would be my duty—but I could never—"

"You were actually tempted to betray us?"

Garth finally stopped at the mouth of a narrow canyon and started to listen. "What's going on? Betray? What are we talking about?"

Apollus was flustered. "That's not true. I've just informed you that I don't want any payment of any kind. But if you must know it all, yes. Of course I was tempted. I'm only a man. What man would not have been tempted? But by the gods, I swear that I will not keep a single coin. Unfortunately, I can't speak for my men. They will require some percentage of the treasure for their silence."

"What treasure?" asked Garth in frustration.

Apollus' expression changed. Garth's befuddlement had been sincere. "The treasure we are on our way to recover," the Roman said uncertainly.

Garth stared at him. Then enlightenment dawned. "You think there's a treasure in this cave?"

"Of course," said Apollus. "Why else would you drag us down into this infernal cauldron in search of a secret cave?"

Garth sighed in deepest regret. "Oh, Apollus. Somehow you've been harboring a terrible misconception. I suppose I'm to blame, with all my talk of secrets and mysteries. Just hang tight, Apollus Brutus. Very shortly all the mysteries will begin to unfold. Come on. The cave is right up here."

We continued up the narrow canyon. Apollus looked greatly vexed. For a guy who'd just willingly rejected a fortune, he seemed grievously disappointed that the noble choice might be denied him. Actually, he didn't seem to know what to think. Nor was I sure what to think of him. I was suddenly grateful that he'd harbored the misconception that he had. If he hadn't, we might never have persuaded him to come this far.

The going got rather steep. It was only a couple hundred yards to the entrance of the small cave, but the terrain kept us from arriving for another thirty minutes. At last the thin, dark crevasse gaped open before us. Sweaty and tired, we peered inside. From a distance it had looked like just another fissure in the rock, no different from any other fissure. Up close, it was apparent that a tunnel cut back to the right and descended down a gloomy corridor. There were footprints all around, and the ashes of a cold fire.

Garth slipped the backpack off his shoulders and unzipped the main compartment. He pulled out a red, plastic-cased six-volt flashlight and hit the rubber button to turn it on. Apollus hardly reacted, just watched in silent fascination. "You'd better light your torches," he said to Apollus. "I only have one of these."

Apollus stared at him, then he produced a small set of flints.

"Here," said Garth. "I might be able to hurry that along."

Apollus stood impassively as Garth took one of the torches from his hand and pulled a single wooden match out of a box. Garth struck the match and put it to the torch's head. The bitumen slowly caught flame until the entire head was blazing and putting off a greasy smoke.

Apollus seemed to take this as a challenge. He retained his next torch and struck the flint. In a single try, the second torch ignited as easily as the other had with the match. Garth smiled. Perhaps some conveniences of the modern world weren't all that miraculous.

Garth handed the flashlight to me. I stood transfixed at the cave's entrance. For some reason, my heart was beating like a timpani inside my chest. It had seemed so long—almost a lifetime—that I had been trapped in this harsh, enchanting world. Was I really at the brink of returning home? The thought transformed so quickly into a tear on my cheek that I had no time to relish the reality. Harry wasn't here. Oh, Father in Heaven, how could we do it? *How could we leave him here? It felt as if we were leaving him behind through the portal of another universe. Garth was confident that there would be hardly a day or two's difference between the moment we left and the moment we returned. But how could he be certain? How could we be sure of anything? What if we returned to find sixth-century Mohammedans or twelfth-century crusaders? Harry would be a long-forgotten memory. His final, horrible destiny would be forever unknown to those who loved him. Somehow I felt sure that the moment I entered that cave, it would be too late. There would be no going back. And yet, what choice did we have? Without some sort of help or resources from the modern world, our search might prove to be just as fruitless.*

Garth seemed to read my thoughts. He put his arm around my shoulder. "We're doing the right thing, Meagan. We're doing the only thing we can."

"What if we're wrong, Uncle Garth?" *I sobbed.* "What if . . . what if we're sacrificing our only opportunity? What if we never see him again?"

"No, Meagan," *Garth said sternly.* "Search your heart. Dig deep down. Listen to the Spirit. You know it isn't true, don't you? We *will see him. Do you feel it? You have to know it, Meagan.*"

I felt the power in Garth's bright green eyes. So self-assured. I did as he asked. I searched my own heart. I concentrated as hard as I knew how. And somewhere below the surface, I did feel something. I can't explain it. I don't know what it was. But I felt . . . brave.

I was ready to enter the tunnel.

Apollus was more reluctant than ever. I saw apprehension in those dark blue Roman eyes. What exactly was *inside that shadowy tunnel? What was he getting himself into? I suddenly felt sorry for him. I even felt a little inconsiderate. Then, all at once, our actions seemed irrational. What in heaven's name were we doing? We'd invited a Roman centurion to witness the twenty-first century! What were we* thinking?! *Had we lost our minds? What would be the consequences of such a thing?*

It was clear that neither Garth nor I had fully thought this out. Somehow, it really wasn't our right to decide. Could we have predicted the consequences of our own presence among the Romans? What made us any different from Apollus?

But then the answer hit me. The gospel. Garth and I knew the reality of our Father in Heaven's kingdom and the Plan of Salvation. Suddenly this difference seemed paramount. Even the scantest knowledge and testimony that I possessed seemed like a special license to see the things that we had seen. At least I'd give the experience its proper interpretation, put things in an appropriate gospel perspective. But how would Apollus react? What would he do with the knowledge he was about to receive? What kind of power were we about to place in this young Roman's hands?

If Garth had asked himself the same questions, it was clear we'd both asked too late. Apollus was already strapping his cuirass tighter across his chest and balancing his bronze helmet on his brow. He held aloft his torch and asked, "What are we waiting for? Let's see these mysteries that you've kept hidden from me for the past six days."

Garth and I looked at each other. It was time to embark.

"All right," said Garth. "I'll lead the way. You two keep—"

In that instant, the three of us caught our breath. The ground shook! There was a tremor in the earth.

I grabbed Garth's arm. After three or four seconds, the rumbling stopped.

"What was that?" I asked in dismay.

"Quake," said Apollus. "Not a strong one. I used to feel them all the time as a boy in Felsina. This one was no cause for concern."

Garth's face told me different. I shared his apprehension. Such a rumbling so close to the entrance of the tunnel seemed too coincidental. Something was happening in the ground below. What could it have been? Was this normal? I didn't remember feeling any such tremors before, either on Cedar Mountain, inside the cave, or below that waterfall near the shores of the Dead Sea.

"Let's go," said Garth. "Walk slowly and stay close."

We crept into the fissure and disappeared from the daylight of 70 A.D. If anything ominous lay at the source of the quake, there was little doubt that we were about to discover what it was.

CHAPTER 7

In my imagination, it hadn't been so bad. I'd envisioned at least two to three men pulling on each of those massive oars. With thirty oars whisking us through the water on each side, as well as a billowing red and white sail, how hard could it have been to propel the ship? I experienced a rude awakening as soon as I saw the steerage room. One man! That's all there was to each one of those fifteen-foot oars.

My ankles were locked into place at a bench on the right, just behind the main mast. This particular ship only had one bank of oars on each side. I glanced upward through a wooden grating and saw part of the ship's deck. The sail was down, tied tightly against the yardarms. The wind was blowing against us.

I peered through the eyelet that held my oar and gawked at the vast, dark ocean. The vision in my right eye was still impaired by a milky blur, but it didn't make any difference; I couldn't see a speck of land. I'd never been on a body of water where I couldn't see some sort of shoreline. Claustrophobia crept over me. Was this the terrible isolation that one feels on the ocean? The feeling was intensified by the shackles on my ankle. If this ship went down, I really was destined to go down with it.

"Four beats per stroke!" a taskmaster shouted at me. He was a horrible-looking man with a smashed nose and bushy eyebrows that seemed to grow together across his forehead, like one long hairy caterpillar. "Raise your oar when the drum stops. Keep it raised if the steersman beats only the drum on the left. Lower it when he beats the drum on the right. If we find out you're slicing with the edge of your oar instead of rowing, you'll be flogged! Is that clear?"

Such was the extent of my instruction. Rowers were expected to catch on quickly. If we didn't, we'd surely lose our job—and in the harshest way imaginable. The steersman raised his hands over the twin drums—his signal that the rowing was about to commence. My ribs started throbbing, as if warning me that if I tried to pull that oar a broken bone would pop right through my flesh. The taskmaster with the flat nose was right behind me, holding a multi-strapped whip in case I showed the least hesitation.

"Steady pace!" cried the ship's commander from his raised platform behind the steersman. He looked more like a college professor than the commander of a slave ship; gaunt with a dull, expressionless face and graying hair. He wore a simple white tunic with a leather belt. I realized that no one in the steerage room wore a Roman uniform. The crew, it appeared, all worked for the slave merchants. If there were any soldiers on board, they remained up top.

The commander's order was repeated, and the rowing began. I pinched my eyes shut to control the pain and pulled at my oar. My ribs hurt so bad I was sure I would cry out, but I held it inside and kept on rowing. After ten or eleven strokes, the pain deadened. I concluded that my ribs were not broken. Or maybe they'd healed. Perhaps by a miracle. I could do this, I decided. I could make it.

After the first hour, I became a machine. It didn't seem to matter that all my joints felt as if they'd been set on fire. One more stroke. I didn't think any further ahead than one more stroke.

Four hours—that was the length of my shift. I thanked God that it hadn't gone the full eight; I'd have never made it that long. I guessed that our shift had been shortened because the skies to the north were darkening. They wanted fresh rowers to try and outrun the storm. It was a futile objective, it seemed to me. But we altered our course toward the west anyway.

When they locked me back in my bunk, it took only a few minutes for my muscles to become as stiff as rigor mortis. I guzzled down my cup of water from the night before—I didn't even care about the food. Then I lay back, certain I would fall asleep instantly.

Amazingly, Micah was still singing. That doleful hymn had gone on all the while I was rowing. By now he was somewhere in Leviticus or Numbers—I couldn't have said for sure. After a moment, the singing stopped. He actually interrupted his hymn to speak.

"It doesn't matter, you know."

I just lay there, not interested in hearing whatever rude thing he was about to say.

"They won't pass you over anymore," he persisted. "The next Sabbath we'll *both* be forced to row."

I was right to ignore him. I didn't want to hear it right now.

After another moment he said, "Thank you."

He commenced singing again. I was already drifting off. Still, his thank-you penetrated. For several hours I slept soundly and peacefully.

When I awakened, the ship was bobbing and swaying. I could hear the wind howling overhead and waves crashing against the sides. The drums had stopped. We were hunkering down to wait out the weather. Slaves in the hold continued muttering and praying despite the setting of the sun and the conclusion of the Sabbath. Like me, most of these men had been landlubbers all their lives. Tension was high. The only thing that comforted me was the fact that the crewmen didn't seem too concerned as they locked the last shift of rowers back into their bunks. This storm, I presumed, was not the worst they had seen.

Before the key-keepers took away their lamps and left us alone in the darkness, I looked over at Micah. He was awake, his eyes flitting about nervously. It was sort of nice to see his human side. He wasn't a total robot. Micah was afraid.

"So how far did you get?" I asked to take his mind off the storm.

"How far?" he asked.

"With your song."

"To the end," he replied.

"End of what?"

"The Torah. The Books of Moses."

I clicked my tongue to show that I was impressed. "That's incredible. You memorized all of Genesis through Deuteronomy? How long did it take?"

"Four years," he said.

"Are all Essenes required to memorize it?"

"We are required to master every virtue we can. The Lord requires no more and no less."

"I see. Makes sense. We believe the same thing."

I felt sure he would challenge that. Instead, Micah was quiet. After a moment he asked, "Why do you believe Jesus of Nazareth was the Messiah?"

The question seemed sincere. I felt I should answer with the same sincerity.

"Because it was revealed to me," I replied.

"Revealed? Who would reveal such a thing?"

"The Holy Spirit."

I think he'd been expecting a more intellectual, doctrinal-type answer. It left him stumped. At last he said, "The Holy Spirit has revealed no such thing to me."

"Have you asked?"

My question seemed to strike him as totally incomprehensible. "I would not tempt God with such a question."

"You think it's tempting God to ask Him to reveal something?"

"Only a prophet may receive God's word and will. This is the law. Without order, there is only chaos."

"That's true when it comes to the whole Church," I said. "But how would you know if a prophet is a true prophet unless you asked? Or how would you know which doctrines are true and which are false?"

"God gave us our wits," said Micah. "We have our intelligence to judge."

"But everyone's intelligence is different. You know that. Are you telling me that every Essene you know has the ability to memorize all five books of Moses?"

"Of course not. Only those with the gift."

"Well, that doesn't seem fair, does it? No, there needs to be a great equalizer—something that will reveal the truth to both geniuses and dummies, like me. That equalizer is the Holy Spirit."

Micah stewed over this. Then he quipped, "We are *not* all created equal. For most, it is not their destiny to find salvation."

"You really believe that?"

"Of course."

"That's where we're different. I believe all men *will* have an equal opportunity to find salvation. If they don't have a chance in this life, they'll have one in the next. That's fair. If God is anything, He's perfectly fair."

I heard Micah sigh in the darkness. "I *do* believe God is perfect. But I'm not so sure that He is fair." There was great pain behind those words.

"Now that makes a lot of sense," I answered, mildly sarcastic. "Think about it. If He's not fair, how could He be perfect?"

He mulled this over. But I never found out if my words had sunk in. Suddenly the ship tipped so violently that if we hadn't been chained in place we might have spilled out of our bunks. Many of the men cried out.

"It's my advice," I said to Micah in conclusion, "that if you ever *do* ask God to reveal something to you, you might want to do it soon."

As the night wore on, there were several more similar jolts. Nevertheless, our ship stayed together. Micah never did reply to my advice. No doubt, like me, he exerted all his concentration to just hold on. Before this night was over, I discovered what it really meant to be seasick.

But the seas didn't stay rough forever. I felt a great deal of peace along with the tension. As our little boat was battered and tossed, I realized how grateful I was to know the things I knew. It occurred to me that my testimony really was the only possession I had left. Everything else was gone. My hopes were dimming that I would ever have anything else. It was true what my mother once taught me as she tucked me snugly into my bed: the most valuable things we own can never be taken away.

I thought about her a lot that night; so many wonderful images. I thought about my father and my sisters, too. I could see all their faces so clearly. It was as if they were hovering around me like angels. Memories—those are also possessions that nobody can take away. I was determined that if memories were all I had left—all that remained of what was normal and good—I'd do everything I could to keep them fresh and alive. So I nestled into those memories and fell asleep. And sometime during the night, the storm subsided and the seas grew calm.

CHAPTER 8

It was the strongest tremor yet, nearly knocking me off my feet. Apollus caught me before I tripped. We'd only been inside the cave for five minutes, and already we'd felt three of these tremors. The cavern filled with dust as stones fell from the ceiling and fissures appeared in the rocks. This was crazy! Any second the whole mountain could come down on top of us.

"Should we go back?" I asked Garth, my voice trembling.

"No," he said firmly. "The Galaxy Room is just a little farther."

Apollus held my hand. He forged ahead with his torch, seeming more fascinated than frightened. Garth's promise that a piece of the mystery would shortly reveal itself gave him all the incentive he needed. I coughed up the dust and followed, fighting to shine my flashlight onto the walls of the tunnel. We rounded a narrow bend and came out inside a wider room that narrowed again at the other end. As we reached the connecting tunnel, Garth grabbed my shoulder.

"Wait!"

Apollus stopped as well. We surveyed the way ahead. Rubble was strewn along the ground. I flashed my light at the ceiling and swallowed hard. A boulder the size of a house was hanging over our heads. Several smaller stones broke loose from its edges and rained around us. Nothing seemed to be holding it up. There was a grinding echo emanating from deep within the stone. I was sure it was just a matter of minutes—a matter of seconds. A billion tons of weight were bearing down. A cave-in seemed inevitable.

"Come on!" urged Garth.

We quickly skirted the rubble and made our way into the next chamber. When we felt ourselves clear of the unstable ceiling, we leaned against the wall and caught our breaths.

"What if it falls?" I asked Garth. "How will we get back through? How will we find Harry?"

"How did you get through before?" Garth asked.

The memory made me shudder. "We fell into a river. It nearly drowned us."

"I'm familiar with that method," said Garth. "I'd prefer not to repeat it."

"How much farther?" Apollus interrupted. He seemed anxious to learn whatever mystery he'd come to learn and get the heck out of here.

"Not far," Garth informed him. "At least to the first juncture—the Galaxy Room. It's just through the next corridor and around another turn."

"Let's go!" urged Apollus.

We stepped away from the wall. Then it happened. A tremor more powerful than all the others combined shook the cavern. From the tunnel behind us came a deafening crash. A whoosh of air and a blast of dust swept over the top of us. I fell to the ground and lost my grip on Apollus' hand. The wall to my left opened up like the jaws of a dinosaur, then crunched down again, as if the monster were attacking. A pillar of stone toppled and crashed at my right. I clamped my arms uselessly over my head and waited in terror as the ear-splitting crashes and echoes reverberated for ten more seconds—an eternity!

Then everything went silent. The tunnel was dark. Both of Apollus' torches had been extinguished. I saw my flashlight a few feet above my hand, its beam cutting a sharper and sharper edge as the dust settled.

"Meagan!" I heard Apollus cry.

"I'm here!" I shouted back. "Uncle Garth!"

"Yes," he responded, coughing horribly. "Is everyone all right?"

"I am," said Apollus.

"I think so," I replied.

I rose awkwardly to my feet, shaking a layer of pebbles and dust off my back and shoulders. I held my hand over my mouth to try and filter the dust. Then I retrieved the flashlight and shined it back at Apollus and Garth. They continued to cough and spit. I shined the light into the tunnel behind us—that is, toward the area that used to be a tunnel. The enormous boulder had broken loose, creating a chain reaction that entirely sealed off the corridor. But this wasn't the most frightening sight that my flashlight revealed. As I shined it in the other direction, it became apparent that the way ahead was also blocked. That pillar of stone was only the beginning of a hundred tons of debris that had fallen and shattered. There was only about seventy-five feet of tunnel left for us to maneuver in!

"We're trapped!" I shrieked. "Both ways!"

Garth took the flashlight and surveyed the situation for himself. He could only confirm what was obvious. The tunnel had become our tomb.

Apollus made a feeble attempt to heft one of the boulders that blocked the way back. When it didn't budge, he dug out some of the smaller rocks around it and tried again. The boulder was as solid as if it had been set in concrete.

Garth searched around until he found one of the doused torches. Then he brushed off his backpack, found a match, and reignited it. Apollus snatched it away and stomped off toward the other end of the cave-in.

"What are we going to do?" I asked Garth.

"Don't panic," he replied. "Let the dust completely clear."

"We might not have that much time!" Apollus said urgently. "If there's another tremor, it could all come down!" His bellowing voice actually created further echoes in the earth, as if he might fulfill his own prophecy.

"Shhh!" Garth said. "Quiet for a minute."

I thought Garth was worried about the reverberations. Then I realized he was listening—listening hard.

"What is it?" I asked in a whisper.

Then I heard it too—another echo in the earth. Strange, I thought. It sounded unnatural—manmade. Like stones being moved, or . . .

"Hey!" I cried. "Help! We're in here!"

Garth grabbed my shoulder and put his finger to his lips. He wanted to keep listening, pinpoint the source. My heart was hammering. It could only have been Apollus' men! Yes! Lucullus and Graccus had disobeyed orders and followed us. They were trying to dig us out! The prospect was hopeless. Even if there'd been a hundred men on the other side of that rubble, it wouldn't have made any difference. No number of men could have moved that first boulder.

But as I continued to listen, I realized the sounds were not coming from the tunnel behind us. They were coming from the tunnel ahead!

Apollus climbed the slope of debris at the other end of the room. He appeared to have pinpointed the source. He called into the wall of rubble, "Is someone there?! Hello! Is someone there?!"

Garth and I scrambled nearer to Apollus. There appeared to be a narrow gap at the top of the debris—too narrow for any of us to slip through.

Apollus began digging frantically at the gap, hoisting out stones and boulders and letting them clatter to the bottom of the slope of debris.

"Hello!" I shouted into the hole. "Can you hear us?!"

Apollus stopped digging. We listened. Then we all heard it—the faint echo of a human voice: "I'm almost through!"

A whole course of emotions rushed through me that I can't adequately describe. The voice was faint and muffled by stone, yet it left a ring in my ears that penetrated to my soul. It couldn't be. It was impossible. I didn't even let the name appear in my thoughts. The odds seemed so utterly incomprehensible.

Garth was also still, his eyes squinted as he strained to hear even one more syllable. For the next several minutes we heard only digging and grinding as Apollus and the man on the other side continued to pry away stones.

And then the voice called again. This time it was unmistakable.

"Is everyone alive?"

I drew in a breath of air, then expelled it as I cried, "Gidgiddonihah? Gidgiddonihah, it's us!"

Never in a million years—yet it was true! It was Gid's voice! He was ahead of us. How had he gotten ahead?

"Meagan?" called Gid with equal surprise.

"I'm here, Gid!" I shouted. "Garth, too. And Apollus! Is Harry with you?"

It was a desperate question, but if Gid was here, why not Harry?

My heart sank as Gid replied, "No, Harry isn't here!"

I could see part of him now. I could see Gid's hand. It was so close that I reached in and touched his palm. He gripped my hand, then released it. I got out of the way to let the digging continue. A half hour later, the gap was wide enough that Gid was able to slip through. He was a dusty mess, like the rest of us. Then I realized that part of the discoloration in his face was from bruises and lacerations. His lower lip had been badly split. He was still healing from his encounter in Caesarea.

Gid stood up straight and looked us over. He lowered his eyes and said, "I had hoped . . . that Harry might be with you."

We all gaped at him. "What happened, Gid?" I asked. "How did you get here?"

"I've been here for two days," he reported. "I was going to wait one more day, then I was going to give up and continue on alone."

"You were waiting for us?" asked Apollus in surprise.

"It was all I could do," said Gid. "I couldn't return to Caesarea. My only hope was that you would try to travel home. So this is where I came."

"Where's Harry?" I asked desperately.

"I'm not sure," said Gid painfully. "When I last saw him, he was lying in the yard at the slave camp, unconscious."

I shuddered. "What was wrong with him?"

"How long ago was that?" Garth asked simultaneously.

"It was the day after we were attacked," Gid answered. "He took a bad blow."

"So you haven't seen him for nine days?" asked Garth.

"No," said Gid. "I was sold to that gladiator, Problius. His intention, if I understood right, was to take me home to Berytus and dispose of me in a wild beast show."

"How did you escape?" asked Apollus.

Gid answered plainly. "I pretended to be in a worse condition than my wounds warranted. My leg was so swollen with bruises that I convinced them it was broken. It gave me a limp for about a week, but the bone was intact. Our second night on the road, they got careless and left my ankles unchained."

"You escaped from Problius of Berytus?" Apollus repeated in disbelief.

"His reputation was greater than his skill," said Gid.

"Was?" asked Garth.

Gid nodded to confirm.

Apollus gaped in utter amazement. "You killed Problius of Berytus?"

Gid studied the Roman's face, I think trying to determine if his amazement was mixed with outrage. He narrowed his gaze as if in challenge and replied, "With his own chains."

I saw that Gid's wrists were still red and chafed from the shackles. For Gid to have escaped, he would certainly have been forced to kill the man who possessed the keys.

"But what about Harry?" I demanded again.

"I prayed that somehow you would have been able to get him released," said Gid. "As it stands, I don't know any more than you."

Garth told Gidgiddonihah about the slave ships departing daily from Caesarea's harbor. Gid reported that he'd seen many slaves marched down to the docks, but he couldn't have guessed which ship might have taken Harry or where it might have sailed.

"We're going home," I confirmed for Gid. "We're going to find Harry's father. We're going to get help, and then we're coming back."

Gid scanned the boulders and debris that blocked the present route back to the Roman world. "We'll have to find some way other than this."

Apollus' patience had reached the breaking point. "All right!" he thundered. "I've waited long enough. It's time I learned why we're here. I demand to know what we're looking for!"

At that instant we felt another tremor, less intense. I latched onto Gid's arm. Another stone or two dropped from the ceiling.

Gid put his hand on Apollus' shoulder. It didn't seem a gesture of friendship as much as a warning. "Calm down, friend. I suggest we crawl through this gap and try to reach a safer part of the tunnel."

"The Galaxy Room," Garth asked Gid, "—is it still intact?"

Gid's face revealed a strange expression, as if the question had no sensible answer. "You'll have to see for yourself."

Each of us in turn crawled through the space that Gid and Apollus had cleared. It was ten yards to the next room. Any second the narrow shelves above and below us might have shifted and crushed us all. I knew that a maze of caverns and tunnels still awaited us. How many more sections might have caved in? But even more compelling—what had caused the instability?

Five minutes later we had our answer—or at least part of it. Actually, I wasn't sure how to interpret the scene which met our eyes. The sight held our gazes fast. For several minutes, Garth and I just stared in amazement. Apollus held back farther than the rest of us, his feet on the verge of fleeing for cover. His arm was held just out of his field of vision, certain that it would be required at any second to shield his face from some blinding, burning sensation.

We'd arrived. We'd reached the Galaxy Room. But it was not the same Galaxy Room that I remembered from weeks earlier. That Galaxy Room had been a swirling parade of colors, all rotating around a dense fireball of crimson red. It had been brilliant, hauntingly beautiful, but perfectly symmetrical. Each layer of color had flowed at a steady, predictable rate. There was a comforting poetry about it all, an impression that there was order in all of the chaos. Now, any feelings of harmony were gone. The chaos was real—crooked, contorted, twisted, writhing.

The fireball that hung suspended in the center of the room looked warped. Parts of it were black and dead, while other parts were spewing *forth explosions of purple and dark orange that went shooting across the room like comets, complete with fiery tails that gathered in on themselves and splattered until the mass of color was absorbed by all the others. There were no more swirling bands, just raging streaks of yellow and red and green with no distinguishable pattern. I noticed bright explosions erupting from the ground, like blasts of magma from a volcano. But these blasts were particles of energy with no force or gravity to guide them. They just fizzled and dissolved like sparks from a campfire.*

I remembered that the energy from the room had filled my body with a tingling sensation, not hot or cold, not painful or uncomfortable. In fact, it was rather nice. Now the feeling wasn't pleasant at all. In fact, it was draining. Each muscle was affected at different moments; just as one limb would recover, another one would weaken. At moments I felt so dizzy I might have fainted, but then the dizziness would disappear.

Did the earthquake create this chaos? Had a shift in the earth's crust thrown the Galaxy Room off balance? Or did the chaos of the Galaxy Room create the earthquake? Perhaps the two phenomena were working hand in hand, throwing everything into greater disequilibrium by the minute.

A disturbing thought struck me as I watched another eruption of particles fly up from a hole in the floor. Harry and I had fallen through just such a hole. A month ago, the floor had been solid. Now it appeared that this hole had been enlarged, with several more pits created around it. Rivers of water continued to gush beneath the semi-transparent crust. I couldn't help wondering if the original flaw in the room's symmetry hadn't been inflicted as Harry and I fell through. The chaos and disorder had been building in momentum ever since. What further pandemonium was still to come?

I recalled Harry's statement that our plunge through the floor had caused thirty years to disappear in the blink of an eye. Dearest heaven! My fears that we would never again find ourselves in 70 A.D. were intensified.

"Let's cross it!" Gidgiddonihah shouted above the roar of energy. The noise was only an illusion—something other than sound. The only real sound was the rushing of water, which intensified as we ventured farther out into the room.

I looked at Apollus. He appeared hypnotized, his mouth gaping as he tried to comprehend the scene. This was the moment I'd predicted. My confidence would give him the assurance to go on. I reached out and took his hand. At first he was oblivious to my touch, but then he looked at me. The sight of my face broke the room's spell.

I was able to lead Apollus into the storm of colors. Gidgiddonihah blazed the trail, and Garth took up the rear. Just as before, the particles of energy swept around us, sometimes crashing directly into us. The colors flew apart without causing any particular sensation at all, except for that queer draining and reenergizing of random muscles. I watched Gidgiddonihah nearly lose his balance and then recover, so I knew I wasn't the only one experiencing this sensation.

We maneuvered around all of the shafts and holes. At a point about halfway across, a hole on our right exploded with a fan of energy, causing us to falter and gasp. But then we moved on. Twice Gid changed our course to avoid areas where the shelf looked thin. The rivers rushed beneath our feet, sometimes splashing up into the room and making the ground slick.

The opposite wall still had the watery, faraway appearance that I remembered from our first encounter. And then—in an instant—the opening in the opposite wall rushed up close, as if we'd passed through a kind of focal lens that distorted space and distance.

We'd done it. We'd reached the other side of the room. I heaved a sigh of relief. The illusory roar in my ears and the zapping of energy to my muscles faded as we entered the opposite tunnel. By "fade," I mean the weakness set in more firmly. It had been exhausting to cross that room. We all showed signs of the same fatigue. After we'd passed into the chamber beyond the Galaxy Room, Garth sat on a stone and caught his breath. Gidgiddonihah leaned against the wall. Oddly, Apollus looked hardly fazed. His adrenaline had kicked in, and he was anxious to see what was next.

"That room," he said, as if struggling to come up with some adjective. Instead he just repeated, "That room!"

"It represents a bridge between your world and ours," said Garth philosophically. "Something, however—the earthquakes, I presume—has sent the fields of energy into disarray."

Apollus didn't care about that. He hadn't seen what the room had looked like before. "A bridge? Your world and mine? I don't understand! How could your world be different than mine? Do you mean there is another world? Another land beneath the crust of the earth?"

We were going too fast for him. Frankly, I wasn't sure how it should be approached. "Something like that," I replied. "Be patient. Everything will make sense in time."

In time. *Boy, that was an odd way to put it. The Roman's head was swimming, racing with a million questions. He didn't know how to put them into words.*

Gidgiddonihah changed the subject. "There are many worlds," *he said, interpreting the subject as best he could.* "And it's time I returned to mine. This is where we part ways."

I stiffened with shock. "You're leaving us?"

Gid nodded soberly. "We both have one desire—to find Harry and bring him home. If Harry is alive, I will find him. But as a warrior, I find myself sorely ill-equipped. I'll go to Zarahemla. I'll return with weapons and supplies that I understand. There may still be people in my land who can help—some who may even remember Harry as a boy living in Bountiful with his father and sisters. I'll seek their assistance and counsel."

Garth nodded regretfully. He understood and approved. I didn't under-stand at all, unless . . . unless Gid was referring to prophets. Nephite disci-ples. Goodness! Was that what he meant? Now my head was swimming. This rescue might involve three different worlds and realms. Maybe that's what it needed. A feat this complicated needed every resource it could muster.

"We should have a plan," *said Garth.* "We'll set a goal to meet back here on an appointed day. How long will it take you?"

Gid mulled this over. "Three days. Perhaps four. It can't take any longer."

"Then that's our plan," *said Garth.* "We'll meet right in this very room four days from now. Agreed?"

Gid nodded. "Agreed."

Garth gripped the Nephite's hand. "Farewell, my friend. And good luck."

"God be with you, Garplimpton."

"Wait!" *I cried. I felt a desperate sense of finality about all of this. The plan was too simple. That raging, swarming Galaxy Room presented com-plications that no one was even considering. It controlled the time bridges, yet it was totally out of whack. Four days. It seemed ludicrous to think that all our clocks would run at the same speed. The discrepancy might add up to weeks—even years!*

But what could I say? Garth understood these variables better than I did. He'd accepted the risks. It was the only option—our only hope.

My eyes filled with tears. I could tell Garth and Gid had read my mind. Somehow this took the wind out of any arguments I might have presented. We'd go our separate ways. Then we'd do the only thing we could—pray.

As a tear fell on my cheek, I reached into my satchel and pulled out a chunk of bread wrapped neatly in a bundle of red cloth.

"You . . . you probably haven't eaten in days," I said to Gidgiddonihah.

He took it gratefully. "Thank you. Don't worry. I'll be fine. I'll see you in four days."

He embraced me firmly. Then he met Apollus' eyes. The Roman centurion still looked dazed. Gid nodded to him, then he turned and slipped into a passage to the right. Once again, the Nephite was gone.

The rest of us turned toward a trail to the left—a crevasse that slanted downward and eventually led to a chamber the size of several football fields with white, foaming waterfalls and a ceiling that glittered every color of the rainbow. I realized that even the Rainbow Room might look different after the earthquake. We'd find out soon enough. From there the trail would become fairly straightforward. Within hours we'd reach the mouth of Frost Cave. After that, I had no idea what to expect. I could only hope I'd be home again, but at this point I wouldn't have been surprised by anything.

Then there was Apollus. Even now he exuded an undercurrent of tension that told me I couldn't possibly predict his behavior. So be it. We couldn't turn back now. In just a few hours, I expected to watch the fireworks erupt as a hardcore Roman soldier came face to face with the twenty-first century.

CHAPTER 9

We'd been on the high seas for just over two weeks, with a brief stopover at a port that someone said was the island of Cyprus, though like most of the prisoners I was prevented from seeing any part of it. A day out of Cyprus, poor Joshua in the bunk on my left died and was cast into the sea. I didn't even realize that he'd passed away. I was so exhausted from rowing that I slept most of that day dreamlessly. The key-keepers and their servants came while I slept and hauled away his body. I can't even say for certain if he was really dead, or if the slave merchants simply decided there was no hope for recovery and passed their final judgment. I might have been the only one left on earth who mourned his passing.

Another Sabbath had come and gone. Micah and I were both required to take our turns at the oars. I'd overestimated Micah's zeal-ousness about the Sabbath. I'd actually feared he might allow himself to be executed—tossed overboard with his throat cut—rather than pull those oars. Maybe that first week, the day I took his shift, he'd have done exactly that. But as time wore on, his spirit softened; his self-righteousness and arrogance waned. Oh, don't get me wrong; he still had an opinion on every subject under the sun. At times our conversa-tions in the dim light of our bunks left me exhausted, convinced there was no hope that he'd ever see things any other way. But the changes *did* come, subtly at first. Then came his submission to rowing on the following Sabbath. He tried to continue his hymn even as he pulled the oar, but the taskmasters stopped his song with a lashing to his back.

It was a tough blow to the other prisoners. They'd come to regard Micah as a kind of hero—a symbol of the religious commitment and discipline that they had all compromised out of fear. Now that last flicker of pride had been snuffed out. Everyone was very depressed. One of the men even glared at Micah in resentment and pretended to spit on the floor (if he'd *actually* spit on the floor he would have been flogged). I was sitting behind Micah. I glared right back at the man from my bench as if to say, "What are you lookin' at, punk?" The man turned away in shame.

Over the last two weeks I'd earned a certain degree of respect from my fellow oarsmen, despite the fact that my eye still looked as purple as a plum. I might have only been fifteen, but I was still bigger than most of these guys. Maybe it was just the respect they'd felt at seeing me survive that first day when I'd taken Micah's place. I'd surprised them all. But somehow I felt it was more than just size or stamina. I noticed that the men began to treat me as if I had some kind of spiritual authority. I'm not sure why. I like to think my testimony somehow gave me a kind of inner strength that the men responded to instinctively, but I couldn't know for sure.

My friendship with Micah developed steadily. He really didn't seem to understand the concept of having a friend. Life among the Essenes had been so different. Friendships were dictated by rank and station, and everything was very formal. Opening your heart showed weakness; a lack of discipline. I was a complete mystery to Micah. Yet I could tell that our mutual trust and admiration were growing.

He didn't use my name. He called me simply, "Christian." It didn't strike me as derogatory. I think he did it to remind himself that the mystery behind the things I did might be explained by that single title.

"Hey, Christian," he said to me one evening after we'd finished our shift. "I'll have you know . . . I prayed this morning. I prayed *your* way."

"Oh?" I replied, wondering if he'd really understood what I'd meant.

Micah had memorized at least a hundred prayers covering every subject—waking, sleeping, sickness, gratitude, peace, war, death, weather, blessings, cursings, eating, bathing—you name it. He'd just apply the right prayer to the right occasion. My suggestion was to make it up as he went along. Just talk to God the way you'd talk to a friend—that is, a friend you held in the utmost regard and respect.

"I spoke to Him using the words of several *different* prayers," Micah explained. "In essence, I made up a new prayer. I might recite it tomorrow morning as well."

Well, I thought, it was progress. "How did it make you feel?" I asked.

"Invigorated."

"That's great," I said, trying not to sound patronizing. "Next time maybe you could make up a prayer that doesn't combine the words of any other prayer at all."

He laughed scornfully. "I'm afraid it's not my gift to speak to God like that. Besides, it's not necessary. I have nothing new to say to God. Nothing that has not already been said."

"Of course you do. You have *tons* of things to say. And the way you'd say it would be different than anybody else."

"I doubt that."

"Do you have a prayer about a slave bound for the rock quarries of Corinth who would like very much to be free again and travel back home to Judea?"

"No, but I have a prayer which speaks of misery and affliction and pleads for relief. Isn't this the same?"

I shook my head. "It's *not* the same. You have to really *talk* to God. Really tell Him your feelings. Talk about every last detail of your own personal sorrows and needs. That's how I think God wants to hear from us. Anything else somehow doesn't quite say it. I'm not saying set prayers can't be good. We have some, too—for baptisms and blessing the sacrament. But otherwise, we try to speak from the heart."

"You mean you say different words every time?"

"Yes, every time. Sometimes the words might sound the same. Sometimes they might be *exactly* the same. But usually only if I get lazy or tired. If I'm sincere, the words are almost always different. Sometimes—and this is very sacred—I feel like the words are *given* to me."

"Given to you by God?"

"Yes."

He scoffed. "You mean God actually *tells you* how to pray to Him?"

"Why not? God knows everything. He knows what we're going to pray for even before we ask, right?"

"Well, yes . . ."

"So prayer is just a way of expressing love and faith. We're telling God how much we love Him. And letting Him show how much He loves us."

He scoffed again. This was the point Micah found most incomprehensible. He'd never thought of His relationship with God like this. To him, such ideas bordered on blasphemy. To think that the Creator of the universe would stoop down to offer *love*, or expect His creations to love Him back, was ludicrous. We were expected to *worship* Him, yes. Fear Him, definitely. But *love Him?* It was just too much to take in. But then I wondered if Micah had ever been taught the concept of love at all. Out there in the harsh deserts of the Dead Sea, someone might have felt like there was no room for such emotions.

And yet Micah's spirit was softening. Even here in the stinking hold of a Corinthian slave ship, part of his soul seemed to be remembering.

"I will attempt what you have said," he replied, almost grudgingly. "But I fear it will be a very short prayer."

"No problem. God doesn't care how long it is. Just that—"

Suddenly my thoughts were savagely interrupted. The key-keeper stood over me, glowering. "You! On your feet!"

The chain was pulled through my ankle ring. I blinked my eyes in confusion. What was going on? Surely he knew I'd just finished my shift. My sweat hadn't even dried. But I didn't question it. If I did, I'd feel that multi-strapped whip on my back. Several other men who'd rowed that day were also being dragged out of their bunks.

"Move!" barked the key-keeper.

Micah watched with great curiosity. So did all the other slaves. We were herded up the ladder and into the steerage room. A commotion was stirring among all the prisoners and crew. Everyone was trying to see through the eyelets on the right side of the ship. Something was out there, and it made everyone very nervous.

It was late in the day. A stiff breeze was blowing out of the west. There should have been a deep red sunset, but an overcast sky had diffused the light, giving the sea a coppery appearance. I squinted toward a tiny silhouette on the horizon. It was a ship, and it was sailing right toward us. I could hear the faint drumbeat of its steerage room. The pace was fast. *Remarkably* fast. Faster than any pace I'd been forced to row. The ship was in pursuit.

It had three banks of oars, just like the fiercest-looking Roman warships I had seen in Caesarea's harbor. There were nearly two hundred oars powering that thing! Adding to their advantage, the sails were hoisted. The wind was perfectly suited to propel them toward us at an angle. They were chasing us with the power of both men and nature. But *why*? I'd thought the Romans had no enemies on the Mediterranean Sea. They controlled the whole thing. What did these people want? Why did the merchant commander look pale with fright?

I was ordered to take my place on the bench. At this hour, most of our rowers were sent below to give the crew a few hours of relaxation. But now they'd rounded up all the strongest men, despite their weariness, and locked them back into place. Whatever contest was about to begin, I felt certain it would have dire consequences. This was just the incentive I needed to grab that oar and row like I'd never rowed before.

I shivered as the chain was pulled through the loop on my ankle. I remembered that scene from *Ben Hur*—the one where all the slaves went down with the ship. In the movie it was a sea battle, and the mood here was just as intense. Except that we weren't turning to fight. This was not a warship; our defenses were minimal. I'd seen about half a dozen Roman soldiers on deck over the past several weeks, but they were fat and soft, likely the standard detachment of all ships that carried insignificant booty. The only booty I had seen on board were some crates tied near the bow. And, of course, us.

"Row!" the commander shouted as the steersman furiously pounded his drums. "Come on, you animals! Row for your lives!"

That confirmed it. This was a matter of life and death. I could still see the other ship through the eyelets. It continued to sweep toward us at an angle. They were gaining fast. This was hopeless! Yet I pulled on the massive oar. Sweat drizzled off my brow.

"Who are they?" I asked the fellow prisoner on my left.

"Pirates," he replied.

"*Pirates?*" I repeated in astonishment. "What kind of pirates?"

"There's only one kind."

If that was true, I might have expected men with eyepatches, peg legs, and parrots. I doubted they looked like that. I just had a hard time believing that pirates of any kind could operate in Roman waters.

As I looked out at the ocean, I saw chunks of land poking up through the waves. Islands. Well, not really *islands*. Just outcroppings of rock, black and jagged. My eyes suddenly stopped. I noticed a *second* ship sailing out from behind one of the outcroppings, as if it had been hiding there. Now it sailed furiously toward us from the opposite direction.

"Another ship!" cried a rower. He barely faltered in his pace, but the taskmaster cracked his whip across the man's back.

"Turn about!" cried the commander.

The steersman altered the beat for the rowers on the left. They slacked their pace slightly while the men on our side continued to pull with all our might. The ship aimed its nose toward the northwest. But it was too late; the trap was complete. The second ship would reach us in less than a minute.

I might have given up—my lungs were already heaving to the limit—but I'd already felt the taskmaster's whip and I didn't want to feel it again. Hope started to stir inside me. These vile slave dealers were about to be attacked. If the pirates were skilled fighters at all, they were bound to win. Could these pirates actually be the answer to my prayers? Might they be the key to our freedom?

"Row, you dogs!"

I recoiled in agony as the strap landed on my back. The lines burned. I gritted my teeth and gave the taskmaster—my old friend with the flattened nose—an acid glance. But he'd already walked on ahead. He was whipping us all at random, just moving down the line.

Then came the impact. I heard a horrible cracking and splintering. Rowers on the opposite side were arching forward in pain and falling into the aisles. The second ship was pulling alongside us, breaking all of the men's oars. Mayhem erupted. All rowing stopped on both sides. The dark wooden hull of the pirate ship eclipsed the view through the eyelets on the left. I could see into *their* ship—the faces of the oarsmen on the first and second tiers. Wisely, they'd retracted their own oars before collision.

Men on deck were shouting. Feet scampered above us. Through the wooden grate I saw a rope fly. We were being boarded. I heard the clash of metal swords. Suddenly the slaves on my side began to scramble and scream. More cracking and splintering. The ship we'd first sighted was pulling up alongside us. I ducked my head as the oars snapped in our hands. Before I could prevent it, my own oar whipped back and hit the face of the slave behind me.

The crew was fleeing from the steerage room. They must have felt their only hope was to reach the deck, fight for their lives, or beg for mercy. The last one to leave the steerage room, making his way from the very rear of the boat, was the taskmaster with the flat nose. He had the keys; every slave in the room knew it. I watched as a thick-necked slave across the aisle took the broken end of his oar and smashed it into his chest.

The taskmaster fell. He tried to rise, but other slaves began pummeling him with their fists and broken oars. The man knew exactly what they desired. I saw the keys in his right hand. As a last act of contempt before a rod of wood was smashed on his head, he threw the keys toward one of the eyelets with all his might. He was trying to throw them into the sea! But instead, they hit the boards and ricocheted. I didn't see where they landed. The slaves fell on him with even greater savagery. I looked away in revulsion.

Just as I turned my head, one of the fat Roman soldiers fell past my eyelet and landed in the water between the ships, his throat cut. I heard more splashes as other men were thrown from the deck. Then the sounds of fighting and screaming ceased. The slaves stopped searching for the taskmaster's keys and listened. We all knew our ship was now in the hands of the pirates. Anyone who had defied them was dead.

We directed our eyes toward the roof. Some sort of argument was taking place between the two pirate commanders. They were trying to decide how to divide the spoils. During this moment I adjusted my bare foot and felt a cold metal edge. I looked down. It was the keys! They were right beside my ankle. The means to our freedom was at my feet. But would they be necessary? It seemed to me that *we* ought to become part of the spoils being divided.

I was about to reach down and grab them when several shadows appeared on the stairway leading up to the deck. Four men entered the steerage room. The pirates were black. That is, their faces were *painted* black. I wasn't sure if this was meant as a disguise, camouflage, or just to make them look more menacing. Nearly all of them had sharp, pointed beards and wore only loincloths and leggings. The man in front carried a long knife and a club. He ordered another man to check the hatch leading down into the ship's hold, where Micah and the rest of the slaves were still chained to their bunks. Then he strolled down the aisle, gripping his weapons. His eyes barely registered our faces. He was looking past us, around us, as if he was trying to locate any other booty that might have been stored below. As he drew nearer, I moved my foot to hide the keys. He and his other two men reached the opposite end. Satisfied, they turned and started back toward the stairs.

The last man emerged from the hold. "Nothing down here," he reported. "More slaves. All Jews."

"All right," said the leader. "Let's go."

"Release us!" shouted a slave near the front.

This started a general clamor throughout the room—begging, pleading for them to unlock our chains, take us with them. The pleas were ignored. The pirates ascended the stairs and left us alone. I heard the pirate commander shout one last command.

"Move those crates at the bow, untie all the lines! *Then torch it!*"

My blood turned cold. Torch it? The *ship?* They were going to *burn the ship?!* All at once, I realized this was their only choice. We were no good to them as spoils. We were *witnesses.* Any one of us might have identified their ships or members of their crews to the Roman authorities. But why would we report them? *They were our rescuers!* Some of us might have even been persuaded to join them! Then I realized that even among criminals, there was a deep-seated prejudice against Jews. Or perhaps they'd come to learn that Jews made terrible sailors.

The slaves around me began howling, dragging at their chains. I felt the keys again under my foot, but I didn't dare grab them. Every man around me might have started groping to take them away. Their excitement might have alerted the pirates. I had to wait until the men left the deck, until the ships cut their lines and broke away, until the first flame was ignited. And yet, what good was it going to do us to unlock our chains? We were in the middle of the ocean! Our ship would be burning!

The islands. Maybe we could reach one of the outcroppings of rock. But without oars, how could we get there? The wind was gaining momentum, the waves lashing higher. The idea that we might swim to any destination seemed suicidal.

As I looked upward through the grating, I saw a flame shoot up the main mast. The two ships began to pull away. More flames reflected on the waters. Oars appeared from the eyelets of the different tiers on the pirate ships. They began rowing. The slaves around me were pulling at the rings on their ankles so desperately that they had begun to tear the flesh. Time to make my announcement.

I reached down and snatched up the keys. "Wait!" I cried. "The keys! I have the keys!"

I had to shout several more times before anyone heard. The men closest to me began clamoring for everyone else to be quiet. The man beside me lunged for the keys, but I fought him back. Then I reached for the lock that lay on the floor two benches ahead and twisted the key in the keyhole. The bolt fell free. Men behind me pulled the chain through their anklets. Someone on the other side tried to take the keys to unlock his own leg. I yanked them away, determined to free all of the bolts myself. I was afraid I'd never get the keys back. I still needed to free Micah and all the other slaves in the hold. And I had to do it before the fire trapped us all.

Four separate bolts secured all the chains in the steerage room. I had to fight to reach each one of them. Nobody trusted me to really set them free. The flames on deck started to roar. Smoke was seeping through the eyelets. After I'd unlocked the last bolt, I pushed my way through to the hatch leading down into the hold.

Before entering, I grabbed the lamp beside the stairway. As I climbed down inside, the lamplight fell across the rows of bunks. The slaves down here were no less panicked than the ones above us, screaming and pounding their fists. I swallowed in dismay. The hold had been built to house about a hundred and fifty slaves. About half were up top; the other half were scattered throughout the room. There was one lock for every stack of three bunks. I'd have to unlock about fifty separate bolts to free everyone. To make matters more daunting, I'd have to unlock every single one by myself.

I said a quick prayer to God, then I went to work. I turned the key in lock after lock. Men scrambled out of the bunks. Without offering any thanks, they crammed themselves into the aisle leading toward the hatch. I reached Micah. He was the only one still locked in his stack of three. He watched frantically as I pulled the chain through his anklet. After hoisting himself into the aisle, he grabbed my shoulder.

"Christian, come on!" he urged. "It's too late to save them all!"

I broke away from him. "You go! I'm right behind you!"

He stared back in befuddlement. "You'll die! You'll die with them all!"

"GO!" I shouted.

He hesitated a moment longer, then fled. I continued as rapidly as I could. Even the weakest and sickest of the slaves found the strength to climb out of their bunks and fight for their lives. Several men squirmed out into the aisle before I reached them, hanging by one shackled leg. I unlocked each bolt. At last I reached the end of the aisle and began working my way back down the other side. Smoke was filling the hold. Men were starting to cough.

I'd gotten about a third of the way back. As I reached for the next lock, I was met by another pair of hands. These hands stuck a key into the keyhole ahead of me. It was Micah!

"God is with us, Harrison!" he cheered. It was the first time he'd addressed me by my real name.

"Where did you find the other keys?"

"Above the lamphook. There was always an extra set hanging there. Let's get out of here!"

He'd unlocked every other bunk all the way back toward the hatch. The job was done! The ladder leading up to the steerage room was still choked with men. Micah and I rushed to the rear of the line. Men were climbing over each other to get out. Smoke was pouring into the hold, coming from somewhere behind us. The sides of the ship were aflame. I could hear the flames roaring through the wood. I feared that every inch above us was also burning. Yet each man continued to disappear up the hatch, into the steerage room. I heard shouting and splashing as men plunged into the sea. Some were shrieking in terror. Had they leaped from the burning ship only to drown?

Only four or five people were still ahead of us. One of the men fell back into the hold. His hands cupped his face. He'd been burned.

Coughing from the depths of his lungs, he heaved out the words, "No use! Can't go that way!"

My heart tightened. There was no other way to go!

I realized the floor was tilting. I grabbed the leg of the nearest bunk for balance. As I looked back, my mind darkened with panic. Water was creeping toward us up the floorboards. The rear bunks were nearly half submerged. The ship was sinking!

The last of the men climbed up the ladder anyway, ignoring the man who'd been burned. But then they covered their faces and fell back inside. The steerage room had become an inferno.

"What do we do?" Micah cried.

I had no answer. My thoughts were racing as the ship continued to tilt. Two of the men plunged into the flames anyway—it was their only chance. We heard their ear-rending screams. The water had reached my ankles and was creeping up my shins. The smoke was so thick I could hardly breathe. There were just three of us now—Micah, myself, and one other slave. Micah's face was taut with terror. How strange that I was suddenly overcome with a feeling of calm.

The calmness was so unexpected that I was tempted to disregard it. Why shouldn't I feel terror like the others? This was the moment of my death. There was no escape. And yet the calmness told me otherwise. I grasped Micah's shoulder.

"Get down," I said. "And hang on."

Micah searched my eyes. His own fears abated a little. The water had reached our waists. It was surging and boiling from some breach at the back of the hold. We crouched down, tightly gripping the posts of the nearest bunks. The last man—the one whose face had been burned—was insane with panic, shrieking and screaming and splashing about. Flames began shooting inside the hatch, searching out the last pockets of breathable air.

Micah started praying—a death chant.

I interrupted him. "Get ready!"

His face looked resentful. Why would I interrupt his last communication with God? But my voice was firm. Confidence was rushing inside me. The slope of the floor became even steeper. At that instant, the ship did something unexpected. It began to twist. The walls, the bunks, the entire room turned onto its side. The ladder leading up to the hatch was now horizontal. I could hear hissing and sizzling as a greater part of the burning wood met the surface of the sea.

The smoke cleared a little. I could see the hatch.

"Now!" I cried to Micah. "Swim for it!"

The slave with the burnt face pushed through before us. We reached the opening and peered into what had been the steerage room. Benches were now hanging down from the ceiling. The room was still engulfed in flames, but a cool, inviting level of water stretched out before us. Several planks of wood collapsed and fell; otherwise, there were very few obstacles between us and the tilted stairway leading to the upper deck. That stairway now led out into the sea.

"Can you swim underwater?" I asked Micah.

"I can't swim at all!" he announced.

This filled me with dread. I should have expected it. He was from the desert. The sea would have been as unfamiliar to him as the North Pole.

"Get behind me!" I told Micah. "Hang on to my tunic, right here at my waist. Don't let go for anything!"

At that moment several rafters collapsed at once, sending up a cloud of steam. We heard the scream of the man who'd pushed out ahead of us. The ship continued sinking. It was starting to tilt upright again. There was no time to lose!

"Hold your breath!" I cried.

All the sounds of chaos went silent as I dove under the surface, pushing off from the rim of the hatch. Micah hung on. I was swimming for two, pulling my arms with all my might. The stairway leading out into the sea was only about ten yards away. Still, I wasn't sure I had the strength to reach it.

The water was dark and murky and filled with bubbles. I could see the glowing embers of the fallen rafters, like lava erupting from the ocean floor. I had to swim under them. This would be the most difficult moment. My legs kicked furiously while my arms clawed at the water. Micah started to let go, his breath spent. I grasped his hand and swam that last yard with just one arm. But as I pushed to the surface, I hit my head. It was the roof. The entire ship was now submerged, being dragged to the bottom of the sea. And we were still trapped inside!

The current began spinning us at will. We were caught in the downtow. Micah released my shoulders as the churning water tried to tear him away. I seized the only part of him that I could find—his hair. Then I swam one last mighty stroke upward.

It was a total surprise when my head broke the surface. I drew in a great breath. Micah gasped for oxygen as well. We'd made it! We'd escaped the ship!

Night had almost completely fallen. There was only a faint sliver of violet light in the west. The first stars glimmered overhead. The wind was fierce. All that remained of the ship were a few floating planks, still burning. I saw the silhouettes of men splashing among the waves. But then I saw another silhouette. This one was massive and black. It was an outcropping of rock! An island!

Micah started thrashing. I was tempted to break away; he could drown us both. I embraced him tightly and kicked my legs to tread water.

"It's all right, Micah! There's land! You hear me? Land!"

I couldn't tell how close it was. The rising and falling waves played with my perception of distance. My muscles ached to delirium, yet the calmness was still there. It strengthened me. Micah stopped thrashing. I draped my own arm across his chest—just like they'd taught us in my lifesaving class—and began swimming toward the rock. Waves overtook us. The rock appeared and disappeared. We coughed water from our throats.

At one point Micah stiffened, as if ready to panic again.

"Be still," I said. "We're almost there."

I kept on swimming, each stroke becoming harder to pull. The black mass loomed closer and closer. I was now convinced the rock was only twenty or thirty feet wide. I wasn't even sure there was a place to hang on. But then I realized other men had taken refuge there. I could hear their voices.

My strength was spent. I couldn't stay afloat any longer. But then a wave washed us inward, and I felt hard stone under my fist. What's more, I felt someone wrap his arm around my shoulder and pull me in from the sea. I recognized him as one of the men I'd unlocked from his bunk. I perceived about twenty men clinging to the rock as waves crashed and surged around it. Those same waves frequently swept around my legs as I lay there, my lungs heaving for oxygen.

We were alive. But we were still holding on for dear life to a mass of stone barely thirty feet wide. This was where we would spend the night. We were like ants clinging to a tiny leaf—so tiny it was reasonable to think that our weight alone would cause it to sink. I hoped the waves wouldn't get any higher. It was conceivable that they could wash right over the top of us, leaving us again at the mercy of the sea. What would we do now? How would we ever reach land—*real* land? I didn't worry for long. God had a plan. He always had a plan. I closed my eyes, certain He would reveal it with the rising of the sun.

CHAPTER 10

"What kind of writing is this?" asked Apollus as he stared at the stone wall covered with graffiti.

"It's English," I responded. "The language of my people."

"What does it say?"

My face flushed. "Well, um . . . it just says . . . actually, it's really not that interesting. Let's move on."

Apollus grinned wryly. "Ah, I understand. The words are vulgar. Am I right?"

I raised my eyebrows. " Yes. How did you know?"

"Roman youths are inclined to write the same things on walls. I have a feeling your world is not really so different from mine."

Boy, *I thought*, this guy is in for a shock. *Frankly, I was surprised at how little curiosity Apollus had shown over the last twelve hours. He'd asked very few questions. Instead, he'd looked stoic and disinterested, the corners of his mouth turned down. He must have had some inkling of the wonders that awaited. He'd seen Garth's flashlight. He'd also seen his electric razor. Garth even offered to let Apollus try it out for himself, though the Roman firmly declined.*

I felt I'd done my best to prepare him. "Now you realize," *I'd told him,* "soon you'll see things that you never dreamed possible. Your life will never be the same."

Apollus had responded by telling me about the grand Coliseum that his emperor was constructing in the heart of Rome and the massive aqueducts that had made it possible for Rome to support a million residents. It was as if Apollus was trying to reassure himself that his empire was still the greatest the world had ever known. I almost felt sorry for him. How cruel to burst his bubble. His whole life was Rome. His whole existence was devoted to the glory of the Empire. How would it affect him to realize that Rome was not the center of the universe? That one day it would crumble and decay, with hardly a trace remaining?

Apollus would have to come to grips in his own way with what he was about to see. A part of me was eager to see him get his comeuppance. But another part was terrified that the things I found most attractive about my Roman—his courage, his bravado, his blustering confidence—were about to be dashed forever.

Apollus followed Garth that last hundred feet toward the entrance of the cave. The tunnel filled with daylight, and our flashlight and torches began to lose definition. I forgot about Apollus and focused on my own exhilaration. There sat that old rusty gate—the doorway to the twenty-first century. Everything was exactly as we had left it. It had been an entire month—the most exciting, harrowing month of my life. And yet as I searched my heart for some sense of fulfillment, I was overcome by depression. Harry's absence felt heavier than ever. This was no happy homecoming. The most difficult part of this adventure hadn't even begun.

Apollus stepped up to the gate. He gazed out at the yellow sun. It was positioned directly in line with the cave's opening. So it was morning, I realized. Nine or ten o'clock.

Garth fumbled in one of the side pockets of his backpack until he produced a key. He unlocked the padlock and swung open the gate. We emerged into the bright, warm world.

Actually, it wasn't warm at all. There was a brisk chill. Goose bumps appeared immediately on my arms. It took several seconds before I realized why I found this so disturbing. When Harry and I had first entered this cavern, it was late April. The temperature was comfortable and cool. By now it should have been late May, maybe the first of June. But this did not feel anything like May or June.

"What's happened?" I asked Garth shakily. "Everything has changed! What time of year is it?"

"October," said Garth with scientific objectivity. "Or perhaps March."

"October?" I shrieked. "March? How long have we been gone?"

He shook his head, trying to figure it out in his own mind. Then he sighed drearily. "Time never moves at the same rate between our worlds. In the past, the discrepancy has never been more than a few months, but with the earthquake . . . we have no way of knowing until we find a calendar."

He tried to sound calm, but his voice had an undercurrent of tension. He was as scared as I was. What if years had gone by? What if our families had aged several decades? I took some deep breaths. There was no reason yet to panic. Find a calendar—someone who could tell us the date. That was the first priority.

Apollus didn't understand our distress. He still wore his stoic frown, looking across the landscape like a shrewd customer at a car lot, not wanting to betray his interest to the salesman.

As we climbed down the stone stairway, things still appeared pretty much the same. The dilapidated walkway hadn't undergone any additional decay. The trees looked about as tall as when we'd left. The landscape had roughly the same shape, despite being blanketed by a wispy layer of snow. But this rising confidence was squashed as we reached the place where I was sure I'd left my Yamaha motorcycle.

"It's gone! Someone stole it!"

"Don't panic," said Garth. "It's right over here."

Garth took several steps down the mountain toward a pile of brush. He removed several branches, exposing the motorcycle's front wheel.

"I took the liberty of covering it over when I first arrived," Garth explained. "Otherwise, I'm sure it would have been stolen."

I removed several more branches to expose the ignition. "The keys! I left the keys right in—"

As I turned, Garth was dangling the keys in front of my nose. He'd been storing them in the same pocket with the padlock key.

"Thank you," I said, slightly embarrassed.

"Don't mention it," said Garth.

I glanced at Apollus. His gaze was riveted on the motorcycle in dreamy fascination. He removed the remaining branches of camouflage himself, and then stepped back abruptly, as if the motorcycle might have been a living thing that could spring to life and attack at any second.

I put my hand on his shoulder. "It's a motorcycle, Apollus. A machine. You ride it."

He gaped at me. "Ride it?" He laughed nervously, shaking his head.

"Oh, don't be such a baby," I said. "It's easy. I'll show you."

But as I got ready to mount the seat, I realized that my ancient pullover was not going to permit this. My underwear was little more than a wraparound diaper. I might have been anxious to get home, but not *enough to sacrifice all modesty.*

Once again, Garth's foresight came to the rescue. He pulled out a pair of safety pins. "Try these," he advised.

I took the pins and stepped away to pin my dress together just above the knees. Apollus couldn't take his eyes off the motorcycle. I think he was actually becoming enamoured.

"You say the wheels are turned by machine?" he asked Garth.

"Yes," said Garth. "You could think of it as an elaborate system of pulleys and gears."

"But how does it stay balanced? It would fall over!"

Garth smiled. "You let Meagan take care of that. I have a feeling she can handle it pretty well."

I finished pinning the hem of my pullover and shivered. The thrill of arriving home was quickly being overtaken by the biting cold.

"Here," said Garth, tossing me an extra sweatshirt from the main compartment of his backpack. "I have another one just like it. You two ride down the mountain and get someplace warm. I'll start down the road on foot. After you've situated Apollus, you can come back and get me."

I nodded and slipped the sweatshirt over my head. I found my motorcycle helmet near the back wheel. After slapping out some dirt and twigs, I slipped it on my head and climbed onto the seat. As I stuck the key in the ignition, I kept one eye on Apollus. I was gonna love his reaction when this thing fired up.

My first effort was disappointing, just a chug. The bike had obviously been sitting here for some time. Apollus slowly backed away. On the second attempt, the bike roared into action. Apollus leaped for cover, shading his eyes with one hand as if the object might explode.

Garth went to his aid. "It's all right!" he yelled over the noise. "That's how it's supposed to sound!"

I revved on the gas to spit out all the dust, then I let up on the clutch. The bike lurched forward. I spun it around and faced Apollus and Garth. Apollus twisted to the side as if he'd just found himself in the path of a stampeding bull. I decided not to push it. I rolled forward very slowly and let the bike idle beside them.

"Come on!" I said to Apollus. "If I don't get you to a gas station, you're gonna freeze to death."

I wasn't sure this was true. That thick armor and wide red cape should have kept him fairly comfortable. But his legs were completely exposed. Apollus looked at me with awe. I could get used to this, I thought. If only all men would react to me this way.

"Right here," I said, patting the back of the seat. "You sit right here and hang on to my waist. It's easy."

He inched closer, looking very tentative. I was loving every minute. I thought back on that moment so many weeks ago when he'd arrogantly pulled me up to sit behind him on his white horse. He'd been so cocky. Oh, there was justice in this universe!

As he started to raise his leg, I further advised him to bundle up his cape so it didn't get caught in the tire or get burned up by the exhaust. At last he'd taken his place firmly behind me. I helped him to kick out the buddy bars to prop his sandals on. I remembered that Harry had left his own helmet at the base of the mountain. Not that it mattered. That plumed hunk of bronze on his head was bound to protect him from any serious injuries if he decided to bail out.

Garth gave us a farewell wave. He watched Apollus, no doubt feeling as much fascination as I was. A Roman soldier in modern America! It blew me away to think of it.

We scooted down the trail and soon connected up with the dirt road. Apollus hung on tightly, fighting with his cape to keep it bunched in his lap. After a while, I felt him start to relax. If this was the most awesome thing to see in my world, he must have felt confident that he could handle it. But then we reached an overlook that gave us a view of the entire Bighorn Basin. Again, his muscles tensed.

I stopped the cycle and pointed. "That's Cody."

"Cody?"

"It's a city. Well, a town actually. More like a village."

It was a golden day. Whatever clouds had dropped this half-inch of snow had been swept away by the wind. The arteries of highway that criss-crossed the valley were as visible as ever. So were the tiny objects moving upon them. Apollus pointed, as if to ask a question. But then he stopped himself. He didn't seem quite sure he wanted to know what all these things were. Maybe it was too much to take in at once. I decided the best thing to do was just give him a baptism by fire. We'd come down this mountain and burst right into civilization. When his questions finally started to fly,

I was sure they'd come out a hundred at a time.

We zipped down the various switchbacks. Apollus continually turned his head so he could gaze out at the town. I could feel his heart racing. I could also feel him shivering, though he never complained of the cold. Adrenaline seemed to be sustaining him.

At the base of the mountain, I hardly hesitated as I zipped out onto the paved highway. Apollus' first sight of a modern automobile was a Dodge Ram pickup, complete with a cowboy in a cowboy hat who craned his neck in amazement. What would he think about a fully bedecked Roman soldier and a girl in an ancient pullover riding a motorcycle? Either we were escapees from a Christmas pageant or a mental institution. Then again, Garth had said it might be October. Perhaps he'd think we were just on our way to a Halloween party. In either case, he'd have thought we were plain idiots for not wearing warm clothing.

Apollus took in all the sights: barbed wire fences, a drive-in movie theater, a rodeo stadium, the neon vacancy signs of several motels, and even the old weathered buildings of a western town—a tourist site situated off to the left. The highway was bustling with sport utility vehicles and sedans. There was even another motorcycle, its rider clad in black leather. I could only imagine what Apollus must have thought of it all. He just clung to my waist and took it all in with his usual stoic frown.

My fingers and ears were stinging from the cold as we pulled into the lot of a convenience store and gas station. As I brought the Yamaha to a halt in front of a pair of pay phones, Apollus didn't move. I practically had to pry his hands from around my waist before I could climb off.

"Are you all right?" I asked him.

He nodded.

"Go inside," I instructed. "I'll be right behind you. I'm just gonna try and call my mom. Understand?"

He stared dumbly.

I reached for one of the receivers. "These are called phones. We use them to talk to people. We speak in here, and our voices are carried . . ."

His eyes seemed to glaze over with incomprehension.

"Oh, never mind," I said. "Just go inside. Warm yourself up."

Stiffly, he got off the bike. But then he stood there at the door, mesmerized by the wide pane of glass, perhaps fascinated by his own reflection in it. I hung the receiver back up and sighed. Was I going to have to show him everything?

*I opened the door and pushed him through. "Don't touch anything,"
I said firmly. "Just wait for me."*

*A red-headed cashier and several other customers were already gawk-
ing. Apollus looked a bit offended by my brusqueness. He didn't appreciate being pushed around by anyone. Nevertheless, I left him standing there
and returned to the phones. After blowing warm air on my fingers, I
dialed an access number for collect calls. The operator took my name and
phone number. I waited in agonizing suspense for my mother to answer. I
wasn't even sure what I was going to say. I hadn't rehearsed a single sentence in my mind. Maybe I'd simply burst into tears. All I wanted to say
was "Mom!" All I wanted to hear was her voice saying, "Meagan!"
Unfortunately, I was denied both experiences.*

"Answering machine," said the operator. "Try your call later."

*I hung up in frustration. Where could she be? When would she be
home? Who else could I call? Harry's father? No, I wasn't ready for that
one. I preferred to leave it to Garth. Besides, I was freezing. I went inside
the store to join Apollus.*

*As I entered, a teenage boy with a sweatshirt much rattier than mine
approached Apollus as he stood near a pyramid of motor oil. "Rad, man!"
he announced, looking over his wardrobe. "Hey, can I see that sword?"*

*Apollus grabbed the hilt defensively. The move was so smooth and
automatic that I feared he might draw it and cut the poor kid's head off.
I intervened swiftly.*

"It's all right," I said to Apollus. Then to the boy I added, "Not a good idea."

*The kid, of course, thought it was some kind of put-on. He strutted
away. "Yeah, right," he said mockingly. "Psycho-warrior." He rejoined a
friend near the Icee dispenser.*

Apollus scowled.

"Calm down," I whispered to him. "They're harmless."

*I stepped over to the cashier. She wore a low-cut blouse and too much
eyeliner. She'd been sucking on a cherry lollypop and looking Apollus up
and down with more than casual interest.*

"Can you tell me today's date?" I asked her.

She kept her eyes on Apollus. "The twenty-fifth."

"Of?"

*She sized me up for the first time, almost as if I was competition. The
way I looked, ratty hair and a layer of dirt on my skin, I'm sure she wasn't*

too concerned. "October, sweetie. You two in a play?"

I saw the calendar behind her on the wall and gasped with relief. It was still the same year. We'd only been gone six months. But then it hit me. Six months! Oh, my poor mother! She must have been crazy with grief. No doubt she'd given me up for dead. Or maybe . . . maybe Harry's father had explained things. Then there was Marcos. Harry had said that Marcos had traveled back here to find Melody. Surely my mother hadn't given up hope.

"Listen," I said to the girl. "We have a friend still up on Cedar Mountain over there. I have to go back and get him. If I could just get a hat and a pair of gloves—that's all I'd need. Heck, just the gloves! My fingers are nearly frozen."

She indicated a pair of work gloves on the back wall. "Eleven ninety-five."

"I don't have any money," I confessed. "Maybe I could just borrow them. I promise I'll bring them right back."

She snorted dubiously. Then her painted eyes lit up and she said suavely, "You gonna leave Hercules here as collateral?"

I frowned. I felt a bit defensive. This girl was much closer to Apollus' age than I was. Not that any age would have mattered to this one. I'd be gone twenty minutes. What could happen in twenty minutes?

"Sure," I said.

She reached under the counter and produced her own hat and gloves. Then she leaned toward me and asked in a conspiratorial voice, "So does your friend look anything like him?"

I stammered. "Um, yeah. Just like him."

She handed over the hat and gloves, then started leering at Apollus again, sucking on the lollypop. Apollus' face was expressionless, body straight, as if standing guard outside his Samaritan fort. Maybe leaving him here wasn't such a good idea, I thought. In twenty minutes he could evoke an uproar heretofore unimagined in the western world.

"Do you have a bathroom?" I asked the girl.

"Through there." She pointed toward a back storage area.

I thanked her, then I took Apollus by the elbow and led him into the back. We found the bathroom. I showed him the push-in lock.

"Stay in here and lock the door," I explained. "Just push this button. Understand? No one will be able to get in. Simple. Clean up a bit if you want. Just wait until I get back. Can you do that?"

"What's this?" he asked, staring at the toilet.

"I think you'll figure it out." I pushed in the button myself and shut him inside.

When I emerged from the back room, the cashier and three other customers were staring at me.

"He, uh . . . had to go," I explained.

I fidgeted a moment. The cashier's eyes narrowed. She seemed to suspect that I'd done something to keep Apollus out of her sight. I fled through the doors before she could change her mind about the hat and gloves. I hopped on my motorcycle. Time to get Garth. Once I got Garth, everything would be under control.

I found my uncle-to-be about halfway down the mountain, wandering along a switchback with his arms hugging his chest and his hands hidden under his armpits for warmth.

"Where's Apollus?" he asked.

"At that gas station down the highway. I locked him in the bathroom."

"You did what?"

"Come on. I don't think he'll stay in there for very long."

All the way back I had visions of coming upon a scene with flashing police lights and dead bodies—all slain by a Roman sword. Apollus was already jumpy. It didn't seem like it would have taken much—some rude comment about his armor and greaves—and Apollus would come unglued.

To my relief, the parking lot looked pretty much the same. Nevertheless, Apollus had not stayed in the bathroom. When I burst through the glass doors, he was standing near the counter, surrounded by about a half dozen teenagers, including the one who had prodded him to show his sword. Now the sword was out of its scabbard. Apollus was giving a demonstration. He spun the sword under both arms and past both ears like a martial arts performer. The red-headed cashier looked on with a smitten smile and stars in her eyes. Apollus finished with a flourish, then deftly tossed the sword back into its scabbard. Several teens applauded.

One boy insisted to a friend, *"I can do that last move with num-chucks."*

The friend shoved his shoulder. *"Sure you can, Bradley."*

"Where'd you learn how to do that?" asked a guy with long sideburns who must have been just about Apollus' age.

"I was taught by Tacticus Ahenabarbus," said Apollus, *"—best swordsmen in the Fifth Legion of Rome."*

Two of them laughed. A third one scoffed as if it was a bad joke.

I moved in then, pretending to laugh with the rest. I clapped my hand on Apollus' armored chest. "He's such a kidder. He's really into this Roman stuff. Now come on, honey. I have to talk to you."

I thanked the cashier and returned her hat and gloves. Then I led Apollus toward the door. I whispered harshly, "I thought I told you to stay in the bathroom!"

"I got bored," said Apollus. "Where's Garth?"

"He's outside, calling his wife."

"Calling?"

"On the phone. Follow me."

When we emerged, Garth was holding the receiver to his ear. There were tears in his eyes. So he'd gotten through. He was talking to his wife, Jenny. The word was out. Soon it would spread like wildfire through all our families. We were home.

"I know . . ." Garth said to her, wiping his eyes. "Fine, I promise . . . no, I'm fine . . . I love you, too . . ."

I started to cry as well. What an extraordinary moment. His family hadn't seen him in six months. I knew it was a private conversation. Still, I strained to hear every word. It was Apollus who provided the distraction. He stepped off the curb to watch a man filling his gas tank. A man wearing an orange hunter's hat in one of the other vehicles whistled a catcall at Apollus and shouted out his window, "Nice legs!"

I tried to pull Apollus back to the curb. "Apollus, please! Stay close to me."

"Is that man insulting me?" he asked, more out of curiosity than contempt.

"Yes," I admitted. "Don't you realize it yet? We stick out like sore thumbs! Nobody dresses this way around here, Apollus. If they want to think we're actors in a play or dressed up for Halloween, please, don't disagree with them."

Apollus pointed back inside the store. "Those people—they acted as if they'd never seen a sword before. Don't they teach men how to fight with swords in your land?"

"Not exactly."

"Are there no battles? Doesn't anyone fight for his honor?"

"Oh, they have plenty of wars," I said. "But it's not quite the same—"

His finger shot toward Garth. "How can he speak to his wife on that box? Is it a trick?"

"No, it's—"

"Why is that man putting a pipe into that machine? Is he filling it with fire? How big is your land? What is it called? Is this the capital city?"

So the moment had arrived. The thousand and thousand questions. Apollus wanted all the answers at once. I promised him I would explain everything, but it would take some time.

Garth continued to talk to his wife. He asked about his children and told her about me. There was so much to say, and yet I think a lot of time was expended as the two of them just struggled to contain their emotions. He told her about Harry. They cried some more and discussed who should be the one to tell Jim.

"I'll tell him," said Garth. "But first you have to get us home."

It was arranged that Jenny would immediately call a travel agency and book a flight on the first plane out of Cody. She didn't even ask who the third passenger was that Garth was requesting a ticket for. They seemed to mutually agree that there was too much to try and explain in a single phone call four hundred miles apart. We were advised to get to the Cody airport as fast as we could. The tickets would be waiting when we arrived. Apollus Brutus Severillus was about to be the only Roman to ever fly thirty thousand feet above the earth.

I stomped back into the store and said to the teenagers still gathered at the counter, "You see that Yamaha 200 out there? I paid five hundred dollars for it. I'll give it to any one of you for a hundred bucks and a ride to the airport. Any takers?"

I closed the deal with the guy who had the long sideburns. His name was Jerry, and he owned a 1991 Chevy Cavalier with cloth seats that I think used to be gray. Now they were so covered with food, grease, and soda pop stains that it might have been more accurate to call them polychrome. He tried to pay me with a check, but when I insisted on cash he produced four twenties, three fives, and two ones from his wallet, along with a handful of change. I guessed he was a year or two out of high school and worked for a local mechanic. There were dozens of odd metal tools and greasy rags on the backseat which he took away and stuffed into the trunk. He asked one of his friends to watch the bike until he returned, then opened the passenger door for me while inviting the others to hop in the back.

Apollus climbed in without hesitation. I had a feeling he was starting to shake off his initial apprehension about all this and get swept up in the adventure.

"*So where are you guys off to?*" *Jerry asked as we pulled out onto the highway.*

"*Salt Lake City,*" *Garth replied.*

"*Oh, yeah? My brother drove through there once. He said it was* big. "

I had a feeling he'd never been outside of Wyoming.

"*Yup, it's pretty big,*" *said Garth.*

Apollus' eyes were still taking in all the scenery. "*What are those?*" *he asked.*

He was pointing at all the telephone and cable wires. I was reluctant to answer, knowing that Jerry would think we were Romulans.

"*I told you we'd explain everything later,*" *I replied.*

Jerry glanced back. "*What are what?*"

"*Those ropes strung from pole to pole.*"

Jerry crinkled his nose. "*The phone lines?*"

"*Ah, phone lines,*" *said Apollus with enlightenment.* "*Is this how you amplified your voice to be heard by your wife?*"

"*That's right,*" *said Garth, impressed at such an astute conclusion.*

"*Is this guy okay?*" *asked Jerry.*

"*Yes,*" *I confirmed.* "*He's just taking his role for the play a little too seriously.*"

I scowled at Apollus, hoping it might encourage him to shut up. Not a chance.

"*How did you build this machine?*" *he asked the driver.*

Now Jerry beamed with pride. "*You like it? I bought this thing for less than I paid for her motorcycle. We put in a new engine, new carburetor—the works. Now it runs like a charm.*"

"*What is the price of a machine like this?*" *Apollus asked.*

"*Oh, I don't know,*" *said Jerry.* "*This is the first car I ever rebuilt. Sentimental value. But, uh . . . what are you offerin'?*"

I interrupted. "*Honey, don't get carried away—*"

"*My name isn't honey,*" *Apollus bristled.* "*I'm trying to conduct a business transaction. I'm willing to pay ten silver denarii.*"

"*Ten* what? " *asked Jerry.*

I spun around and blustered at Apollus, "*What's the matter with you? You can't buy a car, Apollus. We're going to take a plane.*"

"*Is that another machine?*" *he asked.*

Jerry gave Apollus—and then each of us in turn—a deeply concerned glance.

"*Watch the road!*" *Garth piped in.*

Jerry jerked the wheel.

"*Never mind him,*" *I told Jerry.* "*This Rome thing has become an obsession.*"

Jerry didn't believe a word of it. He was sure we were putting him on. "*Nobody likes being the butt of someone else's joke,*" *he said glumly.*

Garth started to apologize. "*Now, there's no reason—*"

"*Let's just get to the airport and be done with it,*" *Jerry interrupted. He faced forward, looking offended.*

Apollus was like a kid in a candy store. Every sight drew a gasp and a question—fire hydrants, traffic lights, the courthouse clock, a trailer with a boat, the flashing lights of a police car, the playground in front of Burger King. "*What are those pieces of glass that woman wears on her eyes?*" *Apollus asked.* "*What makes the numbers glow on that sign? How long will one of these machines operate before you must add more fire?*"

I couldn't get him to shut up! I was sure Jerry would dump us at the side of the road with a declaration that we were all nuts. Fortunately, the drive to the airport was only about ten minutes. Jerry seemed as relieved to arrive as we were.

"*Well, thank you very much,*" *I told him after we'd climbed out of the Cavalier.* "*Enjoy your new motorcycle.*"

Jerry said nothing, just sped away with wide eyes and a heavy frown—an expression that combined the emotions of a man who felt swindled with one who'd just seen Bigfoot.

Apollus was becoming more enthralled every minute. To the left there was a hangar yard with several small private Cessnas. "*Are those planes?*" *he asked.*

"*Those are planes,*" *Garth confirmed.*

"*Are they faster than those other machines?*"

"*Much faster,*" *said Garth.* "*They fly through the air.*"

Apollus paled. "*That's impossible.*"

"*Welcome to the twenty-first century,*" *I said.*

"*Is that the name of your nation?*"

"*No,*" *I frowned.* "*That's the year.*"

The mortal dread that Apollus had first felt when we stepped out of the cave returned. Up until this moment, it had never occurred to Apollus that we had traveled in time—just journeyed to a strange, undiscovered land. I doubted if the concept had sunk in even now. I bit my tongue. We were moving way too fast. Apollus' head was spinning like a pinwheel.

"Never mind all that," said Garth. "Let's go in. Apollus, I'll need your weapons."

"What?"

"Your sword and your knife. I'll put them in my backpack and check it as luggage."

He stood firm. "I'll not relinquish my weapons."

"Apollus," I said impatiently, "you'll get them back in Salt Lake. They won't let us on the airplane if you're carrying them."

"I'm not sure I want to be on this air-plane. If it tries to fly like a bird, we'll all surely die."

I tried to take a more understanding approach. "I know all of this is very confusing. Things just work differently in our world. Haven't you noticed that no one wears swords? And the plane will fly, I assure you. It'll be the most thrilling ride of your life. Now, come on—where's that Roman courage that I saw storming up the slopes on Mount Gerizim? Give Garth the sword. Everything will be fine."

He looked as nervous as a cornered animal. Nevertheless, he relented. Maybe it was hearing a woman challenge his courage. Apollus grudgingly removed his sword belt and scabbard and handed them to Garth. Lastly, he turned over the knife. Garth stuck them in his backpack. The sword was almost too long, and its tip created a peak in the top after he zipped it closed. If the baggage handlers tossed it around, it would likely puncture the material.

I could tell that Apollus felt totally naked and vulnerable. I tried to be sympathetic, but then it occurred to me that maybe this was good for him. Everyone needs to have their security blanket torn away from time to time. Otherwise, how can we ever learn and grow stronger? Yes, this was good for Apollus.

"I'm hungry," said Garth. "Let's find something to eat."

The Yellowstone Regional Airport was the tiniest airport I'd ever seen. There were only two airlines flying in and out. One room, one gate—and the man who checked you in was the same man who loaded your luggage on the plane. There was a modest airport café that exuded the smells of grease and hamburgers, making my mouth water. We quickly retreated into the men's and women's bathrooms to wash away, as best we could, the layers of dust left by Frost Cave.

When we came out we drew a lot of stares, as usual. What excuse could we give them now? Riding around town in ancient costumes was one thing, but why would we choose to wear such garb on an airplane? We addressed the issue by not addressing it. Just let them stare, I decided. I wished I'd asked for a hundred dollars more for my motorcycle, so we could have stopped off at Wal-Mart and bought clothing. But now that I looked at the departure schedule for our airline, I realized there wouldn't have been time. The direct flight to Salt Lake on Delta/Skywest arrived in less than an hour and would depart twenty-five minutes later.

Garth went up to the counter and confirmed that his wife had reserved three seats. We had a little bit of trouble when we couldn't produce any I.D., but a second collect phone call to Jenny smoothed out the tangles. Thank goodness for hometown airports! At a bigger one, I'm sure we'd never have gotten away with it.

I ordered Apollus a double cheeseburger and french fries. He'd become very quiet again, and hardly even looked at his surroundings anymore. Just stared off into space. I became concerned. I'd have given anything to read his thoughts.

Our sandwiches arrived. I showed Apollus how to apply ketchup and mustard. He ate his burger just as Garth and I had demonstrated. But still, his expression showed no reaction. I couldn't tell if he found it disgusting or delicious.

"Bet you've never tasted anything like that before," I said, trying to draw a comment.

"Mm," he grunted, chewing carefully and swallowing.

"Is something the matter?" asked Garth.

Apollus looked at him, but never answered. Beyond Garth was the window to the landing field. Our plane was in sight, making its final approach. Apollus dropped his cheeseburger and stood. He seemed to be walking in a dream as he approached the window and pressed his face to the glass. The commuter plane sank from the sky and touched down on the runway. When I stepped up to Apollus, his eyes were full of tears. Clearly, the modern century was starting to overwhelm him. Yet he'd still seen such a small portion. If this was how he reacted to a twenty-seat commuter plane, how would he respond to a 747? Or a rocket ship? Or an aircraft carrier?

When they called for boarding, Apollus was forced to remove his helmet, then his armor, then his bucklers, cape and even his hobnail sandals before he could finally pass through the metal detector. It was humorous seeing all his things piled beside the tiny plastic container designed to hold coins and keychains. When they were done with him, all he had left was his tunic. He looked utterly pitiful.

Suddenly I felt very sad. I began to wish he'd never come. It wasn't right. I feared I'd committed a great sin. Like removing a beautiful but wild animal from the forest. He was in a cage—a spectacle for everyone to gawk at and point their fingers. We'd made a mistake. A mistake that I knew could never be undone.

Apollus continued his vigil of silence as we boarded the airplane and even as he braced himself for takeoff. For the first ten minutes, his eyes watched the objects on the ground grow smaller and smaller as the earth in all its vastness grew larger and larger. But then he turned away from even this, and stared morosely at the seat ahead.

I put my hand on his and felt tears come into my own eyes. I wanted to say something. I didn't know where to start. I guess I wanted to beg his forgiveness. But what good would that have done? It was too late. The crime had been committed. It would be upon my head forever.

"It's all nothing," I heard him mumble.

"Huh?" I asked. "What's nothing?"

"I am nothing," he replied. "The Emperor is nothing. Rome . . . is nothing."

CHAPTER 11

I was awakened by seabirds and the steady, distant churning of the ocean. The sky was pale—no color at all. The clouds were long, puffy streaks, some crooked, some running side by side like a tumbling, cottony logjam. The wind was still blowing, but not with nearly as much fury as the night before. The sea was choppy, but growing calmer by the minute. Visibility only went on for a mile or two, then the sea was washed out by haze.

I turned to one side, then to the other to count how many survivors had managed to hang on during the worst of the storm. My right eye was still blurry. Nevertheless, I counted twenty. Exactly twenty, including myself. Of the hundred or so slaves and twenty or so crewmembers on our merchant slave ship, only twenty men had survived. We were a miserable-looking lot, all of us barefoot and disheveled. Our only clothes were the garments about our waists. I was still wearing my torn, ratty jeans, which two weeks ago I'd ripped into cut-offs.

Micah was beside me, still sleeping. I looked around again and recognized the man who had pulled me in from the sea—the same one I'd rescued from the hold. He'd climbed to the highest place on the rock, which was only about ten feet out of the water. He was stretched out in exhaustion on the coarse black stone, but his head was alert. He peered off into the haze. I'd seen this man many times over the past few weeks, but I didn't know his name. I'd never learned the names of any of my fellow slaves, except for the ones whose bunks were right beside mine. We didn't get much of a chance to strike up acquaintances.

But the merchants and their taskmasters were gone now. I stood up and climbed to the place where the man was lying, carefully avoiding the other men strewn all about. He saw me approaching and smiled grimly. He had a thick beard, as did most of the men. But strangely, his beard looked almost perfectly clipped and groomed. It just grew that way naturally. He was a little older that the rest of us, mid-forties, with a receding hairline that accented his brooding forehead. Immediately, he reminded me of my father—not by appearance, but by the warmth in his eyes.

"Well, well," he said. "My young savior awakens."

"My name is Harrison," I said.

"I am Nicanor," he replied. He gave the sea another hard look. "Maybe we should have gone down with the ship. We'll all be dead of thirst in three days."

"Then we have to get off this rock," I said.

"A wise suggestion," he said facetiously. "How do you propose it?"

I shaded my eyes and gazed at the water. There was no sign of the ship or any part of it. About a quarter mile to the south stood another outcropping of rock, this one much steeper and more jagged. A half mile farther stood another one, about like ours. And then beyond it— it was hard to tell how far with all the haze—appeared to be the shoreline of a larger piece of land. It was at least four or five miles away.

"Perhaps it's better to die here, as free men," said Nicanor. "If we're sighted by a ship, we'll no doubt be brought back into servitude to the Romans."

"My eye still doesn't see too well," I said to Nicanor. "Does that look like an island to you?"

He strained his own eyes. "Can't tell."

Several of the other men had started to stir. They'd overheard our conversation and were peering at the same spot of ocean.

"There does appear to be something out there," Nicanor confirmed.

His confirmation did little to buoy up the men's spirits. I heard a few of them uttering prayers. Death chants. I climbed back down to where Micah lay and roused him to consciousness. He sat up groggily.

"How do you feel?" I asked.

"Where are we?"

"I don't have any idea," I confessed.

"The Aegean," replied a man nearby. "I sailed these waters as a boy. To the north is Thrace. To the east is Asia and Lycia. To the west is Achaia. And to the south is Creta."

The description sounded odd. Apparently there was land all around us, except on the very spot we happened to get shipwrecked.

"What about that over there?" I asked him. "Do you think it's an island?"

"Could be," he said. "Might be Creta. Might be any one of ten thousand islands in these waters."

"Might it have food and fresh water?" asked Nicanor.

The man shook his head and looked away. I realized he really wasn't sure of anything. Still, the information gave me hope.

"How can we reach it?" I asked Nicanor.

One of the other men answered. "We sprout wings like a bird and let the wind carry us."

His sarcasm drew no laughter.

"Is anyone here a strong swimmer?" I asked.

The question seemed reasonable enough. After all, people in my day had swum the English Channel. Heck, they'd swum all the way from Cuba to Florida. That island was five miles away at the most. I even started to wonder if I might be strong enough to reach it myself. But the question only generated snarls and scoffs.

"Most of us don't swim at all," said one man. "The Jews are not seafarers."

"But you survived last night," I said. "How did you find this rock?"

"The rock found us," he replied.

It was clear that many of them had been washed here by the waves. They'd been saved by Providence. My shoulders slumped in discouragement. Even if I *was* strong enough, it seemed twice as daunting to try it alone.

"I can swim," said Nicanor confidently. "When I was a younger man, I swam from Capernaum to Tabgha on the Sea of Galilee. I was a fisherman there for the first thirty-seven years of my life."

My confidence swelled. "If you go, I'll go with you."

"Are you a strong swimmer?" he asked.

"I think so," I said. Then more assuredly, "Yes. I earned a merit badge in lifesaving."

"Merit badge?"

"All together, I bet I swam a whole mile. Don't worry. I can make it."

So it was decided. Nicanor and I would attempt the swim together. I really didn't think it would be that difficult. First we'd swim to that steep outcropping about a quarter mile away. Then we could rest. Afterwards, we'd swim to the next outcropping. A cinch! I was overflowing with confidence. Perhaps I should have been more realistic. We still had no water, no food. My muscles ached from the night before. There was still a half-pound iron ring on my right ankle. But the more I stared at that hazy island and those outcroppings of rock, the closer they seemed to appear.

"We'll find a boat," I said. "Then we'll come back here."

"What if there are no boats?" asked Micah.

"He's right," said one of the others. "Even if it *is* an island, who's to say it's any less barren than this hunk of rock we're sitting on now?"

"What do you suggest?" asked Nicanor. "That we wait here and let ourselves cook in the sun?"

"If either of you survive, how do we know you'll come back?" asked an older man with streaks of gray in his beard.

These were silly questions. Nevertheless, I kept my patience. I understood their fears. If they really were destined to die, why should they let us fill them with false hopes?

"We'll come back," I said. "I promise."

They stared at us, uncertain.

At last another man with a long face said despairingly, "You'll be eaten by sharks. Or swallowed up by some other leviathan of the deep."

"Pray for us," I said. I was looking at Micah. He at least, I felt, knew how to pray.

Nicanor and I looked at one another and nodded. My heart pounded. Adrenaline started pumping. That was good. I needed all the adrenaline I could get.

Nicanor waited for me to dive in first. I perched myself at the edge of the rock. Then I gathered my last ounce of courage and dove out as far as could, half-expecting that when I raised my head the closest rock would look twice as large, while the rock behind us would look far away. It didn't quite turn out that way. It was true that with every stroke Micah's rock got smaller and smaller, but the rock we were swimming toward seemed to stay exactly the same size.

Nicanor passed me on the right. He was swimming the crawl stroke, just like me. I felt sure he could have left me in the dust, but instead he paced himself and never left my sight. I stopped frequently to rest and check my bearings. After a while, however, it took just as much energy to tread water as to swim, so I forged ahead. Incrementally, our destination loomed closer. But it seemed to take forever. The waves washed around me. Nicanor stayed out in front.

As time wore on, the ring on my ankle began to feel like an anchor, as if it might drag me right to the bottom. I started swallowing water when I meant to take a gulp of air. This was going to be more difficult than I'd thought. I didn't understand. It was only a quarter mile away! How could swimming such a short distance be so hard? In Scouts it had seemed so easy. Then again, in the pool at Hunter High I'd been able to grab the edge and push off before every lap. I'd never realized what a difference that had made.

I was well short of my first destination, my lungs heaving and my muscles burning, when I concluded there was absolutely no way I could swim five miles. No way on God's green earth. This was a job for an Olympian! I began to pray to Father in Heaven that if I could just reach that first rock, it would be enough. I'd never ask for anything more. I sensed that Nicanor was winded as well. This scared me more than anything else. If the old fisherman was ready to give out, I didn't stand a chance. I fought down a rush of panic, then lowered my head and just kept swimming.

I rarely stopped to check distance now. That steep shard of cliff was just a blurry image on the horizon. Then I noticed that it was growing faster than before. This lifted my spirits. I was almost there.

I started counting my strokes. Ten . . . twenty . . . thirty. On my ninety-fourth stroke, I grasped solid rock. Nicanor and I arrived at the same moment. The cliff was almost sheer, but we managed to find an uneven shelf about four feet wide. We dragged ourselves onto that shelf until we were halfway out of the water, then we lay on our backs and heaved for oxygen. For several minutes neither of us spoke a word. But it was clear what we were both thinking: we'd overestimated our strength. Now it appeared that we were permanently separated from our fellow survivors. There was no going back.

"Well," said Nicanor finally, "at least there were no sharks."

He laughed once, but it was broken up by coughing. I leaned back against the rock and assessed how far we had swum. The tiny rock with Micah and the others danced above the waves. I could see them stirring about. I wondered if they could see us against this black cliff. They'd know we made the first leg. But the next outcropping was twice as far. It was out of the question.

"I'm afraid I'm not a young man anymore," said Nicanor.

"Me neither," I replied.

This made us laugh. But it was short-lived. The gravity of our situation settled in.

This particular rock looked to be about three times the breadth of the one we'd abandoned, and four times as high. From a distance, it had seemed more suited to climbing on the left side. We rested about twenty minutes, then slipped back into the water and began working our way around the base. Seabirds screeched at us from above. They'd hidden several nests in the cliff, no doubt convinced that nothing would ever disturb them here.

"You think there might be eggs up there?" I asked Nicanor.

"I don't know," he replied. Then he shook his head. "Not the right season. Winter's coming in just a few weeks."

Still, I was determined to check each nest. As we half-climbed, half-swam around the base of the rock, I made mental notes of their locations on the rocks. My mind was so consumed with this that I almost didn't see the obstruction in our path.

I heard it first—a dull wooden thud in the surf. I'd half expected to see a canoe knocking against the rocks. It wasn't a canoe. It was a log—but not just any log. It was almost twenty feet long.

"It's the mast of our ship!" Nicanor declared.

Indeed, the log showed scars of the fire. It tapered slightly toward one end. A portion of the yardarm was still attached in the middle, though the sail had burned away. We determined that it must have broken away from the ship when it overturned just before sinking. Somehow it had floated here to wash against this outcropping of rock.

"It's the boat we were looking for!" I announced.

The wood itself seemed fairly light. It had been lacquered to keep it from rotting. This also helped it to float. I straddled the log and lay flat on my stomach. I started paddling with my arms. Sure enough, it could be maneuvered and steered.

"We'll paddle it to the island," said Nicanor.

"No," I said. "We should paddle it back to the other rock. With all of us pitching in, we'll reach that island as fast as a motor boat!"

Nicanor never asked what a motor boat was. I guess he figured I knew what I was talking about. It took us over an hour to get back, despite the fact that there was hardly a ripple now on the ocean's surface. We rested frequently, still exhausted from our initial swim. My lips were parched, my tongue swollen from lack of water. Wetting it with salt water made it worse.

I couldn't have said what Micah and the others thought when they saw us kicking and paddling that twenty-foot log back toward them. Their excitement seemed to increase by degrees until, by the time we arrived, they were shouting for joy. Several of them helped pull us in when we got close enough. It took us a good half hour to decide how best to arrange the twenty men along the length of the mast. We decided to straddle ten men along the main length while the other ten hung on to the yardarm and kicked with their legs. We'd rotate at intervals.

Our spirits were high as we shoved off toward the island. Some of the haze had cleared. I felt confident that it was, in fact, a sizable chunk of land. Whether it had any essentials for sustaining life was still to be determined. Nevertheless, my heart swelled with gratitude. It occurred to me that whenever I'd expended the least degree of effort to pull myself out of a jam, the Lord had always carried me the rest of the way. Sitting still—that was the only mistake anyone could make. And even if there was no other choice, there was always prayer. Micah confirmed that he'd done plenty of that.

So I was satisfied now—there was definitely a reason that I was here. If it was only to help save Micah and Nicanor and these other seventeen men, that was enough. But I had a feeling there was another reason. Something more subtle, and perhaps more important. I'd find out soon enough. In the Lord's due time.

CHAPTER 12

As we entered the terminal in Salt Lake City, they were all there waiting for us, arms open to embrace us, faces streaming with tears: Jenny and her two children, Rebecca and Joshua. And Melody—looking so much stronger than the last time I'd seen her. She'd lost some weight, but otherwise she looked as beautiful as ever. There was also a dark, handsome young man who I guessed to be Marcos. Beside them was Melody's eighteen-year-old sister, Steffanie, with a head of more blonde hair than any girl deserves. And finally, in the very center, my mother, who looked more ragged than all of them. I might have thought she hadn't slept in months. Considering the heartache I'd caused her, it was possible that she hadn't.

My face was buried in her shoulder before I even realized it. We were both crying uncontrollably, hugging each other as if we would never let go.

"Oh, Meagan," she whispered. "I'd almost given up. I'd almost given up."

"I'm home, Momma. Will you ever forgive me?"

"No," she said, then changed her mind. "Yes. Don't ever leave me again."

"But I have to, Mom."

I let the statement hang in the air as I accepted embraces from Steffanie, then Melody. In an instant I noticed the conspicuous absence of Harry's father. I looked around in dismay. Melody read my thoughts. "My dad isn't here," she said. "We couldn't find him."

"Where is he?" asked Garth.

"Shopping," said my mother. "He's been running errands for the last two days."

"If you'd have come up through the cave even a day later," said Jenny, "you might have run smack into him."

"Why?" I asked. "What's going on?"

"We were coming to find you," said Steffanie. "And to find Harry."

"They were leaving tomorrow morning," added Melody.

I looked at Steffanie. "We? You mean you and your father?"

"And me," said my mother.

My jaw dropped. I might have laughed, but I was too stunned. My mother in Roman times? Did she think it would be like sightseeing in Yellowstone?

"Where is Harry?" Steffanie asked her uncle. "Aunt Jenny said there's something wrong."

"Is he all right?" Melody asked me. "Can you at least tell us where he is?"

I felt overwhelmed. "There's so much . . . so much to explain . . ."

I realized Apollus had not joined us. He'd lingered back several paces, taking in the scene of our family reunions. He looked utterly out of place and uncomfortable. There was a tenseness about him, like a cat ready to spring. Jenny's children, Rebecca and Joshua, had gathered around him, taking in his Roman outfit.

"Are you a Nephite?" asked seven-year-old Becky. She took his hand as if she felt an unusual kinship to someone wearing an ancient uniform. Apollus didn't reply—just stared at the two children as if gaping at a pair of strange exotic animals.

I made the introductions. "This is Apollus."

Everyone seemed to have noticed him for the first time. Or perhaps this was the first time they realized what they were looking at.

Jenny, looking incredulous, leaned toward her husband. "Is he . . . ?"

"Yes," Garth answered. "He's exactly what he appears to be."

Steffanie walked around Apollus as if walking around a polished marble statue. "My, my," she said. "A real Roman soldier. I never thought I'd see one of these . . ."

Apollus' hand felt for the hilt of his sword—a natural reflex. Fortunately, it was still in Garth's backpack in baggage claim. Other people in the terminal were gawking just like Steffanie. What else could they do? We definitely needed to find Apollus a new wardrobe.

"Come on," said Garth. "We better find Jim. As Meagan said, there's a lot we have to explain."

We piled into two separate cars for the ride to West Valley. Our plan was to rendezvous at the Hawkins' home. Apollus and I rode with my mother, Melody, and Steffanie. We also rode with the dark-eyed young man, who was finally, officially introduced to me as Marcos.

"*I've heard a lot about you,*" *I said.* "*In fact, you're the reason we're all here. Or not here, as the case may be. This all began because we were looking for you.*"

I didn't mean it critically, yet I realized that was how he took it. A shadow of guilt swept over his face. "*I know,*" *he said regretfully.* "*What about Gidgiddonihah? Do you know where he is?*"

"*He's gone back to the world of the Nephites,*" *I explained.* "*But we're supposed to meet him in the cavern in four days. Maybe it's three days now; I've lost track of time. I haven't slept for twenty-four hours. Gid was going to round up some help and then join us to search for Harry.*"

"*Tell us, Meagan,*" *Melody pleaded.* "*What happened to my brother?*"

I filled them in on as much as we knew about the arrest in the Caesarea market and all the slave ships bound for unknown destinations. I told them about the earthquake, and how our original return route had been cut off. Harry's family had all been suffering tremendous anxiety since they'd first heard that Garth and I were flying in from Cody. I felt as if I'd confirmed their worst fears. It might have been better if I could have reported that Harry was dead. There's nothing more horrible than not knowing—wondering if all your hopes are in vain.

"*Then the expedition is still on,*" *said Steffanie with a stiff upper lip.* "*We'll still be leaving for Frost Cave as soon as we can. We'll find another route, and then we'll find Harry.*"

I almost objected. Steffanie couldn't go back; she was only eighteen. Somehow I'd forgotten that I was only fifteen. I had every intention of returning, but that was different. I'd already been there; I knew what to expect. I knew how to avoid enemies and recognize friends. As to the concept of my mother *going back—that one still blew me away. She was my mother, for heaven's sake! I just couldn't see her traipsing around the deserts of the Dead Sea, or subsisting on a meal of figcakes and barley gruel. I was sure that Jim would see to reason. We just had to sit down with Jim and Garth and the rest and explain the dangers. Then I was sure the final list of who would be going back would shorten considerably.*

Harry's father, his hair showing more gray than I remembered, was literally waiting for us in the driveway when we pulled in. Either he'd just arrived home from his errands, or some quiet voice had whispered that we were coming. Jenny and Garth's van pulled into the driveway ahead of us. I watched Jim's eyes radiate surprise and delight as his old friend stepped out to greet him. Then his eyes filled with tears. They embraced, and Jim became animated with questions. His eyes found me as Mom parked in front of their house. He started toward me, seeming to look beyond me at the place where Apollus sat. But then Garth grabbed his arm and spoke a few grave words. Jim listened intently, his face becoming paler. This was the moment I'd been dreading. He'd just been told that Harry was not with us.

I climbed out of the car. Jim looked stricken. His eyes darted from me to Garth, even to Apollus. "Where?" I heard him ask. "How long ago?"

"Ten days," said Garth. "At least by their measurement of time."

"He was injured? How? What happened? Where did they take my son?!"

"Let's go inside. We'll explain it all inside."

I was feeling dizzy as I stepped through the Hawkins' front door. Maybe it was all the emotion. My stomach was churning with acid. I was just so tired. The stress and exertion of the last twenty-four hours had finally caught up to me. I needed to sleep. Just a few hours' sleep, and then I would help Garth explain everything. I'd even help plan the expedition back. But I knew right now that if I sat down, I'd never be able to keep my eyes open.

"Are you all right?" my mother asked me.

"Yes," I said. "I think I just need to lie down for a few minutes."

Melody took over from there. A minute later, I found myself in her bedroom. "Here," she said, leading me toward the bed. "Get out of those clothes. I'll run a hot bath for you. Steff should have a pair of sweats you can wear. Wait right here."

I lay down on her bed to wait. My memories from there are a little fuzzy, but oh, so wonderful. The next thing I knew I was sinking down into a tub of hot water with bubbles and the fragrances of hyacinth and raspberry. This was it, I decided. I'd died and gone to the celestial kingdom.

"Would you like me to buy you some hair color?" said Melody through the door. "Just the rinse kind. Tonight we could try to match it to your original hair color. Would you like that?"

"Sure, sure," I said dreamily.

Coloring my hair to match my roots was the least of my concerns. The cotton sweats I climbed into after drying off felt as soft as oriental silks. So did the sheets of Melody's bed. I snuggled between them and buried my face in a nest of white pillows. That really was the last thing I remembered for several hours.

When I awakened, it was with a jolt. "Apollus!" I said aloud.

My goodness, I'd forgotten all about Apollus! It was dark outside. Melody's clock read a little past six p.m. I threw off the blankets and stepped hurriedly down the stairway and entered the Hawkins' living room. No one was there. Where had they all gone?

"Is that you, honey?" asked my mother's voice from the kitchen. "We're in here."

I rounded the corner and entered the dining room. Garth, Jenny, and their kids, as well as Jim and my mother were seated at the table. I saw a bucket of Kentucky Fried Chicken, two pieces left. The table was strewn with paper plates and crumpled napkins, gnawed corncobs and chicken bones. Garth looked as if he'd also taken a shower. He wore fresh clothing that his wife had brought from their home in Provo. No one else was in sight.

"Do you feel better?" asked Jim.

I nodded. "Where's Apollus?"

"Melody, Marcos, and Steffanie took him to the Valley Fair Mall," Mom replied. "They were going to buy him some modern clothing."

"They took him there *without me?*" I asked in a panic.

"Is there something wrong?"

"He's a stranger in a strange land!" I said frantically. "On the plane I was sure he was on the verge of a nervous breakdown!"

"I had the impression that he and Marcos were hitting it off rather well," said Garth.

"I'm sure they're fine, honey," consoled my mother. "Sit down and have something to eat. Garth says you haven't had a healthy meal in days."

Whether Kentucky Fried Chicken was healthy might be debatable. But it did smell good. My spirit calmed a little. Apollus was in able enough hands. I guess I felt a little jealous—sort of like a parent missing their child's first steps. Apollus was seeing a thousand new sights, and I wanted to be there.

"They should be home shortly," said Jim. "In the meantime, we have a lot to discuss, Meagan."

His tone was serious. I sat down and took an extra-crispy wing out of the bucket. "Yes?" I said, a little nervous.

"Garth tells me you're determined to go back with us. Is that right?"

"That's right," I said. "More determined than anything."

"Are you sure that's a good idea?" asked Mom.

"What do you mean?" I said defensively. "Of course I'm sure."

"I just don't know if it would be wise, Meagan," said Jim. "You're still very young. According to the stories Garth has told us, you're very lucky to be alive."

"You think anyone else could have done better? I'm going back, Jim. Wild horses couldn't keep me here. I could never live with myself if I thought I'd abandoned Harry. Not after all he did for me. I'm sure Garth feels the same way."

"I'm staying, Meagan," said Garth.

I raised my eyebrows. "You are?"

I looked at his wife beside him, holding his hand. Then I looked at his two children, one on either side. "I've already been gone from my family for six months," he said. "I can't bear to think of Harry, but . . . I can't leave my children again." He didn't have to explain anymore. I understood perfectly. I should have expected it.

"Then that's all the more reason I have to go back," I said. "Without me, you'd never be able to retrace our steps."

"If what Garth says is true," said Jim, "there are no steps to retrace. It's a matter of faith now. A matter of believing that God will lead us where we have to go."

"But I know the country," I protested. "I know the hazards."

"What about your friend, Apollus?" asked my mother. "Wouldn't he be able to help us with such things far better than you?"

I shuddered and drew a deep breath. "I'm going back, Mom! No one can keep me here. Someone could try to lock me in a closet, but it wouldn't matter. As soon as I got out, I'd follow you."

Jim and my mother looked at each other. Somehow they didn't seem surprised by my response.

"Then we're all going," said Mom.

"Who's all?" I asked hesitantly.

"Jim and Steffanie. Me and you," she confirmed.

"Marcos wanted to come as well," Jim added. "But I need him to stay with Melody. She's ninety percent back to full strength, but I don't know what the future holds. Besides, I could never separate them again. After all, they're engaged to be married."

My heart fluttered. "They are? When?"

"That hasn't quite been determined," said Jim. He took my mother's hand. "They face somewhat the same problem we've faced. We'd like to know that all our loved ones are safe and well. It's not easy to plan such a sacred, happy event when so much else is in disarray. I hope they'll wait until we've returned, but . . . they're under no obligations."

"We'd like to all be married together," said Mom. "Even the same day." She sighed drearily, then smiled. "Maybe it can still happen. It depends, I guess, on how soon we return."

I was still gaping at my mother. "Mom, be serious," I said. "You don't have to go with us. You don't even like to go camping without a trailer and indoor plumbing. Do you have any idea what you're getting into?"

"I think I have some idea," she replied. "I've listened to Marcos. I've heard what Garth has said. It doesn't matter, Meagan. If you and Jim are going back, do you really think I could stay? Do you really think I could endure six more months like the last?"

The pain was visible in her eyes. I reached out to hug her. "Oh, Momma. I wouldn't want to do that to you again, but . . . we might never get back. What if we found ourselves in the same mess as Harry?"

"We'd be together," she said. "Right now, that's more important to me than anything else."

The idea began to filter through. All at once it filled me with relief. My misgivings about returning to that awful place seemed to lighten. Maybe it would be good to have my mother at my side.

I looked at Jim. "When are we leaving?"

"As soon as possible," he replied. "I was leaving tomorrow. If the time bridge has become as unstable as Garth has described, every moment counts."

"What worries me most . . ." Garth bit his lip thoughtfully. "Time has always moved much faster in the past than in the present. If we were to spend several months in the past, only a few days would have elapsed in the present. This is the first time that more time has elapsed in the present than in the past. What ramifications this might have for your return trip, I couldn't say."

Jim became more agitated. "Even as we sit here, weeks, months—perhaps years—could be pulling Harry and us apart. I'm ready to leave now. We could all be ready to leave by tomorrow afternoon. I have most of the supplies."

"What about things to bargain with?" I asked.

"Bargain?"

"Yes," I said. "That's why we came back. We didn't have enough money and resources to search for Harry."

"What did you have in mind?" asked Jim.

"You mean gold and silver?" asked my mother.

"Not exactly," I said. "To be honest, I thought this might be an area where Apollus could help. If anyone might know what things from modern times Romans would consider the most valuable, it would be Apollus."

"You mean like radios or televisions or cordless telephones?" asked Mom.

"No," I said. "Those things wouldn't do them any good. There's no radio stations—no phone lines. I mean just cheap things."

"I know what she means," said Garth's wife, Jenny. "We spent over six years living among the Nephites. I can't count all the things I wished we'd had. Bobby pins. Thermometers. Things that here are considered practically worthless, but in ancient times would have been worth their weight in gold."

"Exactly," I said. "A magic marker. A spool of scotch tape. Who knows? We might trade something like a butane lighter for passage on a ship that would take us anywhere in the Roman world!"

Garth smirked to himself. "This trip could well play havoc with modern archaeology. I can just see some scientist analyzing a butane lighter that he found alongside a Dead Sea Scroll."

Jim grunted. "He'd probably ignore it. He'd think some other modern explorer got there a few years beforehand and left it. We're talking about my son's life. I'll carry anything if I think it might save him."

We heard a car pull into the driveway.

"They're back," said Jim. "We'll get Apollus' opinion on all this."

But before we could reach the front door to greet them, Steffanie burst inside. "We lost him!" she cried.

"Lost who?" asked Jim.

"Apollus!" she declared. "He wandered away. We've been searching for almost an hour!"

* * * * * *

Steffanie and I sped back toward the mall in her Camry. Mom and Jim took their own car. Melody and Marcos had remained at the mall to search on foot.

"*How can you lose a Roman soldier in full military uniform?*" *I asked Steffanie.*

"*He didn't want to go inside,*" *Steff explained.* "*We had a feeling he was jittery, so we left him in the car.*"

"*I thought you went to buy him clothes!*"

"*Melody figured he was close to Marcos' size.*"

"*So you just left him there?*"

"*Marcos didn't like the idea at all. Five minutes later, we went back. But that's all it took. He was already gone.*"

"*Did Apollus say anything?*"

"*Nothing much. He was very quiet. I tried to ask questions to get him to talk.*"

"*Like what?*"

"*Silly things. How long had he been a soldier? Had he ever seen the Parthenon? Did he have a nice Roman girl waiting back home—?*"

"*A nice Roman girl?*"

"*Just things like that. He wasn't all that talkative.*"

I groaned inwardly. "*Letting him come with us through that cave was the worst idea I ever had. I'm very worried.*"

"*There's something else to worry about. He had his sword.*"

"*You let him take his sword?*"

"*How could we stop him? He got it out of Uncle Garth's backpack.*"

"*You should have explained that people don't carry swords around the mall!*"

"*He hangs onto it like a security blanket. I just hoped he'd leave it in the car.*"

"*I can't believe this is happening!*"

It couldn't have been any worse if we'd let Tarzan run amok in New York City. We pulled into the mall parking lot and met Mom and Jim behind the bus stop.

"*We'll drive around the mall and see if we can hook up with Marcos and Melody,*" *said Jim.* "*You two check out the parking lot in front of Toys-R-Us. Meet us back here in half an hour.*"

As we pulled back into the street, I heard a siren and spotted a police car driving up 35th South, headed east. I shivered. I had a very bad feeling.

"*Follow that police car,*" *I told Steffanie.*

We followed it under the I-215 overpass. We lost it. But then Steffanie pointed to the left. The police car was parked in front of the Chili's restaurant about half a block away. I had the same horrifying vision that I'd had as Garth and I drove up to the mini-market. The first part of my vision had come to pass—flashing lights. There were two police cars. I held my breath to anticipate the carnage I was about to behold.

Turning into Chili's parking lot, we spotted several policemen speaking with four teenage boys in Lancer's football jerseys from Granger High. A crowd of people had gathered in the doorway of the restaurant, looking on. The boys were pretty banged up. One had a torn shirt and held his ribs. Another pressed a cold pack to his head. Another had a broken nose, and was lying back on the hood of his sportscar—a blue Corvette—to keep it elevated. The saddest sight was the poor Corvette. The windshield was smashed, along with one of the side windows. A headlight had been smashed as well.

"A gang fight?" asked Steffanie.

"I don't think so," I replied.

I didn't see Apollus. Was that a good sign? Maybe my instincts were wrong, and it was just a gang fight—nothing to do with Apollus at all. Such hopes were dashed as soon as I climbed out of the car.

A boy yelled at one of the policemen, "How should I know if it was a real sword?! It was real enough. Look what he did to my car!"

I approached, coming up right between them.

"Who did this?" I interrupted.

"Who are you?" asked the policeman.

"I'm looking for a friend. He was wearing a costume."

"That's him! Roman freak! He was headed that way, toward the Hale Theater."

"Is your friend performing at the Hale Theater?" the policeman asked me.

"Maybe," I said. "Why did he do this?"

"He just went nuts," said another boy.

"We were only teasing him," said the first boy. "We weren't really gonna run him over. Man! Can't a guy take a joke?"

The scenario became clear. These tough high school jocks had seen Apollus wandering down the street and decided to have a little fun at his expense. Likely they'd slammed on their brakes in front of him, honked their horn. Apollus wouldn't have known that it wasn't a real threat. He'd reacted in the only way he knew how, first taking a few swings at the car.

Now the boys' anger would have been real. They'd climbed out to take him on. I thanked God that all of them were still alive.

"He tried to kill us!" cried the kid lying back on the hood, his nose bleeding. "We were just defending the car."

"If he'd tried to kill you, you'd all be dead," I said.

"Can you give us the man's name?" asked the policeman.

I became thoughtful. "You know, I don't think it's the same guy. The guy we're looking for was dressed like a vampire."

I hopped back in the car. Steff shifted into gear as the policeman called after me. I shut the door. "Drive that way!" I ordered.

We left the scene of chaos and drove west toward the Hale Theater and the E-Center. The marquee in front of the theater read, "Forever Plaid." Fat chance of finding a Roman in that *play! I peeled my eyes, trying desperately to see a man with a Roman helmet among all the buildings and cars and shadows.*

"Slow down," I told Steffanie.

We passed the hockey arena and the movieplex. No sign. But then something caught my eye. Just past the E-Center stretched a row of tall power lines. The poles extended across I-215. At the base of a distant pole I saw a lone figure. It was lucky I saw him at all; he was a hundred yards away, and the only light was the moon. Yet I was sure I perceived a Roman helmet.

"That's him," I said. "Stop the car."

"You think so?"

"Yes. It's him."

She pulled onto a dirt turn-out just off the left shoulder. The figure didn't move. He was just sitting there, his knees pulled into his chest, head drooping. Steffanie started to get out of the car.

"No, you wait here," I said. "Let me talk to him alone."

"Are you sure?" asked Steffanie.

"He knows me. I think he trusts me. If we both go, he might bolt. Just give us a few minutes. In fact, it might be better if you drove around so the police don't see us parked here."

Steff considered this with some reluctance. After all, she had three years on me. I was afraid she was about to pull seniority. "Okay," she finally agreed. "I'll go around the block a couple of times."

She closed her door and grabbed the wheel. After she pulled away, I approached the figure at the base of the power pole. I'd covered about half the distance when the figure saw me. He looked startled. I was sure now it was Apollus.

"It's me," I said. "It's Meagan."

"Meagan," he repeated, as if it took a second for it to register.

He settled back down in his place and stared off at the traffic on I-215. His sword was still clenched in his right hand. I said nothing more until I was right beside him. I crouched down to see his face. "Are you all right?" I asked.

He hardly stirred as he replied, "Yes. I'm fine."

His tone said he was anything but.

"Why did you get out of the car at the mall? What were you looking for?"

He sighed deeply. "I don't know. I guess I . . . Nothing makes sense anymore. Before I came here, it all . . . it all made sense. I knew my place. My place in the scheme of things. But now . . ."

I reached out and touched his arm. He didn't react. "I'm sorry, Apollus. This is my fault. But you were so insistent. I just thought . . . I guess I wanted you to understand where I came from. Garth and I thought you deserved to know."

He stiffened with resentment. "Deserved? You thought I deserved to see all this? You thought I deserved to have my heritage and pride destroyed? To know that Rome is no more than a nation of peasants and bumpkins?"

"I never meant to hurt you," I said. "And you're wrong. Rome is . . . was . . . a great empire. Why, in your day there was none greater. But . . . this is not your day, Apollus."

"I don't understand!" he raved. "That makes no sense!"

"Don't you see?" I explained. "The cave. The Galaxy Room. We traveled in time, Apollus. This is the future. Like I said in Cody, welcome to the twenty-first century."

"Twenty-first century since what? Since the founding of Rome?"

"We don't reckon our years according to that date," I said. "We measure it based on the birth of our Savior, Jesus Christ."

"Jesus the Jew?"

"Jesus the Savior of the world," I clarified. "I tried to explain all this to you a few weeks ago."

"And this God, Jesus, made it possible for us to see the future?"

"I don't really understand how that all works," I said. "But Jesus made the world. He made it by the command of our Father in Heaven. It's through the Father that all miracles are possible."

"*Why are Romans kept ignorant of these things? Are the gods of the Romans so inferior to this Jesus?*"

Hesitantly I replied, "*The Romans don't have any real gods, Apollus. They're just statues. Just symbols and myths.*"

"*But we are ROME!*" he thundered. He leaped to his feet and began pacing about in a fury. "*We rule all the lands of the Middle Sea! The Jews are a weak, groveling, backwater people. Why should the Jews know the true gods, while Rome is kept in the dark?*"

I considered my answer carefully. "*Sometimes strength isn't measured by armies and navies, Apollus. The Jews are God's chosen people. They kept His name alive for thousands of years. But it doesn't mean that God loves them any more than He loves the Romans. He loves all the people of the earth, in all ages and times.*"

"*But you said the Jews crucified Him. They crucified their own God!*"

My heart became heavy. "*Yes, they did. But the Romans were there too, remember? They carried out the execution.*"

"*We didn't know,*" he declared, as if defending all of Rome. "*How could we have known?*"

"*Maybe you couldn't have,*" I said. "*But Pontius Pilate knew Jesus was innocent. It's over now, Apollus. The Atonement is done. God forgives anyone who repents and comes to Him. Even in your day, God sent missionaries to the Romans. Don't you see? He loves everyone. He loves you too, Apollus.*"

"*I do not know any God,*" said Apollus. "*I've never known any power but this.*" He held out his sword. "*I never believed any other power was necessary.*"

I paused a moment as he struggled to comprehend. Then I asked, "*How do you feel now?*"

Apollus looked at his sword in the moonlight. He looked at it in a way I'm sure he'd never looked at it before. Then he leaned back against the pole and closed his eyes. "*What happens, Meagan? What happens to my country? What becomes of Rome?*"

"*It falls,*" I said quietly. "*One day, all of Rome is completely destroyed. All but a few crumbling buildings, a few old books. It's part of history. But what a great chapter! If it hadn't been for Rome, for the peace and stability it brought to the Mediterranean, the Savior might never have fulfilled His mission. Jesus lived and preached as long as He did because of the laws of Rome. It all works together. God has a plan for everything. The beginning to the end.*"

Apollus appeared to be pondering this. Suddenly his emotions were released. He sank down into the position I'd first found him and started to sob. It was a sight I wouldn't have imagined—to see such a strong, iron-willed man reduced to tears. In Apollus I envisioned that I was watching all of Rome weeping, realizing the fleetingness of its many causes and dreams. I put my arms around him. I was crying a little, too.

"I don't understand this plan of God's," he wept. "I don't understand any of it."

"I'll teach it to you," I whispered. "As much as I can. Anything you want to know."

For several minutes his emotions drained. I stayed with him. After a while, I found I was no longer sorry that Apollus had come through the cave. I was grateful. So grateful that I said a prayer of gratitude. I couldn't have planned it any better if I had tried. I realized this had been my secret prayer all along. What he'd lost was being replaced by something far more substantial. A new perspective and hope—the seed of salvation.

Steffanie returned. We snuck Apollus into the car and drove away. No policemen stopped us, though we did see a patrol car parked at the Hale Theater, undoubtedly checking the costume room.

It was already late, and there was still so much to plan and prepare. Before I knew it, all of the lights and smells and sounds of the modern world would be a memory again. My taste of home had seemed so fleeting. To my bewilderment, a part of me felt like Apollus. I'd come to see myself as a stranger here, as if the ancient world was where I truly belonged. The feeling seemed appropriate enough, because who knew how long it would be before I saw my home century again? We had no idea what to expect tomorrow, but all of us seemed adamant about one thing. We were not coming back alone. Without Harry, it seemed possible that some of us might never be coming back at all.

CHAPTER 13

The current was with us—the current and the hand of God. It nudged us along from behind, or perhaps it was drawing us in like a suction. The twenty of us were so exhausted by the end that we might have rolled off that broken mast and sunk to the bottom. I'd kicked and paddled so long that my arms and legs had no feeling. My tongue was so swollen from thirst that I couldn't swallow. And yet none of us gave up. We all pitched in with equal energy and determination.

I don't know how many miles it was. I know it was farther than I'd first judged. But at last the outline of that island became as bold as a mountain. Its edges cut a line across the horizon that seemed to loom larger and larger. In fact, from a distance it seemed to resemble a cut-out profile of Abraham Lincoln: hairline, nose, beard—it was all there. As we got closer, there was even a white smile cut into the red cliffs in just the right place. Ol' Abe was happy to see us. I can't tell you how happy we were to see him.

Our first close-up view of this rolling mass of volcanic stone didn't appear all that promising. There wasn't a tree or a shrub anywhere in sight. Just a dead lump. It looked no better than the lump we'd just left behind, except that it would give us more room to stretch our legs. From the sea, it appeared to be about a mile wide. As we drew even closer, Micah spotted what appeared to be some bushes along one of the crags. Yet this was still no proof that we'd find anything edible. Or, of more immediate concern, that we'd find anything fresh to drink.

Nicanor spotted a cove almost dead ahead, sandwiched by cliffs that were nearly sheer. The narrow inlet went in about thirty yards, ending at a beach of the purest white sand I'd ever seen. Oh, I looked forward to lying in the softness of that sand! Especially after scraping our feet for so long on those jagged outcroppings! But in an instant, basking on the beach became far less of a priority. The ocean had carved several natural caves into the walls surrounding the cove—there was even an arch that reminded me of the rock formations near Moab in Southern Utah. And inside this arch—drizzling, flowing, cascading from the ceiling—were a dozen arteries of living water.

One by one the men abandoned the floating mast, as it was now shallow enough to stand, and scrambled through the surf until they could drench themselves beneath the saltless flow. There was plenty of space, so I claimed my own cascade. I stuck my head underneath and opened my mouth wide. The water was *warm!* It tasted incredible. I suppose in retrospect I shouldn't have found it so appetizing. The source was a sulfur spring above us. But it was drinkable, and it proved an instant cure for my swollen tongue.

As I stood inside that warm cascade, I could hear the echoes of laughter and splashing all around me. Such a beautiful blue cove with crimson red cliffs and pillowy white sands. We were convinced that we'd just discovered our own Greek island paradise. I immediately dubbed it Lincoln Island. Micah threw his arms around me in delight. In turn, I embraced Nicanor. Without his wits and strength, we wouldn't have made it. And yet to the rest of the men, *I* was the hero of the day. They credited me with saving their lives—and even granting them their freedom. In return, I credited God.

Lincoln Island *was* just a rock for the most part. There wasn't a tree to be found. But there were plenty of scrubby bushes and grasses. All in all, I figured there were only about two and a half square miles to the whole thing. But there were wild grapes, turnips, onions, and another red-looking berry that was a particular favorite of the birds. I ended up being the guinea pig and ate one to make sure it wasn't poisonous. Actually, it hardly had any flavor at all—certainly nothing you'd box up for the supermarket. But I didn't get sick. It was edible. There was also a bush with a stubby trunk that bled a pale white sap which Micah reported to be quite sweet. It was awfully sticky stuff—so much so that if you ate too much it was hard to pull your teeth apart. But it, like the rest, provided the essential nutrients of life.

The island was a labyrinth of coves and shallow caves. The place had so many hot springs and bubbling pools that it could have been made into a resort. There was even evidence that at some ancient time the island had supported inhabitants. On the second day, one of the men found the remains of a stone fence and followed it to a hillside of boulders and broken rocks. Several of us dug around the rocks for a few hours until we unearthed a shaft that led inside a chamber that had once been the interior of a building. There were pottery bowls and intricately carved stairways and colorful murals of birds, men with curled hair, and women in long, elaborate dresses. It was breathtaking. I was Indiana Jones! We'd discovered a lost civilization! By the looks of it, there had once been an incredible disaster on this island that had buried an entire city. Perhaps a volcano or an earthquake. The evidence of hewn stone and broken walls descended all the way to the seashore and disappeared. The bulk of the city seemed to be lying out there beneath the waves. Perhaps we'd discovered the remains of Atlantis herself.

Except for the ruins, there was no other evidence that anyone else had ever visited the place. Or if they had, they hadn't liked it enough to stay. I remembered some of those movies I'd seen as a kid—*Jason and the Argonauts, The Odyssey,* and *Clash of the Titans.* This was it! I was on an actual, authentic Greek island. I half expected the Cyclops to appear, or the Medusa to poke its heads out of one of the caves. We were true castaways. Personally, I felt like a *double* castaway. Lost in time, and lost at sea.

Nicanor set out immediately to make cages and nets to harvest the fish that gathered by the score in the coves and inlets. Other men built snares to catch seabirds. No one seemed to feel any immediate desperation to find a way to the mainland, whichever direction it might have been. After all, we were condemned men—condemned to a life of slavery in the rock quarries of Corinth. What many of the men seemed to dread most was that fateful day when some ship with red Roman sails set anchor in one of our coves. Then our paradise would come to an end.

As for me, I spent the majority of my time those first few days contemplating the mysteries of God, and wondering what He could possibly have planned for my final fate. On the fourth day, Micah the Essene approached me and said, "I want to learn more about Jesus of Nazareth, Harrison."

"I thought you told me you knew everything about Him that you wanted to know," I replied.

Humbly, he clarified, "I want to learn more about *your* perspectives. I want to know why you believe so strongly that He was the Son of God."

So began a series of long, marvelous days and endless discussions. It wasn't long before our conversations had more than one participant, and within a week I felt like a preacher with a congregation of nineteen men. Somehow I became the resident authority on matters of the Spirit. *Me!*—a fifteen-year-old boy armed with nothing but a testimony and an abiding love of Jesus Christ.

The evenings were the worst—those hours when I was forced to stare out at the sunset as it spread its wings across the red, glassy sea. I wept many of those nights, though I tried stubbornly not to. I missed them all so terribly—my father, my sisters, my friends. How their hearts must have been aching! I knew it because mine felt like it was being crushed in a vise. Were they thinking of me? Did they still worry and hope? You can't mourn the loss of a loved one forever; at some point you have to pick up the pieces and move on. When would they move on? Sooner than later, I hoped. Sooner than later.

I had to consider that it might be God's plan for me to remain here in this world, perhaps to the end of my days. Even if I did get off this island, I had no idea where to find the secret cavern entrance whose location was known only to Garth and Gidgiddonihah. As I contemplated the hope that I might someday see my father and sisters again, only one vision seemed to burn brightly in my mind. It was a vision of a land with seven cities—a land that by all reports hadn't forgotten the purity of the gospel. There were prophets there. Prophets and possibilities. As well as a young Jewish girl with a face like a princess. Sometimes when the sun was highest, I would stand on the pinnacle at the north end of the island and swear that I could see this place—or at least the glow of it—shining up through the haze of the clouds. This was my next destination. There was no doubt in my mind. I was going to the Seven Churches of Asia Minor.

Now all I needed was a ship, and a trail paved by God.

PART TWO

CHAPTER 14

I lived the moment again through the eyes of my mother. The five of us stood gaping at the magnificence of the Rainbow Room. It was still there, untarnished and undimmed. This was in contrast to the chaos that I felt sure still raged in the far more mysterious, more electric, and more fragile Galaxy Room. There was a purity and innocence about the Rainbow Room that the other room just didn't possess. I knew Harry thought that one powered the other. I didn't think it was quite so simple. But I'd leave those mysteries for another day.

The previous night had been spent in the room where Harry and I had camped before our escapade in 70 A.D. began. It was also the room where Jim and Steffanie had camped four years before. She and her father shared many memories of their adventures among the Nephites: rescuing Melody from King Jacob of the Moon, and spending nearly a year in the city of Bountiful. They spoke of the appearance of the Savior, which of course left us all mesmerized. Especially Apollus. They both cried a little, too, as they recalled how Harry had been healed by the hand of Jesus. I realized how much Jim's only son and Steffanie's only brother meant to them. It made me grateful for my mother. Family—it's the only eternal thing we take with us to the next life after all.

Our plan was to spend at least one more night in the caverns. Today we wanted to reach the chamber just outside the Galaxy Room where Gidgiddonihah had planned to meet us in four days. I felt we were a little early—that is, if Gid's measurement of four days was equal to ours. Apollus was still wearing his stiff leather cuirass, red tunic, bucklers, greaves, and helmet. We never did manage to get him a nice twenty-first-century outfit. A crying shame. No man might have looked better in jeans than Apollus Brutus Severillus.

Mom did her best to clean his tunic and undergarments before we left. Frankly, we all looked much more fit and prepared than during our last expedition. I now had a clean pair of denims, a beige long-sleeved cotton shirt, warm windbreaker, and a head of hair restored to its natural reddish-brown color. I kept my ancient blue tunic and belt stuffed into my new backpack. One never knew when they might be asked to look the part of a first-century Roman maiden.

Apollus was much more talkative than he'd been at any other time since I'd known him. I rather missed my strong, silent Roman, but he'd become hungry for knowledge. For much of our downward journey, he'd hardly paused long enough to draw a breath before asking his next question pertaining to the gospel and the Plan of Salvation. As we left the Rainbow Room and started toward the Galaxy Room, he wanted to know about preaching in the spirit world.

"So after we die," he said thoughtfully, trying to keep it straight, "if we didn't learn of Jesus while we were alive, we may learn of Him after we're dead?"

I knew he was asking for the sake of his mother, sister, and two brothers, who had all been killed—his mother and sister in a carriage accident, and his brothers in the war with Judea.

"Yes," I said, "along with everything else we might not have learned."

"Then why must we learn these things here?*" he asked. "What does it matter?"*

"Well . . . it matters a lot," I replied. "We're supposed to learn it here, if at all possible."

"But why?"

Steffanie stepped in. "This life is the time to prepare to meet God, Apollus. Knowledge gives us the opportunity to choose. The right choices can bring us great blessings. The more we understand about God and His plan, the better prepared we'll be for the life to come."

"You say this spirit world is not yet heaven?"

I opened my mouth to answer, but Steff beat me to it. "No, not yet. We won't go to a kingdom of glory until after the final judgment, which takes place at the end of the world. In the spirit world we'll still be learning. Or teaching. Many of the people who have the truth will be teaching those who don't."

"So why have this life at all? Why not learn it all in this spirit world?"

"It doesn't work that way," said Steff. "In the spirit world there's no opposition. Believe it or not, opposition is our greatest teacher."

"Opposition?"

"Yes," Steff continued. "The struggle between good and evil. The contrasts of joy and sorrow, bitter and sweet. Here on earth, we're right in the middle of it! We're taught that in the spirit world it's many times harder to learn—many times harder to break bad habits and change. God doesn't let us experience pain and sorrow to punish us. My dad always taught me that He does it because He loves us. It teaches us to be more like Him."

Apollus nodded. He seemed to understand. Inside, I was grumbling. It was childish, I knew, but I was sure I could have answered him as well as she could. I just wasn't quite as fluent in all of it. Steffanie had butted in. Now she and Apollus were walking side by side. She touched his shoulder to warn him of a hanging stalactite.

My brain felt hot. What was wrong with me? Was I jealous? No, no, sweetie. Meagan Sorensen did not *get jealous. It was just all that blonde hair of hers. She was also closer to his same age. More athletic . . .* What was I talking about!? Who cared? *Take a deep breath, girl, I told myself. You're overreacting.*

We reached the fork in the tunnel with the diamond-shaped crevasse. It was the same place where Harry and I had first heard the low moaning of Gidgiddonihah after he'd been struck on the head by the men of Kumarcaah.

"We climb this way," I said to Jim.

He peered up the shaft. "I never noticed this before."

"Just up there is the Galaxy Room," I said. "It's right beyond the chamber where we agreed to meet Gidgiddonihah."

"Galaxy Room," Jim repeated, marveling. He couldn't seem to envision it.

Apollus jumped into the shaft ahead of us. He stood with his feet flat against the rock walls at the bottom of the diamond. "Give me your hand," he said to my mother.

"Thank you."

He pulled her up, and she climbed right past him. I admit, I was surprised at her agility. I knew she worked out at the gym several times a week, but I'd never thought of her as the hiker-rock climber type. When Apollus reached down to help Steffanie she stumbled, forcing him to grab her about the waist. It all seemed a bit too convenient. I had no doubt in my mind now: she was flirting with my Roman.

Jim helped me into position. Apollus reached down, but I ignored his hand. Who needed him? I hoisted myself up without any assistance. He raised an eyebrow, then shrugged. Female thing, *I'm sure he was thinking. I clenched my fist. I'd like to have given him a female thing right between the eyes.*

We reached the chamber at the top of the crevasse. We'd made it. This was the rendezvous point. To the left was the passage Gid had entered. Somewhere beyond here it must have connected up with the tunnel that led to the world of the Nephites. Gidgiddonihah wasn't here yet. I wondered how long we would wait. It might be days. Then I noticed something strange. In the center of the room sat the remains of a cold fire.

"Did you and Garth make this?" Mom asked.

I shook my head, baffled. "No. We didn't have any wood. This is new."

Jim leaned down. "It's not new. This was built weeks ago. Maybe months."

I shivered. What could this mean?

"Look at this," said Steffanie. She reached down and grabbed a small bundle of red cloth. It had been set out in plain sight with only a small stone to mark it. As Steffanie lifted it, several coins spilled out and clanged at her feet.

Apollus studied one of the coins under the flashlight. "Silver denarius. This is a Roman coin."

"Roman?" said Jim. "That doesn't make sense. Are you sure none of this was left behind?"

"Of course I'm sure." Then I gasped. "Lucullus and Graccus!"

"Who?" asked Steff.

"My men," said Apollus. "I left them in the ravine." He considered it, then shook his head. "No. It couldn't be them. The only way they'd have parted with a silver denarius would have been if someone had pried it from their dead hand." He gathered up the other coins. "This is quite a bit of money."

"Then where did it come from?" asked my mother.

I focused again on the red cloth in Steffanie's hand. Suddenly, I snatched it away.

"I know this!" I cried. "I gave it to Gidgiddonihah just before we parted. Remember, Apollus? We got it from that shopkeeper in Joppa. It was used to wrap bread."

"*I remember,*" *said Apollus.*

"*Then the fire* was *Gidgiddonihah's,*" *said Steff.*

"*If it was,*" *said Jim gravely,* "*then he hasn't been here for quite a while. Maybe as long as a year.*"

My heart sputtered. A year!? *But we'd stood here with Gid less than four days ago! The ramifications were incomprehensible. What about Harry? What did this mean for Harry?*

Jim found a stone and sat down shakily. "*The dream,*" *he mumbled.*

"*What dream?*" *asked Steffanie.*

He looked severely distraught. Mom put her arm around him.

Finally, he said, "*On the day after Melody received her last treatment, I . . . I was sitting alone in a restaurant. I'd been up all night. While I was reading the menu . . . I dozed off.*"

"*You had a dream?*" *asked Mom.*

He nodded. But then he looked uncertain. "*I don't know.*"

"*What happened?*" *I asked.*

"*I saw my son. He came to visit me. He was at least fifteen years older than the last time I . . .*" *He couldn't continue.*

"*You mean it was a vision?*" *Steffanie persisted.* "*You had a vision of Harry?*"

Jim shut his eyes in frustration. He didn't seem to know how to interpret it. I almost wondered if Jim believed it was real. *My mind was swirling. I tried to piece together all the evidence. It didn't make sense. This was becoming more bizarre by the minute.*

Apollus pointed at the cloth in my hand. "*What's written on it?*"

I noticed the writing for the first time. Someone had sketched a drawing in black ink. Arrows and markers. And words.

"*It's not in English,*" *I said.*

Jim arose. "*Is it Nephite writing?*"

Apollus leaned over. "*It's Latin.*"

"*Latin?*" *I was stymied.* "*Gid didn't know Latin.*"

Apollus took the cloth. Steffanie shined her flashlight as Apollus read:

Waited three days. Found a passage. Not stable. Returned to leave map. Moving on to Neopolis. Message written by Sergius Graccus, Tenth Legion,

Masada. Map drawn by me.

Gidgiddonihah

We paused to let the words sink in.

"He made it through," said Steffanie.

"Who is Sergius Graccus?" asked my mother.

"One of my men," said Apollus. "The same soldier I left with Tiberius Lucullus. At least . . . I think so."

"You're not sure?" I asked.

Apollus read the message again. He looked confused. "Graccus is in the Fifth Legion, not the Tenth. The Tenth is at Jerusalem, not Masada. But Graccus shouldn't be at either place. He is stationed with my father at Neopolis."

Apollus' face flashed with anger, as if one of his men had deserted his post. But then his expression was replaced with utter bewilderment.

I drew several conclusions, none of them heartening. As Jim suggested, Gid had come and gone from here long ago. As we'd feared, the instability of the Galaxy Room had thwarted our plan to meet again in four days. Gid had waited for us as long as he could. He found an exit, then returned later to leave this note. He'd chosen not to write in the language of the Nephites. No one would have understood anyway. He'd persuaded a Roman to write the message, knowing that Garth or Apollus would have read Latin. It was fortunate that Gid had found a familiar face in Graccus, whom he would have remembered from Neopolis. Apparently Gid had then set out on his own to find Harry. But how long ago did all this take place? Was it really a year? Could it have been longer?

Jim became agitated and impatient. "What does the map say?"

I studied Gid's drawing. Plainly, his arrows were directing us into the Galaxy Room. He'd drawn several curving strokes to represent the turbulence. But he didn't want us to enter the tunnel at the Galaxy Room's opposite end—the one that had collapsed in the earthquake. His course veered into a hole on the far right. This was curious. Every hole I'd seen in the floor of the Galaxy Room had rushed with water. Certainly he didn't expect us to ride the rapids of another underground river. Nothing in the map indicated moving water. Instead, he'd drawn several formations, as if to indicate checkpoints.

"This way," I replied to Jim.

We picked up our packs and continued. After bypassing a forest of stalactites, we entered the circular passage just outside the Galaxy Room. But immediately I realized that something was different. There was no reflection on the wall just prior to the final turn—no indication of the swirling colors beyond. Nor did I feel any unusual sensations of exhilaration or fatigue. I felt nothing. Just the chilled cave air. An eerie feeling settled over me. Something was terribly wrong. We rounded the corner and entered. I stopped. Cold sweat broke out all over my body.

The Galaxy Room was dead.

Gone were the swirling bands of energy. Gone was the deafening sound that had echoed, not in my ears, but in every cell of my body. Gone were the distorted perceptions of distance and space. Even the floor that had once looked so glassy and transparent was now hard and black, pockmarked with dozens of holes like an exploded minefield. It was just a plain dark room, perhaps a hundred yards across and fifty yards high, accented by the faraway sounds of water rushing beneath our feet. Its only distinguishing feature was the rounded nucleus in the ceiling, the power source that had once commanded such a glorious light show. It now emitted a faint purple glow, as dull as any plastic glow-in-the-dark toy.

A tear dropped on my cheek. How could such a wonder—such a miracle—have been destroyed? The others stood on either side of me, torn between watching the dull, purple orb or studying the distress in my face. Apollus seemed to have no opinion. I'm not sure he even knew we were in the same room. I felt my fear increasing. Before six weeks ago, it had never occurred to me how fragile time was. Or how precarious the state of time-travelers. Might the death of this room mean that the passage to the ancient world had been closed off? Was Gid the last person to successfully cross the barrier?

The others moved into the center of the room. Jim stared up at the glowing orb in awe. If only he'd known what he might have seen—what he had missed. But as I joined them, I realized their interest was not totally unjustified. The purple nucleus, though it was no longer the center of a colorful storm, was not entirely dead. Something was still alive inside of it. Like a fetus still kicking around inside a glowing womb. I had the impression that as long as that orb emitted any kind of light at all, our hopes of crossing the barrier to ancient Judea still existed. But there was an *urgency—I felt that impression most strongly of all. If that light died completely, so would our chances of ever returning home.*

The same urgency must have gripped Jim, because he said abruptly, "What now? Where does the map say to go now?"

I glanced again at the red cloth. I began to walk toward the right wall. The floor was like a jigsaw puzzle. Half the pieces had fallen through and been washed away. I weaved through very carefully, expecting the shelf under my feet to give way at any second. Each hole was gushing with an ice-cold stream. How was I supposed to know which hole Gid had meant? He'd made no distinguishing marks. And yet I was sure that if Gid had meant for us to climb down into one of them, it would not be into a raging river. It would be easily accessible—and dry.

I found exactly what I had expected in the very last hole, closest to the wall. Even the shelf that had fallen in was still leaning against the side, creating a convenient stairway. We climbed down. I let Jim take the map. He led us past the next two formations Gid had indicated—a pair of stalactites that came down on either side of the tunnel like a gate, and a pool of still, clear water that was curiously marked with the Roman numeral "II." Another tunnel veering left had been marked "I." Gid had drawn what appeared to be a stone bridge. We followed his arrows another twenty yards, finally arriving at the precipice he had depicted. There was only one problem. The stone bridge was gone.

We stood at the edge and stared down into the blackness. Our flashlights didn't reveal a bottom. I suspected it was several thousand feet deep. The echo of our voices took several seconds to reverberate. There was a warm wind coming up from below, as if heated by the earth's core.

Apollus shined his flashlight at the opposite wall. The cliff was uneven and gnarled. There appeared to be several possible tunnels. But the gap was at least fifteen feet wide, and there was absolutely no way across. We needed a gun that shot a spiked projectile, like Batman. Unfortunately, such a tool was not in our arsenal. I couldn't even tell where the stone bridge had once crossed the chasm.

"There must have been another quake," I concluded. "The bridge fell away."

Jim sighed drearily. "Gid said it was unstable."

"What can we do?" asked Steffanie.

We seemed so close. Gid had only drawn one more arrow beyond this spot. The exit was likely within a hundred feet!

"We need more equipment," said my mother. "Something that would work as a ladder."

I shook my head. "We'd never get a ladder down here."

"What we need to find is another way through," said Apollus.

Jim continued to study the map. "Gidgiddonihah may have already shown us one." He pointed at Gid's drawing. "Does this arrow look like it's pointing straight?"

He indicated a mark beside the pool of still water that we'd passed twenty yards back. It wasn't quite clear if it pointed directly at the pool or if it was just one in the series of arrows directing us toward the stone bridge. And yet Gid had drawn a Roman numeral "I" beside the bridge and a "II" beside the pool.

"I think Gid was offering us a choice," said Jim.

We promptly returned to the pool and shined our flashlights into the transparent water. It was about six feet deep, but on the far right edge, tucked behind a lip of jagged white crystal, was a channel that appeared to shoot upward. It didn't seem logical. It seemed to defy gravity. But it was true.

I swallowed. Visions of a former swim inside the watery tunnels of a catacomb in Samaria darkened my thoughts—a horrible déja vu.

"Do you really think he meant for us to swim behind that rock?" asked my mother.

"How can we?" asked Steffanie. "We'd never be able to take our packs. Most of our stuff would be ruined!"

She was right. It had been my idea to bring butane lighters and pen-lights to bargain with the Romans. They'd be soaked for sure. The ball-point pens might be okay. So might the mini Butterfingers, Snickers, and Krackles that Apollus had recommended. Each piece of candy was sealed inside its original plastic envelope. Perhaps we could devise some way to protect the other things, too. But this problem was secondary. How would we ever get them through in the first place?

"We have to see how far it goes," said Jim. "See if Gid's map really does indicate that this is another route."

"Wait a minute," said my mother. "Turn off the flashlights."

We doused them one by one, then peered into the pool without the aid of any light at all. There was another faint source of light back there. Mom's hunch was right. A light was coming from behind the lip of white crystal.

"Could it be sunlight?" asked Steffanie.

Apollus removed his helmet and began unbuckling his sword. "I'll find out."

He shed everything except his tunic. I felt a surge of anxiety—the same anxiety I'd felt when little Jesse had swum off alone into the dark waters of the catacomb.

"Wait," I said, slipping off my backpack. "I'll go too."

"No, Meagan—" said Mom.

"It's all right," I insisted. "I've done this before. No one should try to do it alone. There should be at least two people."

"It's not necessary," said Apollus. "I'll be fine."

"Sure you will," I winked. My shoes were already off. I stripped off the last sock.

"Are you going to swim in your jeans?" asked Steffanie.

"What do you suggest? My skivvies?"

She looked as if she might suggest that very thing. I glanced at Apollus. Fat chance of that. "If I can't make it swimming in my clothes," I said, "how could we ever make it with our gear?"

"The worry is whether you'll make it at all," said Jim.

"I know what I'm doing," I declared and stepped into the water.

It was warm! Well, not exactly thermal. But far warmer than that water in the catacomb. Mom mumbled something to try and get Jim to discourage me, but I wasn't listening. I turned to Apollus. "You wanna go first or should I?"

Apollus smiled wryly. He seemed to approve of my spunk and determination. "Be my guest."

"Meagan, wait—" said Jim.

That was my cue. I pressed my palms together into a point and dove into the pool. I swam toward the lip of white crystal. Flashlight beams danced around me. I also saw the light that shone behind the rock. Apollus dove in after me. I passed beneath the jagged crystal teeth, then I planted my feet on the floor and pushed upward with all of my strength. My legs kicked furiously. The light seemed to draw closer. There was a surface! I could see it! I also perceived what appeared to be the roof of a cave with a small patch of sky.

Apollus swam beside me, his arms also thrust upward. We broke the surface at the same instant and gasped for breath. I swam to the edge and panted. Then I took in my surroundings. We were enclosed by solid rock, but it wasn't really a cave. It looked more like a pit. A good part of it appeared to have been carved out by men. There was an opening to the left accessed by a narrow pathway with stone stairs. Beyond it was a dim blue sky. It was still very early in the day—six or seven a.m. I guessed that Jim and the others would soon perceive the bright sunlight without having to turn off their flashlights.

Several grooves, like ditches, had been cut into the rock. They emptied into the pool. The ditches were dry now, but in the event of a rainstorm, I wagered they would have flowed abundantly.

"A cistern," said Apollus. "This is a pool for water storage."

Storage for who, I wondered? Were we still in the deserts near the Dead Sea? Apollus climbed out and sat on the edge. It was smooth, inlaid with neatly cut tiles. He reached down to help me. I took his hand, but then he stopped and sniffed the air. I smelled it, too. Smoke. Something was burning.

He finished pulling me out. We stood there dripping. Warily, Apollus surveyed the walls of our chamber. I started to wring out my hair like a rag. As water splattered on the smooth stones, I heard a noise.

We spun around, startled. But the noise was not threatening. It was a cry. A baby's cry. We squinted. There in the shadows at the back of the cistern, partially hidden by a fold of rock, stood several frightened women and children.

"It's all right," I said. "We mean no harm."

They pressed back even farther. Who could blame them for being startled? They'd just seen us appear out of the pool like creatures from the Black Lagoon.

"A Roman!" one of the women shrieked. "They found another way in!"

They'd recognized Apollus' tunic. He started to move closer, but then one of the children—a girl of about ten—screamed. Apollus waved his hands to try and silence her. The sound echoed. I stiffened in dread. These people had been hiding in here before Apollus and I had ever appeared. What were they hiding from?

A woman tucked the child's head inside her robe to quiet her. They were all white with terror. I counted seven—two women and five children, all girls except for two boys, aged about two and four.

We faced the pathway to see if anyone would respond to the scream. No one appeared. Hesitantly, Apollus moved toward the stairway. He cut me a glance to let me know he was about to climb it.

"Hurry," I whispered.

He disappeared up the stairway. I turned back to the women and chil-dren. They continued to watch me, unmoving.

"We're not going to hurt you," I assured again. "Are you hiding from someone? The Romans?"

"Who are you?" one of the women asked. She wore a Jewish shawl and head covering. The others wore Jewish clothes, too. The second woman looked severely distraught. The oldest girl comforted her. I had a feeling she'd had a nervous breakdown. Something had frightened these poor peo-ple to the brink.

"My name is Meagan," I said. "Please don't be afraid. Can you tell me where I am?"

They looked at each other.

"Is this Israel?" I asked. "Are we near the Dead Sea?"

My questions must have sounded monumentally stupid. Who wouldn't know where they were standing? I was too impatient to think of a more tactful way to ask.

A girl of about twelve or thirteen said, "You're on Masada."

My eyes widened. On Masada? How could I be—?

Suddenly I heard Apollus shout. "Meagan!"

I left the women and ascended the path, leaving a trail of water. The pathway cut between two stone walls. As I emerged, I found myself beside an overlook that gazed out across a desert landscape. Apollus was there waiting for me, gazing down. The smell of smoke was thick, yet everything was quiet.

It was true. We were standing at the summit of the fortress of Masada. Behind us stretched several rows of buildings as well as piles of hay and three small catapults for launching stones. The catapults were unmanned. There wasn't a soul in sight. Below us loomed a desert plain, looking east. The sun was about half an hour high. The misty blue expanse of the Dead Sea stretched toward the north. On the desiccated plain we could see sev-eral square encampments and a long wall that seemed to surround the entire fortress—a distance of several miles! The camps were Roman. The wall was a siege wall. Holy cow! We were trapped on Masada! Trapped with the last of the Jewish defenders!

We heard voices to the west. I followed Apollus as he crept around a long building that looked like a storage house. The smoke puffed up from somewhere along the western boundary of the plateau, then was carried off toward the north. We continued around the building and began moving west. There were several doorways and much evidence of grain and baskets and waterpots. I smelled something else. It was a sweetish smell, yet it turned my stomach. Inside the first doorway, I heard the faint buzz of flies. I glanced inside. Suddenly I gasped and covered my mouth with my hand.

I staggered back in horror. The building was full of bodies! *Dozens of them! All of them neatly laid out in flawless rows. Men, women, and children. Their throats were cut. The sweetish smell was freshly spilled* blood! *The floor was oozing with it!*

*A cry escaped my throat. My mind reeled with shock. In a flash I knew exactly where we were—*when *we were. This was the morning of mornings. The siege was* over! *All around us in the inner shadows of the buildings lay the remains of nine hundred and sixty Jewish Zealots. Victims of suicide. They'd taken their own lives rather than become victory prizes to the Romans. The clarity of it all crashed down on me like a tidal wave.*

As I glanced to the right, the view opened up. There, along the western edge, rose the fortification wall. Propped up along the inside of this wall was another wall constructed of wooden beams. The beams were smoldering. Of course *they were smoldering! The Romans had only set them on fire the day before! Plunging through a breach in the middle of this wall was a massive ram's head made of iron. It was attached to the end of a long, steel-plated pole. It must have broken through only minutes ago. The voices we'd heard belonged to the Roman soldiers on the other side. They were about to enter the fortress! In fact, I could see several of them behind the breach, beating out the flames. Within minutes they'd enter the compound and witness this gut-wrenching scene for themselves.*

I turned and stumbled back toward the foot path leading down to the cistern.

"Meagan, wait!" cried Apollus.

But I didn't wait. The horror was too much; I couldn't think. I wanted to get away. I had to warn the others. We had to find another route into the ancient world. We'd stumbled upon one of the grisliest tragedies of all human history. I'd heard about it. Read about it. Seen it portrayed in film. But to really see it. To smell it. I had to get away!

I ran down the narrow stone aisle. Apollus followed.

"Meagan, what are you going to do?"

"I'm going back."

"Back?"

"To the others. To Jim and my mom."

"They won't hurt us, Meagan. Remember, I'm a Roman soldier."

I faced him with a look of absolute incredulity. "Don't you get it? It's been three years!"

"What?"

"It's 73 A.D.! We've been gone for three years!*"*

He stood there dumbly, blinking. I continued toward the cistern. The women and children were in the pathway. They shrieked and parted as I pushed past them. I knew who they were now. Josephus had said that two women and five children had been the sole survivors of the slaughter. They were the only ones left to report what had happened. What would they report about us? *What could* they *report?*

I reached the cistern. I was hyperventilating. I hardly drew any breath as I dove into that pool and swam down into the blackness. I swam and swam. There was no light to guide me. If Jim, Steffanie, and my mother were still shining their flashlights, the beams were too dim. I swam blind. The bottom never seemed to arrive. After a minute, dizziness enveloped me. My consciousness was slipping. Whether I fainted from shock or lack of breath, I don't know. I remember trying to swallow. Then my thoughts became as black as the surrounding sea.

CHAPTER 15

I was awakened from a dream.

"Harrison," said Micah, shaking my shoulder. "Harrison, there's a ship in the bay."

"What?" I said, instantly alert.

"A ship! Come on!"

Coincidentally, my dream was about a ship. The ship in my dream had a huge curved bow in the shape of a lion's head. There was also a great white sail stretching so high that it disappeared into the sky. It was carrying me home through the clouds. Was the ship in the bay the fulfillment of my dream?

Micah and I scurried up the rocky trail to reach the summit of the promontory on the left side of the western bay. Most of the others were already there, their bodies laid out as flat as possible. Nicanor was on the ground at my right. Beside him lay Onias, Baruch, Haman, and the others. It was the largest bay on the island, enclosed by two lofty cliff walls. The water was deep. It was here that the ancient ruins tumbled toward the ocean and disappeared beneath the surface. On many long afternoons I'd sat on this very promontory, imagining that if a ship ever did visit our island, it would be into this bay that it would sail and drop anchor. Now my imagination had proven right.

There had been many times since we had been shipwrecked on this island that we had seen ships, or sometimes an armada of ships, in the hazy distance. But if the vessel was ever close enough to distinguish, it was always flying the eagle flag of the Roman fleet. Despite the fear, the restlessness, the monotony, none of us was eager to make our presence known to the Romans. We had no desire to continue our journey to the rock quarries of Corinth. We were all convinced that life here was infinitely preferable to certain death in a Roman slave camp. I'd searched in vain for a ship of another nation, another people. But how was it possible, when the entire ocean was the property of Rome?

I scooted up close to peer over the edge. Then I caught my breath and reveled in the sight. There it was—straight out of my dream. A ship. A beautiful fishing galley about thirty feet long. It did not have a bow in the shape of a roaring lion, but it did have a large white sail, presently being tied to the yardarm by one of its crew. It was floating about fifty yards out from the beach. Never had we seen a ship this close to the island. It was like seeing something from another world, an entirely different phase of reality. Actually, that wasn't so far off. It was from a world that had been entirely separate from ours for nearly three years.

I strained my eyes and felt sure I could see two—no, *three* men on deck. My right eye still couldn't focus very well, the result of a blow I'd received in the marketplace at Caesarea. All outward signs of the wound on my face had long since disappeared, but the inward weakness had remained, becoming most apparent when I tried to focus on something a long distance away.

The crewman finished tying off the sail. The other two were preparing to lower a small dinghy. They appeared determined to come ashore.

"How long has it been here?" I asked.

"Just a few moments," Nicanor answered. "I was casting my net early this morning when I saw them approaching in the distance."

"Did they see you?"

"I don't think so. I left the beach as soon as I sighted it."

"Where is it from?" asked Onias, a gentle man of about thirty years.

"The design is Greek," said Nicanor. "But . . ."

"But what?"

"Well, if they're fishermen, why aren't they casting their nets?"

I looked again. The nets were still sitting in tangled piles on deck.

"They've come all this way, and they don't plan to fish?" asked Micah.

Nicanor scratched his beard. "I don't know."

I perceived that one of the men was hauling water jars and placing them in the bottom of the dinghy.

"Ah, that's it," Onias observed. "They're voyagers. They've come to our island looking for fresh water."

Frankly, their motives didn't concern me. I began to wonder why we felt the need to hide at all. What was the danger? Had we been here alone, cut off from civilization, wallowing in the security of our own company, for so long? Had the habit of hiding from potential enemies become so ingrained that we could no longer recognize potential friends?

Three years. We'd been here for nearly three years. Unimaginable. At first, being stranded on this island had seemed a wondrous miracle. It was an adventure straight out of the imagination of every boy since Huckleberry Finn: to be alone on an island paradise, to build out of the rough terrain a fantastic new civilization. Over time, however, I'd become convinced that this island was a far worse prison than any pit or abyss into which the Romans might have cast me.

Our first year on the island had been devoted primarily to survival. Nicanor had taught us how to reap the bounties of the sea, including shellfish and crabs, little lobsters and shrimp. Inside a hidden chamber of the ancient ruins, we'd also found an immense deposit of mineral salt. Nicanor showed us how to salt and dry our fish in the sun to preserve them for winter. Bird eggs were also a favorite staple of our diet. I'd become quite adept at climbing the cliff ledges overhanging the sea to gather them.

We'd made living quarters inside the various caves, and had even built channels and a little aqueduct to convey fresh water directly to our front door from the various springs. Our quarters were adorned with pottery, blue-blown glass, and other treasures we had unearthed from the ruins. The most common articles we found were little bronze, clay, and ivory idols of a woman wrapped in snakes. The ancient civilization that had once existed here had been *obsessed* with snakes. Serpents were painted on practically every vial, vase, and jar. I'd begun to think they worshiped them as gods. Perhaps there was a good reason for their obsession. We soon discovered that the island was infested with little chocolate-colored snakes whose fangs carried a lethal venom. That first year we tragically lost four men to snakebites. The second year, like Saint Patrick of old, we spent much of our time ridding the island of every last one. Three more of our number died

of fevers during the first winter, and another had drowned while trying to retrieve one of Nicanor's lobster traps. Each death was deeply
mourned. Our plight had made us brothers, both in the spirit of
cooperation and also in the Spirit of God.

Night after night I'd taught them the gospel of Jesus Christ,
including a retelling of that miraculous day in the land of Bountiful
when the Savior had come down out of the heavens. The Spirit had
been so strong, and had converted them down to the very last man.
Micah, in particular, had become more zealous in his testimony of
Jesus than he'd ever been in the way of the Essenes. I might have baptized them all, founded an entire congregation here in the middle of
the Aegean Sea. But since I didn't have the priesthood authority, they
had to content themselves to wait until the day when we might finally be rescued from our island prison.

So here we had remained for three long years. Here I had grown
from a boy of fifteen to a young man of eighteen. Like the others, my
clothing was tattered and torn, hardly worth calling rags. Like the others, I now wore a beard on my face, though mine was a bit more scrag-
gly and thin. Sometimes I would stare at my reflection in the surface
of the sea to try and see the changes that time had inflicted. I'd grown
at least two more inches—that I could tell. My muscles had toned and
my shoulders had squared. Did I look less like a boy and more like a
man? I really couldn't be sure. I needed others to confirm it—but
hopefully not before I'd had a proper shave and a haircut.

We had often discussed how we might liberate ourselves from our
island prison. The treeless island simply provided no raw materials for
building a boat. Our only option was to light a signal fire from the scrubby bushes that grew along the hills—an option more likely to attract
Romans or pirates than anyone else. So we'd waited, and we'd prayed.

We came to accept that our rescue was entirely in God's hands,
and on His timetable. Sometimes my heart would ache as I thought
about all the experiences I had missed—the revelries of a teenage boy
from the twenty-first century. It was beginning to look as if I would
never drive a car. Never ask a girl to a dance. Never sit in the stands at
a football game, cheering the home team.

Still, my faith remained strong. I'd seen too much during my first
eighteen years to ever let it waver. I knew that God did not act with-

out a reason. At the same time, I'd never believe that Heavenly Father had spared my life so many times, only to allow me to waste away the rest of my existence on this barren hunk of rock. For several weeks before the fishing galley appeared, I'd relished a sweet impression that something was about to happen. God's hand was about to reveal itself, extend His blessed mercy once again, and lead me down a new and wondrous pathway. I was certain that the miserable monotony of being an island castaway was about to come to an end.

Now, as I watched the ship in the bay, I could hardly contain my emotions. It could only be the ship from my dreams, the answer to all of our prayers. I started to rise to my feet, my whole frame shaking with determination.

Nicanor grabbed my arm. "Wait, Harrison. Don't be so hasty."

"Why?" I insisted. "What are we afraid of? There are no Roman flags."

"What if they're *loyal* to Rome?" asked Baruch.

"It's been almost *three years*," I declared. "The war with Judea is over. No one will remember the loss of a slave ship bound for Corinth. We broke our ankle rings; they won't even know that we *were* slaves."

"They'll know we're Jews," said Onias. "It will be obvious."

"But these men are Greeks. They're *fishermen*."

"They're also acting very strangely," said Nicanor.

I studied the ship again. "What do you mean?"

"They seem to suspect that this island is not uninhabited."

I squinted hard. He was right. The crewmen were acting uncommonly wary and cautious. They surveyed the hills and cliffs for long stretches, as if they were searching for signs of life.

"Do you think they might be fugitives?" asked Haman, a stout young man a little older than I.

"It's crossed my mind," said Nicanor. "That boat might have been stolen. If we reveal ourselves, it might cause them to raise their sail and flee."

Nervously, I settled back into place. I wasn't about to risk scaring them off.

"If they're criminals," whispered Onias, "they might be dangerous."

"We can't just sit here and watch," I stressed. "This might be our best chance, our *only* chance—"

"Don't worry," said Nicanor. "We all share your determination, Harrison. You're not the only one who has come to loathe this little island."

Carefully, the three crewmembers lowered themselves into the dinghy. They were ready to row ashore. Their ship was about to be left completely unattended.

"I'll take Micah," I whispered to Nicanor. "We'll climb down to the water and swim out to the ship. We'll take control of it."

"You think you can man those oars?" he asked.

I grinned shrewdly. "Believe me, I haven't forgotten how to row."

"To avoid a confrontation, you might want to bring it around to the east side of the island," said Nicanor. "We'll meet you there."

"What about the men?" asked Haman.

We pondered the problem. We couldn't just desert them. After living here for so long, leaving anyone else in this predicament was a fate we wouldn't have wished on our worst enemies.

"I'll take care of the men," said Nicanor finally. "There are only three. It should be an easy matter to take them and bind them."

We nodded to one another. The plan was set. Quietly, Nicanor and the others backed away from the edge, sneaking down toward the spring. Micah and I crept away in the opposite direction, down the steep embankment.

There was a long stretch of ground where I realized that Micah and I would be perfectly visible to the men in the dinghy. One ill-placed foot could jar loose a rock and blow our cover. We had only one option. I stuck out my arm, causing Micah to stop.

"We'll wait until they reach shore," I said. "Then we'll jump."

Micah's eyes widened. "We'll *what?*"

"It's not that far. Are you afraid you can't make the swim?"

"No," said Micah. "You've taught me well how to swim. It's the *fall* that I'm worried about."

I stuck out my neck and peered over the edge. "It's only fifty feet. Maybe less. The water below is clear. It'll be over in three seconds. Come on. It's the only way we can beat them to their ship."

Micah took a deep breath. He worked up the nerve. Finally, he nodded. We watched the little dinghy reach the shore. The men pulled it onto the beach and began to lug their water jars toward the spring.

"Now!" I cried.

Like Butch Cassidy and the Sundance Kid, we launched into the air, wheeling our arms until the slap of cold water surrounded our bodies. I pushed toward the surface and drew a breath. The Greek galley was only about twenty yards away, just sitting there, ripe for the picking. The crewmen on shore had seen us. They returned to the edge of the beach, but they didn't climb back into the dinghy. They just watched us in surprise. In the next instant, Nicanor and the others appeared from several places, converging to seize them.

I swam furiously toward the rope ladder that hung down into the water. My hand reached out and snatched the first rung. Seconds later I stood dripping on the ship's deck, my sights locked onto that bank of oars at the stern. Micah hoisted himself onto the deck behind me. He glanced back toward shore.

"He has them!" Micah said excitedly. "They've given up!"

"*Who* has them?" inquired a voice from behind.

I spun around, on the verge of a heart attack. A man had emerged from the cabin in the center of the galley. The ship had *not* been abandoned. Someone had been hiding in the cabin! He was an older man with curly gray hair, hardened muscles, and eyebrows that sloped sharply out from his nose. And yet his voice had not been threatening. He held no weapon. He shielded his eyes from the brightness of the sun.

"Who are you?" he asked. "What do you want?"

Micah and I stood there, gawking. I felt more like a kid who'd just been caught in the farmer's strawberry patch than a hijacker preparing to commandeer a ship.

"W—we've been stranded here," I stuttered. "We need a ship."

"My ship is yours," said the man amicably. "Stranded here? For how long?"

"Nearly three years."

His eyes filled with pity. "Oh, my! That *is* long. My, my! How many are with you?"

I glanced back at the beach. As Micah had said, the three crewmen had given up without a fight. Nicanor wasn't even making an effort to bind them. They were showing no resistance whatsoever.

"There are twelve of us," I answered.

"Where are you from, young man?"

"Caesarea," I said with some hesitation.

He turned to Micah. "What about you?" His voice stumbled a little. I had the impression he was attempting to speak a different language. "Where are you from? You're Jewish, aren't you?"

I stiffened. If he'd already determined that Micah was Jewish, he might have also concluded that we were escaped slaves. Micah gave a reply that I would not have expected. He answered according to religion, not race.

"I'm a Christian," he said.

If I'd thought this man had shown us sympathy before, it was nothing compared to the compassion he beamed at us now. And yet he didn't look surprised. Micah's words seemed to confirm something he already knew.

"My name is Stephanas," he said. "I'm a high priest of Melchizedek and a counselor of Bishop Titus of Crete."

* * * * * *

As the ship set sail, we stood at the stern and watched the shoreline shrink away forever. We'd left it all behind—our nets and cages, our pottery and trinkets from the ruins. No regrets. In a way, it felt like leaving behind all of our worldly goods to move on to a better place. Or perhaps it was simply that no one wanted any keepsakes to remind them of our ordeal.

Stephanas recounted the story of how he and his three sons had come to our island. "It was the whispering of the Holy Spirit," he insisted. "Two mornings ago, as I was preparing to set out for my usual fishing waters off the western shore of Calliste, a voice—no, a *feeling*—entered my thoughts and told me that I should sail south as straight as a falcon's flight. 'But I don't fish those waters,' I insisted to the Spirit. Again I heard the voice, 'Today you are fishing for men.' That's what it said—just like the story told by Peter of Jesus calling him forth to leave his boat on the Sea of Galilee. So I did as the Spirit directed, and early this morning we sighted your island. Now look what we've caught without having to cast a single net!"

Stephanas was in his early fifties. He was a Greek from a small fishing village near Corinth. A rustic, I supposed, by the standards of most Greeks. His hands were callused and his face was as hard as beaten leather. But he'd had the humility to recognize the truths preached by the Apostle Paul twenty years before. Paul had baptized him along with his wife, Corista, a brother named Fortunatus, and a brother-in-law named Achaicus. Stephanas had actually renamed his three young sons after apostles—Paul, Andrew, and Peter. Now young men in their twenties, they'd become Stephanas' crew.

Andrew told us that seven years earlier his father had moved them to Crete in the wake of some sort of an upheaval in the Church at Corinth. The leadership of the Church had become entangled in corrupt doctrines involving fidelity and marriage that Stephanas couldn't stomach.

"So are we sailing to Crete?" asked Nicanor. He and Onias were the only ones (besides myself, of course) who could speak or understand Greek.

"No" said Stephanas. "Six months ago we relocated again. We've now taken up residence with Bishop Titus and about thirty others on the island of Calliste."

Bishop Titus, I thought to myself. Where had I heard that name before? Titus was the name of the Roman general who'd destroyed Jerusalem. But no, that wasn't it.

"Why did you leave Crete?" asked Onias.

Stephanas smiled wearily. "I'm afraid the same disease that caught hold at Corinth has now stricken the congregations at Crete. But not to worry. We have great hopes that our exile will not last much longer."

"Exile?" asked Nicanor. "You mean you were *forced* to leave?"

"Not forced exactly," said Paul reluctantly. "It was more of a self-imposed exile. Just a year or so to let things cool down."

"Don't honey-coat it, brother," said Peter. "We fled for fear of our lives, and you know it."

I started to feel nervous. Here my congregation of twelve converts hadn't even been baptized into the Church, and now they were hearing about contentions among Christians. For three years—or as I now calculated more accurately, two years and nine months—we'd all basked in the security of a simple testimony of Jesus Christ. I'd tried on one or two occasions to talk about the apostasy taking place in cities like Pella, but for the most part, I ignored it. I guess I'd hoped that one day we might all find ourselves in the sanctuary of the Seven Churches. Micah and the others could learn at the feet of an apostle before they learned about all the madness in the rest of the world. Maybe I shouldn't have sweated it. No one knew about conflicts of doctrine more than Jews. I guess I'd hoped Christianity would prove to be something different from what they already knew—a religion of perfect unity and cooperation. Such was my fantasy.

Andrew sounded downright frustrated. "I don't understand how the Cretan Saints could reject the words of Titus, the man who brought them the good news of Christ in the first place—a man ordained bishop by the Apostle Paul himself!—in favor of men whose origin and authority are unknown."

"It's because with these new philosophers, the Cretans can worship Jesus and still be the liars and gluttons they always were," spat Peter.

The bad blood was evident. Andrew's words had turned on a light-bulb in my mind. Titus—I remembered now. There was a book in the Bible named Titus. I sang the old Primary song in my head just to be sure: *Matthew, Mark, Luke, John, Acts, Romans* . . . Yes, it was right after Timothy—a letter written by Paul. Could he be the same Titus?

It took us only seven hours with the large white sail and the single pair of oars to reach the port of Thera on the island of Calliste. Seven hours—that's all that had stood between us and civilization for the last two years and nine months. In reality, Calliste was only about twenty or thirty square miles; but to us, who had been crammed into a space less than one-tenth that size, it looked as big as the universe. Its harbor was bustling with ships and pleasure yachts of every kind, while its shoreline displayed hundreds of whitewashed houses reflecting brightly in the sun.

It had been a very long time since we'd been in the presence of so many strangers, and the prospect was a little intimidating. Nevertheless, we couldn't have asked for a warmer welcome than the one we received in the humble house of Titus, exiled bishop of Crete.

He lived atop a rugged hill about a quarter mile inland. Titus was a short, stocky man with ruddy cheeks and a mouth that seemed permanently curved into a smile, even when he tried to frown. Except for a swath of gray hair at the back of his head, he was perfectly bald. The gray hair told me he might have been in his sixties, but his face was so boyish, I might have knocked off ten years just for that. He wasn't exactly the austere, rugged-looking man I might have imagined. But then again, neither was my bishop at home.

"Two years and nine months," Titus repeated with astonishment after Stephanas had told our story. "What an incredible feat. The Lord must have fed and cared for you, just as he did the children of Israel in the wilderness."

Nicanor asked Titus shyly, "Are you a man of authority, as Harrison has described? Can you baptize us into the faith of Jesus Christ?"

The bishop's countenance brightened. "Who is Harrison?"

"I am," I admitted.

"Have you been baptized, young man?"

"Yes," I said. "When I was eight."

"By whom?"

"By my father." Then, as if to confirm the legitimacy of the ordinance, I added, "He's a high priest."

Titus noted that I was not a Jew. "Are you a Roman?"

"Not exactly. I'm . . . kind of a mixed breed."

My companions chuckled. Titus smiled amicably, but he looked determined to receive a better answer. "How did you come to be on a ship of Jewish war prisoners bound for Corinth?"

I shifted uncomfortably. "It's a complicated story."

"He has seen the Savior!" said Onias enthusiastically. "He saw him in a faraway land when he was just a boy!"

Titus digested this and scrutinized me keenly. "Perhaps young Harrison and I could share a few words alone."

I nodded my consent.

Titus turned to his counselor. "Stephanas, you and your sons round up the elders and their wives. Get these men cleanly shaven and groomed, and provide them with fresh raiment. Interview each of them for baptism. God willing, we will initiate eleven new soldiers to the cause of Christ tomorrow morning."

"It will be my honor," said Stephanas.

Micah and the others were ecstatic. Stephanas and his sons led them from the house. The bishop invited me to follow him out a back door and onto a small patio that opened up to a view of the ocean. There were some wickerwork armchairs, and Titus invited me to take a seat. It had been a long time since I'd sat on a real piece of furniture. I lowered myself down, tentatively at first, then eased back and relished the feeling. Titus sat in the chair beside me. He noticed me looking at some trellises with budding grapevines that curled over my head.

He reached up and touched one of the stems. "The landlord tells me if I can get these vines to produce, he'll take a third part off the price of my rent." He sighed longingly. "My wife was the one with the gift for growing things. She died four years ago."

"I'm sorry," I said.

He brushed it off. "It's all right. She's waiting for me. Before she died she was quite adamant that I get remarried quickly, though as yet I haven't found the opportunity. It's not proper for a bishop to be without a wife, despite how some in Crete might refute this."

I listened without comment. Titus' eyes hardly moved from mine. At last he said, "Tell me this complicated story, Harrison-of-a-mixed-breed. Tell me how you came to be on a ship with Jewish slaves."

I swallowed, then said boldly, "I was accused of crimes against Rome. I saved two of my friends—fellow Christians—just before they were about to be killed by lions in a gladiator pit."

Titus nodded. "I see. And where are these friends now?"

My boldness dissipated. I stared out at the ocean. "I have no idea."

"Where is this faraway land where you saw a vision of the Savior Jesus Christ?"

"It wasn't a vision," I said. "He actually came to us."

"*Came* to you?"

"Yes. He came down out of the clouds and blessed the people. Over two thousand. It was in a land across the oceans. We call it America."

He was astonished. "The Savior visited a land across the oceans?"

"Yes," I said. "He came among a people called the Nephites. They were his 'other sheep.'"

"But if this land is across the ocean, how did you get here?"

"It was a long journey," I replied.

"Indeed," said Titus. He leaned back. "Why did you make this journey, Harrison?"

"I came here for my sister," I said. "I came here in search of the man she loved. You see . . . she was—*is*—very sick. I came to tell him. I came to send him home to her."

"Was he one of the men you saved?"

"Yes."

"But in the end, you became a prisoner yourself," Titus concluded.

"Yes," I confirmed, my eyes threatening to overflow with tears.

Titus leaned back, his smile as warm as the Mediterranean sun. "Well, my young friend. You've been away from your home far longer than you intended. Now that you are free, will you try to return?"

I swallowed. "Yes, but . . . I'm not sure how to get there. I was going to Asia Minor. I was planning to find the Apostle John and ask for his help."

Titus raised his eyebrows. "The Apostle John? I'd heard once that John was in Ephesus, but that was many years ago. We haven't heard from any apostles since the deaths of Peter and Paul in Rome. I had feared that there might be none left. I had feared that the end times might finally be upon us."

"End times?"

"Yes. Not the end of the world, but the end of the priesthood. If the flame of truth still burns brightly in your land, Harrison, you have great cause to rejoice. In this land, I fear the final flicker is about to be extinguished. The only keys remaining are those held by a few of us bishops. The prophesied famine is here—not a famine of food, but a famine of the word of God. Very few of us really understood the words of the apostles when they tried to explain what was coming. I don't think I fully understood myself until recent events in Crete, and my subsequent exile."

"What happened?" I asked.

"They voted me out," he said soberly.

"Voted out the *bishop?*"

"I've served as their bishop for eight years, ever since the conclusion of my mission to Dalmatia. But you see, there's no one left to issue a release. Now new voices are emerging. They teach that as long as a man loves Christ, there is no law. No commandments. A man may do as he pleases without fear. It's just a repackaging of the old doctrines that the pagans and philosophers taught in Crete before we introduced the gospel. Now they've mingled these vanities with the ordinances of God. In Gortyna, a baptism is no longer considered pure unless a man or woman is baptized at sunrise, naked, facing east, and confessing his sins to all present. Last year there was an epidemic of dysentery. Half of the infants in Crete died. Several missionaries from Smyrna—adherents to a false apostle—began to teach that without baptism, these children were lost. Parents started pounding on my door, begging me to baptize their little ones. I tried to explain that Christ's mercy is extended to the innocent, and there is no need to baptize them. Several baptisms took place without my authority, and it was reported that the infants recovered from all signs of the sickness. Suddenly the whole Church was in an uproar. In the end, we were forced to flee for our lives."

"A false apostle from Smyrna?" I said thoughtfully. "Isn't Smyrna in Asia Minor?"

"Yes," said Titus. "It's not far from Ephesus."

I *knew* I'd heard that name. Smyrna was one of the cities of the Seven Churches. A false apostle had taken up residence in the heart of the last stronghold of truth?

"Who is this false apostle?" I asked.

"Cerinthus of Jerusalem," Titus reported. "They say he arrived from Judea toward the end of the Jewish war. According to his missionaries, he was ordained an apostle by Peter, Paul, and James, the brother of Jesus, when he was just a boy. He even claims that he was set apart to one day preside over the whole Church."

Cerinthus. I let the name burn on my tongue. It couldn't be the same Cerinthus. It was impossible. *That* Cerinthus had died on Mount Gerizim. I decided it must be another false teacher of the same name.

"What will you do now?" I asked Titus.

"My object is the same as yours, Harrison," he replied. "I plan to return home. I'll sail back to Crete as soon as all the arrangements can be made, possibly by the end of the summer."

"But your life might be in danger."

He shrugged. "It's my flock. I'm their bishop."

"But you could come with me," I insisted. "—you and Stephanas and the rest of your congregation here in Calliste. Together we could go to Asia Minor and find the Apostle John."

He shook his head. "I'll serve the Saints in Crete to the end of my days. Or until I am released, either by the hand of God or one of His servants. And if I am martyred, would I be any better than Paul or Peter, Andrew or James? Would I be any better than Jesus Himself? Harrison, I fear that if you go to Asia Minor thinking that you will find a situation better than here, you will be bitterly disappointed."

I let his words sink in. Then I promptly rejected them. I refused to believe it. There *was* still an oasis of truth left in this world. I'd been depending on that hope for far too long to abandon it now.

"Can you help me to reach Ephesus?" I asked.

"Ephesus is not so far," said Titus. "If the winds are right, you could be there in four or five days."

"But I'll need a ship," I said.

Titus massaged the back of his bald head. "It might be difficult to reach Ephesus from Calliste at this time of the year. Virtually all of the transports are making preparations to sail to Athens. In a few weeks the great festival of the Panathenea will be underway. They'll sacrifice a hundred cattle and feed the meat to the citizens, but they'll also eat an abundance of fish and fish sauce. Right now, our fisherman can garner better prices in Athens than they can get anywhere else in the islands. The Saints are counting on the profits as much as any other locals. We are hoping it will help provide us with the funds we need to return to Crete."

"What about from Athens?" I asked. "Can I find a transport to Ephesus from Athens?"

"Of course," said Titus. "Athens is one of the largest ports in the Aegean. But it might be cheaper to travel by foot. You could take the coast road to Thessalonica and Byzantium, and be in Ephesus well before the onset of winter."

I shook my head impatiently. "We don't know the roads. We have to travel by ship." I squinted one eye. "How much would it cost?"

"For yourself, ten or fifteen denarii, or the equivalent in drachma. For your Jewish friends, I'm afraid it would be twice that price. Jews are frowned upon in Greece, just as they are anywhere else in the Empire. I'd thought with the end of the war the situation would improve, but it's only worsened."

I felt overwhelmed. We had no money at all. "What if we worked here for a few weeks?" I asked. "We could help Stephanas and his sons prepare for the trip to Athens. How much could we earn? We're all very good fisherman."

"You're welcome to help us," said Titus generously. "We would divide our portion with you just as we would with the rest of the exiles. But we only own two boats. My son has one of them in Athens now; he's securing a contract from one of the fish buyers. I expect him to return within the week. But two boats can only hold so much. After we sell our catch, there will only be a small portion to divide."

"What about hiring out?"

"Hiring out to other fishermen may not be practical," he said glumly. "Again, a Jew would not receive the same pay as a Greek. Likely, he wouldn't be hired at all."

I groaned inwardly. Nothing ever seemed to just fall into place. "We'll do the best we can," I said. "If the Lord wants us to reach Ephesus, He'll provide a way."

Titus squeezed my shoulders in admiration. "You're a fine young man, Harrison. If all the young men of your land are as faithful as you, the future of the Church in your quarter of the world is secure."

"Thank you, Bishop," I replied.

The following morning, the baptismal ceremony of Micah, Nicanor, Onias, Haman, Baruch and the others took place as planned. All of our beards were either trimmed or gone. In my case, it was definitely gone. We were so clean-cut that we could hardly recognize each other. Titus baptized my eleven companions in a beautiful spot of sea just north of the city. He performed the ordinance just as I might have expected, invoking the name of the Father, the Son, and the Holy Ghost and immersing them under the waves. The other thirty Christian exiles who had joined Titus in Calliste were all in attendance. Not surprisingly, a good percentage of them were the daughters-in-law and grandchildren of Stephanas.

The Spirit was overwhelming, drawing tears of rejoicing from everyone present. Micah and the rest had been waiting for this moment for over two and a half years. I was sure that no one felt more joy and satisfaction than I did. Nicanor, still wearing his wet garments, pulled me in for a deep embrace.

"Before today," he said, "I thought the greatest gift I'd ever received was my father's fishing boat on the Sea of Galilee. Today I was given a gift greater than I could have ever imagined."

Titus also bestowed upon them the gift of the Holy Ghost. He performed the ordinance after warning the Saints against a policy recently adopted by the elders in Crete that the gift should be reconferred every year at the anniversary of the Savior's resurrection. He reminded them that except in cases of excommunication, the gift of the Holy Ghost was only bestowed once in a lifetime. It was then our responsibility to "receive" it. The only thing that could drive it away was sin. And the only way to restore it was repentance.

Despite their humble circumstances, the Cretan exiles could throw quite a party. We feasted on grilled fish, pig on a spit, lettuce salads, a dozen kinds of colorful vegetables, and wonderful hot brown bread. They also served little mice filled with herb stuffing that everyone seemed to consider a particular delicacy. But I just couldn't bring myself to eat the mice. You see, the little pink feet were still attached, and I . . . well, enough said.

Micah couldn't bring himself to eat the pork, either. I realized that a part of him still clung to his old traditions.

"What's the problem?" I asked. "For three years we've been eating seagull eggs, shellfish—even snake. Weren't those things forbidden by the Law of Moses?"

"Well, yes," said Micah. "But . . ."

"So enjoy!" I said. "Remember, the Savior paid for it. Today you've entered a *new* covenant."

He looked again at the pig on the spit. Then he turned white, as if he was about to vomit. After that I didn't push it. His upbringing had actually trained him to be repulsed by the *smell*.

I had my own peculiar dilemma. Titus' elders had also provided several large pitchers of rich, purple wine. It wasn't the first time I'd faced this situation since arriving in the Roman world. *Everybody* drank wine. Men, women, even *children*. I'd have sworn it was a more common drink than water. Actually, it was always *mixed* with water. Hardly anybody drank it straight. Even at today's feast the percentage was about fifty/fifty. For children, closer to ninety/ten.

I had to remember that in this day and age, the Word of Wisdom hadn't been introduced. The Lord had given the Word of Wisdom to the Saints of the latter days as a special protection and blessing, an extra edge in the battle against Satan. It was into *this* covenant that I had been baptized. So I happily drank my water until the celebration wound down and the sun disappeared into the western sea.

For the next two weeks we remained hard at work fishing in the warm waters off Calliste's west coast, where the cone of an old volcano still puffed out a modest plume of smoke. Our nets were filled with mullet, mackerel, and tuna. At the end of each day, we gathered our catch at the house of the bishop to be salted and dried. The guts of the fish were placed in the sun in large trays to rot and ferment. This "sauce," mingled with various spices, was the most valuable commodity we would be trading in Athens.

It was on one of the last of these fishing expeditions that Nicanor pulled me aside and solemnly announced, "Harrison, I've decided to remain in Calliste. I've spoken with most of the others, and they've decided to stay as well. We wish to join with Bishop Titus and help him in his quest to return to Crete."

The news made my heart well up with pain. I'd miss Nicanor terribly, along with Onias, Baruch, and all of the others with whom I'd shared so many trials and triumphs. Still, I had no right to force them to follow me. After all, they'd had no control over their destinies for almost three years. I only wished they'd been baptized into a less turbulent world. But who was I to promise them that in the region of the Seven Churches they would finally find peace? I realized it didn't matter where they served, as long as they served the Lord.

"I'll go to Ephesus with you, Harrison," Micah said that same evening. "You helped me to discover the true course of my life. I will stay with you until you find yours."

I embraced my friend. It seemed a lifetime since we'd enjoyed those long discussions in the dark hold of that slave ship. I marveled at how far we both had come.

Toward the end of the second week, Bishop Titus became quite concerned. His son, Leonidas, was overdue from his trip to Athens. I felt anxious as well. Until Leonidas returned, I couldn't set out on the first leg of my journey to the Seven Churches. At last, one afternoon in late June, Leonidas' ship was sighted. We met him at the docks. But when Leonidas came ashore, he looked exhausted and distraught.

"I couldn't secure a contract," he informed his father. "All Christians have been forbidden to do business in Athens."

"What?" said Titus with alarm. "What happened?"

"I barely escaped before I was arrested," Leonidas continued. "Most of the Christian leaders and their initiates have been rounded up and cast into prison. They are being brought before the Civic

Council. In the presence of the Governor they are commanded to curse Christ. If they refuse to swear allegiance to the Emperor and eat the offerings made to the pagan shrines, they must face starvation or cxccution."

"I don't understand," said Titus. "Something must have incited it."

"It's the philosophers," said Leonidas. "The Epicureans and the Stoics. They passed the edicts. They hate the idols as much as we do, but they hate us even more. I've heard that a Christian maiden spurned one of the Council leaders, but this is surely only a trifling matter. The situation has been brewing for years. Many Christian leaders have already been crucified. *Crucified!* Right along the Panathenaic Way! Some you know. Barnabas of Cypress."

"Barnabas the apostle?" gasped Titus.

"Yes," Leonidas confirmed. "He'd been serving in Gaul. They said he was on his way to Ephesus when he heard of the crisis. But not just Barnabas. Bishop Silvanus and Zenas the lawyer."

Titus was horrified. They were all old associates and friends.

"They've also crucified a cousin of Jesus Christ," Leonidas added. "The man was old and ill, but they dragged him from his bed and nailed him to a cross below the Acropolis."

I was suddenly breathless. "Who was this man? *What was his name?*"

"Symeon Cleophas," said Leonidas.

My heart exploded. *Symeon!* How was it possible? What was he doing in Athens? I'd thought by now he'd have long since settled in Ephesus. I recalled that his first ship in Caesarea had been headed to Athens. But Athens was only supposed to have been a *stopover!*

I grabbed Leonidas' cloak. "What about his daughter, Mary? And a young boy, his adopted son, Jesse."

Leonidas shook his head. "I don't know these names. No one knows the fate of many Christians. Luke is also said to have been in Athens. There is no news of him."

"But Luke was in Spain," said Titus with surprise.

"He was traveling with Barnabas. He may still be in prison. Nobody was certain."

Luke. The author of the third gospel. I hardly grasped the significance. My mind was still spinning with the news of Symeon Cleophas.

I remembered the words of the old prophet, Agabus. That night in Pella he'd said that Symeon, too, would sing the martyr's song, and in the same manner as his Savior, by crucifixion. Symeon was dead. I still couldn't believe it. *Symeon was dead!*

"I have to reach Athens," I pleaded with Titus. "I knew Symeon Cleophas. I have to find his daughter and adopted son."

Leonidas shook his head. "They know my ship. They know many of our faces. It's likely that they remember Stephanas and his sons from this past season—"

"Please," I begged. "There must be a way. *I have to go to them!*"

"I'll take you," said Stephanas. "And I *will* sell our catch. I have an old friend in Athens who is a dealer at the agora. He's a pagan, but he's an honest man. I'll use him as an agent. I'll sell our catch to him, and he can sell it to the hawkers."

"Don't trust anyone," said Leonidas. "The whole city is in an uproar. Christian property is being confiscated everywhere. The law is meaningless! The Roman governor has turned a blind eye. Because they refuse to sacrifice to the Emperor, he considers all Christians subversives, just like Jews. Before he was crucified, Silvanus tried to send an emissary to Vespasian, but the ship was burned before it could ever leave the harbor."

"All right," Titus agreed. "Go to Athens, Stephanas. Take your ship and your sons. Also take young Harrison and Micah. Sell the catch if you can. But do not bring the profits to Calliste. You will try to use the money to buy freedom for Luke and as many other Christians as you can find, including the daughter and adopted son of Symeon Cleophas."

Stephanas' oldest son, Paul, spoke up. "But what about our plans to return to Crete?"

"There is always next summer," said Titus sorrowfully. "It's in God's hands."

No Christian in Calliste slept that night. We loaded every basket of salted fish and vat of fish sauce into the hold of Stephanas' galley by the light of the moon. An hour before dawn, we were ready to depart. I spent that last hour in prayer.

"Let them still be alive," I pleaded. "Help me to find Mary and Jesse. Please, God, don't let it be too late."

I prayed also for Luke, the physician and companion of Peter and Paul whose writings were destined to illumine the western world. What had become of his holy gospel and the Book of Acts? And what about the other scriptures? What about the Scroll of Knowledge, the gospels of Matthew and Mark, and the other sacred manuscripts that Symeon had brought to Athens? Did they ever reach the Apostle John? Did they even still exist?

Something told me that those books had been just as stranded in Athens as I'd been on that island. If this was true, the purposes of God—a plan and purpose which had eluded me for almost three years—were starting to become clear at last.

CHAPTER 16

My throat filled with water, spilling out both sides of my mouth. I started to cough, choking for air. My eyelids fluttered. I could see hundreds of dancing lights. After a moment, the images coalesced into three distinct flashlight beams. I recognized the faces behind them: my mother and Jim, Steffanie and Apollus. I was back inside the cavern.

Jim backed away after pressing the water from my stomach. "She's okay," he sighed. I could feel the relief sweep through the room. "Give her some space," Jim directed the others.

Apollus drew back a little, but I could still feel his strong grip on my hand. His hair was wet and dripping. Obviously he'd just saved my life yet one more time.

The terrible memories of what I'd just seen at the other end of that watery corridor came flooding back. My coughs transformed into sobs. "Horrible!" I wept. "They're all dead. Throats cut!"

"It's all right, baby," crooned my mother, nestling my head against her chest. "It's all over now."

"Three years! It's been three years!"

"Three years since what?" asked Jim.

"Since we left. It's three years later.*"*

"How do you know?" Jim demanded. "What did you see?"

"We saw Masada," Apollus answered.

"Masada?" Jim repeated in amazement. "The Jewish fortress?"

Apollus nodded. "The underwater tunnel leads up to Masada. There were hundreds of dead bodies. Men, women and children—Zealots. They'd committed suicide."

"But how do you know it's been three years?"

"Because that's how long it took," I said. "It took three years for the Romans to conquer it. When we left it was 70 A.D. They'd just destroyed the temple. Now they've taken Masada. In three days, we've gone from September of A.D. 70 to May of A.D. 73! THREE DAYS!"

"How is that possible?" asked my mother.

"You mean Harry has been there for three years?!" exclaimed Steffanie.

Jim's face blanched. His eyes filled with panic. He took a stride toward the pool. My mother stopped him. "Jim, please. Be calm—"

"We have to get up there," he raved. "I have to find my son!"

My mother embraced him, her eyes full of tears. "There's nothing we can do. Nothing we can change. Wait for Meagan, Jim. Wait for her to recover."

Jim clenched his fists, as if he might try to tear away. Then he melted in her arms and began to sob. Steffanie was crying, too. My own mind was a blizzard of emotions. What had gone wrong? Was time racing so fast in the Roman world that even as we sat here days, weeks, and months were slipping by?

I bolted upright. "Jim is right," I said. "We have to go back to Masada. We have to go now!"

Steffanie understood. "It's true. The longer we wait here—"

At that instant the ground rumbled. It was only a slight tremor, like a freight train on a faraway track. But we all felt it. It elicited a feeling of prescient horror.

"I'll help Meagan," said Apollus. "I carried her through the water. I'll carry her back again."

"She's in no condition," Mom argued. "It's impossible."

"I'm all right," I insisted.

"You almost drowned!" my mother reminded me.

I leaned on my elbow, still breathing deeply. I was too weak to fight her. Yet I had to fight. We couldn't wait. There was something about the tremors. Every rumble in the earth caused the timetable to become more unstable, more unpredictable. I said a little prayer, asking God for strength. If there was another large tremor, we might find ourselves off by another year.

"Can we take the packs?" asked Steffanie.

"We'll have to make two trips," said Apollus.

"Just take whatever supplies we can," said Jim. "If it's ruined, it's ruined. Get ready. HURRY!"

There wasn't much to prepare. Shoes were left on. Apollus abandoned his armor and helmet. Steffanie wrapped some of the butane lighters and penlights in clothing and plastic. She was determined to bring her pack the first trip. Jim told Mom to leave hers.

The only thing holding us up was me. I felt like sleeping for ten hours. But we couldn't wait any longer. For Harry's sake—if there was any hope left—we had to reach the other side of that corridor as quickly as possible. I struggled to my feet. Mom cringed. I'm sure I still looked very pale. I tried to find comfort in reminding myself how much easier it was swimming upward than it had been swimming down.

"Are you all right?" Apollus asked me.

"Yes," I said. "I don't need any help."

I put my shoes back on. My pack was staying behind.

Steffanie entered the water first. She pushed her backpack under the surface. It tried to float, but as it became saturated it started to sink. Jim's pack was made of a more airtight material. As soon as he managed to get it under that white crystal lip, I suspected it would float to the top like a helium balloon. The hard part would be getting it under that lip. Each of us entered the water. Everyone watched me. I was the liability. My knees felt weak. Apollus came over to support me.

"She can hardly stand," said my mother.

Jim looked thoughtful. "I have an idea." He set his backpack in the water and floated it toward me. It didn't appear that it was going to sink for anything. Jim grabbed a large rock and set it on top to help get it submerged.

"Stay near me," said Jim. "As soon as I get this under that shelf, you grab onto the frame. Understand? It should take you right to the top."

I nodded. The idea seemed ingenious. I stood ready. The flashlights were doused. Two of them were waterproof, but we wanted to be guided by the glow of sunlight behind the crystal shelf. I drew in a deep breath. But then I hesitated, letting my breath exhale.

"Hey," said Steffanie. "What happened to the light?"

Jim's flashlight flicked back on. We peered into the water. Where was the glow of sunlight? Something had changed. Time had elapsed—at least twelve hours. It was now night.

We didn't have another minute to lose. I drew a final breath and plunged in. Jim was right beside me, forcing his aluminum-framed backpack to the bottom. I swam toward the crystal shelf and pulled myself into the dark chamber beyond. Jim's flashlight continued to flicker as he pushed his pack underneath. I was already feeling lightheaded as he guided my hands to grab onto the silver frame. Then he planted his feet on the bottom and used both arms to push off the rock on top of the pack. It immediately started to rise toward the surface. I held on. The only thought in my head was to maintain my grip on that pack. It continued to rise, and even seemed to pick up speed.

At last it broke the surface. I sucked in a breath of air. My strength was spent. For an instant I passed out. I felt myself sinking back under the surface, but then Apollus appeared beside me. He grabbed me under my arms and pushed me toward the edge. I draped my arms onto the tiled floor and hung on. Jim was beside me as well. He set his flashlight on the edge and held my shoulders.

"Good, Meagan," he said. "Breathe! You're all right. You're all right."

Indeed, the space overhead that had been filled with blue sky was now filled with stars. It was nighttime. There had definitely been a time change, though it was impossible yet to determine how long.

Someone else broke the surface. It was my mother with the second waterproof flashlight. Jim left me and helped her swim to the edge. Next came Steffanie. As soon as she'd drawn a breath she cried, "I lost it! I dropped my backpack!"

Apollus helped me to sit on the edge. But in the process I accidentally knocked Jim's flashlight into the cistern.

"Oh no!"

I watched it sink and twirl into the gloomy waters. At last its shining beam settled on the bottom. I couldn't quite tell how far down it was. I might have estimated that it was only twenty or thirty feet deep, but something else made it look miles away.

"I'll get it," said Apollus. "And Steffanie's pack. Just let me catch my breath."

"Where are we?" asked Jim.

"It's a cistern," I answered.

"Where's Masada?" asked Steffanie.

"Right above us," said Apollus.

Mom shined her light up the pathway leading to the main level. We paused to listen. The eerie silence that had greeted Apollus and me still prevailed. The women and children were gone. No one was hiding in the chamber.

"Are there Roman soldiers?" asked Steffanie.

"If Masada has been taken," said Apollus, "the army is probably sleeping. But there should be sentries."

"How much time has gone by?" asked Mom. "Maybe the armies have moved on."

No one wanted to believe that. If the armies were gone, it would mean that weeks or months had elapsed. It was all so mind-boggling. By our own reckoning, it had been less than an hour!

"Let's get all this equipment laid out," said Jim. "Don't let it soak in these wet packs."

Mom, Steffanie, and Jim went to work. At no one's objection, I continued to rest. Apollus had recovered sufficiently. He stood with his feet at the pool's edge and got his bearings on the sunken flashlight.

"I'll be right back," he announced.

"Be careful," said Steffanie.

Apollus put out his arms to dive. All at once a cold feeling crawled over my body. The next events happened in lightning succession. Apollus leaned over the edge, but before he entered the water, the ground began shaking all over again. Jim's voice cried out, "Apollus, wait!"

It was too late. The Roman's body slipped under the surface. The tremor lasted several more seconds. Mom latched onto Jim for balance. Then it ended. The ground went still. I came to my feet. Little waves lapped against the pool's edge. Out in the middle, the surface erupted with a gasp of bubbles. Jim shined his flashlight into the depths. Where was Apollus? Jim's flashlight should have revealed him.

He was gone!

Apollus had vanished! What was more, the flashlight beam *was* gone! I could no longer see it at the bottom. Both Apollus and the flashlight had completely disappeared. I stopped breathing. I couldn't speak, as if some great hand had seized my throat.

"What happened?" shrieked Steffanie. "What happened?!"

The ice on my lungs shattered. "Apollus!" I screamed. "Apollus!"

"Where did he go?" shouted my mother.

It had all happened so fast. My mind couldn't take it in. Instinct took over, and I leaped into the water.

"Meagan, no!" cried Jim. He splashed into the water beside me and locked his arm around my chest. He swam me back to the edge. "You can't, Meagan! You can't!"

"Apollus! Apollus!"

"Get her out of the water!" Jim shouted. "Sabrina, help me!"

Hands grasped every part of my body. I fought tooth and nail as they dragged me back onto the landing.

"I have to find him! He'll drown!"

"He's not there!" cried Jim. "You'll only drown yourself!"

I collapsed. "Where is he!? APOLLUS!"

It was no use. My Roman was gone. Time had swallowed him whole. Where and when it might spit him out again was unknown. Or if it would ever spit him out at all.

Then, as if our current level of hysteria, devastation, and turmoil wasn't enough, torchlights appeared in the passageway.

"Who's down there!" boomed a husky Roman voice. "Show yourselves!"

We heard the scrape of swords being drawn. The soldiers of Rome were about to surround us. Our only advocate—the only person who might have vouched for our presence and forestalled our execution—had just disappeared into the black hole of time.

CHAPTER 17

We sighted the port of Athens under a frowning gray sky, the tattered remains of a storm that had kept us at sea a day longer than we'd anticipated. Even from the deck of Stephanas' ship I could see the lofty buildings of the Acropolis, situated on a hill four or five miles inland. This included the legendary Parthenon—or temple of Athena—with its forty-eight creamy white marble pillars supporting a vast red tile roof. It was the second marvel of the ancient world that I had beheld, though I admit it struck me as rather cold compared to the magnificent golden temple in Jerusalem. Maybe it was just the jaded opinion of Athens that I had gained from the tragic report of Titus' son, Leonidas.

Stephanas didn't sail directly into the harbor at the Athenian port of Piraeus for fear that his ship would be recognized. Instead, he opted for a stretch of ground just east of the central bay, where the ruins of an older harbor loomed out of the marshlands. The crumbling seawalls were still standing in many places, but overall the moorings had been allowed to sink back into the mud. This harbor, I learned, had once been the most glorious trade port in all the western world. But a hundred and fifty years earlier it had been sacked and burned, along with much of the rest of Athens, by the Roman general Sulla. Ever since, the Athenians had allowed the old harbor to rot. Nevertheless, the marshy grounds were not completely uninhabited. Here and there I could see tents and makeshift shelters in and around the old ship houses.

"We'll anchor here," said Stephanas. "I'll leave my three sons to guard the boat. Paul will row us ashore in the dinghy. Then we'll walk into the city and search out my old friend and associate, Chrysoganus."

The dinghy was lowered into the water. Micah and I, along with Stephanas and Paul, climbed inside. Paul rowed us alongside one of the seawalls at a place where the old tide-eaten steps still came down into the water. As we mounted the steps, Stephanas told his son, "You will give us until tomorrow night. If we're not back before the setting of the sun, you will draw up the anchor and sail back to Calliste."

"No," Paul protested. "If you're not back, we'll come looking for you."

Stephanas became adamant. "I'll have your oath, son. If we don't return, you will leave our fate in the hands of God. Do you understand? Your mother needs her sons. Now give me your oath."

Grumbling, Paul complied. "All right. I swear it, Father."

"Good," said Stephanas. He embraced his son warmly.

With that, the dinghy shoved off and rowed back toward the galley. Stephanas led Micah and me up the sandy steps and across a field until we found a well-trodden path leading into the congested foothills of the city.

I retold our plans to Micah, who didn't understand Greek. He replied with a question. "Who is this old associate named Chrysoganus?"

Stephanas understood a little Hebrew. Nevertheless, he replied in Greek while I translated. "We've known each other since boyhood. We fished the straits together when we were young. Later he decided he'd make more money *selling* the fish than *catching* them. I'll ask him to purchase our cargo. His price should be more than fair. With God's blessing, he'll also give us news of Luke and the other Christians who have been arrested."

"Can he be trusted?" asked Micah.

"We're old friends," Stephanas stated again, as if in his culture this relationship was among the most sacred. "Besides, he has no love for the Epicureans or the Stoics. Nor the gods of the Athenians. He's a Mithraist."

"What's a Mithraist?" I asked.

"A worshiper of Mithras, god of the Persians, lord of the sun, sacrificer of the white bull, and so forth. He ranks quite highly in the cult, from what I remember. Even sails to Pontus now and again to make an advancement through what he calls the seven earthly grades."

"How does he feel about Christians?" I asked.

"Well, he likes me, and I'm a Christian. Even accused me of stealing some of his ceremonies. The Mithraists baptize their converts in water, just like us. They also partake of bread and wine in remembrance of the day that Mithras shed the eternal blood of the white bull to fertilize all the world."

I cringed. It sounded sacrilegious.

Stephanas noted my discomfort and concluded, "He's the only ally I've got in this city, so pray that he'll give us what we need."

I repeated his words to Micah, who said, "If he's a pagan, we'd better pray awfully hard." I didn't bother to translate the statement for Stephanas.

"How is it," asked Stephanas, "that he understands *your* Greek, but not mine?"

"Well, it's . . . it's just that we know each other so well. Three years on that island, you see."

Stephanas pondered this and smirked a little. I think he suspected something more, but he didn't pursue it.

As we entered the streets and corridors of Athens, I realized how accurate my first impression from a distance had been. I'd been in the heart of Jerusalem at its darkest moment. I'd stood in the wicked city of Jacobugath just before it was pulverized by a fireball of lava. Yet I'd never stood in a place so cramped, so stifling, so lacking in order, or so yellowed with filth as Athens. The narrow streets twisted around, cut back, and turned again with no pattern or logic whatsoever. Human waste was routinely spilled out of chamberpots in upper story windows to splatter on the stones. Except for the rains, which washed the waste into shallow, encrusted gutters, I was confident it was never cleaned. The citizens just traipsed through the filth as if it was normal. Around every corner I was greeted by a mosaic, painted pot, or dangling ornament that made me blush crimson. Naked bodies and body parts decorated *everything!* Micah tried to cup his hands around his eyes, but it was futile. How had a Christian community ever taken root here in the first place?

The people themselves looked wan and yellow, like walking cadavers, their eyes carefully avoiding any contact with strangers. But I didn't sense that it was out of fear or distrust. They simply carried an unmistakable air of superiority—especially to outsiders. Stephanas was a

Greek, but they knew right away that he was *not* an Athenian. This part of town was unfamiliar to him, yet when he asked for directions to the agora—Athens' marketplace—he received no answer. Just a smirk or a grunt, as if he was an idiot for asking. They seemed to feel if he didn't know his way around, he shouldn't be here in the first place. Was this really the city that my ninth-grade civics teacher had called the birthplace of democracy? Hometown to Plato, Aristotle, and some of the world's greatest thinkers? If so, it was definitely a kickback to a reputation from bygone days. Nevertheless, the citizens clung to that old reputation fiercely, despite the filth and obscenity they chose to live in now.

We managed to wend our way through the crooked streets by following the general flow of the population. An occasional sighting of the Parthenon atop the Acropolis helped keep Stephanas on track. At last we connected with a wide roadway bustling with donkey-drawn carts and men with heavy baskets carried up from the main port at Piraeus. We walked along a row of columns that appeared to run straight up to the Acropolis. I felt a shudder of pain as I peered down the wide avenue. Wasn't it here that the Christian leaders had been crucified? Just off the road, on an unpaved patch of earth, we passed several posts stained with blood. The bodies had been taken down, but the horror of what had taken place here just days before tore at my heart.

At last we reached a spacious square with pillared buildings, massive statues, colorful awnings, and the ambience of human voices— the agora of Athens. Here, at least, I could appreciate the grandeur of what this city *used* to be, despite all the rubbish and obscenities that flourished now.

Stephanas took us directly to the avenue of the fishmongers. Tables readily displayed hundreds of salted, dried, fresh, or rotting fish. To the sellers' credit, if a particular sample attracted too many flies, it was cast to waiting dogs. Stephanas inquired where he might find a merchant named Chrysoganus. The stallkeeper raised a finger toward a building across the street. We approached and entered. At one time it might have been a beautiful stone structure. But at some point the roof had collapsed and been replaced by sheets of canvas, still sagging and dripping from last night's rains. Dozens of barefoot workers in rough loincloths gutted, cleaned, and packaged mackerel and tuna in crates. Stephanas scanned the interior. A grim-looking man in a woolen cloak—probably a foreman—watched us warily. Almost resentfully.

Stephanas ignored him. He caught sight of a portly gentleman with a broad mustache sharpened on both ends. Around his neck and on his wrists hung charms and pendants of every variety. He looked like a cross between an English aristocrat and a hippie from the 1960s. He squinted to verify Stephanas' identity, then burst into smiles.

"Stephanas of Corinth! It's not possible! Tell me it isn't possible!" His arms stretched out to embrace his old friend.

"It *is* possible," Stephanas declared as they met, hugging and kissing each other's cheeks. "How are you, old partner?"

Chrysoganus gripped the flesh on his paunch. "Eating better than you, I see. Isn't that wife of yours feeding you?"

"Corista feeds me plenty. But you know me."

"Oh, yes. I know you. Nothing but meat and muscles. Are you and your sons still catching the whoppers in my father's boat?"

"Absolutely. You sold 'er to me for a steal."

"Of that I have no doubt," he laughed.

Stephanas introduced us. "This is Harrison. He comes from a far-away land called America."

"America? Never heard of it. Is it beyond India?"

"Yes," I said. "Quite a bit."

"And this is Micah," said Stephanas. "He . . . doesn't speak Greek."

Chrysoganus appraised Micah with an eye of concern. He drew Stephanas in close. "A Jew?"

Stephanas nodded.

"Please," said Chrysoganus. "Don't be offended, old friend. But this is my place of *business.*"

Stephanas looked at Micah ruefully. Micah understood without any translation. "I'll wait outside," he said.

As soon as Micah walked away, Chrysoganus embraced Stephanas again. "So good to see you!" he blustered, his voice overly cheerful. "Come back to my office. We'll discuss old times."

"I have some . . . difficulties," Stephanas stuttered, "that I was hoping—"

"Yes, yes," he interrupted. "We'll discuss it in my office."

Chrysoganus glanced around, as if wanting to be sure no one was eavesdropping. I noticed that the foreman had returned to overseeing the workers. It struck me that Chrysoganus had guessed something of the nature of Stephanas' visit all along. I even wondered if he'd dismissed Micah, not out of personal prejudice, but because *not* doing so would have aroused suspicion.

The office was a stone shack behind the warehouse. The door was a thin, netted curtain to let in the breeze but keep out the flies. I glanced back guiltily at Micah. I would have joined him, but I needed to hear what the fish merchant had to say.

As soon as we got inside, Chrysoganus checked to see if anyone had followed, then he turned to us with a grave expression. "Stephanas, you shouldn't have come here. Several of my associates may remember you. They knew of your affiliations. Weren't you aware of the edict imposed by the Civic Council?"

"I was aware," Stephanas nodded. "That's the nature of the difficulties that I need your help with."

I sat down on the bench. The office smelled of licorice. There were incense holders filled with what I assumed were anise seeds. On the walls hung tiny wooden cutouts painted with shellac. They looked like symbols of the Zodiac. Mithraism seemed to be little more than glorified astrology.

"It's all an ugly mess," Chrysoganus mourned. "There have been *crucifixions!* Did you know about it?"

"Yes, I—"

"Unprecedented for Athens—even in punishing Jews! If you and your companions are discovered, you'll be tried before the magistrates of the Areopagus. They'll force you to blaspheme your God. If you refuse, they'll starve you until you consent."

"What brought all this about?" Stephanas asked.

"Unfortunately, you brought much of it on yourselves," said Chrysoganus. "For years, not a day has passed that some preacher of yours hasn't taken to the agora forum or Mars Hills or some other platform to boast of miracles, reborn gods, and the like. The other schools had finally heard enough. Amazing, isn't it? In Athens you can preach whatever you like, believe the most unsophisticated blather you choose. But don't go telling anyone else they're wrong, and that you're the only one who's right. You'll tweak the wrong noses. That's what you Christians have done. Don't worry, you have plenty of sympathy from me. I, too, am in the minority in my love of Mithras." He made a religious gesture that reminded me of the Catholic sign of the cross, though his version was to quickly touch his forehead, right breast, left breast, navel and lips in one flowing movement.

"There may have been baser motives, too," Chrysoganus continued. "The president of the Epicurean academy—an eccentric, vile chap named Epigonus—took a fancy to one of your young maidens. A Jewess, or so the gossip says. It was Epigonus who used his influence to pass the edict. He's one of the wealthiest men in Athens. A collector of rare and exotic artifacts. Apparently this girl fit his definition of something rare and exotic."

A foreboding churned in my stomach. "What was this girl's name?"

"I don't know," said Chrysoganus. "But her father was one of the first to be crucified. They say he was a cousin or some other relative of this Jesus of Jerusalem who came back from the dead."

"Mary!" I cried in despair.

Chrysoganus looked at me in surprise. "You know this girl?"

"What happened to her?" I demanded.

"I'm sorry, I don't know. I heard he used his bodyguards to raid the girl's house the very night the edict was passed. The next day they crucified the old man. Epigonus' bodyguards are almost as infamous in this town as he is. They're Scythian horsemen."

"Scythians?" Stephanas repeated with a shudder. "I thought those tribes were extinct."

"They are in the regions tamed by Rome. Some years back, Epigonus read Herodotus' history of the barbarian horseman who once terrorized the Greek colonies of the north. Naturally, he wanted a pair for himself. He sent his agent to Olbia on the Black Sea to hire the most primitive warriors he could find. A year later the agent returned with two of the ugliest savages you've ever seen, complete with their horses and even a pair of tigerhounds. All of Athens knows the Scythian legends of cannibalism and butchery. When a Scythian hunts you, he uses the powers of Neuri, the demon ghost. He won't stop hunting until either you're dead or he is. The people are frightened to death. Ever since they arrived, Epigonus has walked these streets without the least fear of maltreatment. And more than a few of Epigonus' enemies have disappeared."

I persisted to learn more information about Mary. "But there must have been some word. Some rumor of where they might have taken her."

"I haven't heard," said Chrysoganus. "She might have been tossed in with the others. There's said to be over a hundred Christian prisoners in the dungeons below the Governor's palace. Many more have fled the city."

"Can we see these prisoners?" asked Stephanas. "Can we talk to them?"

"I don't know how without revealing your affiliations," said Chrysoganus.

"I have a hold filled with fish and fish sauce," said Stephanas urgently. "My ship is moored right now along a seawall of the old harbor."

Chrysoganus nodded, now fully understanding the purpose of his old friend's visit. "I see. And the fishmongers at Piraeus know your face, eh?"

"Please, Chrysoganus," he pleaded. "We need the money to free our people."

Chrysoganus grunted. "It'd take half a hundred galleys of tuna and liquimen to raise enough money to satisfy the Council."

"Then we'll free who we can," said Stephanas. "I'm begging you. The catch is of the highest quality, and—"

The Athenian raised his hands as if offended. "You don't need to sell me on the quality of your catch, old friend. I'd purchase your cargo at a loss. But you're going about this all wrong. You don't know the politics of Athens. This edict was passed by a very slim but vocal majority. If you stuff the right purses, your problem could resolve itself."

Stephanas looked overwhelmed. "But I wouldn't know who or how—"

"Leave it to me," Chrysoganus offered. "Trust me, old friend. Bring your catch to the second shipping house on the lower pier tonight after midnight. I'll have two lanterns glowing on the dock. I'll be waiting."

* * * * * *

We left the fish market and the agora as swiftly as possible. On the opposite side of the road leading to the Acropolis we gathered at the base of a large, bird-soiled statue. Here I took the opportunity to express my extreme discomfort. "He's an *astrologer*," I complained. "It's just another kind of sorcery. How can we trust a man like that?"

"Our trust is in *God*," Stephanas made clear. "Don't condemn a man in his ignorance. Chrysoganus is bound by an oath. He made it to me twenty years ago. To a Mithraist, an oath to serve a friend is the most binding oath of all. Even stronger than an oath to wife or kin. Besides, for now God has provided us with no alternatives."

I repeated the statement to Micah, who replied, "Perhaps we should give God a little more time."

"We'll go back to the ship," Stephanas insisted. "We'll wait and see what Chrysoganus can arrange. He's a very resourceful man with important friends. In his trade, you have to be resourceful in order to—"

Something flashed in my frame of vision. I grabbed Stephanas' shoulder. The gesture startled him. He turned to see what I was looking at.

"What is it?" asked Micah.

We all watched the canvas behind a fruit stall across the street. I swore I'd seen a hooded face appear and disappear.

"Let's move on," I said.

"Move on?" asked Stephanas.

"Quickly."

We crossed the road and reentered the congested neighborhood that led down toward the sea. My companions didn't ask any questions until I reached a place where I felt sure we were safe.

"What was it?" asked Stephanas. "What did you see?"

"Someone was watching us," I said.

"Watching us? Who?" asked Micah.

"A man in a dark cloak with a hood. He's the only one I saw. There may have been others."

Stephanas looked doubtful. He knew about the weakness of focus in my right eye. "Are you sure?"

"Yes, I . . . I'm *reasonably* sure. What about the men Chrysoganus mentioned who might have remembered you? Do you think they had time to inform the authorities?"

Stephanas looked concerned. He turned to watch the road behind us. "It's *possible*, but . . ."

"Maybe we should keep moving," Micah suggested.

We cut into a narrow street. At a place where the buildings nearly collapsed in on themselves, we made a sharp turn to the right. I signaled the others to stop. We pressed close to the two-story wall of an old apartment. Slowly, I bent toward the corner until I could barely see into the street behind us. The afternoon had become oppressively hot and muggy. The streets were mostly empty. The only living souls I could perceive were a few beggars sleeping in doorways or under trees. We waited and watched. Two minutes later, I saw it.

A pair of beady eyes peeked from around a shadowed building. I pulled back abruptly and stood flat against the wall.

"Is he there?" Micah whispered.

I nodded. I turned my head and surveyed the street branching off to the right. The apartment we were leaning against had an archway veering into a courtyard overgrown with vines. Another archway appeared to exit out the backside.

"You two go on," I said. "Walk steadily, not too fast. I'm going to try and get behind him."

"What if there's more than one, as you first suspected?" asked Stephanas.

"I'll be careful. If we're separated, I'll meet you back at the boat. Otherwise I'll meet you tonight at the second shipping house on the lower pier, like Chrysoganus said."

"If you're trying to ambush him, I should help you," said Micah.

"I'm not going to ambush anyone," I said. "Not if I don't have to. You can't help me, Micah. Forgive me for saying it, but you look too Jewish. You'll draw attention."

Micah wasn't offended. "God protect you," he said.

"Don't worry," I assured them. "I'll catch up."

"If you get into trouble," whispered Stephanas, "go back to the fish market. You can trust Chrysoganus. I feel certain he's on our side."

I nodded. Quietly, Micah and Stephanas slipped off down the street. I wiped a bead of sweat from my forehead and crept across the vine-filled courtyard. I passed through the archway on the other side. Another street wound down a steep hillside. I overtook a man and his mange-afflicted donkey, then cut back up a pathway to the street I'd just vacated, only now I hoped I would be behind the man in the cloak.

But where was he? The street was empty except for a woman hauling water up a rickety stairway. As soon as she disappeared into an upstairs room, I dashed to the next secluded position. I did this several times until I'd covered a distance of about seventy yards. By now I had reached the two-story apartment where I'd left the others. Had I blown it? Did the hooded man anticipate my actions? Maybe he was still watching me, waiting around the next corner with a hidden knife.

Then I saw him. His back was to me. He was lingering under the broken railing of a set of stairs. In an instant he skirted off in the same direction as Micah and Stephanas. I debated what to do. I'd seen no evidence of other pursuers, and I knew I was larger than this man. If I could sneak up on him, I'd pin him to the ground—no challenge. He was the hunter; he wasn't expecting to be hunted. Whatever I did, I couldn't let him escape.

I followed briskly. Soon I caught sight of him again. He was walking out in the open, not quite as reclusive. Micah and Stephanas had gotten way ahead, and he was anxious to catch up. His own noisy footfalls allowed me to creep up close. I was practically on top of him when he spun around in surprise. I leaped with all my fury. His knife flashed, but not before I'd seized both arms and flattened him to the ground. I forced my thumb into the nerve of his wrist. He squawked and dropped the knife. The hood fell away from his face, and I moved in to grasp his throat.

Then I froze.

I stared in wonder. My victim stared back. All at once my muscles melted. We just gaped at each other until at last our eyes filled with tears.

"Harry?" he asked me.

His boyish voice rang in my ears like a sweet chord of music. I hadn't heard it for almost three years. I gathered him up and embraced him with all of my strength.

"Jesse! I can't believe it! Jesse!"

The Jewish orphan from the wilderness of Qumran was twelve now. His hair had darkened, his topaz eyes had deepened, and his height had leaped by almost a foot. Even without the hood, I'd have found it difficult to recognize him.

"Harry!" he continued to chime. "I told myself it couldn't be you. I had to know for sure."

"Why were you following us? Why didn't you just step out in front of me?"

"I wasn't sure. I only caught a glimpse of your face. You look so different. So much older."

I embraced him again. "Oh, Jesse! I found you! I was losing hope." My face became serious. "Where's Mary?"

"The councilman has her."

"Epigonus?"

"Yes. Then you . . . you've heard?"

I nodded. The mood changed instantly. Grief flooded over me. "I know about Symeon, Jesse. I'm so sorry."

Jesse choked up. "They killed him, Harry. He was my father. My *new* father."

I embraced him again. "Oh, Jesse. It's all so horrible. You shouldn't have stayed in Athens."

"We couldn't travel. Symeon became sick. Every spring we made plans to reach Ephesus, but his illness worsened. Why are *you* here, Harry? You and Meagan were going home—"

"I'll explain it all later, Jesse. What do you mean he 'has her'? Where is Mary? Isn't she at the Governor's palace with the others?"

"No. Epigonus took her to his villa."

"His *villa?*" I shuddered in horror. "Are you sure?"

"That's what I heard."

"Where is it?"

"It's in the country. That's all I know. It's why I'm here. I've been following him for two days. I wear the hood because he knows my face. So do his bodyguards. Epigonus also has an apartment here in Athens. I've been waiting for him to go home to his villa, but . . ."

"Yes?"

"I lost him. He was shopping with his servants in the agora. I lost him when I spotted you."

I raised him to his feet. He clutched at his bruised hand.

"Are you hurt?"

"I'm all right." His face brightened again. "It's wonderful, Harry. So wonderful to see you."

"Maybe he's still in the agora," I said. "Should we go back?"

"Yes," said Jesse. "We can try. He had his carriage. I was sure he was on the way to his villa."

"Come on."

We ran back up the narrow street.

"How many Christians are still being held in the Governor's palace?" I asked.

"Only a few," Jesse replied. "Most have been set free."

I stopped running, dumbfounded. "What? How?"

"They . . ." He could hardly say it. "They cursed the name of Jesus. They said whatever the Council wanted. They burned incense and drank wine to the image of the Emperor."

I stared at Jesse in astonishment. "They cursed the Savior?"

"They'd been in prison for nearly a week. They were starving."

My mind was reeling. To curse and deny the Christ. How could anyone . . . ? It must have seemed so easy. Say a few words. Burn a little incense. And yet what it *symbolized!* I felt sick to my stomach.

"Where are these people?"

"Scattered. They were set free, but the people still taunted them. Most have left the city." He added uneasily, "A few have taken their own lives."

This nightmare was growing blacker and blacker. We continued to run.

"What about Luke the physician?"

"He's still in prison," said Jesse. "They say he's dying. I've heard they cut off his water. They want his denial. They know he was among those who first brought the gospel to Athens. They want to see him humiliated. Even if he dies, they'll say he cursed and denied Jesus. It won't be true, but they'll say it."

My head was ringing with disgust. How could I possibly make a difference now? It was too late. There were so few of us. I realized how dependant upon Chrysoganus we really were. Could a pagan really be trusted to keep his oath? But what about Mary? She was beyond his help. It was up to me and Jesse.

"How did you escape?" I asked Jesse.

"I was never caught," he replied. "I was gone when the bodyguards stormed our house. Since then I've been living on the streets. I'm used to that."

It was true. He *was* used to that. If anyone knew how to survive on the streets, it was Jesse. When I'd first met him, he'd been an orphan and a beggar for half his life. He'd lost both parents and a brother. He'd watched his grandfather, Barsabas, die in the ruins of Qumran. He was a battered and hardened little man. Before he left Judea, I was sure real healing had begun. Now to have his heart crushed all over again . . . it was almost too much to bear.

"What about the scrolls, Jesse? What happened to the sacred scrolls?"

Sorrowfully Jesse replied, "Epigonus took those, too."

I stopped running again. My heart sank like a brick. "What?!"

"Sometimes Symeon would invite Church members into our home to see them. One of them was a spy for Epigonus. After the bodyguards attacked, I was told that Epigonus' servants carried them off."

"Why? What did he want with them?"

"I don't know," said Jesse.

The answer seemed plain enough. Epigonus wanted to destroy them. Or perhaps . . . I recalled that Chrysoganus had called him a collector of rare and exotic things. Maybe he'd wanted the scrolls for his collection. It seemed too much to hope for. We'd sacrificed so much to bring the scrolls so far. Three years ago, I'd felt they were my sole responsibility. I'd felt sure it was my job to take them to Asia Minor. Nevertheless, I'd passed that responsibility on to someone else. The guilt burned inside me.

Jesse and I entered the agora. It was about six o'clock. Afternoon temperatures were abating a little. The marketplace was filling with people. This would make it twice as hard to find Epigonus—if he was still here at all.

Jesse led me toward a street where ointments and perfumes were sold. He'd felt sure this was where the councilman was headed when he lost track of him. I'd never set eyes on this man, yet I had a distinct image of his appearance. Maybe it was just the name. In my mind I saw a fat, greasy, lecherous pig.

Jesse stopped abruptly. He pulled the hood back over his head. Then he pointed down an arcade of booths toward a mule-drawn carriage of red and black wood. It was oval-shaped. The design had little in common with carriages I'd seen in western museums or the movies. Nevertheless, its purpose was the same. The driver sat up top with a set of reins to guide a pair of husky, flop-eared mules.

No one was inside. Epigonus and his servants were still shopping. My eye was immediately drawn to a pair of stunning horses ahead of the carriage. A servant held their bridles. Their backs were almost silver, the hair gradually darkening on the legs and underbellies. Their tails were bound tightly with black and yellow tethers, making it look more like the tail of a tiger. I'd never seen horses so muscular. These creatures might have climbed Mount Everest. Their saddles were of hard, pounded leather and the bridles were decorated with silver studs and leaflike designs. What particularly captivated my attention were some articles hanging from the bridle: two cups or bowls sewn up in leather. Locks of braided hair hung out the bottom. There were also several leathery looking squares of material, laid on top of one another like fabric samples. These were also sprouting hair. Then it hit me— they were *scalps*. Real human scalps! The bowls were the crowns of human skulls!

At just that moment, Jesse and I were pushed out of the way by a squabble of servants. I turned my head, and there loomed Epigonus himself. He walked by us close enough that I might have seized his throat. My imagination had been stunningly accurate. He was as fat as a Buddha. His jowls dangled from his face like a basset hound. His shape was like a gourd, with hardly any muscles adhering to his upper body and great folds of flesh gathered around his waist. He only looked to be in his late forties, yet he could hardly propel himself along. Sweat streamed down his face in rivers—a walking heart attack just waiting to happen.

He wore an intricately embroidered toga and a cloth cap with a sun visor, decked in amber-colored stones. He didn't pay us so much as a glance as he passed. But neither was I still watching *him*. My focus riveted on the two men walking in his wake.

In all my life I'd never seen such extraordinary-looking men. They had angular foreheads and narrow eyes. Their long hair was black and straight, tied with colored headbands. Their mouths were circled by coarse beards, red-tinged, as if stained with the residue of whatever meal had earned those scalps. Their pants were red, decorated with suns, moons, and stars. On their chests hung stiff vests lined with felt and fur collars. They each wore a bow and quiver of arrows, plus a very unusual knife whose silver blade divided into two tips, curved outward like a split blade of grass. Every inch of their upper bodies was painted in solid black tattoos, even crawling up their necks and upper cheekbones—leopards and horses, rams and snakes, all arranged in mesmerizing patterns. The largest of the two men had tattoos on both cheeks that looked like striking snakes with spiraling forked tongues. He noticed how I gaped at him, and he gaped back. Jesse turned away to avoid being recognized. The Scythian stared me down. He held my gaze even as he strode by, as if he suspected we might soon become mortal enemies. I swallowed hard.

The crowd was awed to silence by these men. They backed well out of their way. Epigonus scolded one of his servants who was loaded down with a newly purchased package. His voice chirped like a small dog. "Don't hold it so low! You'll tip it! You'll tip it!"

The servants loaded an array of bundles and baskets into a trunk at the rear of the carriage. All the goods looked very feminine in character—gowns, draperies, flower garlands, and many jars and vials of sweet-smelling cosmetics. Even if Jesse hadn't told me about Mary, I'd have concluded that he was trying to woo a female houseguest. This bolstered my confidence. If he was still trying to impress her, he might not have harmed her.

Epigonus was helped into the carriage, which instantly sagged almost to the point of dragging against the ground. The Scythians mounted their horses, and the townspeople moved away. The carriage driver snapped his reins. The servants trotted at the rear as the bodyguards and the carriage moved out.

"Come on," said Jesse. "He's going to his villa. I know it."

For the next two and a half hours, as the shadows lengthened, we followed the carriage down the bumpy stone road and into the hills. Epigonus stopped once to buy pears from a local farmer. We hid in the brush. One of the Scythians trotted his horse out to survey the road behind them. I stiffened. Did he suspect our presence? To our relief, he turned his mount and rejoined his partner.

We did our best to keep as far away as possible without losing sight of the carriage. At last it turned onto a muddy road and disappeared into a grove of trees.

We cut through the woods and soon reached a low stone wall. On the other side was a moat, six feet wide and filled with slimy brown water. Beyond this rose a second wall, about fifteen feet high. We moved stealthily through the underbrush until we caught sight of the gate. It was raised by chains, just like a fortress. The carriage, the horsemen, and the servants were all brought inside.

"Who is this guy?" I asked Jesse. "Does he live in a castle? Why does he need two walls and a moat?"

"He's very rich," said Jesse. "He owns half the land around Athens. He also runs the philosophical school of the Epicureans."

"Why does a guy like that have to take advantage of a Christian girl like Mary?"

Jesse looked at me, then said almost shyly. "I forget that it's been three years since you've seen her."

I guessed his inference well enough. Mary was very beautiful. But this wasn't news; I'd already known that. When I'd first laid eyes on her in the city of Pella, I'd thought she was a Judean princess. How much could have changed in three years? How could you improve upon perfection?

"I want to see what it looks like on the other side of that wall," I said.

"We might find a place to climb over it around back," said Jesse.

Instead, I surveyed the tall trees around the perimeter. None of them were close enough to the wall to help scale it, but the lofty branches would offer a nice perch.

"Give me a boost," I said to Jesse.

He helped me to reach the first branch, then he scurried up behind me. We climbed as high as we dared. At last the area behind the wall opened to our view. The sun was setting, but there was still plenty of light. The estate comprised about ten acres, every inch surrounded by the fifteen-foot enclosure wall. In the middle stood a three-story mansion surrounded on three sides by a small lake. Its architecture looked just as eccentric as its owner—uneven levels and tangled corridors. Oddly, most of the arched and square windows looked boarded up or bricked in. I only saw one small, round window that looked free of boards or bricks, about twenty feet above the front entrance. Epigonus didn't seem to care much for sunlight. In other parts of the estate stood storage barns, a horse stable, and servants' quarters.

"How many servants does he have?" I asked Jesse.

"Plenty," he replied. "But it's not a job to envy. When Epigonus dies, I've heard he's determined that all his slaves will die with him."

I pulled in my chin in astonishment. "Why?"

"It's a custom he learned from his bodyguards. When a Scythian king dies, they slay all his servants, horses, even his wives, and burn them all on the pyre. Epigonus seems to think he's a Scythian king."

We could see Epigonus right now, being helped out of his carriage by no less than three servants. The Scythians were walking their mounts toward the stables. I scanned the place for any sign of where they might be keeping Mary. Only one location aroused suspicion. But no; it was too obvious. Jutting up from the center of the mansion was a single rounded tower. Could she be inside? Again, I dismissed it. Watery moats and damsels in towers—too much the stuff of King Arthur, not ancient Greece. What was next? A fire-breathing dragon?

My eyes searched the grounds and spotted something that seemed almost as intimidating. Near a row of pointy pine trees along the side of the mansion, several large animals were nestled in the grass. Dogs? They must have been guard dogs, but I'd never seen dogs quite like these. They looked like wolves, but they were as big as Great Danes. They had broad snouts and lean, muscular backs. They'd been feeding on the carcass of a dead goat that hung from a post. Were these the tigerhounds that Chrysoganus had mentioned? If so, it was easy to believe they'd been bred to hunt actual tigers, perhaps in the tundras of Siberia. I counted at least six. The original pair must have multiplied.

Rescuing Mary and saving the sacred scrolls was looking more difficult than I could have imagined. Not only did we have to deal with the Scythians, but we had to deal with their dogs.

I noticed one of the bodyguards—the man with the snakes on his cheeks—riding over toward the dogs. The beasts began to bark and wag their tails. I realized they were restrained by chains tied to spikes. The Scythian dismounted and began detaching the chains. Night was coming on; it was time to let them roam free to patrol the grounds. Trespassers weren't the only ones who had to worry. I felt sure Epigonus and his servants wouldn't have dared to step out of their houses.

"We'll need to go in during the day," I said, "when the dogs are chained. It would also be nice if Epigonus and the Scythians were away."

"But we might not find an opportunity like that for days," said Jesse.

"I said it would be *nice*. Not that it would be possible. We're going to need some help. We'll go back and round up—"

I stopped speaking. One of the dogs had started barking wildly.

My stomach lurched. The animal was staring right at us! It was in the middle of the yard, bellowing and snarling at our tree. The Scythian turned his head. He took several steps toward us, then leaned forward and strained his eyes.

"*He's seen us!*"

The Scythian leaped onto his horse's back in one fluid motion. Now *all* the hounds were in a frenzy. The bodyguard galloped toward the gate at a full run. The dogs were following him.

"Let's get outa here!" I yelled.

We dropped down from the branch, landing with a grunt and rolling. My veins were searing with adrenaline. How could we ever outrun a horse and a pack of dogs? We were dead for sure! Our scalps would soon join the collection on that Scythian's bridle. What could we do?

It hit me. "The moat!"

"*The moat?*" asked Jesse.

"We'll never outrun them. It's our only chance!"

We crashed back through the underbrush along the stone fence. The hounds echoed in the background. Suddenly, this seemed like the stupidest idea I'd ever had. These dogs were trained to track tigers. Then again, maybe this was our advantage. We had to do something a tiger would never do.

We ran about a quarter of the way around the estate. I knew if we didn't make our move now, it would be too late. We needed to allow time for the water to settle.

"Here!"

It was a stretch of moat covered with lily pads and other muck.

"Don't splash," I said. "Just slip into the water. Slip in!"

We hoisted ourselves over the short wall, then carefully lowered ourselves into the moat. It was only four feet deep. We settled back until all but our faces were completely submerged. I could hear the hounds. They were scouring the area back near the tree. My faith wavered. This wasn't going to work. The Scythian would easily conclude that we were hiding. Where else could we hide except in the moat?

Nestled in the lily pads, we waited and listened. It was two full minutes before the bellow of the hounds drew nearer. I got ready to hold my breath. We waited a few more precious seconds. Then I nodded at Jesse. We pinched our noses, leaned back, and disappeared. My heart was thundering in my chest. I was sure it alone was creating shock waves in the surface of the moat. I tried to look up through the water. My vision was obscured by the lily pads, but I could see the darkening sky. Thank goodness it was almost night. If the sun had been high, it seemed certain that we would have been completely visible.

I continued to hold my breath. My lungs were nearly spent. I was about to lift out of the water and draw another breath when a hound suddenly threw its front legs over the stone wall directly above us. It tossed its neck from side to side, confused. Then it drew back and disappeared. I had to breathe. I couldn't wait any longer. But then I saw the Scythian. His image looked ghostly through the water, like a stalking wraith. He was riding along the outside edge of the wall. His bow was in hand, armed with a razor-pointed arrow. He glanced once or twice into the moat, but for the most part he studied the trees and the terrain ahead. He rode past—it seemed to take forever—and then finally moved out of my frame of vision.

I shut my eyes tightly. Ten seconds. I had to hold it ten seconds longer! At last I couldn't fight it. I raised up and drew a gasping, wheezing breath. A lily pad was stuck to my forehead. I was sure the noise had alerted every living creature for miles around. But the Scythian and his horse didn't return. The hounds sounded some distance ahead. Finally, Jesse's face broke the surface.

"Where are they?" the boy panted, his lungs desperate for oxygen.

"They're moving around the wall," I whispered.

"Should we make a break for it?"

I thought about it. I thought hard. If I judged wrong, the mistake would be fatal. I waited one more minute.

"Now," I said.

We hoisted ourselves out of the moat and plunged into the darkening woods. The cry of the hounds fell farther and farther behind. So, it seemed, did my hopes of rescuing Mary tonight and finding the scrolls. As the moon rose into the sky, I remembered that we had another appointment: in a few hours, we had to be at the second shipping house on the lower pier. Stephanas was expecting us. There was a lot of ground to cover between now and then. I prayed that Chrysoganus and the others had devised a plan to free Luke and the other Christians. I feared it would take all of our energies, and every ounce of our strength, just to find the sacred scrolls and to save the daughter of Symeon Cleophas.

CHAPTER 18

The devastation closed around me like four granite walls. Apollus was gone. There was nothing I could do to bring him back. We had no idea when or if he might emerge from that pool. The Romans who surrounded us inside the chamber gawked at us like we were insane. They raised their torches and stared into the water, trying in vain to see what we were looking at. Nothing was there.

My emotions were still reeling as we were escorted at sword point down the snake path that descended the eastern slope of Masada. I saw immediately that everything had changed. The building where all those suicide victims were laid out had been torn down. Other areas of the fortress had been ravaged and burned as well. It had been days, perhaps weeks, since Apollus and I had been here. This only heightened my hysteria. That second tremor had been far stronger than the one inside the cave. If the first tremor had changed things by a number of weeks, the second one might have changed things by years. Oh, Apollus! The possibility was becoming increasingly real that I might never see him again.

My turmoil kept me from providing my mother with the emotional support she might have required. She was engulfed by wonder. Yes, I wanted to tell her, this really was ancient Judea. We really had gone back in time. For her, the devastation of losing Apollus was combined with the shock of our new and mind-boggling environment. She kept herself close to Jim.

Jim recalled the name on Gidgiddonihah's note and said to the Romans, "We're looking for a soldier named Sergius Graccus."

"I know Graccus," a soldier confessed. "His cohort went with the general back to Jerusalem."

"Then take us to your general," Jim demanded, sounding a little like a Martian invader. "If you don't," he added, "I promise you the consequences will be severe."

The soldiers were tempted to laugh, but something in his threat sounded genuine. After all, he spoke perfect Latin. We could hardly be considered Jewish troublemakers. Could they afford to take any chances? Maybe it would be better to pass this off to a higher authority. Besides, the familiar controversies surrounding our modern-day equipment cropped up. There appeared to be very little water damage to our lighters, penlights, and ballpoint pens. Everything worked just fine. Frankly, I was beginning to wonder why we ever brought modern supplies at all. They always got confiscated right from the get-go. All that shopping, planning, and packing was a complete waste of time.

Jim's demand almost threw me into a panic. I still believed Apollus could emerge from that pool at any moment. How could Jim suggest that we leave him? And yet how could we stay? We were here to find Harry. What an unimaginably tangled mess!

Before the day was out, the four of us found ourselves marching under heavy guard toward the headquarters of Governor-general Flavius Silva in Jerusalem. We learned that the defeat of Masada and the death of the Zealots had taken place almost two weeks before. Twelve full days had elapsed in what for us was only an hour. In that time period, the Roman army had burned all of the corpses. They'd commenced the destruction of many of Masada's fortifications to prevent any other Jewish faction from ever taking up residence on its heights again. Silva had left his encampment just five days earlier to make his formal report to the Emperor from his permanent headquarters on the Mount of Olives. I remained an emotional wreck during the whole sweaty march. We spent one night camping in the wilderness between Engedi and Tekoa. As we huddled together in our threadworn tent, it was all I could do to keep from breaking into tears every few minutes.

Jim gazed off toward the Romans' fire through the flap of our tent and said in a sober tone, "That was the moment. I felt sure of it as I jumped into the water to prevent Meagan from trying to reach Apollus."

"The moment for what?" asked Steffanie.

He looked at his daughter in all seriousness and said, "If we'd gone back for the other packs—if we'd returned to the other side of that tun-

nel—*I would have never seen my son again. At least not as a teenage boy. My vision would have been fulfilled. The discrepancy would have been more than just three years. It would have been decades."*

"What does that mean for Apollus?" I asked desperately.

Jim looked at me, unsure of how to answer. Then he said, "Apollus wasn't going all the way back. He was only swimming to the bottom of the pool. I don't think it would be . . . exactly the same."

I squeezed off more tears, my heart caught in a whirlpool of panic. My mother put her arms around me. "Calm down, honey. Please don't make yourself sick. At least Jim is convinced that he's still alive."

"But where is he, Mom? He's all alone. I've already messed up his life beyond recognition. We should have never brought him back with us."

"It sounded to me like the choice was his," said Mom.

"I should never have given him the choice. What if he doesn't emerge from that pool for a hundred years? Even if he tries to go back to our century, he'll be utterly lost."

"You care about this young man an awful lot, don't you?" my mother asked.

I wiped my tears, avoiding her gaze. "Of course I do. I feel responsible. If I could just know he's safe; that's all I want to know. He doesn't have any supplies. Steffanie's pack is mostly clothes—a few candy bars. We should have left him something he could use."

"You did leave him something," said Mom. "I heard you teaching him the gospel. He seemed to respond to what he was hearing. You taught him who to pray to. That knowledge is worth all the supplies in the world."

I digested this. Yes, I had taught him how to pray. I'd never actually heard him do it, but at least he knew how. I hugged my mother. My nerves remained on edge, but her words were the most comforting thing anyone could have said.

Steffanie was having almost as hard a time as I was. It felt good to have someone to cry with, despite the tiny seed of jealousy that had crept between us. None of that seemed to matter now. Maybe there were some fringe benefits to having a big sister.

Our tent had four armed guards stationed outside at all times. After Mom and Jim had fallen asleep, I saw Steffanie peek outside to see if they were still there. None of them had moved a single inch.

"These Romans give me the creeps," Steffanie whispered.

"Why?" I asked, though I was fairly certain I knew the answer.

"*They just gawk at us. Especially that one with the big chin. What's his name? Crotus? Every time I glance at him, he gives me this sleazy grin. Ugh! It makes my skin crawl.*"

"*They've been in the desert a long time,*" *I said.* "*Probably too long.*"

"*Do you think we're safe?*" *asked Steffanie.* "*I mean, you don't think they'd ever . . . ?*"

"*I doubt it,*" *I said.* "*They have a whole country to rape and pillage. I think we're safe as long as we're going to speak with their general.*"

"*I wish I was so sure,*" *said Steff.* "*We're nobodies. All we've done is request an audience.*"

"*We're mysterious,*" *I countered.* "*They're wary of us, like witches or sorceresses. In fact, if they try something, that's the tack you should take. Just start muttering gibberish, as if you're casting a spell. Believe me, that'll send 'em scurrying off faster than anything.*"

Steffanie sighed. "*I'd feel a lot better if Apollus were here.*"

I nodded. It was an understatement. We settled in to endure a long, horrible night.

As I'd predicted, the soldiers didn't try anything the next day, though we were hard-pressed to find a moment when they weren't leering.

We continued our march toward Jerusalem. The scars of war were still evident across the land: burned-out houses, abandoned fortifications, and women and children without husbands or fathers. The anniversary of the destruction of the temple was approaching its third year. Now and then we could see some evidence that the citizens were picking up the pieces of their lives: a few fields growing crops, a few oxen and sheep in the grassy hills. Sometimes the rubble had been cleared away and new houses built in their places.

The most savage scar continued to be the city of Jerusalem itself. From the southern hills, we could see that very few repairs had taken place. The bodies of the dead were gone, but the air was still tinged with a sour wind. Some reconstruction was underway, but for the most part, the great city was a wasteland, abandoned and left to itself. I easily identified the square of earth where the Holy Temple had once stood. It was little more than a dirt field now. Even grass and weeds seemed reluctant to grow there. Huge piles of rubble had been pushed off into the ravines on its eastern side, while at another corner some of the precious blocks of stone were being re-cut and refashioned for use in other buildings. The pallor of misery still hung as heavy as a death shroud. For a moment I forgot my devastation at losing Apollus, and found myself weeping for the loss of this great city. Once it had been the most blessed city on earth. Now it was cold. Not in temperature, but in the dearth of the Spirit. In that respect, it was the coldest place I'd ever visited in my life.

The camp of the Tenth Legion was only a fraction of it original size. The tents looked weather-beaten; dumpsites for rubbish took up almost as much area as the camp itself. With Masada vanquished, I had a feeling the Romans would soon disband the entire camp.

The headquarters of the general still looked reasonably comfortable. It was a large, red-checkered tent with flags waving at its pinnacle. Dozens of uniformed aides and sentries scuttled about. The officer in charge of our escort proceeded to show off a few of our modern gadgets to convince the general's secretary that meeting us would be worth the general's time. The flashlights and smaller penlights, of course, attracted the most attention. They hadn't yet figured out how to use the butane lighters, nor had we bothered to demonstrate. But then the general's secretary somehow figured it out by himself. As least that's what I guessed had happened when I heard him shriek, drop the lighter, and suck on his thumb as if it had been burned.

He immediately ordered his men to gather up our backpacks, then disappeared inside the general's tent. As we waited in the hot sun, Crotus, the soldier with the big chin—the same one who had so disgusted Steffanie—approached Jim and said, "I could help you if it goes bad in there."

Jim looked the man up and down. From someone else the offer might have been intriguing, but from this Neanderthal it carried no interest whatsoever. "I'm sure it will go fine," he replied, nodding his thanks anyway.

"I could help you if it goes good, too," Crotus added. "Me and most of these other men—we're getting our discharges today. Going back to Rome to receive our pensions. You was our last official assignment. We're marching to Caesarea come morning. You going anywhere near Caesarea?"

"I don't think so," Jim replied.

"Where are you and your wife and daughters headed?" he asked.

Jim didn't bother to correct him about our relationships. "We . . . haven't decided."

The man persisted. "A man and three women shouldn't travel in this country without protection. You might persuade us to go with you for a ways."

"No thanks," said Jim, his voice a little more firm. "Besides, after we're done in there, I doubt we'll have anything left to pay you."

His lips pulled away from his teeth—a horrible grin that made me feel like lice were crawling all over my body. "Oh, you got somethin'," he assured. "You got somethin'. You think about it. We could help each other. I feel sure."

I realized that at least five of the other soldiers were listening with great interest, grinning to reveal every gap where their teeth had been knocked out or rotted away.

Jim's eyes became as narrow as dagger blades. "I said no." This time his teeth were clenched.

Crotus raised his eyebrows. He almost look surprised, as if he'd been presenting a perfectly legitimate business proposition. The grin disappeared and he backed away a step. His eyes crawled over Steffanie and me again, then returned to Jim. He shrugged as if to say, "No harm in asking," then rejoined his comrades.

The incident disturbed my mother the worst. She was shaking terribly. I'd tried to warn her, I'd tried to warn them all about what this world was like. I wished I'd pressed harder for her to stay behind. Crotus said something, no doubt crude, to the others. They cackled with laughter. To our relief, the general's secretary emerged. He waved for us to follow him inside.

I was the last one to enter the tent. At the last second, I turned back and faced Crotus and his comrades. In a gesture that was utterly childish, I widened my eyes like a crazed sorceress, raised up my hands like spiders and flung my fingers at them, as if sprinkling them with some unholy substance.

"May the fleas of a thousand camels infest—"

I'll just censor my words from there. Suffice it to say they flinched as if the substance had actually hit them in the face. Then they gaped with open mouths. I grinned wickedly and slipped into the tent.

Jim looked at me strangely. Fortunately, his attention was immediately drawn elsewhere. Seated in a little chair that looked like it might fold up as neatly as a director's chair was the commander of the Tenth Legion and the governor of the province of Judea, Flavius Silva. He was introduced by the bellowing voice of his aide. Silva wasn't even looking at us. His arm was propped atop a flimsy table, and he was staring at the flame he'd just created by flicking one of the butane lighters. He was a tired-looking man with sagging eyes, well into his fifties. His skin looked blotched and leathery, probably from all the time he'd spent in the sun at Masada. I didn't think he looked like a man who was easily impressed by new things. Yet he found our lighter thoroughly captivating. At last he raised his eyes and let the flame snuff out.

"Very impressive," he uttered. "Are you the artisan?"

"No," Jim confessed. "But I am the peddler."

Silva frowned. "I'm told you were arrested for trespassing at the fortress of Masada. Is that right?"

"I'm afraid it is, General," said Jim.

"What is your name, peddler?"

"Jimus Hawkinus," he replied.

I raised an eyebrow. Not bad.

"Are you a citizen of Rome?"

Jim considered his reply carefully. "What do you think?" he said, swiftly adding, "sir?"

A corner of Silva's mouth raised into a smile. "I'd say you were from my own home district of Arpinum. Am I close?"

Jim smiled in return. "You know your accents, sir."

Wow, *I thought. Jim was* good. *I'd almost forgotten that he was just about as expert in the art of time-travel as a man could get. Silva's sympathies were immediately ours.*

"Memmius!" Silva barked.

The officer who had escorted us to Jerusalem entered the tent. "Yes, General?"

"This man is a countryman of mine. Why has he been arrested?"

Memmius looked at a loss. "Well, he . . . he was caught in the great cistern. All of them were in the cistern. They were . . . swimming."

"Swimming?"

Jim nodded guiltily.

"How did you slip past the sentries?" asked Silva.

Jim shrugged. "No one tried to stop us."

"Are you being coy?"

"No, sir." Jim cleared his throat.

Silva scowled at Memmius. He was ready to pass off this whole affair as a matter of military incompetence. Memmius squirmed.

Silva indicated our appearance, his face alight with awe. "What is all this? Your clothes, these tools and packs. Where did you get these things?"

"Another part of the world," Jim replied. "We've visited some very exotic places."

"*I can see that. Then are you on your way home to sell these trade goods in Italy?*"

"*Honestly,*" *said Jim, "I can't return home until I find my son. He's been missing for almost three years. Until I find him, my family and I will devote every ounce of our energies to solving the mystery of his disappearance.*"

More sympathy gushed. "Your son. I see. I haven't seen my own sons for almost four *years. How is it that your son became lost?*"

"*He was last seen in Caesarea, General. In fact, one of our motives for visiting Masada was to find one of your soldiers. We received some information that named him as a possible link to finding my son.*"

"*Who is this man?*" *asked Silva.*

"*His name is Sergius Graccus.*"

Silva didn't recognize the name. He turned to one of his legates.

The legate spoke up. "I believe Graccus was in the company that came back with us to Jerusalem. He was one of the men recruited from the Fifth Legion to help us build the siege engine at Masada."

Silva turned back to me. "Then this man has been released to go back to his old unit." To the legate: "Do you know where he was stationed before?"

"*I'd have to check the records,*" *said the legate. "We recruited several dozen men from outposts in the north who had experience with engines and ramps.*"

"*I know where he was stationed,*" *I butted in. "It was at Neopolis near Mount Gerizim.*"

"*Very good then,*" *said Silva. "What is it you hope to learn from this man?*"

"*He made contact with a friend of ours who is also searching for my son,*" *Jim replied. He paused. It occurred to him that Silva might also know something about Gidgiddonihah. He chose his next words most carefully of all. "Is it possible, General, that during your siege at Masada, you came into contact with a man, or perhaps several men, who claimed to be from a part of the world that you had never heard of before?*"

Silva looked down his nose, then chuckled. "A part of the world that I've never heard of before? What part of the world might this be?"

I could tell Jim regretted asking, nevertheless he replied, "Zarahemla."

"*Zera-hemla? No, I'm afraid at Masada there were no opportunities to make new acquaintances from* any *part of the world.*"

The other officers in the room looked equally perplexed.

"*Never mind,*" *said Jim. "We just need to find this man, Graccus.*"

"Well and good," said Silva. "I give you my leave, Jimus Hawkinus. Perhaps you might be interested to learn that many of our legionaries are marching to Caesarea over the next few days. Our work is done in this sun-cursed land. It's time for us all to go home. Would you like an escort to Neopolis?"

"No," said Jim quickly.

Jim looked at me. I shook my head in agreement.

"I mean, no thank you," he said again. "I think we can find our way well enough."

"Suit yourself," said Silva. He looked thoughtfully at the lighter in his fingers. "But before you leave, if you could see your way clear . . . what I mean is, I might be interested in purchasing a number of your articles."

Jim moved toward one of the packs. He asked permission before opening it. "May I?"

"By all means," said Silva. "The items are yours, aren't they? Has anything been taken?"

Silva shot Memmius another stern glance. Memmius shook his head vigorously. Jim dug into the pack and brought out a penlight, two more lighters, a handful of ballpoint pens, and several individually wrapped mini Butterfingers.

He piled them into the general's hands and said, "Please, sir, consider these my gift in return for your magnanimous hospitality."

I stared at Jim in admiration. Astounded. Can I say I was astounded? Jim Hawkins was a natural. He should have been a lawyer or a diplomat. We walked out of that tent with every stitch of our supplies that we had recovered from the cistern. As we proceeded down the pathway and exited the camp of the Tenth Legion, Crotus and his men were watching us every step of the way.

It was starting to grow dark. We huddled in a ravine north of the army camp and consumed several packets of camping rations from our store of supplies. At the same time, we formed our plans for the future—a bitter conversation considering the absence of the man who might have guided our every step.

"How long will it take us to reach Neopolis?" asked Jim.

"Harry said it only took him two and a half days," I replied. "If we left tonight, we might be there by dark the day after tomorrow."

"Is it the same as the road to Caesarea?"

"I think so," I said.

Jim shook his head. "Then we won't start tonight. I don't want to leave tomorrow either. I want to be well behind this Crotus fellow and those other vermin who traveled with us from Masada. Tonight we'll find an inn at one of these smaller villages. Tomorrow we'll wait out the day and leave the following morning."

"Do you really think those men would try to harm us?" Mom asked.

"I don't plan to find out," said Jim. He looked at me. "I don't think your little gesture before we went inside the tent helped any."

"Sorry," I said.

"But, Dad, what's to keep anyone else from harming us?" asked Steffanie. "Crotus seemed to think our status—a man traveling with three women—made us prime targets."

Jim sighed drearily. "I know this much," he said. "Tomorrow we're going to use some of the money Gid left bundled up in that cloth to purchase tunics, shawls, headwraps, and whatever else will help us to blend in. I'm gonna sell these backpacks and buy satchels and travel bags. We'll hide our modern gadgets in those. I might even purchase a donkey if we have enough. The more we can do to keep from drawing attention, the better. But frankly, our best tactic from here on is to put our faith in God."

We found an inn, just as Jim had directed. It was a shabby establishment with twenty unfurnished rooms. I was sure the grubby little Greek proprietor charged us an inflated price. Having left my mother's backpack in the cave, we only had one blanket to share.

The following day we purchased new clothing, bedrolls, and other items we would need for our journey. We even offered a young woman three denarii for her donkey. She took the money with great enthusiasm, leading us to believe we might have overpaid. We whiled away the remainder of the day in the vicinity of the inn. I spent most of the afternoon on the inn's roof—a popular gathering place to escape the sweltering heat inside. I peeled my eyes toward the road going north, called by the locals the Samaritan Highway. Specifically, I was searching for any sign of Crotus and his men. There were plenty of soldiers on the road, but I saw no sign of the creep with the oversized chin. Hopefully, he'd already passed by us earlier that morning.

Secretly, I dreamed that I might see Apollus appear over that rise. I saw it in my imagination a hundred times. I even tensed my muscles in case I had to spring at any moment to rush forward and greet him. It wasn't such a far-fetched dream. Like us, his goal would have been to reach Neopolis. That's where his father was stationed. That was the site of his old command. If Apollus ever emerged from that cistern, this was precisely the road he would travel. I was glad of Jim's decree that we should wait here an extra day. It gave me one last opportunity to hope.

Later in the evening, Steffanie found me alone and sat on the parapet beside me. She read my thoughts like an open book. "You know what I think?" she began. "I think as soon as we find Harry—as soon as we travel back to Masada—Apollus is going to pop right out of that cistern. In his hands he'll be carrying my backpack and your flashlight. He'll look at us strangely for a minute, try to figure out what's different, then he'll see Harry and absolutely squeal in delight."

I pondered this wonderful image. "I hope you're right. There's only one problem. Apollus does not squeal."

Steffanie considered the tone of my reply. She looked at me in all seriousness. "Aren't you afraid you might be a little young for Apollus?"

The hair prickled on the back of my neck. "What do you mean?"

She began picking at the plaster on the edge of the roof. "Well, I'm just saying . . . I mean, it appears to me . . . that Apollus might not be your type."

"Oh? And what exactly do you think my type is?"

"I don't know . . . the Bill Gates type."

I screwed up my face. "A computer geek?"

"No, no," said Steff. "I mean smart, creative. A real go-getter. I think Bill Gates is cute. And very rich."

"What type is Apollus?"

"The athletic type. Definitely. Let's face it. His name says it all."

"You don't think I'd match up with the athletic type?"

"Don't be offended. I'm just giving you my impression. If that's not the way you feel, don't let me change your opinion."

"Oh, you won't," I gruffed. "In my opinion, Apollus is the type who wants a girl who understands him. He's been through a lot. He and I have a lot in common."

I felt my face redden. I'd been determined never to confess my feelings about Apollus. She'd drawn me into this. Did I say I thought there were benefits to having a sister? What was I thinking?

"I'm sure you're right," said Steffanie. "He does seem very sensitive under all those . . . muscles."

I worked up the courage and said, "You like him too, don't you?"

She looked surprised. "Well, I'm not saying I don't find him attractive. But . . . the bottom line is, Meagan, I could never do anything to hurt you."

I leaned closer. "See that you don't."

Steffanie smiled painfully. "Oh, Meagan, I wish any of this mattered. I just want him to be all right. It may be a long time before Apollus can tell us anything about—"

Steffanie stopped speaking. She watched my eyes become as wide as moons. She tried to turn around to see what I was looking at. But before she had a chance, I pulled her away from the edge and forced her down behind the parapet.

"What is it?!" she squawked, startled and annoyed.

"It's them! Oh, my gosh! It's them!"

We crawled back to the edge and peered over the lip of the parapet. In the dusky light, six figures had just marched over the rise and were presently making their way along the curve in the road that passed before the inn. It was Crotus and his five companions.

He hadn't started his march early this morning as he had told us. Something had delayed them. Further observation may have revealed the reason. The men were singing—some song about victory and honor that was no doubt a soldier's ballad. They'd removed their helmets. Their voices were slurred. The men had already started celebrating their release to journey home. They were drunk.

Steffanie turned white. "They're coming this way!"

To our horror, the men were pulling off the road and approaching the inn. Of all the inns in Judea—this couldn't be happening!

"Where's Jim and Mom?" I asked.

"Sabrina's lying down in the room," said Steff. "Dad's around back, checking on our donkey."

"We have to warn them. How can we warn them?"

Steffanie and I were trapped on the roof. The stairway leading down to the ground level was completely exposed to the soldiers' eyes. We'd have to pass right in front of them!

Don't panic, I told myself. I began to crawl to the other end of the roof. Steffanie stayed behind to watch their movements. Upon reaching the opposite wall, I looked down toward the stables. Immediately I saw Jim talking with the boy he'd paid to take care of our animal. I waved my arms to try and get Jim's attention. I couldn't shout; the soldiers would have heard me. But my movements were drawing the attention of every other tenant and servant in the yard as they tended to their camels and other beasts. Any second the Romans would look up to see what everyone found so interesting. Jim continued to speak with the boy. What was the matter with him? Just turn your eyes!

I grabbed a piece of broken plaster from the edge of the parapet and hurled it toward the stable. As it clattered to the earth, Jim was alerted at last. He looked around and saw my arms waving. I urged him to come closer. The other tenants watched with curiosity as Jim crossed the yard and stood directly below me.

I pointed around to the other side of the building. "Crotus," I whispered.

Jim's face flooded with dread. The entrance where he might have warned Mom was blocked. Jim noted that many people in the yard were watching. He motioned me to stay cool and calm.

I leaned away from the parapet to keep out of view, then looked back toward Steffanie. She indicated that the men were directly below her, probably negotiating with the Greek proprietor. As I made my way back, I started to hear the men's obnoxious tones. They were taunting the Greek.

"Since we'll be leaving before sunup," Crotus snarled, "we should only have to pay for half the night." His men grunted in agreement.

"Where's the women?" one soldier boisterously inquired. "You do have women, don't you?"

I realized that the premises had been cleared. The other tenants had taken refuge in their rooms.

"If you'd like to sleep in the yard," said the proprietor, "I'll charge you nothing at all."

"I've been sleeping on the ground for four years in this flea-infested country," barked Crotus. "I want a bed!"

At that moment, the unthinkable occurred. My mother appeared in the entranceway directly below us. At first she took in the scene with a look of innocence, just seeing what all the commotion was about. As her mistake dawned, she tried to melt back inside.

"Hey!" one of Crotus' men announced. "Look there! It's that woman!"

Jim could no longer hang back. My mother's mistake had forced him to come around the building. He walked right through the soldiers and joined her in the entranceway. The soldiers watched, mystified at his boldness.

Mom and Jim disappeared inside, obviously to retreat back to their room. The soldiers suddenly looked very sober.

"Hey, peddler!" Crotus cried out. "Where's your daughters, the witches?" He turned to the proprietor. "Are they boarders here?"

"Yes, they are my guests. Please. I'm a Roman citizen. I don't want any trouble."

"Then you shouldn't cater to witches and charlatans, you Greek slug. Get out of my way!"

Crotus marched toward the building. My heart exploded with panic. The Roman's eyes were glowing with murder.

The grubby little proprietor followed at Crotus' heels. "Wait! I could turn them out. Would that satisfy you? Don't damage my property!"

Crotus stormed inside. One of the soldiers glanced up toward the roof. I pulled back sharply and ducked down. Steffanie cowered beside me.

"What are we going to do, Meagan?"

My eyes searched around. There was no escape!

I could hear footsteps thundering on the stairway. At last the soldier appeared on the landing, his mouth twisted into a brutal smile. "Crotus!" he shouted. "Forget the father! I have the two witches!"

We shrieked and scrambled to the opposite edge. I looked over the parapet. We were two stories up. I'd likely break my leg, but there was no other choice.

In the instant before I leaped, I raised my eyes toward the orange sunset. Why I would look up at that moment was beyond my comprehension. But the action caused me to stop. At the top of the hill overlooking the inn, a figure had appeared in the roadway. The silhouette of a man riding a horse. On his head was the plumed helmet of a Roman centurion.

CHAPTER 19

We were late.

I didn't think it mattered. I knew the cargo in Stephanas' ship would take several hours to unload. What did it matter if we showed up a few minutes after midnight? In reality, it was closer to an hour and a half. Just late enough that by the time we arrived, the disaster was already over.

We found the second shipping house on the lower pier without any problem. The two lamps were still burning on the dock. The outlines of a hundred ships lazily rocked and creaked out in the harbor. Stephanas' ship was moored alongside the stone platform, but there were no workers unloading crates of fish. As far as we could tell, there was nobody there at all. The place was as quiet as a cemetery. A feeling of dread trickled down my back. Something awful had happened. Nobody had to tell me; this was Chrysoganus' doing. Stephanas had been wrong about him. The Mithraist astrologer had betrayed his friend.

But then as Jesse and I crept around a stack of lumber, we saw a man sitting alone in the center of the shipping house. Beside him was a pyramid of vats. They were from Stephanas' boat—the jars containing fish sauce. Several of the vats had been broken. Their slimy contents were spread across the floor, reflecting in the lamplight. I reached into the stack of lumber until my hands found a rounded stick about six feet long. As I retrieved it, other sticks clattered and the man arose with a start. He grabbed his lantern and held it high. The pudgy face was illuminated. It was Chrysoganus, looking distressed.

"Who's there?" he called out.

Jesse prepared to flee, but I held my ground. I wasn't going any-where. Not before I found out what had happened.

"It's Harrius," I said, stepping into the light. Gripping my staff more firmly, I asked, "Where's Stephanas?"

He appeared relieved that I wasn't someone else. "Run, Harrius!" he said. "Don't stay here. The police are out in force."

"What happened?" I demanded.

He came toward me, stopping only when he saw that I was deter-mined to strike him if he didn't stop. "They've been arrested."

I shivered. "All of them?"

"Stephanas, his three sons, the Jewish boy, Micah. Yes, they've all been taken to the Governor's palace."

My eyes narrowed. "You betrayed them, didn't you?"

"No," said Chrysoganus. "It was my foreman back at the agora. As I'd feared, he recognized Stephanas earlier today. He notified the Council. I was followed here. Shortly after Stephanas and the others arrived, the police surrounded us. You shouldn't waste any more time. They've only been gone a few minutes."

"You led them right to him," I seethed. "You broke your oath."

"I swear to you in the name of Mithras that I had nothing to do with this. My heart is as sick as yours."

"And your purse is a lot richer. Nice new boat. A whole cargo of fish—"

"I would never do anything to hurt my friend. On the contrary, I've already spent far more than the value of that cargo trying to help him. Since we parted, I've been visiting friends in an effort to influ-ence the Civic Council to recall the anti-Christian edicts."

"I don't believe you," I said. "You're lying. Why didn't they arrest you, too? I thought doing business with Christians was illegal."

He hung his head. "They didn't arrest me because my foreman told them I was doing business with Christians in ignorance."

"How kind of him," I sneered. "How convenient for you."

"It was neither. Tomorrow he'll use it to blackmail me for every-thing he can."

"And you just watched them haul Stephanas away? Some friend. Some oath."

He bristled a little. "I'm of far more worth to my friend *out* of prison." His countenance fell again. "But you're right. This is all my fault. I'm just a stupid old fishmonger. I should have anticipated my foreman's actions. He blames Christians for poisoning the mind of his wife. But trust me when I tell you that everything that's happened tonight will be nullified tomorrow afternoon."

"Why?" I asked suspiciously.

He looked around, afraid to speak too loudly. He drew a little closer. "Today I offered generous gifts to three principal members of the Areopagus—the Civic Council of Athens. Just enough to sway the vote in our favor. The vote, however, may not take place until after the arraignment."

"Arraignment?"

"Of Stephanas and his sons, as well as the reexamination of any other Christians still in the civic dungeons. The Council will convene at noon. Fabius Grannicus, the provincial governor, will preside. They'll be questioned by Epigonus or by the Stoic leader, Zeno Posidonius. The charge will be joining a dangerous sect. If they refuse to swear a vulgar curse against your Christian God, they'll be returned to the dungeon, starved for several more days, then brought before the Council again. But in Stephanas' case, I don't expect it to go that far. If everything proceeds as planned, he'll be released before the end of the day."

"What if your friends don't vote the way you want?"

"Don't worry about that," said Chrysoganus. "It would ruin their reputations. They'd never receive bribes again. They won't risk spoiling that."

I was amazed that taking bribes could be a reputation worth preserving.

"But it's only three men. How many are on this Council?"

"The Areopagus has seventy members. But the only ones who show up are the ones with financial motives. Usually fifteen or twenty."

"Three men can make a difference?"

"They only get paid if our cause is adopted. If they doubt their own clout to pass a measure, they'll inform me. We'll be given the option of recruiting other Council members on the spot. There's a whole array of signals that the Areopogites use to communicate to us and to each other from the committee well. Our success often depends on how much we're willing to spend."

So this, I thought, was the level to which Athens had sunk. So much for the birthplace of democracy.

I corrected Chrysoganus. "How much *you're* willing to spend. I don't have any money."

"Yes," he said ruefully. "How much *I'm* willing to spend."

I still didn't trust him, and I didn't understand all these political games. But what else could we do? Our only choice was to play it the way Chrysoganus had outlined.

A thought occurred to me. If Epigonus was going to be there interrogating the prisoners at noon, he'd certainly bring his body-guards. Mary and the scrolls might be left relatively unguarded. This might be our chance—perhaps our only chance. Did Jesse and I dare attempt the rescue by ourselves?

I desperately wanted to watch the arraignment, hear the Council vote. I couldn't do it. A chance like this might not come again. In spite of all my doubts and fears, I'd have to trust Chrysoganus one more time.

Chrysoganus looked nervous, as if staying here any longer was toying with fate. "I'd invite you to come to my home," he said, "but . . . I fear the police might be watching."

"We're hungry," said Jesse boldly.

Chrysoganus found a purse under his robes. He loosed it and handed me a few coins. "You might find an eating house still open along the waterfront. I'll see you tomorrow at noon. The Council House is below Mars Hill, west of the Acropolis. Just follow the crowd."

"We won't be able to see you until after it's over," I said. "We have something important to do beforehand."

Chrysoganus looked tentative. "All right. But be warned: if Stephanas and the others are freed, I'll advise them to sail away from Athens very swiftly."

"Tell them we'll meet them here," I said. I searched Chrysoganus' face one more time for a hint of deceit. His eyes looked warm and genuine. I hoped I was judging right. "Good luck. And thank you."

We left the lower pier. Jesse and I wandered along the waterfront toward the main thoroughfare, hoping to find some eating houses still serving food. We had a lot to plan. Tomorrow morning, I expected to be back hiding in those woods outside Epigonus' estate.

We reached a lighted area where several dozen small boats had been dragged out of the water. Ahead of us stood a cluster of people, anxiously conversing over some important matter. As we drew nearer, an alarm sounded in my head. The men were heavily armed, but they weren't soldiers. They could only have been Athenian police.

We couldn't stop walking now. It would look suspicious. We tried to maneuver ourselves to the far side of the platform where we could walk casually past. One of them noticed us and narrowed his eyes. "You there!" he shouted.

We stopped. The other men turned as well.

"What are you doing?" the man asked sternly.

I glanced behind me, as if I wasn't sure he was talking to me.

"Yes, you. Where are you going?"

"We were hungry," I replied. "We're looking for a restaurant."

He took a step toward us. "At this hour?"

I was still holding the stick, though I now tried to make it look like a walking staff. My grip on it tightened.

"Where did you come from?" he demanded. His eyes glanced back toward Chrysoganus' shipping house—the place where several Christians had just been arrested.

"W-we came from the city," I said. My voice had no conviction.

"Are you Christians?"

We stiffened. It was the one question I couldn't have denied.

Another man stepped between the others—Chrysoganus' grim-faced foreman. "He *is* a Christian! I saw him earlier with the Corinthian and the Jew."

We sized each other up for a few tense seconds. The policeman made his lunge. I drew back the staff and swung it like a baseball bat, hitting the man's shoulder. He toppled off to the side. I dropped the stick, and Jesse and I took off at a dead run back in the direction of the lower pier.

"Stop!" a policeman shouted.

They all joined in the pursuit. We reached a bridge that crossed a drainage canal. Instead of crossing, we veered to the right along its bank. The canal was walled in. The water smelled rank, no doubt from the day's runoff. The drop to the surface was seven or eight feet. It was twice that distance to the opposite shore—impossible to clear.

A wooden fence forced us to veer again. The policemen divided to head us off.

"Climb it!" I told Jesse. He was already pulling himself over. I leaped up to do the same, throwing my legs over the other side just as two policemen tried to grab me. The canal on this side of the fence had a lower wall—a drop of only about five feet. Farther upstream, it looked as if there might be places to climb out onto the opposite bank.

"Jump!" I shouted. "Swim upstream."

For the second time today, we leaped into foul-smelling water. It was deeper than I'd thought. My feet touched the bottom. I propelled myself toward the surface and began swimming north. It was pitch dark—no burning lanterns to guide me. I could see the shadows of several policemen following along the bank. I could hear Jesse kicking behind me. A stone building blocked the policemen's progress. Their swords and other encumbrances proved to our advantage. None of them leaped into the water. Two tried to go around the building; several others ran back toward the bridge, presumably to nab us as we climbed out on the other side.

We continued swimming upstream another twenty yards, and finally reached a place where the bank sloped into the water like a boat ramp. The shelf of dry cement was enclosed by high walls. I saw broken buckets and smelled vinegar. It was a place for washing clothes. We stood dripping on the platform, trying to figure out a way to climb out. Ground level appeared to be at the top of the walls. We saw a wooden gate just ahead. I found the handle and pulled, but something tied it shut. It wasn't a chain, just a thick rope.

"Give me your knife," I said to Jesse.

He placed it in my hand, and I sawed the rope until it snapped. The gate fell open. Beyond it stretched a narrow stairway. We climbed it hastily and emerged at ground level.

It was a crossroads. Directly ahead stretched a narrow avenue bathed in moonlight. I started to enter the street, then I hesitated.

Jesse halted beside me. He looked at me curiously. "What's wrong?"

I didn't reply, just stared ahead at the moonlit shapes of doorways and pitched roofs. I felt a strange foreboding, as if something evil was down that path. Yet it was our only escape. The other street left us in full view of the police.

"Let's go," I said.

We started running. The shadowy buildings on either side fell behind us. We'd gone forty yards. All at once we ground to another halt.

From a space between two buildings an animal emerged, its back lit by the blue sheen of the moon. In its throat rumbled a terrible growl.

Terror fanned out from my heart like fingers of ice. A tigerhound? Impossible! What was it doing here? How had it—?

But then from the same thin gap emerged the dark outline of a horse and rider, his long black hair also emitting a blue sheen. The Scythian bodyguard! How could he have tracked us all the way from Epigonus' estate? His face shone, but not with light. It was the specter of something else. What had Chrysoganus said?—a demon ghost who guided Scythians to their prey. I remembered now. Neuri. It was there. I swear it was glowing in his eyes.

My feet were frozen. They wouldn't move, as if attached to the ground by deep roots. Blood pounded in my ears. The Scythian spoke a single word, low and guttural. I didn't hear it. But the dog understood. It broke into a charge.

The roots that held my feet tore free. Jesse's reaction was even swifter. He was ahead of me by several strides. The river. We were both running for the river. Never mind the stairs; we'd launch straight off the wall. I had no doubt that I could clear the shelf, but I seriously doubted my ability to outrun the hound. I could hear it behind me. I could also hear the hooves of the horse.

Just ten more yards. Jesse was only inches from making his leap. But then the dog pounced. Its claws dug into my back and I landed flat on my stomach, the rough concrete grinding into my elbows and knees. I felt the creature's breath as it prepared to bury its teeth in my neck. Jesse's knife—it was still in my grip. I shut my eyes and rolled, swinging wildly. I didn't expect the knife to hit. But it did connect, sinking up to my fist in the flesh of the dog's neck. The animal released a piercing yelp. I let go of the knife and pushed the beast away. Its limp body toppled over the edge, crumpling onto the landing below.

There were no further whimpers. The dog was dead. I looked up to see the thundering hooves of the Scythian's horse flying at me. I twisted out of the way. The Scythian reined in his mount. The horse turned, raising the dust.

I caught one glance—one fleeting glance—of the Scythian's face. He glared down at me from his saddle, the demon ghost still glowing in his eyes. The tattoos of the snakes looked alive and striking. I saw hatred, black and burning.

I turned to run, but I couldn't leap into the river. A stone barrier blocked my access. Just twenty feet, then I'd be clear to leap. It might as well have been a hundred miles. I braced myself for the shooting pain of an arrow between my shoulder blades. After that, I knew I would feel the cold steel of his double-bladed knife as he removed my scalp.

I was almost there—I'd almost reached the end of the barrier—when the weapon struck. But it wasn't an arrow or a knife. I felt the crack of a metal ball on my shin. My legs became entangled, and I tripped onto my hands. The Scythian had thrown a chain. He'd brought me down like a mountain goat. He didn't want to kill me. Just immobilize me. Then he'd have plenty of time to exact his full vengeance for the death of his dog.

Noises erupted in the street ahead—voices. Within seconds I was surrounded by several pairs of legs. The *policemen*. They'd reached me first! Who'd have thought I'd ever be grateful—*grateful*—to be in their custody?

I was hoisted to my feet. I tried desperately to look back and see the Scythian on his horse. Or maybe I'd see Jesse. It occurred to me that I hadn't seen him leap, although I vaguely remembered hearing a splash. Once again, the Jewish orphan appeared to have escaped.

But as for Epigonus' bodyguard—the long street was dark and empty. The Scythian horseman was gone.

* * * * * *

As the cell door slammed behind me, I caught only a brief glimpse of the faces of my friends before the guards swiftly carried away the lanterns. I was limping. The chain with the hard metal ball had left a deep bruise on my shin. Micah and Stephanas found me in the darkness and helped me to the far side of the cell. I was sure I'd counted five or six other men before the light of the lantern faded. Three of them were Stephanas' sons—Paul, Peter, and Andrew. The other three I didn't recognize.

Micah expressed his relief to see me. He was sure I'd been killed by the man in the hood. I told him about Jesse, and about Mary and the sacred scrolls at Epigonus' estate. Stephanas asked several questions. I think I answered them. After only a few minutes, lying on the stone floor with a musty-smelling blanket under my head, I fell fast asleep.

When I awakened, daylight streamed through the barred window in a rear wall. The bruise on my leg was still tender. The others were already awake. Paul brought me a ladle filled with water, which I drank thirstily. I finally had a good look at the other three Christians in the cell. They were gaunt, almost listless. There was an older man with silver hair, a younger man in his twenties whose hair came down to his shoulders, and a third man who was so weak he kept his face to the wall.

"How do you feel?" Micah inquired. "How's your leg?"

"Sore," I answered. "But I'll live."

"You never told us how you were arrested," said Peter.

"Same as you, I guess. I was grabbed by the police."

"Chrysoganus double-crossed us all," Micah declared.

I considered my reply, then said, "I don't think it was Chrysoganus. I spoke to him. He said it was his foreman."

Stephanas nodded. "Caius. Yes, I remember him from the old days. I knew it wasn't Chrysoganus."

"They're *all* against us," said the younger man with shoulder-length hair. "None is better than the other."

"Chrysoganus said there will be a vote today in the Civic Council," I informed them. "He believes the edicts against Christians will be repealed."

"The Council is corrupt," scoffed the silver-haired man. "They only vote when it will make them money. I know. I used to be one of them."

Stephanas made the introductions. The older man was named Dionysius. He'd been a counselor to Bishop Silvanus, who was crucified. Stephanas called him the "first convert of Athens," along with his wife, Demaris, who languished in another cell on an upper level. Also on another level was Luke. They informed me that the old physician was in a chamber called "the pit." No one was certain if he was still alive.

The second man who lay with his face to the wall was named Erastus. Stephanas had known him vaguely from his days at Corinth. Before his arrest, Erastus had served as a treasurer for the provincial governor. His position hadn't made him immune from persecution. He nodded when introduced, but otherwise he hardly stirred.

The younger man was named Ignatius. He claimed his father was a bishop in Antioch. He'd been sent to Athens to serve as a missionary. He wasn't nearly as weak as his cellmates, having been apprehended five days after them.

"I turned myself in," he felt the need to tell me. "I wanted to join in the suffering with my fellow Christians."

I looked at him strangely. What an odd choice. I returned to my subject. "Chrysoganus says he bribed several councilmen to vote in our favor. I believe him. The vote is supposed to take place this afternoon, right after our arraignment."

"An expensive proposition," said Dionysius. "We have many enemies among the Areopogites. A vote is like an auction." He looked at Stephanas. "How much is your friend willing to spend?"

"I don't know," Stephanas replied. "Chrysoganus is an honest man, but I don't know how deep his purse is."

"If Epigonus can introduce his new edict, the price of passing any legislation in our favor will shoot up as high as Mount Olympus."

I sat up. "New edict?"

"It seems that starving us is taking too long," said Dionysius. "Epigonus wants to set an example for the future. If we reject the Council's demand to curse the name of Christ again, he'll call for our immediate execution."

I was stunned. "Are you sure?"

"That's the rumor," said Dionysius. "The guards are good at spreading rumors."

Ignatius piped in. "Good. I say it's about time. It's better than wasting away in here day after day. It's an honor to die for Christ. I welcome it."

Another bizarre notion, I thought. "I'm sure we'd all rather *live* for Christ than die for Him."

Ignatius continued. "Our names would be honored for all generations, like Peter and all the martyrs. Our souls would be guaranteed a seat at the right hand of Power."

Dionysius scolded him mildly. "Now, Ignatius. It's a sin to desire martyrdom. If it happens, it will be a blessing, but only if it's by the will of God."

I gawked at them both. Who in their right mind would *desire mar-*

tyrdom? "I don't know about you, but I'd rather find a way to be honored where I didn't have to die."

"You sound as if you fear it, Harrius," said Ignatius. "Let go of that fear. This is a world of sorrow and pain. It's better to think of the world to come."

"The next world will come in its own sweet time," I responded. "It's better to think about enduring to the end."

"If you've accepted Christ, then you've endured all you need to endure," said Ignatius. "I yearn to seal my testimony with my blood. Then I would cease to be just a voice or a sound. I would become a Word of God."

Wow, I thought. Nothing like having a goal. This was getting too twisted for my tastes. Fortunately, Stephanas came to the rescue.

"Harrius is right. We should think about *living* for Christ. I have a wife and seven grandchildren. If Chrysoganus is determined to help us, I'll put my faith in God that he will succeed."

Ignatius huffed and walked away. *Peculiar man,* I thought. The adage came to mind: be careful what you wish for . . .

Just before noon our cell was unlocked, and the guards marched in and surrounded us. Poor Erastus hardly had the strength to stand. A guard on either side dragged him along. En route we were joined by twenty-four other Christians who'd been kept in different cells. All of them looked pale and ragged, wandering half-consciously as the guards prodded them with their javelins. It was a heartbreaking sight.

Most of the captive Christians appeared to be women—eighteen in all. No surprise there, I supposed. As for the approximately three hundred Saints who'd once been part of Athens' congregation, half had been arrested, the rest had fled. Half of *those* had denied the faith on their first examination, and another third had succumbed after the first four days. Those who remained, beside those of us arrested the night before, were eighteen women and nine men. And of course, Luke the physician, who at the moment did not join us.

We were paraded through the streets toward the Council House at the foot of Mars Hill. I might have expected the citizens to be abusive, tossing garbage and filth. But they just watched us in silence. Some shook their heads, baffled. I'm sure they wondered why we were being so stubborn. Why wouldn't we just recite a few words, drink a little

wine in Caesar's name? We must have seemed to them the most ignorant simpletons. Some of the people looked genuinely sorrowful.
These persecutions had gone to extremes that I don't think they had
expected. Many were shedding tears. A few of these might have been
former Christians who'd denied the faith. Others were family members and friends who were trying desperately to understand why their
loved ones were doing what they were doing.

Erastus was pursued by a middle-aged woman who begged him to
come home. "Do what they want!" she cried. "Say whatever they ask!
Please, my husband. Come back to me!"

Erastus wouldn't look at her. His eyes streamed tears. A guard
finally pushed her back.

It was only a couple hundred yards to the Council House, though
it seemed like miles. The meeting hall of the Areopogites was a round
building supported by eighteen pillars. There were walls between
some of the pillars, but mostly it was open to the outside air. A hole
in the roof illuminated the area where the Civic Council was seated.
A contraption for pulling a canvas over the top was available in bad
weather. Circling around three sides of the House were twenty levels
for public viewing, like an amphitheater. Many places outside the
building were also available if someone wanted to overhear. There
were no chairs or benches; the public sat on the hard stone. Council
members brought their own little folding chairs, made of ebony wood
and other exotic materials. Servants planted each chair in its appropriate place in the committee well.

As we climbed the steps leading inside, I saw Epigonus' carriage. I
also saw the Scythians' horses. My heart tightened. It felt as if my
opportunity to rescue Mary and save the scrolls had passed me by. I
looked around for the bodyguards and saw them just as I entered the
building. They were standing at the topmost tier. Absolutely no one
stood near them, although the rest of the House was filled to capaci-
ty. The one with serpents on his cheeks seared me with his gaze, his
hatred as intense as ever. He looked poised to strike out at me even
now, his fingers curved like claws. I was tempted to blow him a kiss,
but I only smiled.

I was led down to the main floor with the other prisoners. I had
an irrational hope that I might see Jesse. A foolish idea. He wouldn't

risk coming here. But I searched just the same. I needed to know he was safe. I needed to know that after the Scythian had finished with me, his demon ghost hadn't continued stalking Jesse.

My eyes connected with Chrysoganus. He was on the lowest tier, directly facing the Council. He nodded to me subtly. His face was tense; it made me nervous. As I looked at the committee well, I felt I had an inkling why. Hadn't he said that only fifteen or twenty councilmen showed up to these things? There were over fifty guys down there! Counting later, the number was sixty-eight. Only two of them were even missing! Something was up. I felt a coiling in my stomach. This could only have been due to the rumor of Epigonus' new edict.

Upon reaching the floor, I saw Epigonus, his bulbous body spilling over the sides of his folding chair. He'd seated himself front and center, just below the place reserved for the provincial governor. His face was frowning, eyes unfocused. His mouth was closed, but his tongue slithered around inside, polishing and sucking at his teeth.

A few feet to his left sat a bony, long-necked man who reminded me of Icabod Crane. His eyes darted around like a pigeon. This, I assumed, was the leader of the Stoics, Zeno Posidonius. Like Epigonus, he wore a frown, as if to appear the neutral judge of all he surveyed.

It was easy to tell an Epicurean from a Stoic. Epicureans wore far fancier clothes, while Stoics looked rather plain. There were far more Stoics than Epicureans in attendance. I only counted a dozen or so Epicureans seated very close to Epigonus. Epicureans, according to Stephanas, only served the public if there was profit in it. As he'd put it, "Stoics think it's noble to suffer; Epicureans think it's noble to indulge."

The thirty-two of us huddled together. For the first time in days, Dionysius found his wife's hand and clutched it with all of his feeling. It was the only affection he dared to express. The one sad omission from our group continued to be Luke.

Some dark-robed priests entered the building, walking with perfect posture to avoid tipping the towering hats on their heads. Each carried a small marble statue, usually the bust of someone's head. Some statues had animal features, while others represented some creature-shape that I couldn't have guessed. The statues were placed at the edge of the committee well. Idols, I realized. For our arraignment, every deity of Greece would stand as a witness.

All at once, the audience rose to its feet. A man in a white and purple toga descended the steps and sat in the space reserved for the provincial governor. The crowd saluted him with the cry, "Hail Grannicus, Governor of Achaia! Hail Vespasian, Emperor of Rome!"

He was obviously the Governor, not the Emperor. Nevertheless, the audience felt inclined to salute them both. Grannicus took his seat and motioned the crowd to do the same. Afterwards, he tried his best not to look bored.

A brief, memorized prayer was offered to Athena and Zeus, its words lauding the "wise and virtuous" character of the Areopagus of Athens. When it was concluded, the Governor nodded to the Stoic leader, Zeno Posidonius, and said, "Proceed."

Zeno stood and cleared his throat. "Our first order of business, as has been our first order for the last three sessions, is to once again show compassion for our wayward citizens gathered here. We will offer all those deceived by the superstitions of the Jesus cult, as it has come to be known, an opportunity to recant such sentiments, just as most of their colleagues, and receive in response an immediate vindication.

"We have wasted enough of this Council's time discussing the dangerous, immoral, and anti-social influences of this sect. We all agree that its philosophies naturally undermine devotions to the Emperor, the laws of our city, and the common good of the people. I move therefore that we call forth the accused."

"Here, here," muttered a few voices.

A scribe stood and read from a wax tablet. "Dionysius of Eretria!"

The aged counselor of the former bishop reluctantly released his wife's hand and feebly climbed the three steps to the top of a podium that faced the Council.

"Dionysius of Eretria," continued Zeno. "You are accused of illegally practicing the craft of Christianity. For the sake of the multitude, please repeat your plea."

"Guilty," said Dionysius softly, leaning heavily on the wooden bar. Zeno put a hand to his ear. "I'm sorry. What say you?"

"Guilty," he repeated a little louder.

"It is with great mercy that this Council extends to you an opportunity to declare publicly your willingness to terminate any further associations with this society. In token of such termination, you will invoke the gods, reverence the image of the Emperor with incense and wine, and publicly accurse the name of Jesus Christ. Will you submit to these stipulations?"

Dionysius was having a hard time concentrating.

"What say you?" Zeno repeated loudly.

He perked up and shook his head. "No. No, I . . . I don't. Not willing . . ."

"Do you mean to say that you are not willing to discontinue your affiliations with this sect?"

"Yes," Dionysius nodded. "I will not discontinue . . ."

The crowd murmured, but it wasn't in disapproval. I sensed that they were troubled to see a man in such a weakened state forced to endure such a harsh examination. Epigonus looked concerned. He didn't want to lose his thread of public support.

"Dionysius, you are a former member of this body. I am incensed that you would show it such contempt." He turned to the scribe. "The accused will leave the podium. He will remain in custody until he submits to the law."

"The accused, Dionysius of Eretria, will leave the podium."

Dionysius climbed down, his legs barely supporting his weight.

The next Christian was called forth, a woman. Her name was Valentinia. She looked even more frail than Dionysius. As she tried to climb the podium, she collapsed and had to be stood on her feet by the guards. Discontented whispering continued among the people. Zeno offered her the same opportunity to curse Christ and reaffirm her devotion to the gods of Athens. Like Dionysius, she held strong, boldly rejecting Zeno. My heart ached for her, and yet it soared in triumph for the faith of the Saints.

One by one each of the accused was called forth, mustering all of their strength to stand tall and reject the Council, proclaiming their love for Jesus. Stephanas was called up, followed by his sons. "Guilty," they replied solemnly to the accusations. "No," they declared when asked to curse His name.

Erastus took the stand, also helped by the guards. He wouldn't raise his eyes. At first I thought this was out of weakness. Then I realized that it was out of shame.

"Repeat your plea for the gathering," said Zeno.

"Guilty," Erastus replied.

"Will you terminate all Christian affiliations, invoke the gods, and publicly curse the name of Jesus Christ?"

Erastus was trembling. Still unable to look up, he said, "Yes."

The crowd hushed.

Zeno leaned forward. "You will curse the name of Jesus and reverence the image of the Emperor?"

Choked with emotion, he said again, "Yes."

Zeno grinned. "The accused will recite the curse. He will then accompany the priests to the Acropolis to perform the necessary oblations. After which . . . you are free, Erastus."

From the throat of one of the priests rumbled the words of the curse. Erastus repeated every phrase. The words were vile and poisonous. He cursed everything about our beloved Savior: His name, His birth, His parentage, His status in the heavens. I don't remember the specific words; I tried to block them out. But when he was finished, I realized that I was trembling too.

The guards carried Erastus from the podium. With several priests, he left the House, headed toward the temples of the Acropolis. The Christians were shaken, and yet by the faces of Dionysius and Ignatius, I felt that they were not surprised.

Next, they called up Micah. He looked proud, almost jubilant as he climbed the podium. I stood in as his interpreter. The heaviness that had descended with Erastus lifted immediately as Micah professed his faith in the Lord Jesus Christ. My gratitude overflowed to think that God had blessed me with the opportunity to teach and bear testimony to him all those months ago in the dark hold of a slave ship.

Next, the scribe called forth the name of Ignatius of Antioch. Ignatius mounted the stand with all the bluster of a lead actor taking center stage.

Zeno had barely started to speak when Ignatius blurted out, "Yes, I am guilty. *Guilty* in my love of Jesus! *Guilty* in my conviction that His kingdom will one day crush all the kingdoms of the world and damn its inhabitants! And *guilty* in my condemnation of this corrupt Council and all its Satanic officers. Ye who serve the Serpent, beware the torments of hell! Prepare yourselves to face His wrath! In His holy name I declare it! And in His holy name I condemn you all!"

My nerves were set on edge. The resentment of the audience was stirring all over again. By what authority did Ignatius think he could condemn *anybody?* And yet some of the Saints looked upon him with awe.

When Ignatius confessed that he was a Roman citizen, the Council offered to ship him to Rome to plead his case there.

"I will plead my case wherever you send me! To the ends of the earth! Into the very heart of hell! Until the people of this city and all the enemies of God are trampled underfoot, and His Saints given dominion over all the world!"

Guards were dispatched to physically remove him from the podium. I was half tempted to help them. Ignatius was dragged out of the Assembly House, spitting venom and hate the entire way.

It was my unfortunate honor to be called as the follow-up act.

"Harrius of . . ." The scribe squinted at the word. He pronounced it carefully. "A-mer-ee-ka."

Zeno looked at me narrowly. "Harrius of America? Where is this land, America?"

"Across the ocean," I said.

"In Africa?"

"No. The *Atlantic* ocean."

That caused a murmur. But then there were splutterings of laughter.

"There *is* no land across *Oceanus Atlanticus* that may be reached by man or boat. Are you mocking this Council?"

"Not at all," I said. "That's where I'm from."

He asked jeeringly, "Would you mind enlightening us as to how you made this remarkable journey?"

I hesitated, then replied, "You wouldn't believe it."

More laughter. The councilmen looked equally entertained.

"I'm sure you're right," said Zeno. "So in this imaginary land of yours, are they all Christians?"

"No," I said. "Not all of them. But we still try to get along."

"I see. So in this imaginary land there are Stoics and Epicureans, pagans and Mithraists, Jews and Cynics?"

"I'm sure there's a little bit of everything," I said.

"A regular shepherd's stew, I take it, eh?"

The audience laughed.

"Yes," I replied.

"And like in Athens, do you Christians rapaciously condemn all other philosophies, sentencing to hell those who hold opinions different from your own?"

"I hope not," I said. "It would be wrong if we did. We do our best to show love."

"Love?"

"Yes. That's what Christ is all about. He's about love. He's about tolerance and long-suffering. We don't want to force the things we believe on anybody. We just want to share. Christ gives a person hope. Because of Him, we know that we can all live again."

"Oh, I see. So after enduring this life once, we have to endure it again?"

He'd meant it as a joke, but no one laughed.

"It won't be the same. The next time, there's no suffering. We'll be together with God and our loved ones for all eternity. Christ teaches us that all the confusion and grief we experience here are only fleeting things. It's all over before we know it. And it's *worth it*. That's the best message of all. Everything we learn—*every good thing*—we take with us into the kingdom of God and enjoy its blessings forever. That's the message of Christ. It's that simple."

The audience was silent.

Zeno huffed in contempt. "Yes, yes, that's all very lovely and idyllic. If your people are so full of *love*, why do they commit treason against the Empire? Why do they repudiate all the sacred traditions of our fathers? Why do they hold secret meetings before sunrise to engage in ceremonies of incest and cannibalism, eating the flesh and drinking the blood of your dead God?"

I let this sink in, then I laughed softly. "I don't know what religion you're referring to, but it definitely isn't Christianity. We believe in being good subjects to *every* ruler. In fact, we try to be the best citizens we can—the most patriotic, the most loyal, the most hard-working. We certainly don't do any of the things you mentioned. The flesh and blood are symbolic. It's really just bread and wine. We partake of them to honor the Risen Lord. All we ask is the right to practice what we believe according to our own conscience. But I hope we would also defend everybody else's right to do the same thing, as long as their practices aren't harmful and evil."

"Ah ha!" snapped Zeno, certain he'd caught me in a trap. "And there's your loophole! Just call the Emperor evil—call the philosophies of everyone else harmful—and you are justified in your prejudices and crimes. Correct?"

"No," I said. "*Not* correct. We firmly believe that every honest man can judge good or evil for himself, whether he's a Christian or not. There are good people in every society. But there is also evil. The things that we call evil are pretty much the same things you call evil. We believe a person who follows the Spirit and strives to do what is right will cast off evil things and cling to things that are good. That's the whole reason God put us on earth—to work and improve, learn and progress. That's the only way we can truly be happy."

Members of the Council stirred. I had a feeling I'd touched on some of the Epicureans' and the Stoics' own philosophies.

Zeno frowned. He regretted his interrogation. Epigonus looked at his colleague with great annoyance.

Zeno brushed away my words like a mist of smoke. "This is nonsense and double-talk. This Council has declared that Christianity is an illegal and repugnant society. Are you a Christian?"

"I am," I said.

"Will you curse the name of Christ and make offerings to the gods of Rome and Athens?"

I said simply, "No."

"Thank you! The accused may leave the podium."

I calmly took my place among the others. Stephanas smiled at me—a smile of deep respect. The others also sent me looks of appreciation.

Zeno, however, had heard enough from all of us. "Are there any further examinations?"

The scribe studied his list. "None that are well enough at present to appear before this Council."

So Luke would not be appearing. And yet I found hope in the scribe's words. Luke may not have been well, but he was *alive*.

"Return these people to the dungeons," said Zeno. "We will move on to more important matters."

From the corner of my eye, I saw Chrysoganus nod toward the committee well.

A councilman sprang to his feet and spoke. "I move that these people *not* be dismissed. Our first order of business will relate directly to their plight and cause. May the accused remain in the House?"

The question was deferred to Grannicus, the governor, who appeared half-asleep. He stirred enough to reply, "Fine. Proceed."

Epigonus narrowly surveyed his colleagues. He also scanned the crowd of spectators, trying to figure out what was happening.

"The House recognizes Areopogite Modestus," said the governor's scribe.

Modestus stepped forward. Zeno reluctantly took his seat.

"Distinguished members of this Council," Modestus began, "it's high time we reevaluated the ill-conceived edict passed by this body with regard to the citizens displayed before us today. Look at them, people of Athens! Starved and berated, tortured and *crucified!* I am moved to tears to ponder their plight. I confess that their beliefs are crude, but they are the products of blissful ignorance! These people are not criminals. They have not undermined the Emperor. As this young man, Harrius, has so eloquently stated, they are among the most productive and law-abiding of our citizens. Yes, their teachings are unenlightened and obnoxious. Their harangues have been heard in our streets from dawn to dusk. But since when in Athens is it illegal to spout obnoxious rhetoric? If it were so, most of the men of this Council would be languishing in the Governor's dungeon!"

The audience laughed. A few councilmen even seemed to be laughing at themselves.

"I move that this silly edict be stricken from the tablets. I also move that we dismiss any penalties imposed for associating with Christians on any level of business or commerce."

That, I realized, was Chrysoganus' own special provision. It thwarted any efforts by his foreman to entrap him with blackmail.

Zeno came to his feet again. "This a lawful edict passed by this Council. Have you forgotten the principal crime of which these people are accused? They will not reverence the image of the Emperor!"

Chrysoganus sent another signal. Another councilman took the floor.

"I am in agreement with my noble colleague, Modestus. Let us repeal this edict. These people reverence our Emperor as much as any citizen of this land. They are harmless! What are we afraid of? A whim of fashion? A passing fad? Christian beliefs are too puerile to have a long-lasting effect. Do you think its teachings could really compete with the time-tested philosophies of Athens' greatest minds? It lives only because we fan its flames by making its adherents suffer. Do not ennoble this cause by giving it any more martyrs. Let it die the natural death of common sense!"

Councilmen were nodding. A murmur of approval was sweeping through their ranks. Many faces, however, were looking at Epigonus.

At last, like an elephant rising from the dust, Epigonus pulled his feet beneath his chair and stood upright. Just the sight of it demanded everyone's attention. He looked pale and breathless. Beads of sweat dangled on his brow.

"Fellow Areopogites," he began in his squeaky voice. "To even hear such sentiments expressed here today leaves me flabbergasted to the point of insensibility. Harmless? A passing fad? The products of blissful ignorance? Have we really grown so inflated in our own self-opinions that we would fail to recognize a pernicious evil when it tries to spread its infection among us? We can well claim that its appeal is only to the ignorant and superstitious. But I tell you, dear brothers, it is by the ignorant and superstitious that whole societies are obliterated. Do you not recognize it? Love and eternal happiness, indeed! These people threaten our very way of life! Do not be fooled! If they had the power, they would overthrow our emperor, our provincial governor, our laws, our philosophies—our very existence! They would set up their own kingdom in our midst and put us under its heel. They would ruthlessly condemn *anyone* who did not express full obeisance to their Christian God. Do you think they would grant us the same mercy that we have granted them? Would they allow us to recant and repent? Oh, no! I swear to you, we would fall under the sword faster than a serpent's strike. We have all seen the true Christian character; it is evident in the vituperations of the young man, Ignatius of Antioch! To them, we are all the children of hell!

"Do not be deceived by the gilded words of this boy, Harrius, who comes to us from his imaginary land at the edge of the earth. His sentiments are as fictional as his origins. Love, indeed! Perhaps the Council would be interested to learn that last night this loving boy assaulted a peace officer of Piraeus, inflicting an injury that could leave him impaired for weeks. Is this the act of a boy motivated by peace-loving philosophies? No! It is further evidence of how Christianity inclines the mind toward fits of hatred and violence.

"I am here to present a further amendment to the legally ratified edict to rid our community of the Christian scourge once and for all. Let us waste no more of this Council's precious time. Let us establish a precedent, brothers! Let it be known to all who may be tempted to embrace this sect in the future that if they refuse to submit to the will of the Civic Council, they will face swift execution! I call for an immediate vote— that is, before the hearts of too many of our esteemed colleagues shrivel at the prospect of passing a just sentence. Remember, these people have willfully chosen to take their suffering upon themselves!"

The Council stirred like a boiling pot, glancing about in every direction. Signals were flying—winks, coughing into fists, scratching the nose. It was a symphony of signals—some directed at Chrysoganus, some at Epigonus. Some to each other. Were the people of Athens really so dense as to think this Council was anything but a farce? And in the middle of it all, we Christians stood there and watched, holding our breath.

Chrysoganus nodded drearily. Another councilman stood. He moved that the proposal presented by Modestus should receive the first vote. Another councilman argued the case for Epigonus. It was a tennis match, the ball bouncing from Epigonus back to Chrysoganus. After a while, Chrysoganus hardly raised his eyes. He just nodded— just kept consenting to raise the price he would pay to his supporters.

At last a compromise was proposed by a councilman loyal to Chrysoganus. "We will not repeal the illegality of Christianity," he stated. "But neither will we imprison and starve its adherents. Nor will we levy a punishment against those who associate with them. Instead, we will impose a stiff fine against anyone who refuses to renounce his affiliations. If he cannot pay, he—or she—will suffer seven lashes in the public square. This humiliation should be more than adequate to help them ponder the error of their ways. Anyone caught preaching Christianity in public will automatically receive seven lashes. If caught a second time, they will be banished from the province. However, in the case of these poor people before us, how can we conscience a punishment any more severe than the one they have already received? If his honor the Governor will consent, we will now conduct the vote."

Grannicus agreed, and the voting commenced. We watched in suspense. The vote seemed to divide right down the middle. It was the very last vote—the vote cast by Modestus—that finally tipped the table in favor of the Christians.

The Christians of Athens shed tears of relief, but there was no cheering. They had no energy for that. But at least they were free. We'd won. Or so I thought until the bloated body of Epigonus arose from his chair one final time.

His face had flushed red. He was so angry he could hardly speak. His darkest gaze was directed toward Chrysoganus. He knew the author of his defeat. And I knew he would find a way to seek retribution.

"We will hold one final vote," Epigonus uttered. The Council House fell silent. Epigonus paused, still sweating profusely. I half-wondered if he might faint, but then he raged on. "I move that the leader called Luke be given special consideration beyond this newest amendment. Let him serve out his sentence as one of the original propagators of this wretched filth. A tree cannot live without its root. Cut out the root, brothers of the Areopagus!" The final word creaked out of the back of his throat. He was short of breath. At last he recovered and added, "Finally, I propose that Harrius of America be punished for his abuse of a peace officer of Piraeus. A capital crime in any other circumstance! Let at least this boy receive a lawful and just execution!"

I stood there, stunned. What had just happened? My companions stood around me, looking powerless and defeated. I turned to the committee well. The councilmen just sat there. Some shifted uncomfortably in their seats. Others glowered down on me. Not a single member rose to my defense. A feeling of panic began swelling inside me. To them, it was an acceptable compromise. The Council members, fearing the wrath of Epigonus, appeared only too happy to consent to this final injunction. I looked to Chrysoganus. He shook his head mournfully. I knew from that look that the old fishmonger had nothing left to give. He was broke. He'd sacrificed his entire fortune to fulfill an oath to a friend.

I remained there in a daze. The voting was like a whirlwind; it was over in a matter of minutes. I listened as the scribe declared the verdict, my mind sunken into a kind of trance. I was sentenced to death. Not death in a few weeks or months; none of the bureaucracies of the twenty-first century would bog things down here. The execution would take place tomorrow morning. The guards closed in to seize me.

At the last instant I gathered my wits enough to cry out, "Wait! What about the girl, Mary! The daughter of Symeon Cleophas! Set her free! Tell Epigonus to release her! He's holding her captive at his villa in the hills!"

More rumblings filtered through the spectators. Epigonus glared at me. This time he didn't stand. He didn't seem to have the strength. He opened his mouth and said, "The girl, Mary, who was brought to my estate for questioning, committed suicide before I could complete my interrogation. Her body was burned on the pyre three nights ago, along with her filthy collection of Christian books. She is no longer the concern of this Council."

I stood there gaping at the swollen figure of Epigonus. It felt as if all the life had been sucked from my body. The guards started to drag me up the steps of the Council House. Epigonus sent me no expression at all, but I caught the hateful gazes of his bodyguards. They almost appeared disappointed. They didn't seem to want me to die in a public square. They had wanted me for themselves.

In a blur of sound and color, I was whisked from the Council House. I hardly remember the three-hundred-yard walk back to the palace dungeons. Nothing would stay in focus; it was all muddled with confusion. But one face somehow imprinted on my brain just as we entered the corridor leading down to the dungeons. It wasn't the face of someone I knew. I'd never met the man before; of that I was certain. He was standing just across the palace square, leaning casually against the base of a statue of Athena. His eyes watched me. This wasn't remarkable; *everybody* was watching me. But with him the look was different, as if . . . as if he *knew* me. Ridiculous. An illusion. There were literally *hundreds* of faces in every direction. Yet this one burned a lasting image on my mind.

What was so unusual about it? It was just a face. Just a stranger. I felt sure the answer was inside me. I just had to jar it loose.

And then, like a burst of light, I made the connection. I knew why the face had stood out. I'd seen faces like his before. Hundreds of them. *Thousands* of them. In a land on the opposite side of the world.

The stranger was a Nephite.

CHAPTER 20

I heard myself scream his name. I screamed it even before my mind had registered what it was doing.

"APOLLUS!"

I looked for a reaction in the Roman rider at the top of the hill. Steffanie looked at me like I was crazy. How did I know that was Apollus? Why was I calling out to a stranger on a horse? She was right. I was deluding myself. And yet still I watched him, hoping beyond hope. I thought I might have seen the rider raise his head. But then the drunken soldier—the one who had climbed the stairway—seized my arm. He threw me down behind the parapet.

"Shut up, witch! You'll get no help from the gods."

He thought I was calling on Apollo, the Roman sun god. Steffanie tried to run past him to reach the stairway. He reached for her, but she slipped by. She skidded to a halt, however, as Crotus appeared on the landing, his eyes spinning in a drunken rage.

"Nice catch, Regulus," he told his comrade.

Another soldier called to Crotus from below. "What about the parents?"

"Kill the father!" Crotus called back. "Do what you like with the mother!"

Two more of Crotus' comrades ascended the stairs. Now there were four of them, all grinning like cats before swallowing the canary. The remaining two soldiers on the first level went inside to deal with Jim and my mother.

Crotus edged closer. "So you were going north, eh? We wasn't good enough to escort you, eh? Well, witches, you'll be casting no more spells. No more fleas to keep me scratching through the night."

My curse had worked? I doubted that. But I did have a renewed faith in the power of suggestion. Steffanie lunged for the edge of the parapet. She grabbed a sharp piece of broken tile and held it in front of her in self-defense. Crotus and the other three soldiers threw back their heads in laughter. Their inebriation made it far funnier than it would have been otherwise.

We heard the pounding of horse's hooves on the hard dirt yard of the inn. The rider was moving swiftly. I could tell that much. And the hoof-beats had come from the direction of the hill.

Steffanie now stood on the west edge of the building. She couldn't see into the south yard. And yet her ears had pricked like mine. We glanced at each other. We both had a sense—a feeling. She wanted to look, but now Crotus had blocked the way. He was stalking Steffanie like a panther. He didn't even feel the need to unsheathe one of his weapons. A girl with a piece of tile was no real threat.

"Now put that down, honeycake," said Crotus. "Otherwise, one of us will get hurt—and I assure you it won't be me." He sprang to grab her wrist.

Maybe it was his impaired reflexes, or maybe it was Steffanie's unexpected agility. In any case, Crotus missed and Steffanie struck—right in his face. The edge of that broken tile sliced into the lower half of his nose, also catching a piece of his left cheek. Crotus staggered back. At first he didn't even cry out. Just reached up his hands and felt the wound. He looked at the blood on his hands. Finally, his temper exploded. Screaming the foulest of Roman expletives, he drew his knife.

Suddenly a voice rang out from behind.

"Lay it down, soldier!"

I spun my head.

He stood on the landing at the top of the stairs, sword drawn, body clad in bright new armor. Apollus the warrior. Apollus the lion. Apollus the hero of my heart.

The soldiers turned. They looked confused. The man was wearing a centurion's helmet, but he was so young. Less than twenty. Our attackers were hardened warriors in their thirties and forties. Crotus was incensed that he should be interrupted at his moment of retribution. Steffanie used the distraction to rush by him and get to me. She pulled us both into the corner at the southwest edge—the greatest possible distance from the violence that would undoubtedly erupt.

"She cut me!" Crotus raged. "I want her throat!"

"I said put it down!" Apollus repeated. He raised his sword to enforce the command.

The other legionaries backed away, but their hands were on their hilts. They also seemed offended that anyone would interfere with their fun and games—especially some young upstart who in their eyes couldn't possibly have earned the plumed helmet he wore.

"Who in the name of Jupiter are you?" barked Crotus.

"I am your superior officer," said Apollus. "And I command you to drop that weapon. You're drunk. You're all drunk. I want all of you to toss your swords at your feet."

No one moved. The soldiers all looked to Crotus. They weren't about to comply—not unless Crotus complied first.

"You're not my superior officer," said Crotus, blood still dripping from his wound. "What century do you command? A century of flower girls at the temple of Magna Mater?"

"I am Apollus Severillus of the fortress of Neopolis, cohort of the Fifth Legion," he proclaimed.

"Fifth Legion," Crotus huffed derisively. "The Feminine Fifth went back to Syria years ago. The Tenth is in command here."

"Lay down your weapon, soldier," Apollus warned again. "Or I swear you'll be pouring blood from more than your nose."

Crotus tucked in his chin in amusement, his teeth now stained red as the blood seeped between his lips. The knife remained in his grip as his other hand reached for his sword. "And I tell you, you upstart grunt—march your rosy red hide back down those stairs, or me and my men will slice you into pieces so small the ravens won't even bother."

Crotus' men gained confidence. Swords began slipping from their scabbards.

We all heard a crash beneath our feet. My mother screamed. A brawl was underway inside the inn. They were trying to kill Jim! I peeked over the edge and looked down at the window where the noise had come from. There was another crash. The window's shutters whipped open. Part of the plaster surrounding the window frame also exploded outward. A soldier—facing backwards—came flying through with a wooden bench against his belly. He landed on the ground with a grunt. He'd been rammed through the window! Go Jim! The man lay there and groaned.

More crashing and screams reverberated inside. Jim still had to deal *with another soldier. I also heard the wails of the Greek innkeeper. All his worst visions of damage and mayhem were coming to pass.*

Crotus and the soldiers on the roof used the distraction to draw their swords. Two of them rushed at Apollus. He dodged the first man quite neatly, even kicking him in the back to let him sail past and hurl himself over the edge of the parapet. Apollus swung his sword with both hands to meet the second soldier. There was a terrible clang. The attacker was thrown off balance. Apollus twisted around and sprang toward the middle of the roof. The third soldier—the one named Regulus—raised his weapon. Apollus continued his spin and struck first. Regulus tried to thwart the blow, but his aim was inaccurate. A part of Apollus' blade cut a deep gash in his sword arm. Regulus cried out in agony and dropped his weapon.

Crotus rushed into position and struck downward at Apollus' head. Apollus caught the blow with the center of his blade, creating a flash of sparks. Apollus was forced down on one knee. Crotus attempted to sideswipe his blade into Apollus' shoulder. Apollus averted that strike as well, but the force of Crotus' two-hand swing sent Apollus sprawling across the roof. Then, in a move that was pure poetry, Apollus transformed himself into a roll, found his feet, and was suddenly upright again. Crotus charged. Apollus warded off several more blows, sparks flying.

I heard a ruckus coming from the entrance of the inn. Suddenly Jim and his assailant emerged. Jim held a piece of furniture that looked like the innkeeper's own table. It was hoisted over his head to ward off more blows from his attacker's sword. Several swings hacked off the table's legs even as I watched.

The soldier who'd been thrown off balance leaped back into the fray. Apollus now fought two men. Regulus was trying to recover. He gripped his sword with his uninjured arm. I saw no reason to let Apollus fight three men. Following Steffanie's example, I dug my claws into the edge of the parapet and pried off a large stone brick. Before Regulus had pushed himself up from his other knee, my brick came smashing down. Regulus collapsed and fell flat on his face.

Apollus was ducking and dodging sword blows from two directions. Near the eastern edge of the building was a sunroof of sorts—a five-by-five box covered by a thin wooden lattice. During the day it ventilated the area over the innkeeper's office and let in sunlight. It rose up like a short chimney. Apollus had been backed against this box, still parrying sword thrusts.

All at once I heard Steffanie cry out. Her father had fallen to the ground in the entranceway of the inn. The soldier stood over him, ready to finish the job. Without a second thought, Steffanie leaped. She threw herself over the edge of the parapet, landing on the soldier's neck. The man smashed abruptly against the earth, his legs reflexively flipping up into the air. Steffanie tumbled off to the side. Jim leaped to his feet and retrieved the soldier's weapon.

At just that moment, Apollus threw himself to the left to dodge Crotus' strike. The momentum caused both of them to trip into the sunroof. The lattice immediately gave way, and the two men landed with a crunch on the office furniture below. I was desperate to see if Apollus was all right. The last soldier was blocking the way. He leaned over the opening to appraise the situation himself. His face looked stricken; he obviously didn't like what he saw. Then he turned his wrathful gaze squarely on me.

Still gripping his sword, he strode toward me. I leaped for the stairway, but his arm latched onto the material of my cloak. He wrenched it with all his strength and sent me sailing toward the edge of the parapet. The material ripped off my shoulder. Several bricks broke loose from the parapet and rained down. Somehow I kept from flipping over the edge, but the impact left a shooting pain in my left wrist.

I gasped in mortal dread as the Roman seized me by the hair. His sharp nails dug into my scalp. He flipped me over onto my back and set the chinked blade of his sword against my throat. His terrible visage loomed over my face, the eyes flashing lightning.

"At least you'll die, witch," he said in a voice that was surprisingly calm.

His fingers tightened as he prepared to slide the blade across my throat as easily as slicing butter. I shut my eyes in ultimate horror, bracing my heart for the cold certainty of death.

But then there was a dull clunk. The ring was almost musical. Someone was standing behind the soldier. The soldier's eyes glossed over and his body went limp. As his head dropped, my rescuer was revealed. Mom! In her hands was a large clay vase with a slender neck. She held the neck in both hands, having just brought it crashing down on the back of the soldier's head. I scooted out from underneath the fallen Roman and looked up at my mother with awe.

She was looking at the vase with admiration. I think she'd expected it to shatter. There wasn't even a crack.

"Nice vase," she said approvingly. Then she dropped it and enfolded me in her arms.

* * * * * *

The Greek proprietor was having a tizzy fit. His inn was in a shambles. Crotus was dead; he'd landed on his own sword as he fell into the innkeeper's office. Apollus had walked away with hardly a scratch, just a slight dent in his helmet.

My wrist hurt terribly. I felt sure it wasn't broken, just jammed. So I didn't complain. Steffanie, on the other hand, was injured far worse. Her leg had twisted as she landed on the Roman's back. The ankle was purple and swollen, and she shrieked in pain at even the thought of someone touching it.

Apollus leaned over her. "It's broken," he concluded. "It will have to be set and wrapped."

The other guests of the inn slowly emerged from their rooms and gathered around. Jim and Mom had bound the hands of the surviving soldiers. Most were still out cold, their injuries combining with the effects of alcohol. Regulus was conscious, though very dizzy. The Greek proprietor frantically tried to bandage his arm, fearing reprisal from the whole Roman army if he didn't do everything he could.

"You must leave here!" he ordered us. "Take your donkey and go! I've already sent my stable boy back to Jerusalem to lodge a complaint. But more soldiers might not arrive before these men awaken. Please leave before any more property is destroyed!"

Jim knelt to help examine his daughter. "We'll try to set it when we get to a campsite," he said.

"She can ride with me on my horse," said Apollus.

Mom gathered all of our satchels and supplies. Steffanie whimpered as Jim lifted her. After Apollus mounted his horse, Jim transferred her into his arms. She threw her own arms around Apollus' neck for support, and made herself as comfortable as possible sitting in front of him in the saddle. To accommodate my own injuries, I was granted the dubious privilege of riding the donkey. Who'd have thought I could feel jealous of a broken bone?

My instincts concerning Apollus had all been right. I knew we shouldn't have left Masada so soon. Apollus had climbed out of the pool only a day later. After convincing the Roman officers of his name and rank, he was allowed to scavenge among the provisions of armaments left over from the seven-year campaign and dredge up for himself a new helmet, greaves, bucklers, leather tunic, and sword. The new centurion's uniform didn't fit him quite as well as his last, which had been custom-manufactured. But he wasn't about to try and recover the other one.

His first reaction upon emerging from the cistern had been shock. Where had we gone? Quickly, however, he drew his own conclusions. Fortunately, the soldiers informed him that we'd only left the day before. He'd followed our trail straight to Silva's headquarters in Jerusalem. Afterwards, just as I'd predicted, he'd charted a course straight for Neopolis, even drumming up for himself a chestnut-colored stallion. He'd never had any intention of stopping at our inn along the Samaritan Road. If I hadn't screamed out his name, he'd have ridden right on by.

We found a campsite among some rocks just a few miles north and struck a fire. Steffanie shrieked in pain as Apollus and Jim pulled the ankle bone back into place. I wept with tears of sympathy. She fainted in her father's arms as they wrapped the foot tightly in splints and cloth.

Apollus stroked her hair. "When we reach Neopolis, we'll have Demeterus, the camp physician, look her over again."

"That butcher?" I remarked. "Don't let him near her. He nearly killed Jesse."

Apollus tamed me with a smile. "The boy recovered well enough, didn't he? I don't know of anyone better at treating broken bones. Now what about you? How's your wrist?"

"My wrist?" I tucked it behind my other arm. "It's fine."

Actually, it was sore as the dickens, but I really wasn't interested in talking about it. It certainly wasn't worth the kind of attention Steffanie was getting. What if he tried to do something to it like he'd just done to her ankle?

No, that wasn't the reason I didn't want his attention. I wasn't sure what I was feeling. I felt all shy and vulnerable all of a sudden. I hated it. I hated it! I turned away and walked back to the place where I'd laid out my bedroll. Apollus arose to join me, leaving Steffanie in the able hands of Jim and my mother.

"Let me see it," he insisted.

"I told you, it's fine—"

"Now."

I glared at him. I thought about squawking back "no!" in a tone just as authoritative. I couldn't bring myself to do it. Naturally, I gave in and handed him my wrist.

"Don't hurt me," I said.

As usual, he did not obey. He tried to bend it.

"Ow!" I cried, pulling it back.

His diagnosis was swift. "Not broken. Just a sprain."

"I know that," I snapped. "I told you. Thank you very much."

He sat back. "Still as stubborn as ever, aren't you? I can tell you missed me a lot."

That melted me. In fact, it tore me up. My lower lip started quivering. I couldn't control it. My eyes filled up like a fishbowl and overflowed. He regretted his sarcasm.

"Sorry," he said. "I'm sure this has all been as difficult for you as it has been for me."

"We were scared to death," I said, my voice almost scolding. "I thought—we thought—we thought you were gone. Gone forever."

"I didn't go anywhere," he proclaimed. "You did. You all left me."

"I begged Jim to stay," I said. "We didn't know. How could we know when you might—?"

"It's all right," he said. "It's all right. I understand. I'd certainly have done the same. It was quite a shock when I climbed out of that pool. But I must admit I've grown rather immune to shock lately. Nothing surprises me anymore. If that moon dropped out of the sky, rolled down that hill, sprouted legs, and danced a Spanish jig, it would be no less surprising than any other event over the past few days."

I smiled. Then my face grew serious again. "Then . . . you know that we've been gone almost three years?"

He nodded.

"Are you afraid?"

"Afraid?" he repeated, as if I'd chosen a completely inadequate word.

I narrowed it down. "Are you afraid to face your father? You've been gone for a lot longer than he would have expected. He'll hug you, but then he'll probably beat the living daylights out of you."

Apollus snickered. "You know my father well."

"*What if he's gone home to Italy? Crotus said the Fifth Legion left Judea years ago.*"

"*But their cohort is still in command at Neopolis,*" said Apollus. "*I confirmed that in Jerusalem, although I wasn't able to learn any news respecting my father or my old lieutenant, Sergius Graccus. But we'll all be in Neopolis soon enough.*"

He gave a solid nod, as if he had a perfect handle on all of it. But Apollus couldn't fool me. His mind and heart were turning somersaults. His whole world had been flipped upside down. I had the distinct feeling that he didn't feel he belonged here anymore. I wondered if he felt he belonged anywhere at all.

He changed the subject. "*Your wrist will heal better if we wrap it like Steffanie's ankle.*"

"*That's all right,*" *I said.* "*You just take care of Steffanie. She looked very comfortable today on your horse.*" *I was trying to sound sincere. I was afraid it sounded petty.*

Apollus glanced back and gazed at her face by the fire. "*I'm not sure she'll be comfortable anywhere she is for the next few days.*" *His eyes lingered on the vision.*

My heart sank into my toes. "*She's beautiful, isn't she?*"

He turned back, as if surprised by the question. Then he nodded thoughtfully and said, "*Yes. Very beautiful. But I've come to conclude that all of the women from your world are extraordinarily beautiful.*"

He was complimenting me, but I didn't read it that way at first. I knew I couldn't hold a candle to Steffanie. I tried to use the comment to improve my case another way. "*Yes, you're absolutely right. Girls like Steffanie are everywhere in my world. Millions! They're dropping out of trees. What really counts are* other *things, like . . .*" *I'd gotten myself in a tangle here. I couldn't think of any positive attribute that Steffanie might not already possess. Then it hit me,* "*Well, like* history. *What really counts are how* many *memories* two people share. *You know, like how many adventures they may have been through together.*"

"*Really?*" *Apollus rested his chin on his elbow.* "*That's fascinating.*"

Oh, the sly fox. He was reading right through me.

I backpedaled. "*Well, anyway, that's just an opinion. It doesn't mean anything.*" *I began fiddling with my hands. Why was it that at moments like this I could never figure out what to do with my hands?*

He continued watching me. "History. Yes, that's an interesting thought. I'll have to think about that one."

He gazed off toward the moon, making it look convincing that he really was thinking about it.

I did a little staring myself, drinking in every curve of that beautiful, god-like face. My heart was pounding so hard. Oh, how I loved him. There, I'd admitted it! I loved him so much it was twisting my insides into Gordian knots. I knew I was only fifteen—too young to know what love really was. But who cared about any of that? Hook me, clean me, fry me in butter. My heart was his completely. And yet my lip was still quivering like the wings of a hummingbird. I might have been his, but he surely wasn't mine. Apollus didn't belong to anyone. I wondered if he ever would. And somehow, in some twisted way, this only made me love him all the more.

Some of us might have slept that night. I know I didn't. I know poor Steffanie didn't, either. Although Jim had found some Motrin in his travel bag, it was hardly adequate to relieve her pain.

The next day we were off riding again toward Neopolis. I gave my mother a turn on the donkey. Steffanie continued riding the horse. As Apollus had said, she didn't look comfortable at all despite having Apollus ride behind her. Actually, for most of the trip she rode alone. Apollus led the horse by its reins and conversed with Jim. My mother and I walked side by side, talking about everything under the sun. The mood remained tense, but at least our worries were now centered primarily on finding Harry. I knew I would always treasure this time with my mom. We were sharing an adventure that I doubted any mother and daughter had ever shared.

It took us a half day longer to reach Neopolis than it had taken Harry. As the hump of Mount Gerizim loomed larger on the horizon, Apollus forced us to quicken our pace. I watched his eyes, and I could feel the thrill leaping in his soul. When the walls of his fortress appeared in the distance, he beamed with excitement. I suspect it took every ounce of his self-control not to climb on his horse and kick it into a dead run, leaving us all behind. He stayed with us all the way up to the gate.

The sentries at the gate were faces that Apollus didn't recognize. They were younger, fresh recruits from the hills of Italy, not the grizzled old warriors who Apollus had known from before.

"What is your name, Centurion?" asked the gatekeeper.

"Apollus Brutus Severillus," he replied, his chest puffed in pride.

The name practically drew a gasp from everyone in hearing. It was eerie, as if Apollus' return had been something prophesied, something dreamed about.

"We'll take you right to the commander," the sentries announced.

As we were led inside, Apollus did begin to recognize some of the men. Word of Apollus' arrival raced far ahead of us. All along the way, old comrades turned out and saluted their former superior. We marched straight through to the headquarters of the garrison commander. The buildings all looked the same. Stretched before the commander's office was the same wooden walkway with its same sturdy rail. But the man who emerged was not Apollus' father. It was Sergius Graccus—Apollus' former right-hand man. Could it be that his subordinate now outranked him?

"Graccus!" Apollus cried.

The two men rushed forward and embraced each other's shoulders in the manly style of Roman officers. Their smiles beamed as bright as the sun.

"Apollus Brutus!" Graccus exclaimed. "It's really you! This is a greater miracle than the weeping statue of the goddess! By Jupiter, man! You don't look the slightest bit different!"

"Yes, Sergius," said Apollus, his voice carrying some urgency. "My father, Sergius. Where is my father?"

Graccus' smile slowly faded into an expression far more heavy and serious. "He's dead, Apollus. He's been dead for six months."

The light went out of Apollus' eyes. My own heart came into my throat. Oh, how I had adored that old warrior! He'd done so much for me. Tears streamed down my face. But for Apollus the news was more devastating than I could have imagined. His mother and siblings were already dead. His father was his last solid link to the world he knew so well. After all the confusion of the last week, he'd desperately needed to plant his feet on familiar ground, hear a familiar voice, and bask in the presence of the man who had always represented safety and security. Now that opportunity had been denied him.

His voice barely a whisper, he asked, "How did it happen?"

"Stroke," Graccus said. "It was very quick and painless. I was at Masada, so I didn't witness it for myself. But they say he just slumped over at his desk. I was promoted during my service with Silva. When I returned a week ago, the interim commander was released and I took his place."

Apollus suddenly looked dizzy. I feared that the powerful man was about to faint. Jim responded swiftly. He and Graccus started to help

Apollus into the commander's office, but he waved them off. He would go inside on his own volition. Jim and one of Graccus' orderlies helped Steffanie off the horse. We followed them inside. Graccus honored Apollus by seating him in his father's old chair behind the desk. The setting threatened to engulf Apollus with a rush of emotion. Still, he refused to let it overwhelm him. No tears would fall from the eyes of Apollus Brutus, at least not in our presence.

Uneasily, Apollus asked, "Did you get a chance to speak to him after . . . our disappearance?"

"Yes," said Graccus. "Lucullus and I waited in that gully for two days. Then we searched for two more. We returned to Neopolis and gave him our opinion that you had been captured by the Zealots." Graccus looked again at Apollus, then at me, his face full of wonder. "This is remarkable. It's as if it was yesterday. Apollus, you must be twenty-two years old now. She must be eighteen. And yet . . ."

We didn't respond. We just let Graccus mull it over. At last he seemed to put it all together. "It was the cave, wasn't it? The cave was responsible for this miracle."

"Yes, Graccus," Apollus replied soberly.

"We searched for the cave. There are so many caves in those hills. So many strange feelings."

Jim leaned forward. "What do you mean?"

"It's a mysterious place, the Judean desert," Graccus responded. "There were several caves that Lucullus and I found. But the feeling inside was so peculiar that we turned around and departed. And then later, when I met . . ." He stopped.

Jim persisted. "Met who? Who did you meet?"

"The man called Gidgiddonihah," said Graccus. "The one who fought with us on Mount Gerizim when we defeated Simon Magus. I met him in the hills above Masada when I was surveying the earthworks. He told me that he had emerged from a cave." He turned again to Apollus. "I was sure it must have been the same cave where you, and the girl, and the man named Garth had disappeared."

"Was Gidgiddonihah alone?" Jim asked.

"No," said Graccus. "He'd brought with him twenty men—the most unusual men I've ever met. They called themselves the men of Nephi—Gid's countrymen. Gidgiddonihah said they were looking for the boy, Harrius."

"How long ago did this happen?" Jim demanded.

"It was at the end of last summer," said Graccus. "Perhaps nine months."

I could no longer contain myself. "Where did they go? Were they captured by the Romans? Are they still alive?"

Jim grabbed my shoulder. One question at a time.

Graccus continued. "It may have been auspicious that at the time I encountered Gid and his warriors, I was under orders to return to Neopolis to recruit more engineers to complete the earthworks. Gid and the Nephites accompanied me. Your father was thrilled. He remembered Gid quite well. Gidgiddonihah assured your father that you were still alive and perfectly well. The news filled him with immeasurable joy. He wept openly as he sat behind that desk."

Apollus closed his eyes, his own burden of guilt somewhat relieved. "Then my father knew the truth. He didn't die believing that he had lost his last remaining son."

"No," said Graccus. "He believed Gidgiddonihah implicitly. Gid informed him that you might return at any moment. He also said you might be in need of money for supplies. Commander Severillus gave to Gidgiddonihah all the silver he had on hand. Gidgiddonihah left his men stationed here and returned with me and my recruits to Masada. He asked me to write a message in Latin on a piece of cloth. Then he wrapped your father's money inside the cloth and returned to the cave. I didn't see Gidgiddonihah after that, but I heard later that he rejoined his men here at Neopolis. Then they moved on."

I repeated my question. "Where did they go?"

"In search of Harrius, I presume," said Graccus.

"Did they say anything more?" asked Jim. "Any hint of their next destination?"

"Yes," said Graccus. "He did mention one possible destination. But I didn't understand what he meant. Gidgiddonihah stated that he might embark on a journey to a land of Seven Churches. But I couldn't tell you where this land is."

"I know where it is!" I blurted out. "He went to Ephesus in Asia Minor." I turned to Jim, Steffanie, and Mom. "He went to find the Apostle John. I know it! We can follow him, Jim. His exact same trail!"

So it was that our time in Neopolis was cut miraculously short. Apollus was only given a single night to enjoy the sociality of his old com-

rades. To be honest, I don't think he had any regrets. There was nothing left for him here, and he knew it. Graccus didn't even hesitate in granting him leave to accompany us on the remainder of our journey.

So in the morning, just like the weary Roman veterans who had successfully concluded the Jewish war, we too would be seeking passage on a ship in the harbors of Caesarea—a ship bound for the center of spiritual civilization in the Mediterranean world. In the land of the Seven Churches, we hoped to find Gidgiddonihah and the twenty brave Nephites who had come to help him in his quest. But more importantly, we prayed that we would finally find Harry Hawkins. With the blessing of God, it would become a destination that would reunite our families once and for all.

CHAPTER 21

My mind was a jumble of emotions and questions. I was hard-pressed to sort them all out. Each demanded my full attention. The face of the Nephite. Mary's reported suicide. The burning of the scrolls. My fate at sunrise. As I walked through the corridors of the dungeon beneath the Governor's palace, I was forced to draw a host of uncertain conclusions.

As for Mary, I didn't believe it. I'd *never* believe it. Epigonus was lying. He *had* to lie. If he'd told the truth, the Council would have demanded her release. But in his terrible lie were also sewn the seeds of Mary's fate. Now he *couldn't* release her—ever! When he was finished with her, he would be forced to dispose of her. Give her over to his despicable bodyguards. *And it was my fault!* If I hadn't spoken up— if I'd just kept my mouth shut—Epigonus might have let her go. Now he couldn't let her go. He couldn't risk it. Though I doubted if a man as powerful as Epigonus could ever be convicted of a crime, letting the Council discover his lie might damage his political clout.

I didn't believe the scrolls had been destroyed, either. God wouldn't have protected them this long to see them destroyed by a lecherous swine like Epigonus. Again, the councilman was lying. Epigonus' passion was collecting rare and valuable things. He'd never destroy anything that might add to his collection.

But the biggest mystery by far was the Nephite. Who *was* he? What was he *doing* here? I knew of only one link that the world of the Romans had with the world of the Nephites—Gidgiddonihah. It wouldn't have surprised me to learn that Gid had escaped from his captors in Caesarea. Would he have embarked on a quest to find me?

Friendship and honor were the codes of Gid's life. But how would he have possibly known that I was in Athens? I hadn't known it myself until a few days ago.

Somehow I must have been mistaken. That man *couldn't* have been a Nephite. Surely there were dozens of races with similar features. But even if he *was* a Nephite, why should I think he was here with Gidgiddonihah? Maybe he was a trader. A world traveler. Maybe he'd come through the tunnels *in search* of Gidgiddonihah. Whatever the truth, it seemed far too remote to think this man could alter my fate at sunrise. How many times could I expect the cavalry to show up at the last moment? But then I reminded myself—with God such opportunities were limitless. As long as I kept the faith.

That thought continued pounding in my heart as we reached a room in the center of the dungeon. It was accessed by a metal-plated door with no windows. The guard turned the key. It opened with a screech that set my teeth on edge. Beyond the door there appeared to be nothing. No floor. No ceiling. Just blackness. It was like a doorway into the emptiness of outer space.

"You can jump, or we'll push you," said the guard. "You got one second to decide."

I gave them a baffled look. I nearly lost my chance to choose when the guards raised their arms to push me. I jumped at the last instant. Jumping was better; I might have some control over my landing. But I couldn't see the floor! How could I brace for impact? Thankfully, the depth was only about six feet. My bruised leg buckled and I landed on my shoulder.

The door slammed shut. I pushed up on my hands, spitting dirt from my lips. The room reeked of mildew. I peered into the darkness. A sliver of light crept beneath the doorway, allowing me to perceive the shape of a man near the far wall. He wasn't moving. Was he dead?

Then his whisper pierced the shadows. "Are you hurt?" he asked.

I knew who it was. It was Saint Luke, former traveling companion of Peter and Paul, author of two of the greatest books in the New Testament.

"No," I replied breathlessly. "Not badly."

I'd met hundreds of people since I'd arrived in the Roman world. But none before now had taken my breath away. He arose unsteadily to his feet. I was astonished. He'd been starved for a week. He'd been denied water. Such a man should have been flat on his back, gasping his final breaths. He stood over me and offered his hand to help me stand.

"I can do it," I said. As I tried, I winced in pain.

"Don't move," he said. "Let me feel it."

"It's all right," I insisted. "It's not from the fall. It was injured last night."

He knelt down beside me. His gentle hands felt the bruise on my right shin. I gazed at his face. His features were Greek. The face was covered with gray stubble. His hair was dark, also streaked with gray. I guessed he was about sixty, perhaps a bit younger. His lips were cracked; otherwise I couldn't see any physical evidence of thirst or star-vation—that is, other than the unsteadiness of his legs. He was about my height, maybe a little shorter, and his limbs looked remarkably agile. His eyes seemed to shine in the darkness.

"It's swollen," he concluded. "Likely bruised to the bone. But it's not broken. How was it injured?"

"It happened just before I was arrested," I said. "I was tripped. A chain attached to two metal balls."

"Unusual weapon."

"Scythian," I said.

"Scythian?" he said with surprise. Then he nodded in understand-ing. "Epigonus' bodyguards."

"That's right," I confirmed.

"My name is Luke," he introduced.

"I know," I said with awe. "I'm Harry Hawkins."

"Strange name," he said.

"Yes," I concurred. "I'm not from . . . not from these parts. But I'm a Christian. And I've . . ."

I stopped myself. Was I really about to say "I've read all your books"? Goodness, I'd have sounded like a groupie. I settled for, "I know all about you."

"Do you indeed?"

"Well, I . . . at least I know some of the things you've done."

"I'm surprised," he said. "I've been the servant of many great men, but I've never recounted my own deeds."

"Where I come from, we *all* know of you. I know you were a companion of Peter and Paul."

"Yes," he said. "I was. Though nothing I did was able to prevent their deaths." I sensed it was a painful subject.

I stood upon my feet to prove that I was all right. "There."

"Very good," he said.

I looked into his face. I was still amazed at his fitness after such ill treatment.

"I didn't expect you to be so strong," I said.

"Oh, I'm hardly strong," he said. "In fact, my head is spinning. Help me over to the wall, would you?"

I took his arm. We sat together against the cold stone.

"They said you weren't receiving any water."

"I'm not," said Luke. "Not for three days. But God provides."

He pointed toward the far corner. The sound was very faint, but I heard a trickle. "A leak in the plumbing," said Luke. "Directly above us is the Governor's fountain. The water is brackish at first, but believe me, after a day or two it becomes as sweet as nectar."

I shook my head in amazement. The way God had preserved his life and strength was nothing less than a miracle. But I felt a twinge of pain in my heart. I realized he hadn't heard the news. He didn't know his own fate.

"The Council voted today," I said. "The edict against the Christians has been repealed."

"Repealed? Are you sure?"

"I was a witness," I said. "Everyone has been set free."

He was delighted. "That's marvelous!"

The excitement faded as he realized that my face remained serious.

"For you and me the sentence is different," I said. "The Council voted for our execution."

He nodded solemnly. Despite it all, the news didn't seem to surprise him. "When?"

"Tomorrow morning."

"I understand why they might make an example of me. But what do they have against you?"

"I struck a policeman," I said. "But I don't think that's the reason."

"Oh?"

"I think it's because I killed one of the Scythian's tigerhounds. It attacked me just before I was arrested."

"I've heard about these dogs. I'm surprised that you're still in one piece."

"Luck," I said.

Luke scoffed at that. "The fortunes of God are never luck. More likely you have a destiny to fulfill. The Lord will preserve His faithful servants until their appointed time. Long ago, Peter promised me that I would not die alone. If your final destiny was simply to be here with me, at this moment, then it is enough. If I'm to die tomorrow, Harry Hawkins, I'm honored that I will die with you."

I wanted to tell him about the Nephite. I wanted to communicate my premonition that it was not our destiny to die. What could I say? I'd sound like an idiot. I finally said, "Surely Peter meant that you would die among friends. Not with a stranger."

"If you're a Christian, you're no stranger. We're brothers in Christ."

"I don't believe our destinies are fulfilled," I said.

"Is there something you feel that you've left undone?"

"*Many* things," I said. "I couldn't count them. But there may be one thing over all the others. Here in Athens there are some books—some scrolls that were in the possession of Symeon Cleophas. They're the words of the Apostles. I've always felt it was my responsibility to take them to Ephesus and give them to the Apostle John. I tried to give that responsibility to someone else. Now I realize I made a mistake."

Luke listened. He nodded thoughtfully.

"Maybe that's *your* destiny too," I added. "Your books should be in the same collection. Maybe our destiny is to carry them to Ephesus together."

"*My* books?"

"Yes," I said. "The one you wrote about the life of Jesus. And about the acts of the apostles."

He shook his head. "I've written no such books."

I stared at him. "Of *course* you did."

He shrugged. "These things are passed down by the mouths of the prophets. They are far too sacred to be written. The Jews and Gentiles would only mock them."

I was dumbfounded. "Are you serious? You've never written any books?"

"I'm a physician, not a poet."

I leaped to my feet. "You've gotta be kidding!"

Luke became concerned. "Sit down, Harry. You seem upset."

"Upset! How could you—? Don't you realize—?" I bit my tongue. How much was I allowed to say? Not a poet?! How could he say that? One day his words would be the most widely read literature in all the western world! I wanted to quote "Star Wars"—*Luke, it's your DESTINY!*

My hope ignited more brightly than ever. Saint Luke couldn't die! The disaster would be incomprehensible! His book contained the only full account of *Christmas!* Bethlehem, the manger, shepherds, heavenly hosts—it was all in *Luke!* These things weren't mentioned in any other book of scripture. A billion nativity scenes throughout history would never be erected. Furthermore, Luke was the only one who'd ever given a history of Paul. Without the Book of Acts, the apostles' letters might have never made it into the Bible. This was just the beginning! Who could measure the extent to which history would change? If God was sending the cavalry, it wouldn't be to rescue me. It would be to rescue *him.*

I sat down again. "Listen to me. You're not going to die tomorrow. Neither am I. Something is going to happen. I'm not sure what, but I promise you it is. You still have things to do. Don't ask me how I know. I just know."

He looked into my eyes with mesmerized disbelief. My conviction was so forceful that it couldn't help but be contagious.

We waited out the day in silent darkness, our ears tuned to the slightest noise in the chambers above us. Most of the noise came from my stomach. Luke's stomach was beyond the point of making noise. I'd overestimated the quality of his health; he really was quite frail. For most of our time together, he had no energy to move or speak.

The hours slipped by. I was sure it was night. I began to doubt all my instincts. Were our rescuers really coming? *Patience,* I told myself. *Don't lose faith.* I marked the passage of time in my mind. With every passing minute, I was sure the opportunity to stage a rescue was shrinking. Maybe we wouldn't be rescued until we actually met our executioner, our necks laid out on the chopping block. I couldn't take that kind of suspense. *Let it happen*, I cried in my heart. *Let it happen now.*

Moments later I heard a sound, far away, in another part of the building. It must have been two or three o'clock in the morning. Luke was also stirred to consciousness. We listened. My heart pounded. For nearly a minute there was perfect silence. Then another sound. Voices! Someone shouting commands.

I listened for the clash of swords. Everything went silent again. This was nerve-wracking! I stood and walked toward the sliver of light beneath the doorway. More silence—two full minutes. *What was happening?*

But then the sliver of light was partitioned by shadows—human legs! People were outside the cell door! I braced myself. It occurred to me that I might have horribly misjudged the passage of time. Was it morning already? Were the guards here to march us forth to meet our fate?

I heard a key in the lock. My heart plummeted. Only the guards would have a key. Anyone else would have smashed in the door with a sledgehammer. But then it flung open with the same horrible screech. Our sunken cell was filled with lamplight. Luke and I squinted our eyes. A figure stood in silhouette, the lamplight glowing around his shoulders like the points of a star.

But then another lamp was brought into view. The man in silhouette held it aloft to light the chamber. I saw his face. My heart swelled as big as Zarahemla. It was Gidgiddonihah!

"Harry!" he cried.

The mighty Nephite was armed from head to foot with sword, bow, long knife, and hatchet—just how he'd looked when I'd first set eyes on him so many years ago. He leaped into the pit. More men appeared behind him in the entranceway, all armed with swords and bows. One of them was Micah! The others were Nephites.

I embraced Gidgiddonihah with tears of jubilation. "Gid! How did you find me? How did you get here?"

"Later," he said. "Guards in other parts of the city may have been alerted. We have to go."

Micah called down from the doorway. "Stephanas and the others are waiting at the harbor!"

I turned back toward Luke. He was struggling to rise to his feet, his eyes wide with amazement.

"Luke has to come with us," I said.

"Fine," said Gid. "But hurry. We don't have much time."

We helped Luke to walk across the cell. Micah reached down with one of the Nephites to hoist Luke into the hallway of the dungeon. I recognized the Nephite's face—it was the man I'd seen that afternoon. More arms reached down to help me out of the pit, and then Gidgiddonihah. As I was hoisted into the hallway, I counted no less than a dozen Nephite warriors. There were also six guards, disarmed and scowling in resentment. Now I understood where Gid had gotten the key.

"Inside!" commanded the stern-looking Nephite I'd seen beside the statue of Athena.

Grumbling, the guards jumped down into the cell. They gazed back at us with bitter malice as another Nephite slammed the door. As soon it was locked, the guards began shouting for help.

"Go!" cried Gidgiddonihah.

We began running toward the outside doors. Luke struggled to keep up. Another Nephite—a man at least as burley as Gidgiddonihah—finally lifted him onto his back and carried him. Five more Nephites were standing watch at the entrance to the dungeon. No less than seventeen men! Gid had brought an entire Nephite army!

We entered the courtyard below the Governor's palace. Voices were shouting and feet were running on the balconies above us.

Gidgiddonihah indicated the lanterns at the top of the ramp. "Kill those lights!" he commanded.

Several of Gid's men snubbed out the wicks, and the area darkened. Gid gave the signal and we crossed the courtyard, passing through the various marble statues of Athenian gods. We continued up the narrow street into the warehouse district of the city marketplace. Gid's assault on the dungeon had been flawless. Not a drop of blood had been spilled. Leave it to Gid to plan and execute a jailbreak.

The street cut back to the west and ascended a steep hill that partially overlooked the palace. We found an area that looked like a city park, thick with trees and a large bronze monument dedicated to some long-dead Athenian statesman. Luke was set down on a stone bench. He looked breathless, despite being carried. We turned toward the palace grounds and watched torches flitting about as men tried to figure out what had happened. In the light of the full moon I could also see the ocean and the port of Piraeus, four miles distant.

I looked at Gid again with eyes of wonder. He flashed me his familiar grin and said, "You look well, Harryhawkins. If you get any taller, I might feel a bit intimidated."

"No way. Not you."

He made some introductions. "This is Jashon," he said, referring to the stern-faced man I'd seen that afternoon. "He's a kinsman of mine from Zarahemla—the great-great grandson of the prophet and general, Gidgiddoni. That makes him my great-nephew." He introduced the large man who had carried Luke. "This is his brother, Heshlon."

My astonishment widened. "You went *back?*"

"Yes," Gid admitted. "These are *all* my kinsmen. Everyone I knew from my days in Zarahemla had aged over thirty years. This is the next generation of warriors from our noble bloodlines. Strong in spirit, but soft in the arts of war. I had to whip these boys into shape. They don't teach war anymore among the Nephites. We didn't even have any swords until we received these gifts from Apollus' father, the commander of Neopolis."

The Nephites scoffed in good humor. Jashon said, "Actually, we were afraid this old soldier might drop dead on the trail and make us carry him. After all, he's almost eighty years old!"

Gid and the rest of the soldiers laughed. Micah listened in fascination. I found the whole scenario absolutely incredible. It was true. To these men, Gid would have appeared to be the youngest-looking eighty-year-old man they'd ever seen.

"How did you know I was in Athens?" I asked.

"I didn't," said Gid. "We first went to Ephesus. I figured if you ever escaped, that's where you'd go. In Ephesus, I'd expected to find Symeon, Mary, and Jesse. When we didn't, I remembered that their ship had been headed to a city called Athens. I came here on a hunch, thinking if I found them, I might find you."

"Have you seen Jesse?" I asked.

He nodded. "Our ship dropped anchor the day before yesterday. We found Jesse this morning. That's how we knew where you were."

"Is he all right?"

"Perfectly," said Gid.

"Did he tell you about Mary and the scrolls? Did he tell you where she—?"

Gid stopped me. "He told us everything, Harry. He's waiting for us right now with three of my men."

"Where?" My eyes widened. "You mean at *Epigonus' villa!*"

Gid nodded. "They're staking out the area until we get there. Jesse said you'd know the way."

"But what if you hadn't been able to rescue me?"

"That," said Gid, "was not an option."

"When we reach this villa," added Micah, "we might not face as much resistance as we might have expected. Epigonus collapsed this afternoon at the Council House."

"Collapsed?"

"Yes," said Micah. "It was shortly after you were taken back to the palace dungeons. He had to be carried out on a litter. No small feat, I assure you."

"Is he alive?" I asked.

"Alive enough to be taken home in his carriage," said Micah.

This was an odd development, but not completely unexpected. Still, I had serious doubts that it would mean we'd face less resistance.

"We'd better reach Jesse and the others," said Gid. He spoke to Heshlon, referring to Luke. "Can you take this man to the ship?"

"No problem," Heshlon replied.

"Take Muloki and Amnon," said Gid. "We'll meet you there before dawn. Tell Priscus to have our ship ready to sail."

I took Luke's arm before he was hoisted back onto Heshlon's back. "You're in good hands," I told him. "These men are Nephites. They could carry you to the ends of the earth."

"I have no doubt of that," said Luke.

Heshlon lifted him again. They moved off toward the harbor at Piraeus with Muloki and Amnon.

"Where did you get the ship?" I asked Gid.

"The owner, Priscus, is a Christian. Timothy, the bishop of Ephesus, asked him to help us. He was a bit reluctant at first, having no crew, but in a matter of a few weeks he trained my men to become regular sailors. An admirable feat, considering that most Nephites hate the water—including me."

We turned west, toward the hills. Along the way, I did my best to describe Epigonus' estate—the mansion with its tangled corridors and tower, the dogs, and the Scythian horsemen. We moved as swiftly as possible. I'd made this trip once already in the dark. We were able to keep to the fields and hills without having to walk along the main road. I was afraid the sight of a dozen foreigners armed with swords might alarm any late-night travelers. But there was another reason: I had an eerie feeling that the road leading to the villa was being watched.

In a little over an hour, we came in sight of the woods surrounding the estate. Gidgiddonihah paused to watch for several minutes.

"Is something wrong?" I finally asked.

"I don't like it," he said.

"Don't like what?" asked Micah.

He chewed on his lip. "I'm not sure."

My adrenaline started flowing. I knew better than to question the instincts of Gidgiddonihah. If he didn't like something, there was definitely something not to like.

At last Gid sighed, more like a growl. "Let's find Jesse and my men." He signaled for everyone to move out, keeping low.

We stealthily crossed the field toward the woods. The Nephites grasped the hilts of their swords, partly to be ready to draw them and partly to keep the hilts from knocking against their belts. The moon was as bright as a searchlight—even more luminescent than the night before. I wished it would go behind a cloud. We were as exposed to peering eyes as we would have been in the middle of the day.

At last we entered the woods. Gid stopped again. We listened hard. Where were Jesse and the other Nephites? About thirty acres of woods surrounded the ten acres of property inside the walls. They might have been anywhere, though I suspected they were at a place where they could watch the front gates.

"This way," I whispered to Gid.

He followed me, but with a reluctance and caution that made me all the more nervous. His kinsmen remained close behind, with Jashon and Micah at our sides. Several had drawn their weapons. The light of the moon could hardly penetrate the lofty branches of the trees over our heads. The stillness of the woods was broken only by the occasional snap of a twig as we moved carefully across the forest floor. I could feel evil—it was as palpable as heat or cold. My muscles were as tense as piano wires; at any second I was expecting the ghostly, tattooed visage of a Scythian warrior to burst forth from the undergrowth.

The walls of Epigonus' estate loomed through the trees. We forged ahead until I could see part of the fortress gate. But where was Jesse? Where were the three Nephites who had accompanied him? This wasn't good. Anybody in the immediate area would have heard us coming. I raised my hand to my mouth to call out quietly across the road.

But before I could utter a sound, one of Gid's men released a gasp of horror. Electricity shot up my spine. I turned to my left and saw the man staggering backward, his eyes riveted on something in the grass. He was caught by his kinsman. Then they began howling with lamentation. Gid and Jashon pushed their way through to see what had caused so much distress. I held back. I knew what they had found, and I didn't want to see it. It would have surely torn my heart in half. But then my eyes fell upon another grisly sight. Just ahead, the shadow of another body was lying on the forest floor—another of Gid's men.

My soul wrenched out in grief. They were dead! All three Nephites were dead! Throats cuts, heads scalped. I took two steps toward Gid's fallen kinsman and dropped to my knees. It appeared as if he hadn't even had time to draw his sword. Gid examined each body. He shuddered at the way they'd been desecrated. His eyes blazed with fury.

"What did this?" he asked.

"The Scythians," I replied with certainty.

Gid was astonished. "Two men did *this?!*"

I nodded. He turned back toward the gate, his teeth clenched. The Nephites pulled themselves together. They'd never known war. They'd never known death—not like this. Their determination started boiling.

Jashon approached Gid. "The boy isn't among them," he reported.

Hope pounded in my chest. Jesse wasn't dead. But where was he? Did he escape? This idea quickly dissipated. If he'd escaped, these woods would have been crawling with dogs. Jesse had been taken alive; it was the only explanation. His face would have been known to Epigonus, and to the Scythians. They'd taken him inside with Mary. Maybe they felt his life could be used to blackmail her. Or maybe they simply wanted to inflict on him an even more terrible fate than the Nephites.

"How do we get over the wall?" asked Jashon.

Gid contemplated the problem, the wheels of his military mind spinning. He looked at me. "What opens that gate?"

"It raises up," I said. "There's some sort of mechanism that lifts it with chains."

"Are these Scythians his only warriors?"

"He has a lot of servants," I said. "They might also give us some trouble. Then there's the tigerhounds. Five of them."

"I'm not worried about dogs," said Gid, grasping his bow. "In fact, we'll *need* the dogs. At least in the beginning. We'll need them as a distraction. To climb the wall we'll form a human pyramid. At least five of us—perhaps six—should reach the top. Those who climb the wall will divide into two groups. The first group will occupy the dogs. The second group will use the distraction to infiltrate the house. Kill two or three of the dogs if you like. Then let them *win*. Let them drive you off—all but one man. That will be you, Jashon. You'll remain in hiding at least twenty minutes. Use your own judgment. Then open the gate."

"I understand," said Jashon.

"If they realize we're here," I said, "they might kill Mary and Jesse. They might destroy the scrolls."

In soberness, Gid said, "I suspect they *already* know we're here. Or at least they know we're coming."

I'd had the same chilling suspicion. I felt I understood Gid's strategy: making them think we'd been driven off was our only chance to gain any element of surprise.

"How many will try to get inside?" I asked.

"Two," said Gid. "Just me and you."

I nodded. I was ready. We'd have twenty minutes to locate Mary, Jesse, and the scrolls before Jashon opened the gate. There were so many variables; anything might go wrong. I crushed out all negative thoughts and followed the warriors of Zarahemla to the low wall that ran alongside the moat.

Gidgiddonihah leaped into the water. The rest of us followed, sinking up to our waists. Gid chose the largest men to make up the base of the pyramid. They lined up along the wall. The depth of the moat made the height close to twenty feet. Three men climbed out of the water to stand on the shoulders of the four. Two more, with difficulty, stood on the shoulders of the three. Now for the greatest challenge. The remaining five, including myself, Jashon, Micah, and Gidgiddonihah, began climbing the arms and legs of the other men

as if we were climbing monkey bars at a school playground. The men
on the bottom winced, but they maintained their balance by pressing
their hands against the wall. I was the first to reach the two men at
the top. One used his free arm to help me into place. I planted my
feet on their shoulders. Then I reached for the wall's edge. My hands
could barely grasp it. Straining, I hoisted myself upward and draped
one of my legs over the side. The wall was two feet wide. The bruise
on my shin was throbbing. I reached down and helped Jashon, then
together we helped Micah and another Nephite named Antipus. At
last, to the profound relief of everyone below, we hoisted up
Gidgiddonihah.

But Gid wanted one more man. "Uzziah," he whispered harshly.
"Grab my ankle! Climb!"

Gid clung to the edge. We held him in place as Uzziah struggled
to climb his body. Finally, he grabbed Gid's tunic. The tunic started to
rip. Micah reached down and grasped Uzziah's other hand. Just as he
was hoisted to safety, the pyramid started to collapse. The men
splashed into the moat in a tangled heap. The noise was thunderous,
and the tigerhounds inside the yard were alerted. They bolted across
the grass to our position, howling and barking.

"Separate!" ordered Gid.

Jashon, Micah, and the other two Nephites walked swiftly along
the wall toward the gate. Gid and I went in the opposite direction. This
balancing act would have been challenging enough in daylight, but in
the dark it was downright unnerving, especially with the racket of the
dogs. Micah and the others began taunting the hounds, shouting and
whistling. The tactic worked. Four of the beasts stayed with them.
Only one stubborn animal followed us. Gid pulled an arrow from his
quiver. This problem had to be eliminated quickly. Taking careful aim,
he let the arrow fly. The dog yelped once, then fell silent.

We continued our tightrope walk, keeping low. The woods behind
us might have helped our camouflage, but I knew it was imperative
that we jump down as soon as possible. Gid selected a spot behind a
row of narrow pine trees that looked like folded umbrellas. We hung
down from the edge as far as possible. Then we dropped.

I hit the ground, collapsed, and rolled. Gid landed on his feet. We
recovered, then crawled through the grass over to the row of trees. Gid

unsheathed his sword and handed it to me. "Here," he said. "Be ready to use it."

The dogs continued barking viciously at Jashon and the others. They'd almost reached the gate. I focused my gaze on the mansion. It seemed strange that no one was stirring—no moving lanterns. No running feet.

Then two horses sprang from the stables. The Scythians were riding toward the gate. I could see bows in their hands. Gid and I didn't breathe. My heart beat wildly. Jashon and Micah were sitting ducks! I wanted to warn them, but I couldn't risk exposing our position. One of the Scythians loaded his bow and fired an arrow. I heard one of the Nephites cry out. It was Jashon! He dropped from the wall, and I heard his body splash into the moat. Micah and the others fell out of sight. It was too dark—I couldn't see where they'd gone. Were they inside the yard? Had they fallen back into the moat? I heard the twang of another bowstring. A dog yelped. There was another splash. More arrows were fired by the Scythians. What was happening? I couldn't see!

Then everything went quiet. The Scythians rode slowly up to the gate, which was enclosed within an arched tunnel. The mechanism to raise it must have been inside. Jashon had been shot. Who would raise it? Would it take more than one man? One of the horsemen disappeared inside the tunnel. If Micah or another man was hiding inside, I was sure they would be found. The second horseman climbed off his mount and approached the body of one of the dogs. Three more had been killed. The last surviving hound stayed near its master. Gid and I remained perfectly still.

The second horseman emerged alone from the tunnel. He rode his horse along the inside of the wall, all the way to the place where Gid had shot the first dog. Then he stopped his horse. But he didn't dismount; he just sat there in the moonlight. I swallowed the knot in my throat. Did he suspect our presence? His dog had been killed too far down the wall. Surely he'd guessed that there were two separate groups. I swore that the Scythian's demon eyes were looking straight at us.

My hand gripped the sword. I was sure this was it—the final confrontation. It would start as the horseman ordered his last dog to attack. Then the two Scythians would surround us, firing arrows.

But the horseman didn't move. He grabbed the reins, turned his mount, and rode back toward his partner. Then the two of them rode together back toward the front of the mansion, their dog following close behind.

My heart sank back into my chest. I heaved an incredible sigh of relief.

Gid looked bewildered. He narrowed his eyes. "That man knew we were here," he said softly.

"Then why did he ride off?" I asked.

"I don't know," he replied thoughtfully.

My stomach knotted again. "Should we regroup with the others?"

Gid thought another moment. "No. Let's keep moving."

We crept down the row of trees. I could see the sheen emitted by the surface of the lake. I knew that it surrounded the mansion on three sides. By all appearances, there was only one way to approach the house. To our left stood the servants' quarters. The place was completely dark except for a single dim lantern burning above the entrance. As we moved past it, I noticed something peculiar on the ground ahead. It was a mound of earth, overgrown with grass. On the near side, a cavity sank into the mound. As we drew closer, I was able to see down inside. There was a muddy stairway leading down to a door. A root cellar, I wondered? But why would a root cellar be so far from the house?

I descended the muddy stairs. Gid hesitated; I'm sure he was wondering what I was trying to do. The door was bolted by a large iron padlock, cankered with rust. It didn't appear to have been opened in years. I stuck Gid's sword through the eyelet, then I placed the tip against the hard wood and yanked. The lock broke. I shoved the door open with my shoulder, revealing a dark corridor. It seemed to run toward the mansion, directly under the lake.

I turned back. "Gid, look!" I whispered excitedly.

Gid had seen it. He disappeared, returning thirty seconds later with the lantern that had hung over the entrance to the servants' quarters. I peered into the tunnel. I speculated that at one time it had been used by the servants to get to and from the main house. But why wasn't it being used now?

Gid joined me at the bottom of the stairs. "There's not much oil in this lamp," he said. "It could burn out at any moment."

We continued into the corridor, our reflexes primed for an ambush. The tunnel was humid, and sweat trickled down my forehead. The corridor sloped slightly downward. At the place where I estimated that the lake began, the path turned sharply to the right and descended another stairway. A peculiar iron wheel, about four feet wide, was positioned there on the wall. I had no idea what it was for, and there was no time to find out. The stairway descended about thirty steps, then turned again toward the mansion. At the bottom there were six inches of standing water. So, I thought, that explained why the servants no longer used it. Apparently the lake was starting to seep in. It would have been drier to take the long way around to the front entrance.

Gid and I sloshed through the water. He continued to hold the dim lamp out in front. We reached the place where water was leaking in. In the ceiling there was a block of stone about six feet wide. It looked sort of like a plug. Water dripped steadily from its edges. We passed beneath it and continued another hundred feet to another stairway that curved to the left. Like the other, this one ascended about thirty steps. At the top it curved straight again, revealing another hardwood door. As I'd feared, it was locked.

I tried shoving against it. The door budged a little, but then the padlock on the opposite side caught it. This was a true dilemma. We couldn't slam our bodies against it. The noise would echo through the whole house.

"Try the sword," said Gid.

I shoved the blade into the groove. I could hear the padlock jiggle on the opposite side, but there was no leverage to try and break it.

"Here," said Gid. He pulled the bone-handled knife out of his belt and laid the handle across the edge of the door. "Prop it against this."

I placed the end of the sword against the lock and lifted the blade until it was flush with the knife's bone handle. Then I jammed my hand upward against the sword's hilt. The bone handle broke. But so, it seemed, did the lock on the opposite side. The door fell open under its own weight. Another stairway was revealed, dusty and streaming with cobwebs. Gid stuck the knife, its handle now broken in half, back in its sheath. We pushed through the spider webs and found yet another door at the top of the stairs. This one was unlocked.

Gid set down the lantern and armed his bow. I held the sword tighter and pushed the door open slowly with my foot. As the interior lamplight hit our faces, we hung back, fearing an onslaught of arrows. The room was still. We edged forward. Before us stretched a magnificent array of tapestries, mosaics, statuettes, furniture, artifacts, and antiques. It was like a museum, or an Egyptian tomb. The artworks filled the room from floor to ceiling—much of it gold, silver, and ivory. There were treasures from as far away as India and China. Some of it looked as old as civilization itself: crystal vases from Babylon, ebony tables from the courts of Pharaoh. There were unicorns and griffins, sphinxes and dragons.

Our eyes took in the wooden rafters overhead, as well as the tall wooden shelves. The shelves were free-standing; many of them held ancient books, neatly rolled up and bound in leather or sheepskin. My heart starting racing. I scanned the shelves for a glimpse of the sacred scrolls. They had to be here. Where else would they be? I didn't see them on the shelves.

But then my eyes rested on a large red table, and my breath caught in my throat. I took several strides toward the table. Gid stayed close, his bow at the ready. They were all here! The Book of Matthew, the Scroll of Knowledge—all eleven scrolls that we had carried from Jerusalem were just sitting on the table, as if waiting to be catalogued. I reached out to gather them into my arms.

Then we heard the scream.

It was a man's voice. It sounded far away—somewhere on the other side of the mansion. We crossed the room to a thick double door and pushed. It wouldn't budge a single inch. Something heavy was barring it on the other side.

We heard another muffled scream—a woman. Not Mary; I felt sure I would have known Mary's voice. We searched the room, desperately looking for some other way out. There was another stairway on the far side that led up to a balcony. At the end stood an arched doorway.

We flew up the stairs three at a time and burst through the doorway. Then we froze solid in our tracks. It was a bedroom. It had one circular window twenty inches wide and a tiny yellow lamp. Sprawled out in the center of the room was an enormous round bed, a dozen feet across, surrounded by six spiraling pillars. Over the back hung a heavy curtain embroidered in gold. It portrayed a scene from a Greek dinner party.

Lying on the bed, nestled in a mound of pillows and blankets, was the councilman himself. Epigonus looked as pale as a ghost. His eyes were closed. He drew a deep, gasping breath. It was clear that he had suffered some sort of serious attack—a heart attack or a stroke. Epigonus was dying. The eyes fluttered open. He turned his head, trying with difficulty to focus his gaze on us. We stood there gaping in surprise. Where were his servants? His nursemaids? His bodyguards? Would they really have left him alone to die?

As he finally recognized me, his eyes widened. "You!" he squealed, his lungs straining for breath.

I gathered my wits and stepped closer. "Where's Mary?" I asked sternly.

"Dead," he wheezed. "I told you. She's dead."

I narrowed my eyes. "You lied."

He paused. Then laughed—a horrible, choking sound. "So I did. It doesn't matter. She'll be dead soon enough. My Scythians will see to that."

"*Where is she?!*" I demanded again. "*Where's the boy, Jesse?!*"

He watched me another second. He seemed amused by my desperation. Then his eyes turned back toward the ceiling. "The gods do have a sense of humor after all. To mingle my ashes with so many Christians. Welcome to my funeral pyre. You're a part of it. Everyone . . . is a part of it."

From a distant room of the mansion we heard another scream. In a flash I realized what was happening. Jesse had mentioned it—the Scythian custom. Slay the wives. Kill the slaves. The horsemen were fulfilling their master's last wishes!

The bedroom had two entrances. Another doorway stood open across the room. We sprang toward it. Yet another stairway was revealed, this one curving downward into darkness. It also went upward, revealing a faint source of light. We heard no more screams. But for the first time I smelled smoke. Horror, like the legs of a spider, crept up my spine. *Welcome to my funeral pyre.* Epigonus couldn't be that crazy. Would he try to make a funeral pyre of his own house?

We bounded up the stairs. After about forty steps, we reached another doorway. This one was quite narrow—three feet wide, four feet tall, and bolted by no less than three chains. It was the tower! I felt sure it was the same tower that Jesse and I had seen from the tree. Light was coming from underneath the door.

"Mary!" I shouted. "Mary, are you in there?"

"Harry?!" called back a voice. It was Jesse.

"Jesse! I'm here with Gidgiddonihah! Is Mary in there?"

"I'm here, Harry!" cried the voice I remembered so well.

Gid had already set to work on the chains.

"Are you both all right?" I asked.

"We're fine!" said Jesse. "But hurry! The Scythians are killing the servants. They're going to burn the house!"

No news there. Though I suspected it wasn't just the servants they planned to slay. I looked back, half expecting to see one of the Scythians climbing the stairs.

Gid groaned in frustration. "The chains are new! I can't break them!"

I started to panic. We couldn't afford to waste any time. Gid felt along the chains until he came to the bolt attached to the door.

"Give me your sword," he demanded.

I complied. He stabbed it into the door above the bolt. The wood splintered. He raised the sword and did it again. The blade dug in behind the bolt, and Gid twisted it outward. The bolt pulled loose. He stabbed downward one final time, then yanked the bolt out of the wood. He repeated the action on the next bolt. This time as he twisted it, the tip of the sword broke clean off. Undaunted, Gid hammered downward until the bolt broke away. I pulled open the door.

As the two occupants came into view, my eyes relished the sight. Jesse's face was bruised, no doubt from the ill-treatment of the Scythians. I drank in the features of Mary, my beautiful, dark-haired Judean princess. Her hair was long and flowing. The last time I'd seen her, it had been short. She'd cut it off to pose as a boy—an ineffective disguise, in my opinion. Jesse had been right; she'd grown up. She looked more stunning than I could have envisioned. Her eyes were already swimming with tears as she drew me into her arms. Her emotions overflowed.

"It's all right," I whispered in her ear. "We're here now. I'm here."

She embraced Gidgiddonihah. He accepted the embrace, then ended it abruptly. "The house is burning! Let's move! Let's move!"

He pushed us ahead of him through the doorway. Jesse picked up the broken sword. I held Mary's hand. The stairway curved around, and we saw the yellow light emanating through the doorway leading into Epigonus' room. A pall of smoke now filled the sloping corridor. Something struck me as wrong. I reached out and grabbed Jesse's shoulder.

"Jesse, stop," I said.

I peered into the gloomy darkness of the stairway beyond Epigonus' room. I'd seen something. A flash. Like the flash of a weapon.

Gidgiddonihah suddenly pushed his way between us. His bow was in hand, armed with an arrow. But before he could draw it back, the snap of another bowstring reverberated in the shadows. Gid was struck! The arrow hit his side, spinning him around. He recovered and stood up straight. With incredible concentration, he drew back his bowstring and fired into the darkness.

We heard the thud as the arrow hit its target. The attacker shrieked—the inhuman cry of the Scythian. Then we heard his body tumbling deeper into the stairwell.

But then another shape lunged toward us—this one baring its teeth! A tigerhound! The creature leapt for Jesse's throat. He swung the broken sword downward, and the blade hit home. The dog fell onto the stairs, then rolled back into the same smoky darkness as the Scythian.

Gid leaned against the wall in pain. Mary and I helped him to walk down to Epigonus' room. In the lamplight we were able to assess the injury. The arrow had pierced through his abdomen on the right, just below the ribcage. I couldn't tell if it was centered enough to have pierced any vital organs.

The Nephite reached down and broke off the shaft. In an astonishing burst of self-will and fury, Gid yanked out the arrow himself and tossed it aside. Still gritting his teeth, he set his sights toward the arched doorway that led out onto the balcony. "Let's keep going!" he declared.

With hardly a limp, he marched forward, one hand pressing his wound, the other still grasping his bow. We followed close behind. I happened to glance at the councilman in his bed. His eyes were open, but they were glossed over. Epigonus was dead.

Even before we reached the doorway, I could see the smoke rising into the room from below. I gasped in dread. The museum room was on fire! *The scrolls!* We stepped out onto the balcony. The shelves, much of the furniture, and the tapestries had been set aflame. Even the wooden door leading down to the servants' passage was burning! My sights riveted on the red table with the sacred scrolls. The furniture around it was raging! The flames were licking at the scrolls!

"No!" cried Mary.

She leaped down the stairway, her only thought to rescue the precious manuscripts that had been in her father's care for so long. With alarm, I suddenly realized that these flames hadn't started themselves! Mary reached the bottom. I was five yards behind her. She rushed toward the table, dodging the flames. I'd almost reached the foot of the stairs when I saw the shape rise from behind a burning couch. The man's face was tattooed with striking snakes. The Scythian! His arrow was aiming *straight at Mary!*

I leaped over the sloping banister, my feet still running as I hit the floor. I dove, tackling the horseman just as his bowstring fired. The arrow was thrown off target. The Scythian and I crashed into a table, sending an arrangement of marble statuettes shattering across the floor. The powerful bodyguard tossed me aside, then reached to his right and grasped a staff with the stone head of a crocodile. As I came to my feet he was facing me, ready to swing. I ducked as the crocodile swung over my head. He swung again—this time lower. I dropped and rolled. He pursued, hammering down. I grabbed an orange pot with handles shaped like ram's horns. The Scythian's staff shattered it in my hands. He raised it again. I turned my shoulder. As he stabbed it downward like a javelin, the staff scraped against my shoulder blades, ripping my tunic.

At that instant, he threw back his head in agony. Gid's arrow had struck him in the back, the arrowhead piercing through his shoulder. My arms latched onto the staff to prevent him from raising it again. I planted my feet on the horseman's chest. Then I thrust out with all my might. The Scythian flew into the midst of a burning shelf. Fiery scrolls spilled around him. The shelf teetered. I leaped out of the way. The free-standing edifice came crashing down on top of him.

Gid appeared above me and helped me to my feet. We heard Mary cry out in desperation. She was fighting the flames to gather up the scrolls. Several had already caught fire! She'd burned one of her hands. We had to pull her away from the flames. In her arms were only five of the eleven manuscripts. The rest were being consumed, crackling in the flames. My heart groaned in despair.

Fire was engulfing every wall. Our old entranceway was an inferno. We couldn't escape!

"Epigonus' room!" shouted Mary. "The window!"

The window was less than two feet wide. We'd never fit through. It couldn't save us, but it might save the remaining scrolls. We fought back up the stairway to reach Epigonus' room. Jesse had already opened the window.

His head poked back inside when he heard us. "The Nephites have opened the gate!" he announced.

I pushed my head through the opening. Smoke billowed up from all around the base of the mansion. I saw Micah below us—he and the others had managed to raise the gate. Now they were trying to break through the mansion's front entrance.

"Micah!" I yelled.

He and the Nephites looked up.

"We can't get in!" cried Micah. "All the entrances are blocked from the inside!"

Mary pushed me out of the way. She hoisted the scrolls up to the window. "Catch these!" she implored. "Protect them with your lives!"

She thrust them through the opening. I didn't see if Micah had caught them or not. I was suddenly thrust forward, and my chin smashed into the stone. Gidgiddonihah had pushed me into the wall! I heard the whir of an arrow. Gid wrenched out another cry.

There in the opposite doorway leaned the Scythian who had fallen back into the stairwell. Gid's arrow still protruded from his hip. He'd survived! He'd managed to climb back to Epigonus' room and reload his bow. Gid had taken the arrow *meant for me!*

Despite his double wounds, Gid was still on his feet. He reached for his favorite weapon—the hatchet. The Scythian loaded *another* arrow! Gidgiddonihah took one stride toward him and raised his weapon overhead. At the same instant that Gid's hatchet was released, the Scythian's bowstring snapped. Gid's aim was lethal; the Scythian was struck in the head. He sprawled onto his back for the last time. Gidgiddonihah collapsed to his knees. The third arrow had gone straight into his stomach. The other arrow had penetrated his ribcage on the right side.

"Gidgiddonihah!" I cried in terror.

The Nephite warrior tried to stand. His powerful hand broke off the shaft of the arrow in his stomach. I reached under his arms to offer support.

"Break off the other one!" he commanded.

Jesse fulfilled the command, breaking the second shaft to keep it from interfering with Gid's arm movement. The warrior's strength wavered, and he nearly collapsed again. Mary positioned herself under his opposite arm. Gid stayed on his feet.

Mary's eyes were flowing with tears. "What can we do? We have to get him out of here!"

The pall of smoke was so thick I could hardly see the massive body of Epigonus in his bed. Mary and Jesse were coughing. An idea struck me.

"Jesse! Grab that curtain!"

I pointed toward the thick woolen curtain at the head of Epigonus' bed—the one depicting Epigonus' favorite pastime, a dinner party. Mary and I continued to support Gidgiddonihah while Jesse tore down the curtain.

"Throw it over us!" I told Jesse. "We're going back the same way we came in!"

As the curtain was draped over our heads, the four of us made our way to the balcony and down the stairs. Gid's legs threatened to buckle. We fought to keep him upright. Because of the curtain, all I could see was the floor under my feet. As we reached the base of the museum, I raised its fringe just enough to see the doorway leading down to the tunnel. It was hanging by one hinge. Flames still licked around its edges.

I glanced back toward the fallen shelf. Something struck me as peculiar, but it didn't quite register. All my concentration was focused on reaching that door. A tapestry broke free from the ceiling and swooped in front of us, the material molten with flames. A storm of sparks erupted. I pulled the curtain over our faces and forged ahead.

We reached the door. Using a corner of the curtain to protect my hand, I tossed the burning wood aside. We plunged through the ring of fire and entered the smoky stairwell. Immediately, I tossed the woolen curtain onto the stone steps. The material was scorched and smoldering. Several holes had burned through it near the back. Gid's weight became too much for Mary. He sank down onto the steps.

"Gid," I pleaded in distress. "Hang on. It's just a little farther."

He looked dazed. Mary and I were covered in his blood. I feared

Gid didn't understand me. But then his eyes filled with comprehension, and he nodded. Again we hoisted him to his feet. Jesse found the lantern that we'd first brought from the servants' quarters. It still glowed the tiniest flame. Gid stepped awkwardly down the stairs; I could tell every step sent pain shooting into every part of his body. As we reached the first corridor, I stopped. My eyes strained to see the floor.

"What is it?" asked Mary.

"Jesse," I said. "Shine the light!"

He brought forth the lantern. I reached down and touched a moist stain. It was blood! Another series of stains reflected on the ground a few feet farther. A trail! Now I remembered what had struck me as so peculiar a few moments earlier. The fallen shelf had looked different— it had been *moved.* Somehow the Scythian had managed to crawl out from under it. He was still alive!

"We have to go back!" I clamored. "He's in the tunnel!"

"No!" said Gid sternly. "Keep going."

He was right. Forward was our only choice. To go back now meant asphyxiation—certain death. Smoke was continuing to pour into the stairwell. We knew the Scythian was seriously wounded. Probably burned. We'd take our chances with him. We arrived at the sharp left turn that took us into the passage leading under the lake. In desperation we descended the final stairway into the stretch of tunnel flooded with six inches of water. Jesse raised his lantern to see down the long corridor. There was no sign of the Scythian—just the steady percussion of dripping water. My stomach churned with a deep foreboding. Gid continued sloshing forward with a determination that I didn't understand. As we neared the center, I heard the strangest sound. It was a grinding echo coming from the ceiling above us, like the hoisting of chains. I looked up in consternation.

"Keep moving!" cried Gid. "Keep—!"

Suddenly the stone plug in the center of the corridor lifted out of its foundation. A torrent of water poured in. Mary shrieked. Jesse's lantern fizzled out. Gid leaned forward. We forged on, passing beneath the central stone, our bodies drenched. Then the stone was removed completely, and the full fury of the deluge was unleashed. The lake poured into the tunnel in a raging waterfall. The wave washed us down the corridor, tumbling our bodies in the darkness. I lost my hold on Gid, on Mary. I struggled to push myself upward for breath. I was flipped upside down. Someone grabbed onto my hand. It was Mary. Our heads broke the surface. I could hear her gasping for breath. I latched onto her waist and swam furiously with the current while Jesse splashed ahead of me. Where was Gid? Had the deluge washed him the opposite direction? How could he swim in his condition? He'd surely drown!

A flickering light appeared ahead. I could see the stairway at the opposite end of the tunnel, sloping upward. The wave slammed against the back wall and washed back over our heads. I continued clawing at the walls to reach the stairs. Finally my fingers grasped the corner and I hoisted myself around it, pulling Mary behind me. Jesse also emerged into the flickering light, coughing and choking. The water was climbing the stairs fast. I scrambled to keep ahead of it, my hand still grasping Mary's wrist.

Someone else's hand seized my throat.

I looked up into the flaming eyes of the Scythian, the demon ghost glowing in his face, the black tattoos of the snakes blistered and raw. His arms and neck were also burned. Gid's arrow still protruded from his shoulder. In his free hand he gripped his terrible double-bladed knife. A burning torch leaned against the wall behind him. Mary screamed. Jesse lunged forward to defend me, but the Scythian kicked him in the face. I was slammed against the wall. The Scythian raised his knife to slash it cleanly across my throat.

I caught the horseman's wrist. Clenching my teeth, using all my strength, I held the knife at bay. My other hand wrapped around the shaft of the arrow embedded in his shoulder and twisted. He howled in agony. My elbow smashed his forearm. The knife fell from his hand. It bounced onto the steps and soon became immersed in rising water. I propelled my fist into the tattoo of the snake on the Scythian's face. He flew back against the wall, nearly crashing into Mary. I yanked her out of the way as the horseman crumpled onto the steps, his body half submerged in water. The Scythian's eyes narrowed in rage. He reached into the water and found the knife. His arm reached back to throw it like a tomahawk. I shoved Mary to the floor, falling on top of her. The knife ricocheted off the stone just above my head and clattered onto the steps. But then I heard a loud splash.

When I turned my head, Gidgiddonihah was lunging from the water. His hand gripped the broken knife with the bone handle. He buried the blade deep into the Scythian's belly. The horseman wrenched out a cry of death. He fell forward, limp and lifeless. Gid collapsed on top of him. But then he rolled off the Scythian and lay there panting, the water rising around his legs.

I pulled myself to my feet. "Jesse, Mary, help me!"

We hoisted Gid up the final flight of stairs until we reached the last corridor. I glanced at the iron wheel—the mechanism that had raised the stone plug out of its foundation. We continued on. Gid had a hard time lifting his head.

"It's all right," I said to him. "We'll find a horse, Gid. We'll take you to Luke. He's a physician. He'll take care of you. Just hang on."

Footsteps were running down the tunnel toward us.

"Harry!"

It was Micah!

"Micah, Uzziah, help us! Gid's hurt! Help us carry him outside!"

The Nephites gathered around and gently lifted their kinsman. I followed closely. "Hang on, Gid! You'll be all right. Hang on."

We reached the exit and carried Gid into the open air. We laid him in the grass, the flames of the burning mansion illuminating his face. Jashon was there. The Scythian's arrow had only grazed his arm. It was bound in a makeshift sling.

Gid's eyes were closed. I held his head in my arms.

"Gid!" I cried, tears burning my face. "No, Gid! You can't! *Father in Heaven! Please, no—!*"

His weary eyes opened, and he looked up at me. "Harry," he whispered.

"Yes, Gid. You won't die in this land. I promise you." I looked at Gid's kinsmen. "We need a horse! Find me one of the Scythians' horses!"

"The horses are dead," said Micah solemnly. "There isn't a living thing on this entire estate, other than us."

Gid drew a ragged breath. There was blood in his mouth. He closed his eyes. *Oh, God!* I braced his shoulders. This couldn't happen. Gid couldn't die. A stripling warrior was invincible. I had to keep him alive. My self-will, my own life force, would keep him alive.

When Gid opened his eyes again, there was no pain in his features. Just a calm smile. It widened into a grin. The same familiar grin that I'd seen a thousand times.

"Harry, do you remember?" he asked. "Do you remember?"

"Remember what, Gid?"

"His face. Do you remember His face?"

I didn't have to ask. I knew what face he meant. It was the one face neither of us would ever forget. I tried to clear the tears from my eyes. "Yes, Gid. Yes, I remember."

"It's all right," he said. "It's all right."

"No!" I pleaded. "You can't leave me. You're the best friend . . . the best hero I ever had."

"No," he said. "Just a soldier . . ."

"The greatest," I said. "The greatest there ever was."

"She's calling me," he said. Then he whispered the name of his long-deceased wife. "Rebha . . . my little one . . ."

Rage exploded inside me. I wouldn't let him go! But then I looked again at his eyes. I was entranced by the peace I saw in them. I buried my face in his neck. My heart broke, and I gave in. I realized I had no right—no right to hold him here. "Then go, Gid," I whispered through my tears. "Go with her."

Slowly, Gidgiddonihah closed his eyes. There in the stillness, I felt his heart beat its last pulse. I continued to hold him, rocking him, weeping in furious desolation. The firelight reflected on the warrior's face. It made it seem as if the face was still living, still surging with strength. I was tempted to cover it, to shade his eyes. But the fire helped me remember. A life of power. Unconquerable fury. The right-eousness of a warrior of God.

I held him under the night sky, my tears mingling with those of Mary and Jesse and his kinsmen. And there in the blazing moonlight, God's mighty warrior embarked on his final glorious adventure.

CHAPTER 22

For twenty-two days we rode the high seas of the Mediterranean from Caesarea to the mouth of the Cayster River in Asia Minor. It wasn't exactly a luxury liner that Jim and Apollus had booked for our passage, but the accommodations we received in exchange for four penlights, six butane lighters, a handful of pens, and a bag of mini Snickers bars (well melted) were nevertheless the best the ship had to offer. We had our own private cabin, complete with services from the ship's steward. Most of the other travelers were wealthy pilgrims on their way to Ephesus to worship at the great temple dedicated to the goddess called Artemis, or Diana. Despite all we had been told about the strength of the Christian community in the region of the Seven Churches, it seemed that it still ran a distant second in popularity to the traditional cults of the pagans.

The city of Ephesus was actually located a mile and a half upriver in an ancient port that constantly had to be dredged of silt and sediment to make it passable to trade ships. The city itself was nestled against a mountain whose summit was bisected by a thick defensive wall. From the deck as we approached the little harbor, my mother pointed in awe toward the gleaming platform, carved pillars, and massive roof of the Temple of Artemis just northeast of town.

"That may be the most gorgeous building I've seen," she crooned.

"It should be, Mom," I responded. "It's one of the seven wonders of the ancient world."

We debarked ship right during the hottest part of the day, when most of the city's residents were snoring away at their afternoon siestas. Steffanie was still walking with a pair of crutches provided by the garrison doctor at Neopolis. The waterfront was lined with inns and public baths. I was eager to find lodging and soak for a few hours in a Roman spa. Jim, however, had other ideas. His mind was set on finding someone who could give us information about the local Christian community. Up until now, it had been a touchy subject—one that we had been unwilling to broach on board ship for fear that it would offend the devoted patrons of Artemis. But now that we had arrived at our destination, we had little choice but to take our chances with the locals.

As we made our way across the gangplank and set our feet on Asian soil, I couldn't help but notice that our every move was observed by a certain beggar sitting cross-legged in the shadow of a boat house. He had a short gray beard, a round, rosy face and sparkling eyes, despite the fact that he was dressed from head to foot in the most awful, smelly rags. In his hands was a wooden begging bowl. At present it was empty. I felt sure he'd already put in a full day trying to woo the citizens to drop in a few coins, but so far no one appeared to have shown him much sympathy.

I found it curious that he would watch us so intently when other, wealthier passengers debarking from the ship must have appeared far more apt to donate to his cause. I guess we just had that look—the vulnerable, generous look that beggars trained themselves to spot.

We made our way toward the main thoroughfare, a magnificent street paved in marble that led to the famous theater where Paul and his companions had stirred up such a commotion on their first missionary visit. Steffanie's condition made our progress slow. Apollus offered to help, but Steff gently refused. She wanted to do this on her own.

Our turtle's pace was interpreted by the beggar as an opportune moment to make his approach. He arose from his patch of shade and stepped toward us in the middle of the marble street. The begging bowl was left at his side, as if at the moment he wasn't interested in receiving a handout.

"You're travelers from far away, am I right?" he inquired.

"That's right," Apollus replied warily. "You'd better be about your own business, old man. We don't have any coins to spare."

My mother objected. "Nonsense, Apollus," she scolded. (I loved to see Apollus get scolded.) She turned to Jim. "Can we give him something he might sell?"

Jim leaned toward her and tried to say in confidence, "I'd be happy to give him something, Sabrina. But I'm afraid in his . . . circumstances . . .

he'd have a hard time selling anything without being cheated. He'd be better off with coins."

The beggar overheard. "That's all right," he said. "The laborer is worthy of his hire. I would never expect to receive without giving in return. Perhaps . . . you're looking for something. Something that I might help you to find?"

Jim seemed to appreciate his straightforward tone. "As a matter of fact, we are *looking for something.*"

"Ah!" said the beggar. "I knew it when I first laid eyes on you. I knew you were not ordinary pilgrims come to our fair city. I told myself, 'These people are searching. They're searching for something very important.'"

Jim chuckled at his insight. I found the old man utterly charming.

"We're looking for information," said Jim. "If you can provide it, we could give you some things that might make you far better off than you are at present."

He smiled warmly. "Oh, that would be nice. But how could I be better off? I already have everything I could ever want." He spread his arms as if to show us that the whole city of Ephesus belonged to him exclusively.

We laughed.

"I'm happy to hear it," said Jim. "Just the same, I promise we'd do all we could to show our gratitude."

"All you could? My, that is *a lot* of gratitude. Perhaps you'd better ask your question."

Jim decided not to beat around the bush. "We're searching for the gathering place of the Christians."

The beggar's eyebrows shot up. "Gathering place of the Christians?" He clicked his tongue. "You've made a very difficult request."

Here we go, I thought. We were about to find out a beggar's going rate for information in this town.

But then he asked, "What do you know of these Christians?"

Jim hesitated, then replied, "Well, we . . .we've heard there is a large community of Christians here. We're looking for their leader. A man by the name of John."

"John, yes," said the beggar. "I've heard of John."

We stopped in our tracks. My heart raced with excitement. Could it be this easy?

"Do you know where he lives?" I asked. "Can you take us to his home?"

"Perhaps," the beggar said shrewdly. "Why do you wish to see John? Does he have something you wish him to give you?"

"No," said Jim. "I mean . . . perhaps, but . . . John is a special man among Christians."

"What could be so special about John?"

"He's a special witness. He can personally testify to all of the things Christians believe. He was there. It all happened right before his eyes."

"I see. Then you believe this man is an apostle?"

We scrutinized the beggar in surprise. He knew more about Christians than he'd first led us to believe. A peculiar feeling stirred inside me. I looked into the beggar's eyes. I'd often heard the expression that eyes could twinkle. This man's eyes were glistening.

"Yes," Jim replied. "An apostle. A special witness of Jesus Christ."

"What do you think this man looks like?" he asked.

Jim shook his head, "I wouldn't really . . ."

The beggar continued, "Would he be dressed in the toga of a rich man? The robes of a king? The gowns of a merchant? Or might he come to you . . . in the rags of a beggar?"

The peculiar feeling swelled into something else. A burning in the bosom. A feeling so overwhelming that my knees felt weak.

"He might," said Jim, his voice subdued, "come to us as any of those things."

"Would you be more inclined to believe his testimony if he were a rich man or a beggar?"

"It wouldn't matter," said Jim. "He would still be a special witness of Jesus Christ."

The man stood up tall. "What if I told you that I was John?"

We stood there transfixed.

Jim replied solemnly, "Then I would know that you are an apostle of the Lord."

A radiant smile slowly climbed his cheeks. None of us uttered a word.

"Forgive my appearance," said John playfully. "I sometimes dress this way when the Spirit whispers that there is someone to meet at the harbor. Before you knew me, I wanted to have a chance to know you."

My heart was dancing, spinning in delighted somersaults. Hadn't Joseph Smith done something like this once as he greeted new converts from Europe? We just stood there, our eyes soaking in every part of the beloved apostle's face. At last he opened his arms to embrace us.

"*Welcome to Ephesus,*" *he said cheerfully.* "*Welcome to the seat of the Seven Churches of God.*"

CHAPTER 23

In an unmarked Christian cemetery among the ruins of the old harbor of Athens rested the bodies of four brave men from a promised land on the other side of the world. It wasn't the proper place. They should have been buried in their homeland. Especially the greatest warrior of them all, Gidgiddonihah.

I knelt over his grave, the grief so consuming that my mind felt numb. My friend was dead. My hero. If I could have done it, I'd have sacrificed everything I possessed to have carried him back to Zarahemla. I knew he would have wanted his body to rest under Zarahemla's skies, surrounded by its lofty volcanic peaks, in the warm earth of the land whose freedoms he had fought so hard to preserve. It wasn't in my power. Because of it, my grief burned even deeper.

On his grave I laid the broken sword that he had wielded in my defense, and in the defense of Mary, Jesse, and his kinsmen. It was surely only one of a hundred weapons he had raised in defense of the people he loved. And it seemed appropriate to me, somehow, that the tip was broken. To me it symbolized that in the world to which he'd ascended, he would never have to raise a weapon again. His days of fighting were over. Now he would enjoy the rest of a righteous soldier in the bosom of God.

In his last effort, Gidgiddonihah had saved not only the three of us, but he and his comrades had helped to save the five sacred scrolls. Five of eleven. I might have named them without even having to see them. They were the Gospel of Matthew, the Gospel of Mark, the Epistle of James, Paul's Epistle to the Hebrews, and a letter from Saint Jude. We'd lost the Book of Isaiah, the Book of Daniel, and the Book of Ezekiel, though I felt certain that many copies existed in other places. The most tragic losses were a manuscript written by Peter outlining the organization of the Church, a second epistle of James, and the infamous Scroll of Knowledge that we had fought so hard to obtain in Jerusalem as a ransom for Meagan's life. All in all, I suppose I should have been awed by the miracle of what we had managed to save. As for the rest, I knew the Lord had already restored the information in the Scroll of Knowledge, as well as the true organization of the Church. My heart swelled with gratitude. Maybe other copies of those books still existed, waiting to be uncovered by modern archaeologists. Whatever might happen, I was sure that the Lord would always bless His righteous people with whatever knowledge they desired, insofar as they were willing to abide by His laws.

Shortly after the funeral of Gidgiddonihah and the other Nephites, all the Christians of Athens, Gid's surviving kinsmen, Stephanas and his sons, Chrysoganus the Mithraist, Micah, Jesse, Mary, Saint Luke, and myself gathered at the place in the harbor where the ship owner from Ephesus named Priscus had anchored his boat. Stephanas' boat was also anchored nearby, ready to sail back to Calliste to rejoin the cause of Bishop Titus.

Stephanas had managed to sell his catch, but all the proceeds had gone to help pay the debt incurred by Chrysoganus to repeal the anti-Christian edict. Chrysoganus was flat broke. He'd lost his business and he'd lost his standing among the merchants of Athens. In spite of it, the old fishmonger looked content and proud.

"Come back with us to Calliste," Stephanas urged his former partner. "There's always room for another hawker of fish sauce on our small island."

Chrysoganus accepted. "It certainly sounds better than any prospects I have here. But I warn you, old friend, in time I may convert you to the ways of Mithras."

"And I warn you," said Stephanas, "in time I may convert you to the glories of Jesus Christ."

So the two old partners were reunited. I said farewell to Stephanas and his sons—Peter, Andrew, and Paul. Before their ship set sail, I asked Stephanas to give my love and regards to Nicanor and my old, eternal friends from those long months on Lincoln Island.

"Tell them they'll always have a precious place in my memory," I said. "And tell Bishop Titus that I hope one day he fulfills his dream to return with his congregation to Crete."

"Thank you, Harrison," said Stephanas. "But wherever the Lord chooses to let us live out our days, I hope we can always live the pure and undefiled doctrines of Christ."

I feared the same would not hold true for the Christians of Athens. Shortly after the funeral, Dionysius, the former Areopogite, announced that he would be assuming the office that had been vacated by Bishop Silvanus, who had been crucified. Almost as if mounting a political campaign, he declared that he would restore unity and order to the scattered congregation of Athens. The starved and beleaguered Christians showed every sign that they would flock to his guardianship. Frankly, I think they'd have flocked to anyone who showed a shred of willingness to lead.

It was Jesse who had the nerve to ask Dionysius, "How can you be bishop if you haven't been ordained?"

Dionysius replied calmly and straightforwardly, "If I refuse to lead them, who will? Who will continue to tell the people the good news of Jesus Christ?"

I pondered his question, and it penetrated deeply into my heart. There was a sad and lonely resonance to it, and yet it expressed the same dilemma faced by all of the scattered believers everywhere the apostles had preached. The authority of the priesthood had been lost, but their humble love of the Savior remained. What were they supposed to do? Forget about Jesus? Forget His mission? Forget that He had died for their sins?

The answer was simple. They would do the best they could. That was all they *could* do. It struck me how marvelous it was that the basic doctrine of the gospel would survive for the next two thousand years. In spite of all the schisms, debates, conflicts, corruptions, church councils, and even bloodshed, the essential message that Jesus was the Savior of the world would remain intact. The preaching of Peter, James, John, Paul, and the rest of the apostles hadn't failed. It had planted something permanent in the heart of the western world. How successful would Joseph Smith have been if his mission had been in a land where the love of Jesus wasn't at the core of the people? It was men like Dionysius who would keep that love forever burning. Rather than condemn the new bishop of Athens, I wished him Godspeed. Then, like so many others, I looked to the day when the priesthood would be restored and the Savior would once again establish His kingdom on earth.

I tried not to let those thoughts be spoiled by Ignatius of Antioch, who had also been released from prison. In him I saw the bigotry and arrogance that would hinder Christ's mission in all generations, including the generation in which I had been born.

"We must continue to show these vile pagans the superiority of Christ," he declared just before he boarded a separate ship bound for Antioch. "One day the sword will be in *our* hands, brothers and sisters. Be ready for that day! We will crush our enemies to dust, or we will glory in our own deaths as martyrs of God!"

Our own ship left Piraeus the following morning at sunrise. Its passengers included Micah, Mary, and Jesse, as well as Jashon and the rest of the Nephites. Also on board was Luke, the beloved companion of Peter and Paul. He spent most of his time on a cot below deck, gathering strength after suffering for so many days at the hands of the Civic Council. I think his mind was also considering the idea that he might soon undertake a certain writing project—one that would change the face of history and inspire greater faith in billions throughout the world.

My own mind was still too consumed with grief to think about much else. As I watched the sun setting across the ocean that first night, tears again filled my eyes. I couldn't believe he was gone. The world was a much grayer, more dangerous place without Gidgiddonihah. I was sure the pain would never completely heal. The hole would always be there until I was reunited with my friend.

Mary found me gazing off at the sunset and put her hand on my shoulder. I realized that she, too, had been crying. "I was thinking about the first time I saw him," she said nostalgically. "It was when you and Gid stormed out of the hills to save us from the bandits. Do you remember?"

"Yes."

"He was swinging that big gladiator's sword. Like Samson of old. Between the two of you, I'd never felt so safe in my life."

"Everyone felt safe with Gidgiddonihah."

She looked up at me. "It was *you* who reached me first, rushing in like a lion, swinging that club, no thought in the world except . . ." She lowered her eyes. "Except saving me. When I was in that tower, all alone in the darkness . . . I thought of you. . . your face from that day on the Samaritan Road. I knew you were oceans away, and yet . . . I knew you would come."

"Your face has appeared in my thoughts a few times too," I said.

She looked at me tenderly.

I turned away and chuckled. "I remember that time you cut your hair to pretend you were a boy. Worst disguise I ever saw."

She reddened and shied away. "It that how you remembered me? Short hair, dirt on my cheeks?"

I shook my head. "No. When I thought of you all those days on the island, I saw you the way I *first* saw you, leaning out the door of your father's house in Pella. A hood over your head. A lock of hair curled under your chin. I thought . . ."

"Yes?"

"I thought you had the most beautiful . . . eyes. Is that too cliché? I thought you were a princess."

Her face resonated with affection. A rush of warmth filtered into my veins.

She looked solemn again and faced the sunset. "I stood on the deck of a ship like this once before. It was sailing away from Caesarea. You were standing on the pier, growing smaller and smaller. My heart felt . . . I was sure I would never see you again."

I recalled my own premonitions about that day. "Were you really so sure?"

She looked up at me again. We tried to discern each other's thoughts. I read hers by her silence. So she *hadn't* been sure. It was in her heart, too, that we were destined to meet again. We tried to interpret the meaning. It was still uncertain, but it felt electric. A living warmth.

I embraced her, held her against the purpling sky, smelling her skin and hair, again plagued by all the impossibilities of such a relationship. After I gave the scrolls to John, I was going back to a place she'd never have understood. How could I uproot her from her world? And yet . . . what did she have here? Her future was an unwritten book. I began to see possibilities. Tender. Frightening. But that was all part of what made it electric.

It took four days to cross the Aegean Sea, four days to cast visions of the future and mourn the loss of my friend. Jashon, Heshlon, and the rest of the Nephites filled the time with tales of Zarahemla and descriptions of their remarkable society of peace and faith. It was inevitable that Micah and Jesse would find themselves enthralled. It sounded glorious—so much more hopeful than scenes that were shaping up on this side of the globe. Here they'd known only war, suffering, and racism. How could they *not* be captivated by the prospects of a land where every citizen loved Jesus Christ?

Even among the Nephites, I knew it wouldn't always be that way. Nevertheless, it stirred the imagination. Even *I* was tempted. Micah and Jesse, however, were hooked. Jews among the Nephites—was it really so disturbing? After all, they were blood relatives. If only I didn't have such a nagging sensation that such things weren't meant to be. But who was I to question the order of the universe? Maybe this was how it was *supposed* to be.

On the fourth day, Luke arose from his bed, much stronger than before. He remained with us on deck. In fact, it was Luke who first sighted the mass of land rising on the eastern horizon. "There it is," he announced. "The mouth of the Cayster River. After fifteen years, I still know it as well as the doorway to my childhood home."

Captain Priscus announced that we would reach Ephesus' harbor by nightfall. My heart swelled. I'd made it. After three years of daydreaming, I was finally here—the bosom of the last stronghold of the gospel of Jesus Christ in the Roman world.

I'd reached the land of the Seven Churches.

CHAPTER 24

Ephesus was everything I had expected—a thriving Christian community with families from many parts of the Empire. It reminded me of a modern stake, with wards in seven cities. Smyrna, Pergamum, Thyatira, Sardis, Philadelphia, and Laodicea were all within a hundred miles of the stake center, Ephesus. Each was governed by its own bishop. The Apostle John visited as often as possible to strengthen and edify the saints. Rumors of persecution and apostasy in other parts of the Church were rampant, but news in 73 A.D. didn't travel very fast, so the Saints of the Seven Churches kept to themselves and struggled to hold together their little flocks.

The Church had its enemies in Asia Minor, too. Ephesus had an economy completely dependent upon the cult of Artemis. Idols and ornaments of the goddess, as well as sacrificial items for the temple, were sold in every stall. A convert to Christ meant one less customer for Artemis. The conflict was as old as the days of Saint Paul. At present, people investigating the Church were taught in the seclusion of private homes.

The main effort against the Church was directed at John. He was a wanted man. The authorities were convinced that without Saint John of Galilee, the Church would fall apart. If they ever caught him, they were determined to exile him to the penal colony of Patmos just off the coast. Because of the warrant, many bishops and elders were never quite certain of his location. He moved almost like a ghost throughout the congregations, suddenly appearing in their midst to bless them and offer counsel. I almost wondered if he was conveyed by the Spirit, like Nephi, the son of Helaman. His status as a fugitive helped explain why he'd first had to appear to us as a beggar.

After our meeting, John directed us to the home of Bishop Timothy. It was, of course, the same Timothy mentioned in the New Testament—the *close companion of Saint Paul. After pointing out his doorway, John promptly walked up the street and disappeared into the crowd.*

Timothy was younger than I might have imagined, just a little over forty. The features of his face were soft and filled with wisdom. He wore a short beard, like John, and he had a young wife and no less than five children, all under ten years old. They gathered around us in the entranceway of Timothy's two-room apartment, eyes alight with excitement. It was rare enough to be visited by a Roman soldier like Apollus, but to also be in the presence of four exotic and mysterious foreign travelers was an extra special treat.

Timothy invited us inside, then he gently directed his children to go upstairs. Jim helped Steffanie into the apartment with her crutches. We sat on various couches and stools and introduced ourselves. Jim quickly confessed the reason for our visit. "We're looking for my son," he explained. "We're also looking for another man who might have been searching. His name is Gidgiddonihah."

Timothy perked up. "Yes! I know Gidgiddonihah. He was here not long ago with his band of men from the land of—" He struggled to pronounce it. "—Zera—Zerahem—"

"Zarahemla?" I offered.

"That's it!" said Timothy.

Timothy told us that Gid was no longer in Ephesus. He'd gone to Athens to find Symeon, Mary, and Jesse. I was deeply concerned to hear that our old friends had never reached their destination. Our stay in Ephesus was looking like a short one. I knew we'd be continuing on to Athens as soon as possible.

"Please," said Timothy. "Stay with us tonight."

"Thank you," Jim replied.

"Tomorrow is the Sabbath," he added. "We'll be breaking bread at sunrise, provided that my congregation doesn't stay out too late."

"Where is your congregation?" asked Mom.

"I hope they're in their homes," said Timothy. "That's where I counseled them to remain. But I fear that many of them are determined to hear the preacher from Smyrna. His emissaries have been advertising his arrival for days."

"Preacher?" asked Steffanie.

"They say he's a miracle worker. He claims to be an apostle from Jerusalem."

"*What's his name?*" *I asked nervously.*

"*Cerinthus,*" *Timothy confirmed.*

Apollus and I raised our eyebrows in surprise. According to Timothy, Cerinthus had been stirring up trouble in the Seven Churches ever since his arrival two and a half years before. I realized his debut would have been shortly after I'd seen him in the marketplace at Caesarea. Nobody could confirm his origins, but his popularity had been growing steadily in spite of sound condemnations by John and many of the bishops.

"*I've even heard that he is sending missionaries to other parts of the world,*" *said Timothy.* "*He claims to be the true heir of all the rights and authority of the Holy Priesthood—says he was ordained when he was just a small boy under the hands of Peter, Paul, and James, the brother of Jesus. I'm afraid his story has been embraced by many listeners. Even the bishop of Smyrna has become an ardent supporter.*"

"*But he's a* fake!" *I declared.* "*We knew him in Samaria. He's never met an apostle in his life. He was the apprentice of Simon Magus!*"

"*Simon Magus?*" *Timothy said in surprise.* "*There are many in Ephesus who know of the sorcerer Simon Magus. Simon once visited this region on his way to Rome to contend with the Apostle Peter. Can you confirm this association?*"

"*I can confirm it,*" *said Apollus.* "*I remember Cerinthus. He and his bald-headed companions—the Sons of the Elect—often bought supplies in the village of Neopolis.*"

"*If the people knew of his connection to Simon Magus, I'm certain he would be perceived in an entirely different light,*" *said Timothy.* "*Some have even compared Cerinthus to John the Baptist. They call him the voice of one crying in the wilderness to make straight the paths of the Saints before Jesus again shows Himself to the world. Whenever he speaks, men cheer, women swoon, and disorder erupts. Strangers always come forward claiming to be stricken with some foul disease. Cerinthus then proceeds to perform a miraculous healing in the midst of the people. Some say he often heals the same person over and over. The afflicted are known charlatans and thieves who have duped the citizens of Asia Province in times past, but the people seem to have short memories.*"

With a heavy sigh, Timothy expressed his fear that the plain truth was that the people wanted *to believe Cerinthus. The quiet faith of a devoted Christian wasn't enough for them anymore. They wanted drama. They wanted theater. It was far easier to put their faith in a miracle worker than it was to follow the admonitions of men who continued to parrot the same old themes of faith, hard work, hope, and endurance.*

"I don't understand," said my mother. "What does this man want? What is his motivation?"

"The same thing that motivates many false preachers," said Timothy. "Cerinthus seeks contributions from every listener. He claims he needs their gold and silver to build a kingdom on earth worthy of the Savior's return."

"Where is he speaking?" I asked urgently.

"On the hillside overlooking the stadium the Ephesians have built for their chariot races," said Timothy.

Mom was shaking her head before I could even ask.

"But Mom, please!" I said. "We can tell the people what we know!"

Only after Apollus agreed to go with me did my mother finally, reluctantly consent. We set out immediately.

The stadium was quite visible from a distance. As we approached, we could see the torches burning on the hillside. We climbed a winding path and soon found ourselves in the midst of the crowd. Almost two hundred people had come. Cerinthus was standing at the highest place, his face illuminated by torches on either side. He looked about the same: still that handsome, almost effeminate face that looked like it had been molded in plastic. We pushed our way to the center of the group without drawing his attention.

"Listen to your hearts, brothers and sisters!" he continued to shout. "Listen to the spirit that works within you! I am not the deceiver that some have proclaimed." He put his arm around a stubby-looking man standing at his left. The short man looked up at Cerinthus in puppy-like wonder. I half expected him to start licking Cerinthus' face.

"Would this man be able to stand before you tonight if it was not for the power vested in me by the Holy Spirit?" Cerinthus asked.

Several people in the crowd shouted back, "No!"

He continued, "I tell you, this man would have been condemned to crutches for the rest of his life. Judge me by my works, oh hearers of the Word! By my power the blind see, the lame walk, and evil spirits flee. I am come to you by the grace of God from the homeland of Jesus Christ. I was ordained under the hands of Peter, Paul, and James to prepare the hearts of Christ's people to unite His earthly kingdom with His heavenly king-

dom forevermore. My doctrine is the doctrine of the highest God. I am the follower of no man, but only the humble servant of mankind—"

"What about Simon Magus!" I shouted, hands cupped around my mouth.

Heads turned. Some looked irritated. Others looked surprised. Cerinthus should have been used to hecklers by now, but my words almost made him choke. He squinted to see the faces beyond the torches, though I suspected that he might have recognized my voice.

"Who speaks such blasphemy in my presence?" said Cerinthus, visibly shaken.

"I do," I declared, taking several steps forward.

He knew very well who I was, yet he said, "And who are you, young lady? Are you sent here by John to sow the seeds of discontent?"

"I came here of my own accord," I said. "I came to tell the people the truth. Why don't you tell them yourself, Cerinthus the Divine? That's what Simon used to call you, isn't it? Tell them how Simon once handpicked you to be the sole heir of the Sons of the Elect."

Cerinthus had recovered sufficiently to point his finger at me in fierce derision. "This girl is the author of lies! I remember her now. She has been an enemy of God from her childhood. A witch! A prophetess of darkness! I have personally witnessed the destruction caused by her black arts. It is because of demonesses like her that Paul proclaimed his doctrine that women should keep silent in the churches."

"Then listen to me!" cried Apollus. He wasn't wearing his helmet, but everyone recognized the uniform of a soldier of Rome. "It was my garrison that destroyed Simon Magus on Mount Gerizim in Samaria. This man was among them. He was helping to distribute the poison that Simon gave to his followers to take their own lives!"

The crowd murmured in confusion. Even Cerinthus' closest followers, who had gathered near the front, looked completely beside themselves.

I drove the point home. "Listen to the two of us! This man is a fake and a fraud. He was never in Jerusalem. He never met Peter or Paul or James. I watched as the Sons of the Elect burned eleven of twelve sacred testimonies of Jesus written by the original apostles of Jesus Christ. I was there when Cerinthus claimed to have the gifts of prophecy and seership, tongues and healing—not by the power of Christ, but by the power of the Unknown God of Simon Magus."

"It's all lies!" Cerinthus ranted on the verge of hysteria. "These two *witnesses have come to spread the spirit of Satan. Let them be subject to the laws of God. Just as the Father, the Son, and the Holy Ghost are witnesses of all truth, if they cannot provide* three *witnesses to confirm what they proclaim, let it be a sign of their deception and cunning. Let them be dragged from the midst of this congregation!"*

Apollus and I drew closer together. All eyes were upon us. Several of Cerinthus' followers clenched their fists. I was sure they were about to lead the crowd forward in a frenzied rush to tear us apart.

"I am a witness!" resounded a voice near the back.

The crowd parted. Apollus and I stood in bewilderment. My breath froze in my lungs. There, in the midst of the crowd, stood three people. Three visions. Three apparent angels from the sky.

"I am also a witness!" shouted a girl, about eighteen.

"And so am I," proclaimed a twelve-year-old boy in the center.

My heart soared as high as the heavens.

"Harry!" I screamed. "Oh, Harry!"

It was him! Two inches taller and shoulders as broad as an oak tree! And it was Jesse and Mary! Harry was grinning widely. As the audience began threatening Cerinthus, demanding that he get out of town, I fought through the crowd to reach my step-brother. My future *step-brother. Oh, just my* brother! *My big, wonderful, courageous, beautiful brother!*

I threw my arms around his neck. He spun me around twice and set me back on my feet. We cried and laughed and embraced again. Next, I smothered Jesse. Oh, my wonderful Jesse! I kissed every inch of his face. He blushed bright red and I loved it. Then I embraced Mary, sweet Mary. Apollus tried to content himself by slapping Harry on the back, but Harry wouldn't have any of it. He hugged that tough Roman by lifting him off his feet. Apollus laughed heartily.

After Cerinthus slunk away with his tail between his legs, the audience surrounded us. They knew something special was happening. They could feel it. So the joy of our reunion was multiplied by their presence. But I think everyone's feelings paled in comparison to a father's joy. Nothing could compare to the moment when Harry saw Jim coming up the path.

I saw my father drawing near. I knew that Luke, Micah, and the others had gone first to Timothy's home. From them, Dad would have learned all he needed to know. At first I wasn't sure it was him, but then the light of the torches illuminated his face. My father stopped before he reached me. We stood looking at each other, our hearts so full of emotion that we couldn't speak. My father looked the same, just like Meagan and Apollus. They hadn't aged. The sight of me must have been a surprise. A total shock. But my father seemed to exude relief, as if he'd expected far worse. Huge tears welled in his eyes as I went to him. I had almost four inches on him now. We embraced, and our exhilaration was released in a cascade of tears.

"I love you, Dad," I wept. "I love you so much."

"My boy," he whispered. "*My boy* . . ."

Then I looked him in the eye. "Melody?" I asked, bracing myself for the answer.

"She's all right," Dad replied. "The cancer is in remission. She's with Marcos. But she misses her brother terribly."

Again I was caught up in jubilation. But then suddenly I was once more overwhelmed by sadness. "Gid . . ." I said mournfully. "Gid didn't make it."

We grieved together for the life, the heroics, the righteousness of this great warrior. Then we returned to Timothy's house where I was enfolded in the arms of my beautiful sister, Steffanie, and my mother-to-be, Sabrina.

Mother-to-be? Was that still true? I looked at my father.

"Are you—? Have you both been—?"

"Not yet," said Dad. "How could I have a wedding without my best man?"

All that night we talked and wept and laughed. We exchanged our tales of all that had transpired. I told them about the slave ship, Micah, and the pirates—

We recounted our journey back through the cave, Apollus' disappearance, and his timely reappearance on the Samaritan Road—

—the shipwreck, Bishop Titus, Athens, and the death of Gidgiddonihah. We held each other through the night and watched the sunrise behind the Ephesian hills. Then, despite our exhaustion, we gathered with the Saints in a clearing north of the city, partook of our Lord's supper, and wept again in overwhelming gratitude for the blessings, mercy, and joy bestowed upon us by our Father in Heaven.

Cerinthus had indeed left Ephesus with his more devoted cronies. Nevertheless, Timothy warned the congregation that the imposter would likely be back. So would other men like him. So long as people were inclined to let down their spiritual defenses, deceivers like Cerinthus would continue to scatter the flock of God.

Apollus listened intently to Timothy's sermon. As the sun rose higher and the congregation began to dissemble, Apollus remained seated on the ground, his eyes focused a million miles away. I sat in front of him and jarred him out of his trance. He smiled slightly, then looked at the ground. His face was full of distress.

Awkwardly, he said to me, "I would like to be baptized."

My heart thrilled at the announcement. I threw my arms around his neck. "Oh, that's wonderful, Apollus! Wonderful!"

But then I realized that the news didn't bring him any joy. I sat back and looked into his eyes again.

"I want to be baptized because . . . because I think . . . that is, I feel . . ." He sighed. "I'm not sure what I feel."

"The Spirit," I said. "You feel the Spirit. That's what testifies of things that are true."

"No, that's not . . . I mean yes. Yes, I'm sure that I have felt the Spirit. I know that Jesus is the Savior of the world, but . . ."

I launched in with more advice before hearing him out. "That's all that matters. Everything else will take care of itself. God will strengthen your faith. Just follow your heart and do what you feel is right—"

"That's what I'm not sure about," said Apollus.

"What do you mean?"

With difficulty he said, "It's my own destiny that I don't understand. I've listened to the things you've said. I know what's going to happen to this world, to the Church, to my nation and way of life. It all becomes a memory. I don't want to be a memory, Meagan. I want . . ." He shut his eyes.

"What do you want, Apollus?" I asked solemnly.

He looked at the rising sun. "I've lost everything, Meagan. And yet I've gained so much. My family is gone. The things I used to know, the codes I once lived by, have all been shattered and reshaped into something I don't yet understand. I need to find out what makes sense, Meagan."

"The gospel makes sense," I replied. "It's all that makes sense."

He nodded, but then he shook his head. "The gospel is only the begin-

ning. If I embrace it, that's *when the journey really begins. I just feel . . . I'm not sure it's a journey I should make here. Not in this world. It's a journey I want to make in* yours.*"*

My heart pounded. It was my secret dream, unexpressed even to myself. Did the journey include me? I doubted it strongly. I had a feeling he wanted to make it alone, at least for the moment.

Meekly I replied, "You're welcome to come to my world. Stay as long as you like, Apollus. Even forever."

Somehow I'd taken it upon myself to be the ambassador for the twenty-first century. Still, my invitation touched him. He seemed to take it as an official granting of permission. He embraced me and I hugged him back, my heart whirling in uncertainty and apprehension.

The baptism of Apollus Brutus Severillus took place in the river the following day. It was performed by my father, with me and Bishop Timothy standing as witnesses. Micah, Luke, the Nephites, and nearly every Christian in the city was in attendance. Like all services and ceremonies of the Christians, it was performed in relative secret.

As Apollus came up out of the water, many of the children cheered, much to the distress of their parents. It was the traditional whoop given whenever a Roman soldier marched in defense of his subjects. Baptizing a centurion was a novelty in Ephesus, and many prophesied that it was a sign of good things ahead. I hoped it was true, however I feared it was not. I found myself mourning for the people of this land. It was so hard. I prayed for them in my heart. If the Church was doomed to fall, I prayed that at least these good people would be able to endure to the end.

After the baptism, Meagan looked around for the Apostle John. Like her, a part of me had hoped he might attend; I hadn't yet met him. I realized that participating in a baptism in broad daylight was probably too dangerous. Even so, I'd harbored a foolish hope.

I still had an important reason for wanting to meet John. The five sacred scrolls were still in my possession. Years ago I'd promised the prophet Agabus, as well as myself, that I would hand them to the apostle personally. After all we had endured, I felt more motivation than ever to fulfill that promise to the letter.

We remained in Ephesus for several more days, basking in the joy and friendship of the Saints, awaiting a ship that would carry us on our return voyage to Caesarea. Steffanie's ankle had healed enough for her to finally abandon her crutches, and she enthusiastically cast them aside. On that very day, we knew it was time to go home.

I finally decided to show the scrolls to Timothy. He fingered them with careful regard, reading some of the words and relishing them with all his soul.

"I wanted to give them to John," I explained. "But I don't know when he might appear."

Timothy considered me thoughtfully. I knew he had some knowledge of John's whereabouts—perhaps information that was kept secret by all the bishops of the Seven Churches.

"Tell your family to meet me in the morning," he said. "I will take you to a place where we might find him."

We gathered at sunrise in the same field where we had held sacrament services. My heart was racing with expectation. Jesse, Mary, Micah, Jashon, my father, Steffanie, Sabrina, Meagan, and Apollus were all in attendance. Mary carried the scrolls; it meant as much to her to see them finally delivered as it meant to me. We hiked into the hills for about an hour, finally reaching a small cottage in the woods. There were no paths or trails, and the house was hidden in the trees. Unless someone had accidentally stumbled upon it, I doubted it would ever be found.

As we approached, I noticed a garden in a small clearing. Kneeling in the soil, gathering up a basket of lettuce and radishes, was a plainly dressed man with a short beard. He looked mildly surprised by our approach, but then he recognized Timothy. His cheeks brightened into a rosy red as he stood to receive us.

"Greetings, Elder John," said Timothy.

"Greetings, Bishop."

John embraced him. He also reached out to embrace my father and Sabrina, then Meagan and Steffanie snuck in for a hug of their own. As the rest of us were introduced, we simply gawked and nodded, certain that he could see right through to the very state of our souls. But there was no judgment in his eyes. Only love. I hadn't seen such peace and confidence in a man's features since Bountiful. Not since I'd gazed into the face of Jesus Christ.

Reverently, Mary stepped forward and presented her gift. "My father . . . my father wanted to give these to you. And Harry, too, and . . . "

John took them from her. He looked them over, his excitement growing. "You brought these from Jerusalem?" he inquired.

"Yes," I confirmed.

He studied us with an awe and respect that I felt sure I didn't deserve.

"I'd thought these words were lost. You've performed a priceless service. These will be placed immediately in the hands of scribes." He looked at Timothy. "They will be copied and read throughout all the Churches."

Timothy nodded. I didn't know about Mary and Meagan, but my heart was glowing. The long-fought mission had finally come to an end.

John studied Mary a little closer. "You are the daughter of Symeon Cleophas."

"Yes," said Mary.

John's eyes lit up. He embraced her as if reuniting with a long-lost relative. "Sweet girl! I knew your father and mother. And your grandmother."

"My father died in Athens," said Mary sadly. "My mother in Pella."

Her words sounded terribly lonely, and a tear pricked at her eye. She'd always imagined this moment with her father at her side. I think she felt the pain of his loss more acutely than ever. John became pensive, as if his mind was considering some important problem. He surveyed the gathering. At last a wide smile climbed his rosy cheeks.

He looked at Mary again and asked, "What is your name, child?"

"Mary," she replied.

John's eyes brightened with pure pleasure. "Wait here a moment."

He carried his basket of vegetables and the five scrolls toward the cottage and slipped inside. We all stood there, dazed with curiosity. All but Timothy. He seemed to know exactly what was happening.

At last John appeared in the cottage doorway. "Come inside, everyone," he invited. "But only for a moment."

As Mary approached, John took her hand. We entered the room. The furnishings were simple: a clay hearth where John had put his vegetables, a table where he had placed the scrolls, some chairs, and a sleeping mat. John led the daughter of Symeon Cleophas toward a small room at the back. The rest of us hesitated, but Timothy urged us all to follow.

The room was dark, except for the flicker of a small lamp on a side table. Sunlight tried to creep around the edges of a modest square window, but its brightness was subdued by shutters and a wooden mesh. There was only one piece of furniture—a sleeping couch. It had thick cushions and a high wooden back covered in felt and fur.

Lying upon the couch, the coverings pulled back, was an old woman. She was sitting up, a smile creasing her wrinkled but dignified face. She must have been ninety years old. Still, there was a beauty—a nobility— to that face that drew me in, captivated me. The feeling in the room was indescribable. Like stepping into an exalted place. I gasped inwardly as I felt the tears trickling down my cheeks. I knew who this was. Oh, I knew it, and my heart was burning like the sun.

Oh, Heavenly Father, in all my life, who could have imagined such an honor? But there she was, her hand rising to greet her great niece. It was her, *the mother of the first millennium. The woman whose name would be blessed for all generations of time: Mary, the mother of Jesus Christ.*

I remembered one of the things the Savior had said as he was dying on the cross. To his faithful mother, who had remained with him to the very end, he pointed to John and said, "Woman, behold thy son." And then to John he said, "Behold thy mother." It was one of the last sacred utterances from the Savior's mouth, and its purpose was to insure that Mary would be cared for to the end of her days. John the Beloved had not faltered in that request. All these years he had kept his promise to the Master, nurturing and caring for her to the twilight of her days.

Young Mary, the daughter of Symeon, tearfully grasped the old woman's hand. "Great Aunt Mary," she said, recalling her face from some memory in her early childhood.

"Yes, child," the woman confirmed, her voice surprisingly clear and resonant.

Young Mary laid her face in her great aunt's lap. The eyes of the Lord's mother moved across us all. At last, they settled on me. She reached her other hand toward me. I edged forward a little reluctantly.

"What is your name, young man?" she asked.

"Harry," I said. "Harry Hawkins." I glanced behind me. "This is my father and his fiancée, Sabrina. And my sister, Steffanie, and Sabrina's daughter, Meagan."

They all nodded, but kept their places. She reached out to them, insisting that every one of us take her small hand and peer deeply into her bright blue eyes—the single feature that I knew firsthand had been passed on to her Son. We were all trembling with joy, completely lost in wonder.

Steffanie wanted to say something. I think she felt silly, but she just had to let her know. "We . . . we've seen your Son," she whispered.

Mary smiled. Such a glorious, penetrating smile. "You have? Oh, I'm pleased. I've seen Him, too. Where did you see Him?"

"In another land," said my father. "Among a people who love Him with all of their hearts."

"Yes," she said, as if she understood perfectly. "It must have been a very long journey."

"Very long," said Dad. "And very difficult. But to see Him . . . to meet you . . . it was worth every step."

"Great journeys always are," she declared. "We're all on a golden journey—every one of us. A journey inspired by golden dreams, and at the end awaits a golden crown of righteousness. For me, that journey is almost over. But for most of you, the journey has only begun. Please remember that every step is to be cherished. Every single one. Now listen to an old woman. I love you all very much."

Of that we had no doubt. Nor, I felt sure, would we ever again doubt the object of our journey. A golden crown—the reward of the righteous in the realms of heaven.

CHAPTER 25

Good-byes.

They always loomed at the end of an adventure like an unwelcome sting. It never got better, and it never got easier. We endured each one with tenderness and tears. Our farewells to the Apostle John were exchanged outside his cottage. Like the Savior's mother, he expressed his love for us and blessed us with peace and safety. He walked with us part of the way back toward the city. But somewhere along the way, he faded back and disappeared. We were caught up in our conversation; then suddenly we looked about us, and he was gone. I realized this was the pattern that would characterize the rest of his sojourn on earth as he witnessed the workings of God's children to the end of the world.

Next we bid farewell to Timothy and his family, as well as to the Saints of Ephesus. After I had embraced Saint Luke, I said to him, "Remember the books. And don't forget Christmas. You have to tell us all about Christmas."

I wasn't sure the word had even been invented. But Luke seemed to understand. He smiled and said to me, "I've already begun. In the cottage of John, there's someone who can give me all the source material I might require."

That was the end of our good-byes for now. Jashon and the Nephites sailed with us from the harbor of Ephesus to the mouth of the Cayster River and into the heart of the Mediterranean Sea. Our passengers also included Micah and Jesse. The young orphan and the converted Essene were bound and determined to join with the kinsmen of Gidgiddonihah and visit the world of the Nephites. Also aboard was Apollus, much to the pleasure of a fifteen-year-old girl named Meagan Sorenson.

Only fifteen for a few more weeks, thank you very much. Before we reached the cave, I fully expected to turn sweet sixteen. Old enough to get a license to terrorize all the highways from Arkansas to Alaska. Also old enough to be a dream come true for every young male brave enough to pick up the phone and dial my number.

Now, Meagan, did you really want to hear any other male voices on the phone?

Oh, Harry, you do know how to rub it in, don't you? No. Okay? Other males didn't even cross my mind. Only one. And as far as I was concerned, that's all there would ever be.

Oh, please, don't drool all over the page if you can help it.

Very funny. What are you so smug about? Why don't you tell about the last passenger on that ship?

I was just about to. And I confess, there were no regrets there either. The final passenger was Mary, the daughter of Symeon Cleophas. She'd decided to come back with us to the twenty-first century. I couldn't wait to show it to her—to live all the miracles of technology vicariously through her eyes.

I knew my feelings for Mary were strong, stronger than they'd ever been for another girl. I also knew she felt strongly about me. I still couldn't believe a girl like her could ever fall for a guy like yours truly. But however our feelings might have been defined—if they were love, if they were eternal—I felt I still had plenty of time to let them blossom. I was only eighteen years old. Besides, the greatest dream of my life was still calling to me—a goal that I'd nurtured ever since my mother had held my little hands to make them clap as she sang along with me, "I hope they call me on a mission . . ."

I didn't care that I'd just spent three years in a world so far from my own. I wanted to serve my Savior in the century where I had been born, to fight for the cause of righteousness in my own land and time. I knew now how precious the truth really was, how fragile. I would do everything I could to insure that the light that was quickly fading here would never fade there.

I was almost afraid to tell Mary. When I finally did, she gave me a reaction I hadn't expected. Her face was beaming. Her excitement for me was sincere and heartwarming. "I'm so proud of you, Harry. Always know that an extra pair of hands will be clasped together in prayer in your behalf."

I felt overwhelmed. Where in the universe would someone ever find such a girl? I leaned in and kissed her. We held each other and looked up at the stars shimmering above the Aegean Sea, wondering if someday we might build a bridge together to reach them.

Wow, Harry. And you wonder what a girl might see in you? I guarantee, my brother, it's not that hard to see.

Why, thank you, Meagan. I think that's the best compliment you've ever given me.

Don't let it go to your head.

Oops. Too late.

That's what I figured.
If you don't mind, I'll take it a little ways from here.
Thanks to Jashon, we were able to find the entrance to the cavern without having to do any more underwater acrobatics in that cistern at Masada. There was a slight delay as we built a fifteen-foot ladder to take us across the gulf where the land bridge had collapsed. I admit it was a little frightening, especially if you were dumb enough to look down, but even my mother managed to get across with very little coaxing.
A short ways farther we reached the Galaxy Room. Harry looked stricken by what he saw; it had all changed so much. But for me, there was actually a new spark of hope. The last time I had stood here, I'd been sure that the dark purple orb above our heads was dying, and that its death would mean an end to any further opportunities to go visit the great worlds of the past.
There were still no swirling bands of energy. No firestorm of incalculable power. But the orb that had only emitted a dull glow on our last visit was now entwined by a delicate circle of sparks—blue and red, orange and

gold. It was like witnessing the rebirth of something primordial. Something volcanic. Something at the edge of the known universe. Or perhaps something at the inception of time itself. There was a new expansion underway here. I felt sure that something more beautiful, more glorious, and more spectacular than ever was just beginning to emerge. Only its Creator could have known what powers and potentials were about to be unleashed. But eventually someone would discover it, some new adventurer. And from the ashes of the old Galaxy Room would arise an opportunity beyond anyone's wildest imaginings.

Shortly thereafter, the moment arrived to bid farewell to Jashon, Heshlon, Uzziah, Amnon, Muloki, Antipus, and the rest of the army that Gidgiddonihah had assembled in his quest to find me. Their objective had been met. Not only had they saved me from the dungeons of Athens, they'd helped to save Mary and Jesse and the sacred scrolls. It was a particularly heart-felt good-bye for my father. He credited them for making the reunion with his son possible. For me, saying good-bye dredged up the familiar pain of losing Gid.

"In my kinship, his name will always be remembered," said Jashon.

"In mine too," I responded.

I turned to Jesse and Micah. This was going to be difficult. I knew it was unlikely that I would ever see them again. They were going to a world of indescribable peace, a place where the gospel of Jesus Christ ruled the hearts of the people. What could ever entice them to leave? But then again, I knew better than to try and predict the future.

As I embraced my friend of the Essenes, I felt again the rush of memories, those long conversations in the dark hold of the slave ship, and building a home on our isolated island in the middle of the Aegean.

"I was born in the desert," Micah said to me. "Who'd have thought that God would bless me to see so much of the world?"

"I'm sure His blessings for you have only begun," I said. "Good-bye, my friend."

Jesse was surrounded by women. Both Mary and Meagan, and now even Steffanie and Sabrina, had let the boy stake a claim on their hearts. I think he faltered for a moment, wondering if he really wanted to go. But his sense of adventure prevailed. Soon he would become a permanent fixture in the jungles of Zarahemla.

"I feel sorry for any cureloms or cummoms who might get in your path," I said to him.

"What are those?" he asked.

"You'll discover soon enough. If there are any left, I guarantee *you* will find them."

"Don't forget me, Harry. Or I'll have to come and conquer your land as soon as I conquer this one."

"I believe you would," I replied. "So I won't forget."

I embraced him. Then he embraced Meagan and Mary one final time and returned to the company of Micah and the rest of the Nephites. They descended into the cavern and disappeared.

Now for the weddings. I get to tell about the weddings.

By all means. Only a girl could properly tell about weddings.

It was a double wedding—the most beautiful event anyone could possibly envision, and it took place only four weeks after our return to Salt Lake City and the twenty-first century.

The passage of time between our worlds was almost identical this time. For Melody and Marcos, we had been gone about six months. For myself, Jim, my mother, and Steffanie, it had only been a few weeks longer. I was sure it had something to do with the forces at work in the Galaxy Room, but don't ask me to do any of the math. From here on out, no one was taking any chances—the weddings would not be delayed another minute. Who knew when another fantastic adventure might call someone away?

For Melody and Marcos, and for Jim and my mother, it was an unforgettable and glorious day. They were married for time and all eternity, one right after the other, in the sealing rooms of the Salt Lake Temple. Melody wore the same gown as her mother, Renae, while Sabrina wore a dress that she had made for herself during the first six months of Harry's absence.

There were two receptions—one the same day as the sealings and one the day after, all decorated in unique colors and marvelous furnishings. Garth and Jenny and their children were there. So were Jim's older brothers and their large families. The center of attraction for all of Harry's cousins—particularly the females—was Apollus the Roman, who was subtly introduced to them as "a friend of ours who is an expert in ancient weapons." The fact that he now looked completely out of place in one of Jim's Sunday suits did little to dispel his magnetism.

After the weddings, the cakes, the presents, the pictures, and the tears, Marcos lifted Melody into her arms and carried his bride across the yard to their Toyota 4-Runner—

—well decorated in shaving cream and Oreos, I might add. Oh, to be foolish and childish again!

Then the two of them drove to the airport to embark on a two-week honeymoon in Cancun, Mexico.

For my mother and my new father, the honeymoon was quite a bit simpler. I think they'd seen enough exotic places for a while. A week in the mountains at the Homestead Resort in Heber City was about as much as they wanted to handle. As Jim put it, "Sabrina's the one I want to see. There's not a sunset in the world that can stand up to her."

During the reception we looked and looked for Dad's car, determined to give it just the proper aesthetic appearance, but to no avail. Unbeknownst to us, that sneaky father of mine had purchased a *new* car the day before. He'd left it parked right in front of the stake center, and we didn't even know it. It wasn't so bad, however—especially since Dad told me that I had inherited the old one. It was parked at home in our garage. The next step, I supposed, was to finally get a license to drive.

After my mother's reception, I looked around for Apollus. To my surprise, he was nowhere to be seen. For the last month he'd been living at Harry's house, where he and Marcos had tried anxiously to teach him the ways of the modern world. For Apollus, there was much more frustration than I would have anticipated. And the discontent was building in him, much to my serious dismay.

I wondered again if we had made a horrible mistake in bringing him here. My feelings of guilt returned. He'd found the gospel and embraced it; nevertheless he was still like a lost soul, trying desperately to decide what his role should be in the new world.

Steffanie quickly drove us home with Harry and Mary to see if we could find him. I wondered why Apollus couldn't be more like Mary, who seemed to be slipping into her new environment with incredible ease. She could hardly get enough of the new century. She drank it all in with tireless excitement, reveling in every new sight and sound with unquenchable wonder and joy. Maybe it was a male thing. Apollus seemed to feel the need to carve out his own niche in the wilderness, and here he wasn't even sure where to begin.

As we pulled into the driveway of Harry's house, I felt a tickling of dread. The feeling was confirmed as we entered Apollus' room—formerly Jim's den—and discovered that nearly all of his new clothes and other personal belongings, as well as his Roman sword, were gone.

We made another discovery that was even more disturbing. Shortly after we'd arrived home from the cavern, Jim had bought his son a new motorcycle. It was an older bike, much like his last one, except that it was larger. Over the last several weeks, Harry had taught Apollus how to ride. The former Roman centurion took to the new hobby like a natural, and Harry soon found that he had to take a number to get a chance to ride his own bike.

As we entered the garage, Harry's motorcycle was gone. At first I felt relieved. For all of Apollus' rough edges, I knew he was not a thief. "He'll be back," I said to Harry. "He'd never steal your bike."

Harry shuffled his feet and confessed, "The bike wasn't mine anymore, Meagan. I gave it to Apollus."

"You did WHAT?!"

"When Dad told me he was going to give me his old car, I decided to give the motorcycle to Apollus. I knew he was feeling down, and I thought the bike might cheer him up. I told him just a few hours ago at the reception."

"Harry, do you realize what you might have done? Do you realize?!"

We drove around town in a panic, looking for some sign of him. My mind sank into oblivion. I couldn't believe Apollus would just leave. How could he do that do us? How could he do that to me?

Long after dark, we arrived back at Harry's house. I checked the garage one last time. The motorcycle was still gone. Apollus hadn't returned.

"Would you like a ride home?" Steffanie asked.

"No," I replied, my heart throbbing with pain. "I'll walk. I need to walk."

"Don't panic," said Harry. "He might just be gone for a day or two. There's no reason to think the worst."

I nodded, then I turned toward home, leaving in my wake a trail of despair. When I reached my front yard, my head was still hanging. I bypassed the "For Sale" sign my mother had posted near the mailbox and stepped up the sidewalk toward my front porch. I didn't notice Harry's motorcycle parked across the street in front of the Hunsakers' old playhouse.

Our porch was enclosed by a square brick wall. I entered the enclosure and reached into my pocket to find the keys. I was startled by a deep voice off to my left.

"Meagan."

I gasped. But the fear left me in an instant. As Apollus rose to his feet, the motorcycle helmet still in his hand, I threw my arms around him in relief.

"Oh, Apollus! Where have you been? I was terrified! Don't ever do that again. Please, please, don't ever do that again."

Apollus said nothing. I moved back so I could see his eyes. He continued to look at me with longing and regret. He didn't have to say a word. I knew what he was about to tell me. The grief swelled in my heart all over again.

"You really are *leaving, aren't you?"*

"Yes," he replied.

Tears welled up in my eyes. "Why, Apollus? What's wrong? What are you looking for?"

"I have a whole new world at my feet," he replied. "I want to see it. I want to understand it. I want to become a part of it. Don't you see? You've given me so much, Meagan. You've changed everything."

"I changed it for the worse."

"No," he insisted. "For the better. You brought me to the Savior. Yes, Meagan you've made everything so much better. And I love you for it."

I raised my eyes. "You love me?"

"Oh, yes. I can't deny that. I love you more than anyone I've ever known."

"Then how—" I choked down a sob. "—how could you leave?"

He smiled painfully. "Right now I have nothing to give you. But I hope that I will one day. First I have to find it. Then I'll come back. As soon as I find it, I promise I will be back."

I held him again and buried my face in his shoulder, still weeping like a little girl. "But you can't go. What about Harry and Steffanie and everyone else? You haven't even said good-bye."

"I'm not very good at that," said Apollus. "You tell them for me, will you?"

"But you came back to say it to me."

"That one I couldn't resist."

"Oh, Apollus, Apollus. I can't let you go. Why can't you find what you're looking for right here? Maybe it's right in front of you. Did you ever think of that? I could save you so much time. Maybe you don't have to look any farther than right under your nose."

"Maybe you're right. But since I've never yet seen beyond it, how could I know for sure?"

I continued to sob. Then, trying to be brave, I said, "Well, don't expect me to wait for you. Do you hear me? I'm not a slab of bacon that you can just put on ice."

"I never thought you were," he said soothingly. "You're still very young, Meagan Sorenson. I have a feeling there are a few things left for you to discover as well."

We held each other again. Finally I whispered in his ear, "I love you, too, Apollus."

He pulled back slightly. His lips found mine and he kissed me. I thought again of that night on Mount Gerizim. I thought about the moment before he left me in the cave to go get help. I was sure he was about to kiss me then, but it turned out to be just a peck on the forehead. Not this time. This was a kiss that carried all the passion I might have expected from Apollus Brutus Severillus.

After the kiss, he held me again in the light of our porch, though my feet were somewhere in the clouds. Then he put the motorcycle helmet back on his head, threw his backpack over his shoulder, and walked into the night. With my head still in a daze of love, grief, and tears, I watched him ride away.

Then I sat on the porch, hugging myself against the April chill. I let my mind flit through all of the events and memories of the last year. It all seemed like a dream now—and indeed it had been. The greatest, sweetest, most exciting of dreams. I smiled to myself and wiped the tears from my eyes. Apollus was right: there was still so much to discover. What a wondrous universe God had created! I felt so honored to be a part of it. What was even more wonderful was that I still had my whole life ahead of me— and a newer, stronger testimony of truth that I could use to make it into whatever I wanted.

So watch out, universe! Prepare yourself for the inevitable! Meagan Sorenson is about to be unleashed upon you, and she takes no prisoners.

I'll rein you in with only the power of the Spirit. That's all I'll need. That's all I'll ever need, as long as I remember that I'm a daughter of God.

* * * * * *

The letter came in late August. I'd been awaiting its arrival for two and half weeks. Mary and Steffanie had been checking the box every day. But today the mailman had come a little earlier than usual. Steffanie had taken Mary to get her hair done in a genuine twenty-first-century style. My father and Sabrina were at their office downtown, once again building their advertising business, letting everything settle back into its normal patterns of peace and havoc. I was all alone when I checked the mailbox. And there it was—a letter from the Missionary Department of The Church of Jesus Christ of Latter-day Saints.

Perhaps I should have waited until my family could have been there to share in the moment. But I'd never had that kind of discipline. I mean, come on! What was I supposed to do?

Maybe it's to my credit that I at least had the self-control to place the unopened letter on the passenger seat of my car. I drove past Hunter High School to the old bike trails that had given me so much pleasure when I was younger. I may not have had a motorcycle any longer, but I still drove as far as I could down the narrow dirt turnout. Then I parked and hiked to the place where I'd once sat with my oldest sister, Melody, and poured out my feelings about life and the future. This was, of course, just before the accident that had catapulted us into the adventure we'd recently concluded. Maybe I was trying to recapture that feeling a little—the simplicity, the innocence—as I seated myself at the top of the knoll and looked again at the letter in my hands.

It was a clear day with high clouds and a cool breeze blowing out of the north. For a moment I couldn't hear anything around me, not any traffic or birds or even the gentle scrape of the grass as it was disturbed by the wind. Just the sound of that envelope as I tore it open.

I pulled out the letter and unfolded the creases. Then I held it before my eyes. I skipped the opening words—who ever reads those words until the second time through?—and searched until I found the name of my destination. It didn't take long.

Athens, Greece.

I actually laughed out loud. I laughed with pure joy. The wonder, the inspiration, the irony. It was perfect. I bowed my head and thanked my Heavenly Father. Suddenly I felt an incredible rush of eagerness to share the news with all the world.

But I fought it down for just one more moment. I sat back and felt the coolness of the breeze and the warmth of the Spirit. Athens, Greece. It'd be a lot different this time. For one thing, I'd finally have to learn the language. No problem. I was ready for it.

But then a heaviness settled over my heart. From the corners of my mind emerged the powerful image of a man with an iron jaw, rippling chest, and arms like Samson. In one hand he held a sword, in the other the stone blade of a hatchet. The man was grinning—a grin that I was sure I would see for the rest of my days.

Tears came to my eyes and a lump formed in my throat. "Gidgiddonihah," I whispered. "I still need you, my hero, my friend."

I found myself wondering about guardian angels. How did such a thing work in heaven? Could a guardian angel be the spirit of a righteous warrior from another age? Surely the Lord had a multitude of ways to defend and protect His missionaries. Still, I wondered if I might ever feel Gid's presence. After all, I was returning to the city where he had fallen. Maybe his spirit was still there; maybe he'd been awaiting my return for the last two thousand years.

Foolishness, I thought. A silly fantasy.

But then, for an instant, the wind seemed to change. It blew at my back, instead of my face, as if urging me on. I suddenly wondered if Gid had ever really left me. He was still at my side, encouraging me to conquer any obstacle in my path.

So I looked forward to the future. So many hopes were bouncing around in my thoughts that I could hardly sit still. Who could deny that during my first nineteen years I'd led the most extraordinary life that a boy might imagine? If this was just the beginning, I marveled to think what might be ahead as God continued to unfold for me His magnificent plan.

EPILOGUE

My name is Jim Hawkins.

My son is home. My children surround me. And I am the richest man in the universe.

I said from the beginning that reality is what we make it. Fate is always in our hands, so long as we conform to the greater fate of heaven. It's not an easy lesson. By now I might have thought it would have become second nature to me, but sometimes I forget the things I already know. I suppose when all of our lessons are perfectly learned, it's time to return to our immortal home. With that in mind, I'm sure I still have a long life ahead, filled with joy and sadness, thrills and adventures, weddings and grandchildren. I particularly look forward to the last two. Melody has just announced that she and Marcos are about to submit their paperwork to adopt a little girl. At last I'll have someone I can really spoil. I glory in the blessing of knowing that my daughter is in the hands of such a stalwart young man. If all of my children's weddings can bring me as much happiness and security, then tomorrow holds no fear.

As for myself, I feel I can see the future quite clearly in the eyes of my new bride. Oh, how I love her! And how I've waited so long to call her mine. I still remember that awful morning when I watched the clock mark the advent of my fortieth birthday. The inclination was so real to just give up, to quit, to pray that God might take me home. I'm so glad the Lord doesn't always answer our prayers. I feel as young now as I've ever felt. I feel as young as that spunky kid who once rode his bicycle with a gawky thirteen-year-old boy named Garth Plimpton to see a certain stone mural painted on the canyon walls of the Shoshoni

River. Life has never felt so fresh and full of excitement. And I know that my excitement is shared by a very special spirit in the world to come—my eternal first wife, Renae.

As for Sabrina, there's been a look in her eyes lately that one can only see in the eyes of a woman. The look can be quite frightening, yet there's no denying its irresistible fascination. In short, my new wife, thirty-seven years young, has expressed a desire to have another child. Did anyone say adventure? Well, I feel sure that I am about to embark upon one of unfathomable proportions.

But it's all part of the golden journey. That same journey filled with golden dreams so beautifully described by one of the most beautiful women there ever was. Most of all, I want that crown. I can see it in my mind. I can feel the warmth of its reflection on my face. All the treasures of the Milky Way will forever pale beside it. And to think it is available to everyone. Every soul in our Father's vast kingdom. Or, more surprisingly, to think it is available to *me*. That is the most incomprehensible thing of all. Yet it remains the surest vision of my mind, growing ever brighter with the years.

But for now, let the Lord prepare all things in His own good time. And if ever again I hear the voice of high adventure, I will always know the source from whence it springs. It will be echoing from deep within the heart of a mountain in northern Wyoming, beckoning me back to the worlds of eternal sunsets.

PHOTO BY "PICTURE THIS...by Sara Staker"

ABOUT THE AUTHOR

Chris Heimerdinger was born in Bloomington, Indiana, and joined the Church during his first semester at Brigham Young University when he was eighteen years old. From a very young age he has been enamoured with the art of storytelling, having completed his first novel when he was in the fifth grade.

For over ten years, Chris Heimerdinger has brought adventure and fantasy to LDS readers. With *The Golden Crown,* Chris completes his seventh novel in the *Tennis Shoes Adventure Series.* This concludes the story of Harry Hawkins and Meagan Sorenson in the world of the New Testament, a three-part adventure that began with *The Sacred Quest.* Chris explains, "This was the most difficult of the Tennis Shoes books that I have written to date, and the most rewarding. The Great Apostasy is a difficult subject in any forum. I hope that by exploring some of the causes and effects of the loss of priesthood authority in the meridian of time, we can better appreciate the glorious blessing of having the fulness of the gospel in our day, and do all we can to insure that the Kingdom of God remains strong and vital."

Chris lives in Riverton, Utah, with his wife, Beth, and their three children, Steven Teancum, Christopher Ammon, and Alyssa Sariah.

Check out Chris' web site and become a registered guest at **www.cheimerdinger.com.**

TENNIS SHOES
A D V E N T U R E   S E R I E S

by CHRIS HEIMERDINGER

1. TENNIS SHOES AMONG THE NEPHITES

Thirteen-year-old Jim Hawkins has a bad attitude about every-thing—and especially about the Church. Garth Plimpton, on the other hand, is pretty much a religious fanatic. Through an unusual chain of events, these two opposites become best friends and begin a fantastic adventure that takes them back through time to the lands and peoples of the Book of Mormon. In a series of heart-stopping adventures, they meet Nephite prophets and generals, Lamanite kings and marauders. Once you've read this riveting book, you'll never read the Book of Mormon in quite the same way again.

2. GADIANTONS AND THE SILVER SWORD

Jim and Garth are now in college at BYU, and their earlier adven-tures in Book of Mormon lands are revisited in a most unusual way when evil men from the past (Gadianton robbers from Nephite times) pursue them and disrupt their lives with danger and violence. This is a spine-tingling, explosive saga that transports the reader from the familiar settings of Utah and the American West to the exotic and unfamiliar settings of southern Mexico and its deep, shadowy jungles, where Jim must take a mystical sword once wielded by the Jaredite king, Coriantumr.

3. THE FEATHERED SERPENT, PART ONE

Jim Hawkins is now the widowed father of two teenage daughters, Melody and Steffanie, and a ten-year-old son, Harry. Jim finds himself embarking on his most difficult and perilous adventure—a quest for survival against unseen enemies and an evil adversary from the distant past. He must also solve the deepening mystery of the disappearance of his sister, Jennifer, and his old friend Garth Plimpton. Once again he returns—this time with his family—to ancient Book of Mormon times; but now the civilization is teetering on the brink of destruction. It's the time just prior to the Savior's appearance in the New World . . . a time of danger and uncertainty.

4. THE FEATHERED SERPENT, PART TWO

Jim and his family continue their perilous adventures in Book of Mormon times, using all of their instincts and resources to find Garth and his family and deliver themselves from the clutches of one of the most treacherous men of ancient America—King Jacob of the Moon. They encounter murderous and conspiring men, plagues, a herd of "cureloms," hostile armies, and finally earthquakes and suffocating blackness as the Savior of the world is crucified. Along the way, members of Jim's family discover their loyalty and love for one another, and the importance of the gospel is in their lives, culminating in the glorious visitation of our Lord Jesus Christ to the city of Bountiful.

5. THE SACRED QUEST

Jim has just learned that his daughter, Melody, now age 20, has a very serious illness. During their last adventure in Book of Mormon times, Melody fell in love with Marcos, son of King Jacob of the Moon, who had been converted to Christianity. Now Jim's son Harry, 15, is determined to go back in time, find Marcos, and bring him back to be with Melody. He and his stepsister-to-be, Meagan, embark on this journey, but are sidetracked and end up in New Testament times, about 70 A.D. They encounter both believers and antichrists, consumed with finding a mysterious manuscript called the Scroll of Knowledge. The epic climaxes with a breathtaking confrontation between Harry, Nephites, and gladiators, but Harry's adventure of a lifetime has only begun.

6. THE LOST SCROLLS

Harry and Meagan continue their heart-stopping adventure as they face the awesome challenges of courage and survival in the hostile world of Jerusalem in 70 A.D. While Meagan and Jesse, a young Jewish orphan, are held hostage by the evil Simon Magus and the Sons of the Elect, Harry and his friend Gidgiddonihah must make an impossible journey to Jerusalem to find the Scroll of Knowledge, which may contain the ultimate power and mysteries of the universe. They have only a few days to find the scroll and deliver it to Simon Magus, or Meagan and Jesse will be killed. Our young heroes face breathtaking danger and high adventure as they encounter flames, swords, desperate villains, and perhaps the greatest loves of their lives in this sixth volume of the award-winning *Tennis Shoes Adventure Series*.

DANIEL AND NEPHI

A Tale of Eternal Friendship in a Land Ripening for Destruction

Welcome to 609 B.C.! In a world of infinite mystery, when caravans rule the sun-swept deserts and mighty empires grapple for ultimate power, the lives of a young prince named Daniel and a trader's son named Nephi become entwined in an adventure that takes them along the razor's edge of danger and suspense as they struggle to save the life of a king—and the fate of a nation.

Join Daniel and Nephi as they learn the lessons of friendship, fortitude, and faith that shape two young boys into great prophets of God.

Carefully researched and scrutinized by scholars, *Daniel and Nephi* offers a breathtaking opportunity to explore the world of Jeremiah and Lehi.

"In Daniel and Nephi, *Chris Heimerdinger has once again breathed life into significant characters in biblical and Book of Mormon history."*

—BRENT HALL, FOUNDATION FOR ANCIENT RESEARCH

AND MORMON STUDIES

EDDIE FANTASTIC

When the Powers of the Universe Are in the Hands of a Teenager

Eddie Fanta is a fifteen-year-old boy entangled in tragic secrets which leave him questioning life, questioning justice, and questioning God. Louis Kosserinski is a savagely scarred and crippled old man who has remained in utter seclusion for the last forty years.

Mysterious circumstances bring these two characters face to face, where Eddie discovers the old man's unprecedented genius for electronics and microcircuitry—a genius which has spawned a series of inventions which could change the universe forever! Although Eddie sees Louis' inventions as an opportunity to improve an imperfect world, he ends up wreaking havoc at every hair-raising turn.

Join Eddie in his incredible journey through time and space, reality and spectacle, until at last he discovers an ultimate wisdom and understanding about our universe's Creator.